Anglesey Blue

Dylan H. Jones

Dedicated to my wife Laura, and
my daughter Isabella.
I will be forever grateful for your unwavering support and love.

My patient and insightful readers.

Laura Russell-Jones, Gloria Cerul-Flores, Hugh and Grace Jones, Sandra Easton, Andrea Schweizer, Kathleen Welter, Mike Moellering.
Everything you said, mattered.
Thank you.

Thanks also to Jim Kealy at **2Hemispheres** for the cover design. As always, you delivered more than I could have hoped for.

Prelude

They meant to kill him. He understood that now. There would be no time to process this thought, or plead for his life. Decisions had been made, plans were to be executed, and loose ends disposed of. It was the natural order of things, as inevitable as the slow rise of the sun, which had chosen this moment to cast its ghostly radiance over the late October dawn. The captain, speaking from behind the chamber of his pistol, addressed the crewman in a deliberate manner, as if speech itself might absolve him of the act he was about to commit.

"No witnesses," he said, pinching back the trigger.

Fear clotted in the crewman's mouth like a dry cloth. The remaining seconds unspooled before him, as if in slow motion: the captain's eyes narrowing into a cruel, merciless squint, the unlit cigarette falling to the deck, the crush of the captain's heel over the thin wrapping of tobacco, the inevitable crack of a firing pin, shattering the morning's brittle silence.

The bullet shattered the crewman's shoulder, narrowly missing the vital web of arteries and veins. To his left, he heard the grind of machinery slipping from its gears. The sharp corner of a metal lobster basket struck his temple, whirling his senses into a blur of indiscriminate shapes and colours. Stumbling, he reached for a lifeline, finding only dead air to cling to.

As he descended through the dark mass of seawater, he felt a swell of adrenaline surge through his veins. If he were a religious man, he would have thanked God for this thin sliver of mercy, but his faith was in practicalities and facts, not miracles and fairy tales. This was merely his body's primal need for survival, pushing upwards towards the shallow filter of sunlight.

He broke the surface, and gulped at the oxygen-rich air. Pain gnawed at his shoulder and temple, as the saltwater seeped into the open wounds. If nothing else, it was a sign he was alive, and if he was alive, there had to be hope.

As he pulled the surrounding landscape into focus, he scanned the horizon for any familiar landmarks, but this was no place he recognised, at least not in this light. He'd always considered himself a strong swimmer, but already, his muscles were struggling. *How long could he survive out here? Hours, maybe less?*

Ahead of him, the grind of the boat's engine spat a final insult of saltwater, before fading into the thick swell of fog. He was alone—the revelation fell on him like a rock.

As he drifted, his hand brushed against something thick and solid. His chest tightened. He reached for the object, and felt a momentary sense of elation at his good fortune; the driftwood was large enough to support his weight. He folded his arms around the knotted timber, laid his head down, and rested.

Where was he? They were scheduled to dock in Liverpool later today. *Hadn't they passed the coast of Ireland some hours ago? Or was that yesterday?* Lights blinked along the mainland, as the inhabitants woke from their sleep, warm in their beds; he envied them those most mundane of luxuries. He should have studied the route more carefully, asked more questions. But, this was his maiden voyage; he was instructed to keep his head down, do what he was told, and if he worked hard, they might hire him again. Only yesterday, the Captain had offered him three hundred euros to carry six crates from the secondary hold and onto the deck. 'Easy money,' the Captain had said. His mother would have called it by another name: the devil's penny.

He thought of his wife, Katia. She'd be at the apartment now, making breakfast. *Was she thinking about him? Or was she worrying about the day ahead?* She worked too hard, worried too much. But, that would end. He had promised her this at the dockside. He could still sense the dampness of her tears on his cheek as she kissed him. She had said nothing, just smiled, and then pulled away, as if she herself were retreating into the scenery—drawn back to the routine and rhythm of her life.

The image of his father passed through his mind. He remembered the factory Viktor had worked at since he was a boy—the sort of work that broke a man's body—a relentless grind which had shaved the layers off his heart until it was fit for nothing but scrap. He'd sworn to never permit life the satisfaction of beating him down like that. He would never be like his father; this he had promised himself. But, at this moment, he would have gladly stepped into Viktor's boots, sweating under the filth of the steel-works, his eyes scorched by the hellish molten liquid spilling like lava into the colossal iron buckets.

Maybe he'd been too rash in dismissing the apprenticeship his father had secured him. 'A job for life, son,' Viktor had explained to him, as if that was all that mattered. He saw it differently; it was a life traded for a job. A bargain struck at the age of sixteen, the contract fully obligated at sixty, then, if you were lucky, a handful of years in retirement, before death came to claim its inheritance. Maybe it was like his father had always said: a fool dreams of riches, a good man dreams of happiness, but to end up with neither, what did that make him?

Hours later, or was it days, his body was dragged further out into the open sea. Discordant memories flickered before his eyes, yet he felt strangely at peace, as the images played out their acts. Maybe he was becoming resigned to his fate, and death would come to claim him like a soft, dark palm pressing down until he no longer felt its sting.

As the cold and now familiar darkness drew over his eyes, a flash of light appeared to the east, like a large, silver-winged fish fracturing the surface. It travelled rapidly towards him, skimming across the ocean, until its transparent wing obscured the day's scant sunlight. His fingers curled tighter around the driftwood.

Above him, the great billowing wing shredded the air with noise. He closed his eyes and prayed: a childish, nursery rhyme of a prayer he remembered from school. Shadow and cold fell over him. Then, the impact, potent and precise—a direct hit to his sternum, which emptied the last remaining pockets of air from his lungs. The crewman sank, without complaint, into the unforgiving darkness, the crumbs of the half-remembered prayer still unfinished on his lips.

PART ONE
Redneck Roulette

Chapter 1

"I'll do you for a fiver," the barmaid said, extending her long, perfectly manicured fingernails across the bar, and sliding a freshly poured pint his way. "Make you feel like a new man, but don't go telling every man Jack or they'll all be expecting discounts."

Detective Inspector Tudor Manx took a slow, considered sip of his bitter. "A new man? Still got a few miles left on the old one yet, thanks."

"Oh, right! Proper George Clooney you are, too. Got a couple of them supermodels waiting back at the semi-detached, like?"

"And they love me just the way I am, bad hair and all," Manx said, leaning back and puffing his chest, as if to emphasise the point.

Gwen smiled. "Just the hair, is it? They didn't have the heart to tell you about that jumper, then?"

"Finest Anglesey wool," Manx said, running his hands down the length of his jumper. "They don't shear them like this anymore."

"Thank Duw for that. Probably a health hazard by now."

Manx dropped his chin, and assessed the article of clothing in question. There was no doubt it had seen better days. Its once snow-white hue had turned a jaundiced yellow, resembling the fingertips of a life-long smoker. He was sure it possessed some sentimental value, but couldn't, right now, pinpoint where, or why. The fact he was even wearing a jumper was testament to the sharp, cold turn the weather had taken. Manx's choice of wardrobe had always been uncomplicated and predictable: a limited colour palette of white Oxford shirt, a slim, black necktie left loose at the collar, black straight-legged jeans, a black sports jacket (either

1

wool, linen, or leather, depending on the weather), and black, chisel–toe Blundstone boots, which he purchased off the internet, directly from the factory in Tasmania.

Manx sipped at his bitter, and tugged absentmindedly at a loose strand of wool—one of many trailing, like an unfinished sentence, from his sleeve. The material unraveled rapidly, gaining twelve inches in length in the short time it took him to dispose of the errant thread.

"Keep pulling, and I'll have to throw you out for indecent exposure," Gwen said.

"Probably be the most excitement you've had round here for a while."

Gwen finished scooping the inside of a beer glass with a towel, and leant over the bar. "If it's excitement you're looking for, you're a day too late. His landlordship holds these pub quizzes, every Friday night. Reckons it makes customers spend more on booze. Anyway, it was Pop Trivia night, so the place was heaving."

"Everyone thinks they're a pop music expert," Manx offered.

"You're telling me. Nearly had a bloody riot on my hands. Should have had you lot on speed dial." She retrieved a scrap of paper from under the bar, and read it aloud. "Try this one. How many number one singles did the Swedish Super Group, Abba, have in their eighteen-year career?"

"UK, or worldwide?"

Gwen smiled, and laid down the paper. "See, that's why you're a copper, asking the right questions. Didn't bloody say, did it? So, Dewi Diesel and Mick the Chimney go at it, hammer and tongs. Had to give them both a pint on the house to calm them down. Honestly, men! They're no better than kids sometimes."

"Well, that's the problem with pop quiz nights, isn't it?" Manx paused before continuing. "Winner takes it all."

Gwen thought for a moment. "Very bloody funny!" she said, slapping her hands on the bar like a punctuation mark. "Right, can't be standing here all night gabbing with you. Aiding and abetting they call it, yeah?"

"More like co-operating with police enquiries," Manx said, waving his nearly finished pint in her direction.

"Well, it's not like much happens round here that needs enquiring about, is there? Proper peaceful haven, we are."

"Quiet as the grave," Manx said, handing over his empty pint glass.

"You should take me up on that haircut, before I put up my prices. Once word gets out, you could be waiting for days."

"Days?"

"I'm renting the old salon next to the wool shop. Nothing fancy, mind. A couple of stations, and one of those big hair-dryers, but you've got to start somewhere, right?" Gwen skimmed a few, frothy centimetres off the top of the beer, and slid it over the bar.

Manx reached for the pint, and caught a glimpse of his long, thin face in the mirror behind the bar. It made him wonder for a moment as to the identity of the middle-aged man staring back at him from behind the bottles and optics. The harshness of the florescent light was hardly flattering, not that it mattered—Manx's face wore his years too comfortably, he thought. He had longed for some rebellion, some rage against the onset of age, but his face appeared to have surrendered without much of a fight. The dark, puffy rings that puckered beneath his eyes, the three-day old stubble, and the slightly too long sideburns peppered with grey did little to distract from the overall impression of a forty-nine-year-old policeman, with little time for personal vanity, but, as of yet, had not given up completely.

"Might take you up on that offer, after all."

Gwen nodded. "I can fit you in Tuesday afternoon."

"Outstanding. Tuesday, it is," Manx said, turning his gaze from the mirror's exacting judgment.

"And don't be a stranger. We could do with some new faces in here, even if it's just your ugly mug."

There was little chance of being a stranger here, Manx thought. He'd been back on the island precisely fourteen days, and each one of them had ended in the exact same location; the lounge bar at the Pilot Arms, Moelfre.

Not much has changed since he was last here, either. The neat regiment of cracked Toby jugs still held court over the fireplace, casting their beady enamel eyes over the clientele. The wide bay windows were still festooned with a rag-tag weave of old fishing nets. In the main bar, a scrap of young men clacked balls around the pool table, and in the snug, a coven of young girls huddled around a table, all hushed secrets and loud makeup. Along the bar, the older men in flat caps and corduroy trousers occupied the barstools that had, by now, shifted and familiarised themselves to fit each of their buttocks with comfortable precision. *The pub must have seen better days*, Manx thought, but he struggled to remember when. Maybe the Pilot Arms was one of those establishments whose better days were yet to come.

Was he really back where it all started? It wasn't hard for Manx to recall his teenage self, flirting with the barmaid, and pestering the members of the Young Farmer's Club to buy him drinks, before being thrown out on his ear at closing time. *You can take the boy out of Anglesey, but you can't drink the Anglesey out of the boy*, he thought to himself, and savoured another mouthful of beer, as if to prove his own point.

Gwen winked at him from the other side of the bar. It was a casual sort of wink; the sort you give your friend when you're in cahoots about something. Manx guessed she was in her early thirties, give or take a couple of years, and possessed the pale, almost pearlescent Welsh complexion, with the requisite blush of pink around the cheekbones. Her hair was coal-black, and she wore it up in a tousled bun which left two strands to fall in a nonchalant fashion across her cheekbones.

It was Gwen's eyes, however, which captured most peoples' attention. They would inevitably linger a second too long on her eyes, as if they couldn't imagine a colour that striking existing naturally—a deep green, tempered by flecks of almond around the pupils. Someone had mentioned to Manx she had a young boy, six or so, but the father had left for Saudi Arabia a few years back. Manx couldn't blame the man for escaping the island; he'd done the same himself, but leaving behind a kid and a woman like Gwen Schofield seemed like a rash decision he'd come to regret.

Manx was about to sink the remaining drops of his sequel and order the full trilogy, when his mobile vibrated anxiously across the bar. He checked the number: work. He contemplated not answering, but they'd eventually track him down, and send over a junior to knock on the door of his neighbour and landlady, Megan Evans, who appeared to know the whereabouts of everyone in the village at any given time.

"Manx," he said, with an abruptness he hoped would ensure whoever was interrupting his off-duty Saturday night, would keep it short.

PC Kevin Priddle's voice was loud and over-excited. The hue and cry of a rainstorm rumbled and cracked in the background as he spoke. Manx looked out. In the past hour, the weather had turned from a chilly October evening into an ugly, full-throated thunderstorm. Along the faint horizon of the Irish Sea, several container ships were already anchored, their pilot lights twitching nervously through the fog. They'd be there for the night; no port this side of Liverpool was going to let them dock until the storm had passed. Manx moved closer to the door.

"Where did you say you were?" He sensed an edge of urgency and maybe even a twinge of excitement in the Constable's reply. "Jesus! And you can't locate another senior officer? No, it's fine. I'll drive myself."

Manx hung up, and returned to the lounge. He placed a twenty on the bar, and instructed Gwen to keep the change.

"Leaving me already?" she said.

"Can't keep those super models waiting. They're very temperamental; goes with the job," Manx said. "Oh, and by the way, nine number one's in the U.K., and no one's completely sure about the worldwide. In case it comes up again."

Gwen smiled. "Fount of knowledge, you are," she said. "And don't forget, Tuesday at eleven. Make a new man of you."

***

The rain swept sideways into Manx's face, as he stepped from the shelter of the pub. He walked briskly past the sea-front car park, all but abandoned for the winter, and towards the narrow slip of road leading to the Bryn Mawr housing estate. Turning up his jacket collar, he felt a cold trickle of rain trace down his spine. He shuddered. *Welcome to fucking Wales*, he thought, and ducked his head against the elements he felt were just beginning to conspire against him.

Chapter 2

It took Manx several turns of the key and a string of romantic phrases he'd be too embarrassed to utter in the bedroom, before the Interceptor cooperated. When it finally rumbled to life, the large V8 engine purred out of the driveway and onto the main Amlwch road. A midnight blue, 1971 Mark Three Jensen, with a seven-litre engine was hardly the most practical choice of transport, but the car was a gift, conferred on him by his father, Tommy, and had been in storage for the best part of a decade.

The car, Manx had concluded, suited him in a manner that, ten years ago, he would have dismissed as ridiculous. The worn leather interior, the temperamental nature of the electrics, the grumpy reluctance of most of the moving parts were all strangely comforting, as if the Jensen itself was empathetic to his own state of mind and bodily condition. Trading the car in for a younger, perkier model would have seemed like a betrayal, carrying with it an odour of middle-age desperation he was not willing to surrender to; at least, not yet.

PC Priddle was at Cemaes Bay harbour, a fifteen-mile drive via the A502. As Manx drove past the overgrown hedges hemming the dual carriageway, he was reminded of how abruptly night could fall here, like the unexpected drop of a theatrical curtain mid-performance.

At eight fifty-five, Manx pulled up at the harbour, and peered through the rain-soaked windscreen towards the sway of boats, tossed like toy models in the gale. He stepped from the car, and flipped up his jacket collar. Somewhere in the cacophony of wind and rain, there were frantic shouts.

"Inspector! Inspector! Over here!"

Manx recognised the scrawny outline of PC Priddle, looking in his high visibility vest like an under-filled, neon windsock. To the right of Priddle, two other officers shuffled their feet, unsure of why they were there, and wishing they were elsewhere.

"Why isn't the area cordoned off?" Manx shouted. The wind tore the words from his throat.

"What's that?" Priddle said, leaning closer, and providing Manx with an unpleasant, vinegary whiff of his fish and chip dinner.

"The caution tape," Manx shouted.

"Oh, right! Bloody storm blew it out to sea, didn't it? Bloody lucky it didn't carry us with it. Dai here reckons it's the worst we've had in ten years."

Dai, the larger of the two officers, nodded solemnly.

Manx felt the hairs on the back of his neck stand to attention, as he listened to Priddle's thick, North Wales accent. Having been away for over a quarter of a century, Manx had forgotten how fully chewed-on the English language could sound in the mouth of a native North Wales speaker. His own accent had been eroded over the years to such a flat, non-descript burr most people would be hard-pressed to pinpoint to any specific region other than, "not from 'round here."

Manx took a quick inventory. "Make sure no one else comes past the harbour entrance before forensics arrive."

"Got it, sir," Priddle said, his attention distracted by large slip of green, wind-blown tarpaulin scraping across the harbour floor like a ghost.

"Didn't call me away from my pint to admire the weather, did you?" Manx said, with a stiff edge of impatience.

Priddle stood to attention. "Oh, yeah! Follow me, sir," he said, walking towards the harbour wall. "And be careful, the seaweed's bloody lethal."

At the harbour's edge, Priddle directed Manx's gaze towards a small fishing boat, no more than thirty feet long tethered to the mooring pegs. A large wave caught the keel of the boat, and raised her several feet above the waterline to reveal the name: *Bendith Magdalen*. "Magdalen's Blessing," Manx translated to himself, as the boat levelled for a moment on the crest of a wave then crashed violently into the harbour wall.

"Jesus!" Manx said, stepping back from the violent spray of seawater.

"Gets worse, sir." Priddle directed his torch at the boat's port side.

Manx squatted, his eyes tracing the path of the beam. There was something attached to the boat: a pig carcass, thick, pink, and fleshy. He wiped the seawater from his eyes. As the tide hauled the boat upwards, the figure rose, like an alien creature, from the surface. Manx stepped back.

"Jesus Christ."

He was right; it was a carcass, but it was human, not swine. The body was naked, bound with thick ropes around his wrists and ankles. Manx's first impression was the man had been crucified. His arms were spread outward, his head leaning towards his left shoulder. As another wave surged forward, the boat rose and slammed into the wall. This time, the body took the brunt of the impact. Manx winced as the bones crunched against the ancient stonework.

"They'll have a bugger of a time identifying the body," Priddle said.

The boat reeled back. "Anyone else been down here?"

"Just the two specials." Priddle gestured at the two Community Service Officers, their heads bowed low against the rain.

"I hope you kept them clear of the crime scene," Manx said. "Not that there's any evidence to botch, even for that lot."

He watched as the boat rolled under the swell. "Not much chance of boarding either, until this storm blows itself out. ETA on forensics?"

"Half hour, or so," Priddle said.

"And the photographer?"

"On his way. Weren't too happy being called in on a Saturday night."

"Yeah, welcome to the club."

"Aye, sorry sir. I know it's your night off, an' all, but it looked serious-like, so I had to contact a senior."

"You did the right thing," Manx said. "Who called it in?"

"Dick Roberts." Priddle indicated to the man in a yellow sou'wester, sitting on the wooden bench outside the lavatories. "It's his boat."

Manx looked at the fisherman, who was attempting to light a cigarette.

"Told me he came down to check on the boat, because of the storm. Called us as soon as," Priddle added.

Manx nodded. "Secure the boat," he said. "Radio the Coastguard. Throw some anchors and ropes, or something, over it, and tie it to the harbour. Pinky and Perky over there can give you a hand while I talk to Captain Birds Eye. And, for fucks sake, don't drop him in the brink."

"Mr. Roberts?" Manx asked, shaking the rainwater from his jacket. The fisherman nodded, and kept a fixed, steady gaze on the sea, as if he were waiting for something to materialise over the horizon. Manx wiped the drizzle from his face, and sat. "Jesus, this rain, gets right in my bones."

Dick Roberts kept his gaze seaward, and pulled hard on his roll-up.

"Used to come down here all the time when I was a kid," Manx said, gesturing towards the crescent-shaped bay below. "There used to be a cafe down by the beach, with a big tin roof on it. Made a hell of a din when it rained. Good place to meet girls, if I remember, decent jukebox, too." Manx smiled, caught in a memory he hadn't tapped into for several decades.

"I know who you are," Dick said. "You're Alice Manx-William's son. Left years ago, didn't you? Why you back, then? Run out of money?"

Manx reached inside his jacket, and carefully peeled a length of a King Edward Cigar from its wrapper. "Maybe I just missed the friendly locals."

Dick flipped the butt of his cigarette onto the ground.

"Do you mind?" Manx said. "Always leaving mine at home."

Dick passed over his lighter. Manx had smoked King Edward's since he was sixteen. He'd bypassed the whole teenage, cigarette rite-of-passage and opted for the fattest, cheapest cigars he could afford. It was another one of his bad habits he had every intention of breaking, someday. He drew on the cigar, and watched the smoke dissipate into nothing.

"Tough job, fishing, these days, I'd imagine, especially on a small boat."

The fisherman man spat on the ground. "I do all right."

"All those commercial trawlers? Must cut into your income, though?"

"Why are you interested? Got a better offer, or something?" Dick said, meeting Manx's eyes for the first time. Manx noticed how the vein in his neck twitched, as if he resented every word he was required to utter.

"So, what's the catch of the day? Mackerel, flatfish?"

"Anything I can sell. Pubs want it fresh, don't much care what, so long as it's still wet."

"Gastro pubs, eh? I bet you can't flog a lobster, without some chef wanting to know where you caught it, and who its next of kin are."

The fisherman looked to the ground.

"Why did you come down to the harbour tonight, Mr. Roberts?"

"Had to check the boat."

"Many fishermen do that?"

"They do, if they've got something to lose."

"Not much you could do though, was there? I doubt you could even board with the sea that rough. Then again, I'm no fisherman." Manx let the sentence hang; Roberts resisted the bait and kept looking out to sea.

"Was there anyone else here at the harbour when you came down?"

Dick shook his head. "Just saw that bloody mess. Called you lot, as soon as I realised what it was."

"About what time was that?"

"Seven, maybe. Don't remember exactly."

"Really? I was enjoying my first pint of the evening about then. There was no sign of a storm where I was, not until around eight-thirty."

"Depends where you are. Storm works its way around the island."

"And you're sure you saw no one else? No cars, strangers?"

"Told you already, no one."

Manx leant his arms back on the bench. "We'll need to take a statement. Any plans to leave the island? No tropical vacations, exotic safaris?

"Expect you'll be all over my bloody boat, too?"

"Shouldn't be more than a couple of days."

"You won't find nothing, you know," Dick said, licking at a freshly rolled cigarette, and settling it tightly between his lips.

Manx turned up his collar, and gestured toward the boat with his cigar. "It's a crime scene, Mr. Roberts," he said. "It's unusual if we don't find something."

Chapter 3

Manx pushed open the mortuary door, and stepped into the perfectly chilled air. The overhead lights buzzed like flies, and the hum of classical music played at low volume from a speaker on the desk. The aroma was familiar to him by now: an acrid mixture of antiseptic bleach and diluted ammonia, which caught in his throat, and would linger in his nostrils for the next few hours. He heard a voice coming from beneath one of the gurneys.

"Be right with you. Just tweaking the undercarriage."

The voice was deep and slightly strained, and belonged to the resident pathologist, Professor Richard Hardacre. Moments later, he appeared, like a garage mechanic, from under one of the gurneys. "Cut backs," he explained, brandishing a spanner in Manx's direction. "Requires a certain degree of ingenuity to make sure we stay ship-shape and up to code." He clunked the spanner down onto the stainless-steel counter. "Wouldn't have happened in the old days. But, looking on the bright side, I didn't have all this technical wizardry to make my job easier," he said, gesturing towards the computer. "Life's all swings and roundabouts at the end of day." Hardacre bit down on his lower lip, as if contemplating his own philosophy, then reached for a handkerchief to mop his flushed and ruddy face.

"Dr. Richard Hardacre," he said, offering Manx a fat, clammy hand. "But, most people call me Hardy."

"No Laurel?" Manx asked, with a wry smile.

Hardacre paused for a moment. "I have a wife called Lauren," he replied in a tone, which suggested he'd just that minute recalled he had a wife.

"Lauren and Hardy? Close enough," Manx said.

Hardacre grimaced. "Unfortunately, far from close these days." He sighed, long and sustained like a minor chord. "Divorce on the cards, messy state of affairs all round, not to mention the solicitor's fees. At this rate, I'll be working here until they lay me out on one of these damned gurneys," he said, tightening the plastic apron around his beach ball-like waist.

Hardacre looked the inspector up and down, as if sizing up a cadaver. "You're a tall drink of water. What are you, six two, six three?"

"Six three; give or take."

"You're new?"

"It's a long story," Manx said.

"Good man, spare me the details. I'd probably forget, anyway."

Hardacre wheeled a squeaking gurney to a stop directly in front of the inspector. "We're a busy holding lot. As you can imagine, North West Wales is not an insignificant area. We're always hosting a few John and Jane Does here. Way of the world, these days. However, this guest may be one of the most intriguing I've encountered in quite some time."

"I hope you can deliver on a build up like that," Manx said.

Hardy smiled. "Oh, I think we can." The pathologist swept back the sheet with a flourish, reminding Manx of a magician revealing the "tada" climax to his act. "Not his best look," Hardacre said.

Manx couldn't argue. From the shoulders up, the body was barely recognizable as human. The cheekbones and lower and upper jaws had been pulverised. The nose was flattened, and pushed to the right, so it was skewered inwards, and the forehead seemed formless and liquid, having been driven into the centre of the skull. It was as if someone had taken a sledgehammer to the man's face, and kept on pummelling.

"Male, obviously," Hardacre said. "Just over a hundred kilos. Height: a tad under one point seven metres, and approximately sixty-five years old. Deceased no more than forty-eight hours, and looking at the overall bloating and high saline content, has probably spent the majority of those in the Irish Sea. Also, signs of hypothermia. Not a surprise, but there's minimal water in the lungs, so we can rule out drowning as the C.O.D. We have major internal and external injuries, skin ligatures at the wrists and ankles, fractured skull, fractured crown, and significant bone and dermis damage I'd expect to see from someone who's been walloped against a harbour wall for several hours. There's significant bruising around the chest plate, torso, and lower abdomen, and of course, as you can see, the skull, mandible, and jaws are completely disfigured."

"If he didn't drown, then what?"

"Glad you asked," Hardacre said. "Asphyxiation. But, here's where it gets interesting." He peeled the sterile tissue from a steel pan to the left of the gurney. Inside were two, grey lumps, of what Manx took to be gristle.

"Found them wedged in the hyoid."

"In English," Manx said, examining the fleshy lumps.

"The u-shaped bone which supports the tongue muscles," Hardacre said, opening his own mouth to illustrate the point. "It's at the base of the tongue. Whoever lodged them there didn't want them to come out."

"Them? Do I need to phone a friend, or are you going to tell me?"

Hardacre drew down the remainder of the sheet, so it covered the man's calves. He carefully lifted the flaccid, circumcised penis with the edge of a scalpel, and positioned the organ towards the man's left thigh. "Testes," Hardacre said, trying unsuccessfully to hide the smattering of excitement which had crept into his voice.

Manx glanced gingerly towards where the Professor was pointing, and looked over the shredded mess of loose muscle and veins slacking from the man's groin.

"Not the most pleasant way to depart this realm," Hardacre said.

Manx took a deep breath. The air was thick, and he felt the first twinges of nausea in the pit of his stomach. "OK, so let me get this straight," he said, composing himself. "Someone cut off this poor bugger's balls, choked him with them, then strung him up on a boat, like a carnival attraction?"

Hardacre nodded. "I found tape residue around the mouth and nostrils. His gag reflexes would have compelled him to throw them back up, the tape keeps his mouth shut, and the testes are in his throat. On the bright side…"

"There's a bright side?" Manx interrupted.

"The suffocation would have been swift," he continued. "Oh, and that's not all." Hardy took one of the man's hands, and turned its palm upwards. "Sans fingerprints. They've been removed. Ditto on the other hand."

"Recently?"

"Probably some years ago, an artisan effort, too, I'd say. Usually people just melt them off, hold them over the ring of a hot stove, that kind of thing, but this seems to be a very skilful graft."

Manx stood back, and rubbed his palm over his stubble. "So, we have a male body, testicles removed and used as a weapon, and no fingerprints. What about the tox report?"

"Blood alcohol level of zero point one eight three, which probably means the poor sod was unconscious when it happened. We won't get the full run for a few days, but in the meantime, I'll take some dental x-rays, though God knows if I'll find anything conclusive in there." Hardacre sighed, and wheeled away the gurney. "I'm afraid he's just another John Doe, until we know otherwise."

***

Driving back across the Britannia Bridge towards Anglesey, Manx felt the familiar dingy caste of the scenery lurk over him like a bad mood. To his North, the Snowdonia mountain range was half hidden under a thick roll of clouds, and ahead of him, Anglesey was like a grey shadow, drained of colour and substance. The weekend's storm had passed, but it had left a heavy, sodden weight in the air. *The promise of more of the same*, Manx thought.

A hundred feet below him, the waters of the Menai Strait flowed as they always did, fast and unpredictable. A fine bank of mist had begun to roll in from the Irish Sea, obscuring the small islands and inlets along the waterway. Manx thought back to last night, how the body was crucified to the bow, as if it was being hung up for display. This wasn't just a murder; it was a message. And messages, he knew from experience, rarely arrived without a follow-up.

Chapter 4

It was late Monday afternoon when Manx arrived back at Llangefni Station. PC Mickey Thomas was on duty, his elbows stretched like great, hairy causeways across the desk, and his eyes dutifully scanning over the day's Page Three offering. His outsize, bear-like presence had been a permanent fixture at the old Station for over thirty years, and amidst the pristine cleanliness of his new habitat, Mickey gave the impression of a recently excavated relic, transferred with care and prudence to its new location. Not that this would have concerned him; meditating on his situation would have required a level of self-awareness Mickey Thomas, even this late in his life, would have been incapable of cultivating. Mickey was one of life's constant optimists, always ready with a smile and a warm word, and was due to retire in a few weeks. Over the past few weeks, it had occurred to Manx that Mickey was intent on perfecting the art of doing as little as possible in preparation for that day.

"Weather's cleared up, then," Mickey said, taking a sip of steaming hot tea, the colour of treacle.

"It'll ruin your eyesight; didn't your mother warn you?" Manx said, as he checked out what had captured Mickey's attention.

Mickey blew out a thin, appreciative whistle. "Can't teach on old dog new tricks. Mind you, I'd fancy teaching this one a thing or two," he said, holding the newspaper at arms-length, then tilting it to the right and left, as if he expected the model to tumble out of print and onto the desk.

"Got a code ninety-nine just brewed, if you want one," he said.

"Why not," Manx said. "So, what's the crime du jour?"

Mickey sighed in a loud, exaggerated manner. "Oh, been a veritable hive of criminal activity today, boss," he said, finger reading across his computer screen. "One missing Shih Tzu, whatever the blazes that is. Still at large, by the way. And Dotty Williams from Pentre Berw paid us her weekly, wanted us to evict the German POWs holding out in her hydrangeas. Told her we'd send in the SWAT team, pronto."

"Outstanding. I'll be in the MIR," Manx said.

Mickey looked at him, puzzled.

"Major Incident Room."

"Rightio. That's what they're calling it these days, is it?" Mickey said. "Oh, before I forget, Chief says he wants a word, when you get a minute," he added, before turning his attention back to Terri, the "*nineteen-year-old trainee dog groomer from Southampton and her 36DD puppies.*"

Manx stood facing the incident board, and pinned up the last of the photographs. He'd arranged them in chronological order, starting with the harbour at Cemaes, the body crucified on the boat, and then, Hardy's autopsy shots. Apart from the statistics concerning time and cause of death, and John Doe's probable age, weight, and height, Manx had no other compelling evidence to present. What little evidence he did have pointed to one simple fact; this wasn't a spontaneous act. Most murders were committed in the heat of the moment—a fistfight gone too far, an argument escalated, a robbery interrupted. This was carefully planned, and there was no attempt to hide the body; in fact, the killer had gone out of his way to display the carcass, as if it were a Christmas decoration. There were acres of farmland and forest on the island; you didn't have to be a criminal mastermind to bury a body here, and keep it hidden.

"Right!" Manx said, tapping the white board with the dry eraser. "I will assume, for the sake of time, you've all read the incident report."

There was a low mumbling of what he took to be yeses from the small investigation team he'd been assigned.

"Priddle?"

"Sir?" the young PC said, startled.

"Time of death?"

"Um, sometime Saturday night, sir?"

"Cause?"

Priddle fumbled through the pathology reports, dropping them to the floor as he did so.

"Have you ever worked a murder case before, Constable?" Manx asked.

"Not like a human murder, no, sir," Priddle said.

Manx chose not to pursue the remark. Priddle seemed keen enough, but still had an acre of freshly spawned, green moss lodged behind his earlobes.

"OK, rule number one. The path report is your B.F.F in a murder investigation. That's Best Fucking Friend, in case you were wondering."

"Asphyxiation!" Priddle said, suddenly recalling the report. "Strangled," he added, as if to clarify his answer.

"I know it says that," PC Delyth Morris said. "But, there's no mention of any bruising around the neck. Wouldn't there be some kind of ligature marks, if he was strangled?"

Delyth Morris was the youngest on the team, a year out of Police Training College. The older officers already had a nickname for her, Morris Minor, on account of her height; five-foot dead in police flats. She had the build of a gymnast, or a swimmer, Manx thought, stocky, wide shouldered, muscular, probably a fast runner.

"Correct, Morris," Manx said. "Normally, strangulation would be accompanied by bruising around the neck, which is why, Priddle, he was not strangled but asphyxiated."

"Says here the victim has no fingerprints, either. His face is too fucked up to cross-reference dental records. Unless his DNA's already in the database, we have no fucking clue who he is," Detective Sergeant Maldwyn Nader said, shrugging his wide shoulders, and leaning back nonchalantly in his chair.

DS Nader was the most senior officer on the team, and had been on the island since he was a trainee; a fact he insisted on reminding Manx of as often as he felt necessary. Manx hadn't made up his mind about Nader yet. He always seemed to be looking at Manx through the corner of his eye, as if he were trying to figure him out, or catch him out—he could never be sure.

"On the positive side, here's what we do know," Manx continued. "Our victim is in his mid-sixties, looked after himself. Evidence of hair implants, his nails, what's left of them, were manicured, and looks like he spent time in the sun recently."

"Not from around here, then," Nader offered.

Manx handed out a photo. "OK, let's turn to the nasty little addition to the case," he said. "It's not in the incident report, because we want to keep this particular detail from the rags, for the time being."

"Looks like my wife's cooking," Nader said.

"John Doe's testicles," Manx explained. "Extracted and implanted in the throat cavity."

"Jesus!" Nader said, pulling the photograph closer. "Is that what they look like?" He turned his attention towards PC Morris. "Hey, Minor, ever had a pair handed to you on a plate before?"

"If you're offering, Nader," Morris said, making an exaggerated snipping action with her fingers.

"Nader, you've worked the island a while. Ever come across anything like this before? It could be a warning, or some kind of message?" Manx said.

"Shit! I'd remember if some poor bastard came in with his knackers stuffed down his throat."

"Ok, let me put it another way," Manx said. "Anybody you know who might have the profile or mindset to do this?"

"I heard Mickey's wife say she'd cut off his bollocks next time he comes home with a belly-full. We should bring her in for a statement."

Manx held his breath, and counted to five. He'd come across the class jokers before. They loved the attention, but it didn't mean they were bad coppers; they just required precise directions. "Nader, I want you to approach your CIs. See who's been pissing on whose turf, that kind of thing."

Nader shrugged his shoulders. "Not many of them confidential informants round here, boss. We're not exactly the crime capital of the western world. Probably just some nut-job with a grudge."

"It might be farming related," Morris said. "When they castrate lambs? Farmers used to do it with bricks or stones. They use a special tool these days to make a clean cut, more humane."

"Oh, aye? Know a lot about that do you, Minor? Castration?" Nader said, nudging Priddle with his elbow.

"My dad kept sheep," Morris explained. "He'd hire blokes to come over to do the castrations in the spring."

"Jesus, Minor! It's like Silence of the fucking Lambs over here," Nader said, making a loud sucking noise with his tongue. "You want to sauté my liver with some baked beans?"

"It's fava beans," Morris said, shaking her head.

"Good," Manx said. "Find out if any farmers have reported their..." Manx paused, "...implements stolen."

"Emasculators, sir, that's what they call them."

"Right. Check the local farm supply stores, see if anyone who doesn't fit the profile of a farmer bought any of these emasculator things recently."

Manx checked his notes. "Priddle, you'll be on door-to-door around Cemaes. Ask if anyone saw anything unusual in the last few days. And, while you're down there, rattle Dick Roberts's cage some more. If he gives you the silent treatment, threaten to bring him down to the station for a consultation."

"Anything specific you want me to ask him, sir?"

"Questions. Ask him *questions*, Priddle. I'll assign a uniform to sift through the missing person's database, and see if anyone matching John Doe's description comes to light."

Manx walked back to the incident board. "This is the first phase of our investigation. We're looking under rocks, eliminating the obvious. Remember, there's a reason we call them John Does, a reason we give them a name. He's someone's son, husband, or father, and we owe it to them to find his killer, before we're in here pinning another victim to the board."

"You don't think it's a one-off, sir?" Morris asked.

"I think we can't rule anything out, at this point. Our killer is a showman. He wanted us to find the body, which means he's either sending a message, or he's a sick individual, who wants to share his handiwork with the world. I realise we're understaffed for a major murder investigation, so I'll ask the Chief to free up a few more uniforms, but, in the meantime, I expect hard work, clean evidence gathering, and for all three of you to work like a team. Anything unclear in what I just said?"

There was a communal shaking of heads.

"Outstanding. Let's get to work."

***

Manx sat in the Chief's office, tapping his leg impatiently, as Detective Chief Inspector Ellis Canton carefully pruned the leaves off his Japanese Maple Bonsai Tree. He was surprisingly delicate for a man with such large hands, Manx thought, as he watched the Chief pluck at fragile branches with a pair of miniature butterfly trimmers. After a few moments of deep concentration, he leaned back in his chair and surveyed his plants, as if he were sizing up a gallery exhibition.

"It's all about the symmetry, Tudor," Canton said. "You have to remember, it's a tree, not a bush. Trim upwards, always upwards. You've got to tease the bugger to grow the way you want it to grow; otherwise it's Bonsai bloody anarchy." Canton brushed the sides of his thick fingers gently up the length of the plant, then swivelled on his chair to face Manx.

"Got my message, then?"

"Here, aren't I?" Manx said.

"Never one for small talk, were you?" Canton said. "Your transfer papers," he added, sliding two A4 sheets across the desk. "Came in this morning. One for you, one for our records, just need your autograph, and you're officially under my jurisdiction,

God help me," he said, shaking his large, bald head, which reminded Manx of an over-sized Christmas ham. Manx quickly glanced over the papers; his foreseeable future laid out in black and white. It was a sobering thought.

Canton sensed Manx's hesitation. "Did I tell you how many strings I had to pull to make this happen, Manx?"

"Several times, Chief," Manx said, bristling.

Canton sighed. "You had a choice, Manx. It was either this, or a career pushing boxes around an evidence room until they pension you off."

"So, no choice at all, then, Chief."

Canton cleared his throat. "There's an old Japanese proverb, Manx: wake from death, and return to life. It means no matter how desperate the situation, you turn it around as quickly as you possibly can. From death to life, in one swift move."

"Read that on the back of a Sushi box?"

Canton grimaced. "Free proverb with every Bonsai tree," he said, and tended to a stray piece of lint on the front of his uniform. "There's opportunity aplenty here, Manx, should you care to look. When they re-assigned the North Wales Constabulary divisions, yours was the first name I put forward. I'm already nursing a few bruised egos from certain officers, who thought they had it in the bag, which means you'll have to brush up on those people management skills the force is so hot on these days. Oh, and one more piece of advice, don't be a prick. My prick-ness tolerance is running pretty low these days. I'll put it down to old age."

"I didn't ask for any favours," Manx said.

"Case in point," Canton said, wagging his finger. "That thing I just told you about not being a prick? For future reference, that was a prick-ish remark. Now, please autograph these so we can both get back to work."

Manx quickly signed, before he changed his mind.

"Welcome to the North Wales Constabulary, Inspector." Canton extended his hand. Manx took it, and offered up a weak, thin smile. "You join us at exciting times, Tudor, brand new station, wired, so they tell me, with the very latest technology. And, let's not forget, the second-in-line to the throne and his lovely wife's presence on the island, which has everybody, even the Welsh Nationalists, it seems, giddy as schoolgirls."

"Not much of a monarchist myself, Chief."

Canton huffed. "I trust you'll keep your political views to yourself when I introduce you to the Royal Security Detail. They'll need to put a face to the name, know who's in charge, if I'm out of commission."

"So long as you don't expect me to curtsey."

"I expect you to be professional, and show suitable deference."

"Deference is my second name," Manx said.

Canton looked at him through squinted eyes, and decided to ignore the remark. "Any progress on that nasty business down at Cemaes?"

"I need more feet on the ground," Manx said.

"Ok, since we're negotiating, I can probably rustle up a couple more warm bodies. Now, your turn."

Manx paused. "Forensics pulled a blood trace off the lobster basket. We've sent it to the lab, and should have the results back tomorrow."

"Any hunches?"

"A little early for that."

Canton sat back, and looked Manx directly in the eyes. "I'd recommend you don't play this one too close to your chest, Tudor. I want to know everything you know, the second you know about it. Think you can handle that? None of this maverick, Lone Ranger fuckery."

"Fuckery, chief?"

"Fuckery, Manx. I made it my priority when we opened this station six weeks ago, it would be a fuckery-free zone. So far, it's working, so don't fuck up my good work."

"Got it. Anything else?"

"Since you ask, yes," Canton said, and slid Manx a colourful, glossy folder, featuring a smiling policeman shaking hands with a line of kids dressed in Halloween costumes. Written across the top, in bold letters, was BANG: *Be A Nice Guy this Halloween and Bonfire night.*

"Community Policing. Thirty hours a year, to include on-site training and community integration. How's your Welsh, by the way? We could do with a few more native speakers in the ranks."

"If you want someone with the verbal capacity of a five-year old, then I'm your man."

Canton rubbed his hands together, vigorously, as if he were attempting to spark a fire. "Still, never say never, eh? Being back on the island might inspire you to brush up on the mother tongue."

"You'll be the first to know," Manx said, edging towards the door.

"Oh, before you skip off into the sunset." Canton handed Manx a flyer. "You can put the time served against your community hours."

Manx unfolded the paper. "A.M.A.D.?"

"Anglesey Mothers Against Drugs. They hold their monthly next week. Groups like this are sprouting up like mushrooms these days. Websites, Facebook, Twitter, can't keep up with it all myself, but I do know they'll post anything, if it makes a noise. Truth, fiction, they don't seem to care, so long as it promotes the cause. In short, Manx, don't say anything that's going to bite me on the arse, or get the force involved with one of those damned hashtag campaigns. Play nice with the other kids in the playground. Understood?"

"No fuckery, Chief," Manx said, folding the brochure into his jacket pocket.

Canton nodded. "Glad we're on the same page, Manx."

Chapter 5

S hanni's tongue felt like a thick slice of raw liver, as the man wedged an elbow against his throat. He was seconds away from passing out, when the man finally removed his forearm.

"What the fuck?" Shanni said. The words burned at his throat.

The man said nothing, and stretched his arms skywards, cracking his knuckles. He was tall and wide—the image of brick shithouse came to Shanni's mind. The light was too dim to make out the man's face, and anyway, his eyes still had spots dancing in front of them.

"Jesus, fuck! You could've crushed me fuckin' vocal chords."

The man sat across from Shanni, and flipped a long, sharp knife from palm to palm. "And so would end your Karaoke career. A sad loss to the world, I'm sure."

An hour ago, Shanni Morgan was minding his own business, fixing the head gasket on his Ford Capri S. Now, he was sitting in a barn, which reeked of sweat and cow manure, looking into the dead, cold eyes of a black English Mastiff, the size of a small pony, that hadn't taken its gaze off him since he'd arrived.

The two goons, now standing guard at the door, had dragged Shanni into a van, tied him to a chair, slapped his hands, palms down, and then spread out each of his fingers between several wedges of wood that were attached to the table. It happened so efficiently, he barely had time to register what was going on, until they clamped his wrists down with a metal rod and secured it with two screws. He tried to move his hands, but they were spread out like a fan, vulnerable and exposed. Shanni knew most of the muscle for-hire around the island, but he didn't recognise either of them. They looked professional, Shanni thought, not in it for the thrill of a punch up and beer money. They were probably Eastern-European—hairy, dark bastards with low foreheads and stoic, dead-eyed stares.

The man poured a double measure of eighteen-year-old Macallan into a shot glass. Shanni's focus gradually began to re-calibrate itself. The man had a taut, sinewy face both wide and muscular. *Like one of those freakish, steroid pumped body-builders,* he thought. His head was shaved to the nub, and his biceps bulged conspicuously under his t-shirt sleeves. On his neck, Shanni noticed two thirds of what he guessed was a Union Jack tattoo. The man said nothing, as he sipped at his Scotch, but watched Shanni with the intensity of a panther stalking its prey. Shanni's mouth was suddenly as dry as powder.

"Do you know what you look like?" the man said, after a long pause. He had a polished, English accent. *Proper Queen's English,* Shanni thought. "You look like a rat, a pathetic, neutered rodent, like one of those hamsters stuck on a wheel. Round and round you go." He spoke deliberately, as if he was carefully plating his sentences before serving them up, and illustrated his point by circling his finger in a continuous motion. "What kind of name is Shanni, anyway? Sounds like something I'd use to clean my windows. You do that, clean windows? Steady work in this economy, I'd imagine."

"It's just a nickname. Had it since school."

"Kids can be so cruel," the man said. "But, as we're on the subject of school days, do you remember Edward Longshanks?"

Shanni shrugged. "Maybe. What form was he in?"

"Very amusing," the man said, leaning back in his chair. "History, Shanni, is at its best when it serves to illuminate the present. Edward Longshanks, or Edward the First of England, cut his teeth on the crusades, and acquired a taste for spilling blood at an early age. Back in those days, I'd wager, there wasn't a Welshman within a hundred miles who wouldn't have sacrificed his life for a chance at drawing a sword through his back. Longshanks, of course, hated the Welsh. They were a thorn in his side, a nation of odious, rebellious nationalists which needed to be tamed. He spilled rivers of Welsh blood, but then again, the Welsh had their own share of bloody victories: quid pro quo, so to speak. You probably know the castles around here were built by Edward to keep the Welsh in check. Most people believe, incorrectly, they were built to protect Wales from the marauding masses; nothing could be further from the truth. A smart strategy, unless you happened to be Welsh, of course."

"You a history teacher, or something?" Shanni asked.

The man tensed his body like a cobra waiting to strike. "Point being, Shanni, people quickly forget their history. A few centuries of relative calm, and it's all water under the bridge. Personally, I've never bought into that holier than thou, don't bear grudge, libertarian claptrap. When I turn the other cheek, I'm just inviting someone to poke me in that one, too. Seems reasonable, wouldn't you say?"

"I really have no fucking idea what you're on about," Shanni said. "You sure you've got the right bloke? There's a couple of Shanni's around, maybe you got us mixed up, mistaken identity, or something?"

The man laughed—a short, one note bark. "You're a character, Shanni, I'll give you that," he said, unscrewing a pill bottle, and laying a powder- blue, cylindrical tablet on the table. "I'm sure you're familiar with these."

"On the Viagra, then? Don't have the need for it myself," Shanni said.

"Let's try again, shall we?" The man loomed over Shanni, pushing his knuckles deep into the back of his hands, as if he were kneading dough.

"Jesus! I don't know, do I?"

"Look. Closer."

"Never seen 'em that colour, before," Shanni said, reading the M embossed on side of the pill.

"We inject food dye early in the manufacturing process."

"Yeah? Is that why you brought me here, show me a pill? Seems a bit over the top, mate."

"I'm not your mate, Shanni," the man said. "But, I expect we'll be seeing a lot more of each other."

"Yeah, how's that, then?"

"Just a hunch. It's a small island; people like to talk, especially about your little distribution business."

Shanni bristled, as the man leant closer.

"You really should choose your business partners more carefully."

"Nah, you got wrong bloke, mate. Now, there's a Shanni Evans over by Talwrn. I hear he's into some dodgy shit, smuggles exotic birds..."

Before Shanni could finish, he felt the cold edge of a blade pass slowly over his Adam's apple. A small trickle of blood dripped to the table.

"You're becoming tiresome, and I really don't have the inclination to play games," the man said.

Shanni's heart pounded. "OK! Put the fucking blade down. I'll listen. No harm in listening, eh?"

The man wiped the small trace of blood from the knife on Shanni's shirtsleeve. "I have a business proposition," he said.

Shanni chuckled nervously. "What? Like, an offer I can't refuse?"

"You can refuse anything; I just wouldn't recommend it, as a preferred course of action."

Shanni stalled. "Don't do business with people I don't know. Too risky."

"You require references?" the man asked, raising an eyebrow.

"No," Shanni said, realising how stupid it sounded. "But, a name would be helpful, like."

The man nodded. "Scuttler," he said.

"Scuttler? You just make that up?" Shanni said.

The man flipped the knife around in his palm.

"All right. Say, I am the Shanni you think I am, and I know something about whatever the fuck it is you're talking about. Why would I do business with you?"

"Because, despite your appearance, you're not stupid. I'd say, you're tired of foraging around for scraps, like a rat. That's no way to provide a stable future for yourself and your family."

Shanni bristled at the word 'family.' His thoughts rushed to his wife and six-year-old son, who were probably at home starting dinner without him.

Scuttler continued, "What's your take? A few hundred a month? By the time you pay your distributors, can't leave much in your retirement fund."

"What's your point?"

"I can provide you twenty times what you're moving right now, maybe fifty times more," Scuttler said. "I supply the channels of manufacture, you provide the distribution. The way the economy's nose-diving, I imagine people like yourself will be clamouring for a few hours release from their shitty lives, and we, Shanni, can offer them salvation. Alternatively, you could continue breaking into clinics, keep on with that junkie routine which gets you a few hits, but you're in a game of diminishing returns. Sooner or later, you will run dry."

Shanni took a deep breath. "OK, so let me get this straight. You want me to sell this shit for you? On the island?"

"You already have a network in place, and more product on the street equals more money in your pocket. You will have to step up your game, of course, and you'll be working for me, which has its benefits."

"A company car would be nice," Shanni said, beginning to relax a little. "I got a supplier already, though. You'll have to cut him in."

Scuttler laughed. "Stokes? Don't worry he's completely on-board. You won't hear a word of complaint from him." Scuttler threw a large brown leather bag onto the table. Shanni's eyes blossomed like dawn mushrooms, as Scuttler ran his hands through the stacks of fifty-pound notes.

"Nice carrot," Shanni said. "Where's the stick?"

"Well, since you ask," Scuttler said, and sat on the edge of the table. "I'm a big believer in preventative measures. There's nothing worse than entering this kind of transaction without clear expectations on both sides, muddied waters and all that. "He lifted the knife by the handle, so it hung twelve inches above Shanni's fingers.

"What the fuck?" Shanni said. A trickle of sweat dripped from his forehead and into his eyes.

"In the more rural communities of the deep American South, I believe they call it Redneck Roulette," Scuttler said, swinging the knife, like a pendulum, back and forth between his thumb and index finger.

Shanni stiffened. "No! No need for this mate, I'm in! Whatever it is, count me in." He felt the breeze from the knife, as it cut through the air, and splintered the table with a dull thud. It missed his skin by a hair's breadth.

"Lucky you," Scuttler said, extracting the knife. "Let's try again."

"No! Shanni shouted, squirming in his chair. "I don't fuck people over. If partners, partners, right?"

The knife fell again, this time slicing through the thin membrane of Shanni's index finger. A thin trickle of blood ran off the table and onto the floor. The mastiff stirred, and slurped lazily at the meagre offering.

"Fuck!" Shanni bit his bottom lip. "I'll sell it, whatever you've got. I know people with dough, serious money." Sweat poured into Shanni's eyeballs, creating a thick, impenetrable mist. "I got it, point made, mate."

"Now we're getting somewhere," Scuttler said, placing the knife in the fold of his fist. "Are you familiar with the phrase, flipping the bird?"

"Yeah, what about it?" Shanni's eyes were now laser-fixed on the blade.

"For example, if you sell my merchandise, but retain some of the profits, that would be a sign of disrespect, requiring swift justice, correct?"

Shanni swallowed hard, as Scuttler stabbed at the air between his fingers with the knife in slow, steady motion. Thud. Thud. Thud.

"Now, if I were to discover you were selling your own merchandise, along with mine, that would also be a betrayal of trust, don't you think?"

Thud. Thud. Thud. The stabbing grew faster. Scuttler looked directly into Shanni's eyes, as the knife tip dug into the table—it was a fatal, thudding metronome, hypnotising Shanni, as it skipped over his fingers.

"Then, there's the risk of you absconding with the merchandise. That would be tantamount to flipping me the bird, correct? A big fuck you?"

Shanni felt the veins in his neck pulsating like jack-hammers.

"But, if I were to metaphorically speaking, eliminate that temptation…" Scuttler said, stabbing the knife harder and faster into the table. "Round and round she goes, where she'll land, nobody knows."

Thud. Thud. Thud.

The knife was a blur of steel, skipping over Shanni's hands.

"Jesus fucking Christ!"

The blade landed with a clean and precise cut.

"FUCK!"

Shanni barely felt the blade sear through his middle finger—the pain would come later. A spurt of blood oozed from the small remaining stump. Any words Shanni intended to utter were lodged thick in his throat. He attempted to scream, but could only mouth the action.

Scuttler sat back, and reached for the scotch bottle. *Thank Christ*, Shanni thought, *a fucking drink*. He widened his lips to receive the paltry benediction of mercy, but Scuttler only smiled and slowly dripped the Scotch over the bleeding finger. This time, he did scream: loud and prolonged. The dog pricked up its ears and sat to attention.

"That should stop any infection. And don't worry. No major arteries there, so you won't bleed to death." Scuttler picked up Shanni's severed finger, and inspected it. "Very dirty nails. You should take your personal hygiene more seriously. They're breeding ground for all kinds of bacteria. Still, one less digit to worry about now."

He threw the finger to the floor. In seconds, the Mastiff had scooped it into its mouth, and slunk off to the other end of the barn to chew on it. Scuttler signalled to the two heavies.

"Get him out of here."

The goons grabbed Shanni's armpits, and dragged him across the floor.

"No evidence in the car," Scuttler said, throwing them a roll of surgical bandages. "Drop him at the nearest surgery. Make sure no one sees you."

Shanni felt the welcome rush of cold air, as the barn doors swung open.

"If the pain gets too much, you can always take this," Scuttler said, stuffing one of the blue pills into Shanni's jacket pocket. "I'll be in touch."

Chapter 6

Thinking back on the incident later that day, Gareth Pearce concluded if he'd tacked three seconds earlier, he could have easily avoided the dark, bloated shape in his path. As was his fate that day, his trajectory was perfect. His longboard ploughed into something soft and fleshy, and bucked Gareth, headfirst, into frigid waters at Rhosnegir Beach.

The impact was as sharp as it was cold. He tried to push back to the surface, but the sail had formed a thick and impenetrable ceiling of Darcon laminates and Monofilm above him. He kicked at the sail, twisting his body as he did so, but his waist was tethered to the boom by the harness lines. His lungs pressed urgently against his ribcage, as he struggled. *Don't panic*, he told himself. *There's a way out of this.* He was an engineer, that's what he did; he solved problems.

The harness had rotated a hundred and eighty degrees, the clasp now at his lower back. He reached for it, but his fingers were too thick and numb to unbuckle the mechanism. Then, he remembered—his gloves.

The thick neoprene came off easier than he expected, and was quickly carried away by the currents. The cold blunted the feeling in his hands, as he worked at the buckle—finally, it relented. Gareth kicked hard at the water, propelling his body from under the sail, and broke the ocean surface.

As he slumped over his board, an uneasy stillness gathered around him. He was used to the familiar orchestra of water and wind swirling in harmony as he surfed, but drifting here, alone, he suddenly felt vulnerable, an insignificant mass of meat and bones.

Gareth looked around for the object he'd hit; maybe a dead seal or debris from the Holyhead to Dun Laoghaire ferry, but there was nothing but slow-drifting seaweed. A hundred metres to his north, the thin outline of the shore was already fading in the shadowy twilight. He had two choices: haul the sail from the water and catch a strong wind back, or he could swim, and hope he made it back to shore before it got too dark. The decision, it came to pass, would be made for him.

A violent tug on the neck of his dry suit dragged him from his board and back into the water. Primal instinct compelled him to turn. What little blood left in his cheeks quickly drained. He was inches away from a ghost: a desperate, white-faced ghoul, bruised and bloodied, with a wild-eyed expression in its pale blue eyes. The ghost was so close, Gareth could feel the fetid stench of its breath, as if death itself were breathing on him.

Now, he panicked. He twisted his body right and left, hoping the ghost would relent, but it pulled tighter. The ghost's legs clutched around his waist, taking him back under the surface. A thick wall of water pressed down on him. He'd be dead in seconds, if he didn't act fast. He looked down at the ghost's hands, now wrapped round his neck, and bit down hard. The ghost released his grip. Gareth seized the slim window of opportunity and kicked. He surfaced a few feet away, shivering with fear and cold. He watched as the ghost curled its fingers around the edge of the board, and dragged itself to salvation, muttering as it did so, as if reciting an incantation.

Gareth turned and swam, in fast anxious strokes, back to shore.

Chapter 7

"Will he live?" Manx asked the on-duty doctor. It was ten at night, and Manx could tell the young man was dog tired. There were dark sacks under his eyes, and his skin had a grey pallor that spoke of too few hours of sunlight, and too many days under the harsh glare of hospital fluorescents.

"He'd do a lot better with less undue stress and attention," the doctor said, repositioning the clipboard at the foot of the bed.

After a brief working-over by the paramedics, the Anglesey Air Ambulance had flown the man to Gwynedd Hospital in Bangor. Nobody had extended much hope the man would survive the helicopter flight let alone the night, but the man had an intense determination to live, which, for a moment, Manx envied, before reminding himself that the object of his envy was lying in a coma, with thick plastic tubes inserted into his oesophagus, and the fragments of a bullet lodged in his left scapula.

"We'll have an officer on duty outside, just in case," Manx said.

"In case of what?" the doctor asked.

"No wallet? Papers, anything?" Manx asked.

"It's all in there." The doctor gestured at the plastic bag on the table.

"Clothing?"

"In the cupboard. We've induced a coma, which should give his body some time to heal, but don't expect miracles. He could be like this for weeks, or he may not recover at all; it's out of our hands. Now, if you'll excuse me I've got other patients that need my attention."

"No objections if I hang around?"

"Would it make any difference if I did?" the doctor said wearily.

Manx pulled up a chair, and felt the flimsy weight of the plastic bag in his hands. The wedding ring seemed new, probably recently married. The watch looked expensive—a Rolex, according to the label. Manx lifted it towards the light. It had the weight of a fairground trinket, and a spit of salt-water had pooled inside the face—definitely a fake. He inspected the man's clothes; heavy trousers, a thick woollen sweater, and a dark, blue quilted jacket, still damp. He lifted up the jacket and looked at the bullet hole. Any closer to the heart, and Hardacre would be conducting another post-mortem. Manx sat back in the chair and looked at the man's face—it seemed so translucent that it might soon fade completely into the pristine, white pillowcase supporting it.

Two men in two days, both hauled in from the ocean. Manx had briefly entertained the idea it was just a coincidence, but he knew better. Neither man had ended up in the water by accident. There was motive and purpose to both. All he knew for sure was the man fighting for his life had been shot somewhere on the coast, discarded like litter into the ocean, and survived through sheer luck and grim determination. The other man had not been so lucky.

Before he left, Manx returned the clothes to the cupboard, and replaced the plastic bag to the bedside table. "Who are you, and what the hell happened?" he whispered, as he looked at the man's face. The only response was the rhythmic, shallow panting of the artificial respirator and the digital pulsing of the heart monitor, taunting him with its insistent, life-affirming bleeps.

Chapter 8

Manx eased the Jensen into the parking space outside Woolly Backs, and tugged hard on the failing handbrake—another mechanical flaw requiring his attention.

The wool shop was situated at the end of a row of terrace houses on the peak of the hill overlooking Moelfre beach. Set against the slate-grey hue of the sky, the shop stood out like a prissy dollhouse left out in the rain. The window frames, once bright red, had now faded and cracked like day-old lipstick, and a jumble of multi-coloured jumpers, cardigans, and scarves filled the dusty bay window. The shop's exterior walls were studded with specks of stone that, when caught in the right ray of sunlight, sparkled like cheap gemstones. *What was it with pebble dashing around these parts*, Manx thought. The fad should have died out with The Bay City Rollers and tight-fitting, cheesecloth shirts.

He peered through the window. The shop floor was rimmed on all sides with yarns and knitting supplies. Behind the counter sat a woman, whom he assumed was the owner. She looked to be in her fifties, with bleach-blonde hair gathered up into a wannabe beehive, which itself looked like a yarn of wool. An unlit cigarette dangled lazily from the corner of her lips, and she was deep in conversation with two men in large black overcoats. She was doing most of the talking, while the men nodded, their necks bowed forward to avoid scraping their heads on the low ceiling. Manx could only see their backs, but they looked out of place— two bulls in a wool shop. Manx decided to wait a few minutes, before ringing the bell for "Hairs and Graces. Style by Gwen," situated next door.

Several minutes later, the men left the shop. "Didn't have your shade then, lads?" he said, as they passed. They gave the Inspector a quick once over, and carried on walking. Manx watched them stroll down the hill and into the Pilot Arms. He took one last glance in the shop window. The owner was still in the same position, her hands moving to the knit-one, pearl-one rhythm of her needles, as if she was working over the beads of a rosary, and the cigarette, still unlit, hung like a spare limb from her mouth.

***

"When was the last time you had this mop cut? Queen's Silver Jubilee?" Gwen asked, running her hands through Manx's hair so it settled in limp strands between her fingers.

"Waiting for the right occasion," Manx said.

"Got a hot date, then?"

"Prefer a hot cup of tea," Manx said, hearing the electric kettle on the far side of the salon click itself off.

"Sad, isn't it, old age?" Gwen said, patting Manx on the shoulder. "More interested in a cuppa than finding yourself a good woman."

"Well, you know where you are with a cup of tea. Women, on the other hand, complete mystery."

"Maybe that's how we like it. Keep you all guessing," Gwen said. She walked over to the kitchen. "Two sugars or one?"

"Two, and don't drown it in milk… please."

"Anything else you'd like? Biscuits? Cake? Manicure or pedicure? We are a full-service salon," she added, placing the mug down carefully on the narrow ledge of her workstation.

"Many men come in asking for manicures?" Manx asked.

"You're joking, right? Bloody miracle if I can get any bloke 'round here to sit still for ten minutes for a short back and sides. Why? Do you need some new acrylics, or are you looking for a man with good nails to help you out with your enquiries?"

"Something like that," Manx said.

"I read about that horrible business in Cemaes, mind you. Surprised you had time to come in. Thought you'd cancel on me."

"I heard the tea was cheap."

Gwen folded her arms, and sized up the inspector. "Now, what did you have in mind for this?"

"You're the expert. I'll leave it in your hands," Manx said. "Just don't make me look like a policeman."

"Roger that, Inspector."

As Gwen snipped methodically at his hair, Manx found himself examining his reflection closely in the mirror. The ceiling spotlights glared down on him, and seemed to accentuate every flaw in his long face. His cheeks were becoming jowly; an unwelcome addition he'd only just noticed recently. At least he hadn't put on weight. He was still the same seventy-nine kilos he weighed at twenty-five, but he couldn't take the credit for that; he'd inherited those good genes from his mother. His father's side of the family, on the other hand, had been a short-legged, barrel-chested clan, built for tossing hay bales and pitchforking manure. In contrast, Alice Manx's family had been blessed with a leaner body form and sharply sculpted facial features, which would be described as handsome by any person passing even a cursory glance over the Manx family albums.

"You've got a good head of hair, mind," Gwen said, momentarily derailing his train of thought. Manx felt a string of goose bumps prickle at his neck, as she combed. "For a man your age. Probably lose your marbles before you'll lose your hair."

"Well, I've got that to look forward to, at least."

"I'm here to help," Gwen said, reaching for the scissors.

Gwen's body felt warm against his as she cut, gently brushing against his shoulder or arm as she manoeuvred her way around his frame.

"What do you know about the wool shop?" Manx asked.

"Mandy Fag's place, you mean?" Gwen said, cocking her head to one side to make sure Manx's hairline was symmetrically correct.

"Unusual surname."

"Funny bugger. She's always outside smoking, could set my clock to it, most days."

"She been here long?"

"A year or so. Took over the lease when the last owner, Mrs. Jarman, was taken ill. Pretty sudden, it was. Took off to Marbella, or somewhere, to recover."

"So, it's just her running the shop?"

"Bought the place for cash, too, I heard," Gwen said and leant in closer, her breasts brushing momentarily at Manx's right shoulder. "Honestly, I don't have much to do with her. I pay my rent and say a quick hello, just to be pleasant. She's always going on about her son, who lives up North somewhere, not that I've ever seen him visit, mind. Lot of people like that around here. They come here to retire, look forward to the peace, and quiet, then everybody forgets about them. Quite sad, I suppose."

"Mam! Mam! Did you see that car parked outside? It's bloody brilliant!"

Gwen's son, Owain, burst through the salon door, like a kid-sized dust devil, and threw his backpack onto the sofa in the waiting area.

"I'm hungry! Can I have a banana sandwich?" Owain folded his arms in a gesture which implied he wasn't moving until his request was met.

"Number one, Owain Schofield, language. Bloody is not on the list of acceptable words, is it? No matter what your granddad says."

"But, taid Arwyn says bloody all the time, he…" Owain began, before his mother cut him off.

"Number two, pick up your backpack and hang it on the peg, And, number three, no 'I wants,' without a please. You know the rules."

"Ugh! Please, I want a sandwich, Mam," Owain said, opening his backpack, and scrambling inside for scraps of leftover sweets.

"In a minute. I'm busy," Gwen said. "Inspector Manx, this is my son Owain. He's not always this bad mannered, only on days that end in a y."

Manx turned around. Owain was dressed in his school uniform, the same blue colour Manx himself had worn at that age.

"Nice to meet you, Owain."

"You really a policeman?" Owain shuffled gingerly towards Manx, unsure whether to be impressed or worried. Manx took out his badge.

"Cool!" Owain said. "Is that your car outside? American, yeah?"

"No. It's a Mark Three, Jensen Interceptor, one hundred per cent British. Which is why it breaks down a lot."

Owain's face fell a little as Manx spoke, but quickly perked up again when an idea struck him. "Can I have a go?" he asked.

"Oh, good driver, are you?"

"Yeah, Mam says I'm very good at driving her up the wall."

"I bet you are," Manx said.

"Owain, don't you have homework?" Gwen said.

"No!" he said, and stared gloomily at his feet.

"Owain?"

Owain slumped his shoulders, and pulled out a few scrunched sheets of coloured paper from his backpack.

Gwen smiled, and finished trimming the back of Manx's hair. "There. Not too policeman-like for you?"

Manx nodded his approval.

"Want to see the back?"

"No, I'll take your word for it," Manx said, brushing himself down. "Fiver, right?" He handed Gwen a crisp note from his wallet.

"One time offer. Next time, ten quid, and I expect to see a line of blue outside now I've got the approval of the local constabulary." Gwen paused, the spark of an idea forming. "Maybe I should put up a sign: Stylist to the Detective Inspector of Anglesey."

"Business woman of the year in the making," Manx said.

"Well, can't be a barmaid all my life," Gwen said. "The pay's terrible, and the customers don't tip."

"You'd leave me all alone with all the old codgers at the bar?" Manx said.

"Stay there long enough, and they'll be saying the same about you."

Manx nodded, put that particular thought to the back of his mind, and stepped out to the brittle, late morning.

Chapter 9

Manx walked down the narrow, coastal path towards Moelfre Lifeboat Station—a simple, stone-built structure with a steep concrete slip protruding into the open sea. The lifeboat house had been here since before Manx's grandmother was born, eighteen thirty-three, according to the metal plaque on the wall.

"You the policeman who called, then?"

The voice took Manx by surprise. He turned around. Frank Bingham, a squat man with a shock of white hair, pulled open the door to the rear of the station.

"Detective Inspector Tudor Manx." Manx offered his hand. Frank shook it efficiently, as if he had more important things to do with his day.

"Frank Bingham, coxswain. You'd best come in."

Inside, the lifeboat occupied most of the available space. Its sparkling hull locked in place by metal chains and various brass and steel mechanical paraphernalia that seemed to Manx as unknowable as ancient artefacts.

Manx passed his fingers softly over the hull. "Impressive," he said.

"Aye, the old girl's more impressive when she's out there, mind you," Frank said, nodding his head seaward. Manx noticed Frank's back straighten as he spoke, as if the mere talking about the boat required a certain level of dignity and respect.

"Tyne Class, all-weather. Take a nuclear bomb to sink her." Frank slapped the bow playfully, as if he were giving his wife an affectionate tap on her bottom.

Manx noticed the photograph on the wall; Frank with ten of his volunteer crewmen squinting in bright sunlight on the launch ramp, the sea deep green and calm behind them.

"Tradition, that is,' Frank said. "The RNLI make us all take a new one every year. They tell me it's on the Facebook, or something or other. Even had those Royals down here last summer, some publicity thing, made me wear a bloody suit for it and all."

Frank gestured at a framed photograph of himself striking an uncomfortable pose in an ill-fitting checked sports jacket. William and Kate stood either side of him, the Prince in a grey, double-breasted suit, the Duchess in a navy-blue dress and a wide-brimmed hat. Despite his remarks, Manx noticed Frank's back stiffen with what he assumed was pride.

"Can't be bothered with all that stuff myself. It's all for the bloody tourists, but if it gets people to open their wallets to keep the station operational, you won't hear me complaining. Not that it would do any bloody good, if I did." Frank held up a large, battle weary kettle. "Want a cuppa, if you're going to be here a while?"

"Why not."

Frank handed Manx a steaming mug of tea the colour of scorched toffee. The airbrushed faces of William and Kate grinned back at him.

"The wife brought it. For the station," Frank explained. "Take them or leave them myself. All this fuss over nothing, trying to make out they're just like everyone else. Load of old bollocks. They're not, are they? The wife saw her couple weeks back, the Duchess, at Waitrose in Menai Bridge, couple of big security guards and a brand-new Range Rover. How many people do you know go shopping with bodyguards?"

"Not many," Manx said.

"You don't look much like a policeman. Not undercover, or something, are you?" Frank asked, passing a cursory eye over Manx's jeans, black jacket and loosely knotted tie combination.

"I couldn't tell you if I was, could I, Frank?"

"Aye, good point." Frank seemed satisfied with Manx's answer and split open a fresh packet of Marie biscuits with his penknife. He removed two biscuits, slathered a blade full of butter across each side, and slapped them together until the butter oozed from the centre. Manx remembered his grandfather used to do the same—a Marie biscuit sandwich, the only filling required, warm, full-fat, salted butter.

Frank noticed Manx staring. "Hungry?"

"No thanks, I'm partial to my arteries. Thanks all the same."

Frank shrugged, and bit into the crisp biscuit. "So, what's this about? Police business, or just curious to see the old girl before we trade her in for a new model?" Crumbs fell like snowflakes from Frank's mouth as he spoke.

Probably not used to many visitors, Manx thought, as the coxswain wiped his mouth with the sleeve of his sweater, and brushed the buttery detritus from his chest.

Manx explained they'd found a man washed ashore, without revealing the full extent of his injuries. Frank wiped his palms down the sides of his trousers, and slid open a large drawer built into an antique glass cabinet on the opposite wall. "We've got four Lifeboat Stations on the Island. Moelfre and Beaumaris on the east side, and on the west, you've got Holyhead and Treaddur Bay," Frank spread out a large, laminated map with a complex pattern of numbers and charts. "Our responsibility is the east side of the Island, up to Cemaes Bay. Holyhead takes over from there."

"We found him here," Manx said, pointing to Town Beach, Rhosenegir. "Most likely been in the water about a day, at the most."

"And he was still alive?"

"Still is alive," Manx corrected him.

Frank let out a sharp snap of a whistle. "Bloody miracle. You might want to make sure wasn't walking on the bloody water."

"This maybe a crackpot idea," Manx said, "but I was thinking because we know where he came shore, and approximately how long he's been in the water, we could work out roughly where he fell in."

"Fell in, did he?" Frank asked, his eyebrows twitching like rabbit tails.

"Let's just call it an accident."

Frank traced his fingers over the contours of the map. "I reckon you've got a couple of scenarios. That's what you lot call them, right, scenarios?"

Manx nodded.

Satisfied, Frank continued, "The currents flow east around here, so he probably drifted to Rhosnegir from somewhere in the Menai Strait." Frank pointed at the long stretch of water dividing Anglesey from the mainland. "He could have fallen in further out, mind you, in the Irish Sea, but he'd have probably hit shore well before, most likely Beaumaris or Bangor."

Frank reached for a well-leafed copy of the *Nautical Almanac* on the bookshelf above him, and flipped through the pages.

"Best guess?" Manx asked, peering at the lines running across the map, which meant as little to him as the paraphernalia hung on the station walls.

"And it's only a guess, mind you," Frank said. "The currents move fast in the strait, gets up to seven to eight knots. I'd say you're looking at three possibilities. He could have fallen in on the mainland, probably around Bangor or Caernarvon, or he could have landed in the drink from the island side, Beaumaris or Menai Bridge."

"And the third option?" Manx asked.

"He didn't fall in from the shore."

"What do you mean?"

"Idiots fall out of boats all the time, tourists and Sunday sailors mostly."

Fuck! He should have thought of that, but it made sense. There were no missing persons reported from either the island, or the towns along the mainland. "If he did fall, it wouldn't have been from a large ship, right?"

"Unless the captain was drunk, or had a death wish. I've seen plenty of those in my time," Frank said, swallowing a large slurp of tea.

"So, a small boat could make it through at low tide?"

"Nothing over thirty foot," Frank said, biting into his second biscuit. "It's just a guess. Don't be calling me into court to testify, like."

"You've been very helpful, Frank," Manx said, handing back his half-drunk mug of tea.

Frank gestured at the yellow donation box attached to the wall. "Aye.

Well, you can show your appreciation on the way out."

Manx shrugged, and patted his pant pockets. "Sorry, I just got wiped out by the hairdresser in the village," he said.

"Fleeced, were you?" Frank said, smiling.

Manx nodded, and returned the smile. "Keep up the good work."

"Someone has to," Frank said, as he poured the remainder of Manx's tea down the sink. He carefully washed the mug and set it back on the shelf, making sure Kate and William were turned towards the world as was only fitting, face-forward.

Chapter 10

PC Kevin Priddle wiped the moisture from the day's rain from his face, and knocked again on Dick Roberts's door. Silence. He knelt down, and flipped open the brass letterbox. "Mr. Roberts?" he shouted through the slim opening. "It's PC Priddle, from North Wales Constabulary. Can you open the door? Quickly, like." He whispered the last couple of words, and stamped on the ground.

Maybe Dick was still asleep, or maybe he'd sailed off to Marbella or somewhere. Either way, Priddle had a nagging suspicion this wasn't going to be swift. He'd probably be late for dinner again—the third time this week. His wife, Rhian, wouldn't be happy, give him the silent treatment for a few hours, before finally thawing out sometime before bedtime.

He stepped back a few feet from the house, and took stock of the property. It was a nondescript bungalow, smaller than the others on the road but with the identical pebbledash façade and slate roof. To his left, an old gate clattered noisily against its latch. Priddle shrugged, then edged past it into the back garden.

He was standing to the right of Dick Roberts's vegetable patch, naked and neglected for the winter, when the first sense of unease flitted through him like the unexpected skip of a heartbeat.

He pressed his face against the kitchen window. The table was laid for breakfast—an open box of Cornflakes, a carton of milk, and a teapot wrapped in a woollen tea cosy. Priddle moved to the adjacent window, which he guessed was the bedroom. The curtains were pulled tight. He pulled optimistically on the back door. *Locked. Shit!* He'd have to request a search warrant, and that could take hours. He saw his supper with Rhian slip, like a fading memory that had yet to happen, from his mind.

He was about to radio Manx with the update, when a loud crack from the rear of the garden made him snap to attention. He turned. It took him a few moments to locate the source. His nerves flutter anxiously, as he looked towards the shed at the end of the lawn, its door swinging noisily on its hinges in the stiff breeze.

"Mr. Roberts? Mr. Roberts?" Priddle called out, as he walked towards it, hoping to find some reassurance in the volume of his own voice but finding little. He called out again. "Are you in there? Mr. Roberts?"

His unease was growing like a small tumour in the base of his throat. He looked down; he was treading over shoeprints which had been forged earlier. They were smaller than his, but they looked fresh and ended abruptly at the shed entrance, as if the owner had walked across the garden then vanished.

A violent gust of wind hammered the fragile wooden door against the shed frame; the whole structure shook. Priddle stopped, his adrenaline pumping hard and twisting his stomach into knots.

Six feet from the shed, he stopped and looked back at the bungalow. *Had he missed something obvious?* It wouldn't be the first time. The wind had momentarily subsided, leaving a tentative, expectant silence that unsettled him more than the slapping of the door. There was something else in the air now, too; a strong aroma coming from inside the shed and directly into his gut, something fetid and rotten. He took a deep breath, waited for the nausea to pass, then walked on.

Another slam, this time like a shock of thunder. Priddle's heart lodged itself firmly in his throat, as he edged closer. The smell was so thick and present now, he could almost swallow it. The shed door swung loosely on its hinges, slapping against the frame, like an encouraging round of slow applause beckoning Priddle to move closer, then closer still.

At the entrance, the stench was overpowering. He craned his neck to peer around the edge of the door, keeping his feet firmly planted on the grass. There was a ponderous, slow creaking, as if the shed itself were alive, breathing in and out through its joints and joists. The only light fell from a dust-covered skylight, throwing a thin wedge of sunlight onto the workbench. He looked down. The shoe prints had stopped here—the point of no return. Priddle held his breath against the odour, and reached instinctively for the light switch, which he guessed correctly was to his right.

The fluorescent lights flickered to life. It was as if he were watching a trailer for a horror movie, a montage of fast cuts with bright, white flashes distorting the action, teasing out specks of the story. When, a few seconds later, the lights steadied to a quiet hum, Priddle's gaze was pulled towards a single object filling the space between the shed roof and the floor.

He brought his palm to his mouth.

Dick Roberts's body was hanging from the ceiling, swaying in time with the creaks and groans of the shed, his face contorted into a grotesque expression, which seemed to be staring directly at Priddle. Below him, a swarm of flies buzzed excitedly over the pool of liquefied faeces still dripping from the inside of his overalls.

Priddle's stomach lurched. He felt his legs buckle under him, and he fell to his knees, retching the final remnants of his breakfast over Dick Roberts's final imprint in the world.

Chapter 11

"Did you know, that out of the ten bodily functions which continue after death, erections and reflexive ejaculations are amongst the most common?" Richard Hardacre said, as he examined the body.

Manx looked down. Dick Roberts looked like a child, a boyish, skinny frame, which seemed lost inside his over-sized fisherman's overalls.

"In times of stress, the body eliminates waste," Hardacre continued, as he raised the fisherman's right arm to illustrate his point. "The body's muscles suddenly and instinctively relax, and…" Hardacre allowed the arm to fall to the floor. "Out it all comes. Defecation, urine, semen even."

Hardacre took his pen from his pocket, and waved it over the groin area, as if he were conducting an orchestra. "When one dies in an upright position, or, as in this case, probably completes the deed themselves, elementary physics dictates bodily fluids will be pulled downwards by the force of gravity. The fluid stops at the first obstacle in its path, the bladder or bowels, or in some cases the penis and testes." Hardacre traced his pen around the stiff bulge and telling wet patch on Roberts's crotch area. "Hence, he looks as if he's overdosed on Viagra, before shuffling off this mortal coil."

"Jesus," Manx said, as he leant closer in. He wouldn't have even noticed it, if the doctor hadn't brought it to his attention.

"When rigor mortis sets in, the muscles tense again, forcing out this small amount of ejaculate we see here. Think of it as his final fling. *Vita post mortem*, if you will. Quite literally, life after death," Hardacre explained. "It's one of the many reasons they eventually abolished public hangings. The trauma of witnessing a family member hung was shame enough, without the added humiliation of post-mortem defecation and what not. Of course, took us centuries to conclude it was cruel and unnecessary punishment. We're a slow-moving lot, we humans."

"Any conclusion on the actual cause of death?" Manx asked.

Hardacre breathed heavily. "Hand, please!" he said, as he began the strenuous task of hauling himself from kneeling to standing. Manx offered his arm, which Hardacre took immediately, using it as a lever to hoist himself. He was heavier than he looked.

"Don't get old, Manx, it'll bloody kill you," Hardacre said, and brushed himself down. "In my opinion, for what it's worth thus far, the victim's been deceased between two and four hours. No visible signs of violence, other than the abrasions around the neck area, which are consistent with hanging. Did he leave a note of any kind?"

"Not that we noticed."

"Too bad. Anyway, I'll need to prod around some more. Unless you have any pressing use for him, I'd like to escort him back to the mortuary."

"Be my guest," Manx said.

Hardy signalled to his two medics. They bagged and zipped up the body with striking efficiency. Manx felt a cold shadow pass through him, as they slotted Dick Roberts into the ambulance. It was a depressing coda to a life, dying alone in a woodshed on a cold November afternoon, on a slab of rock in the Irish Sea. *Would that be him one day? Would they find his body slumped over the kitchen table, face down in last night's Indian takeaway, and an empty bottle of Spring bank on the floor?* He imagined his own body, slipped with little ceremony into the body bag, and the eternal darkness which would accompany the final ratcheting of the zipper.

"Manx, Manx?" Someone was calling his name, but it sounded as if it was coming from afar, like a softly dissipating echo.

"Lost you there for a second, Manx," Hardacre said, patting Manx lightly on the shoulder, as if he were trying to wake him from a deep slumber.

"How long?" Manx asked. His words sounded thick in his mouth.

"How long, what?"

"The autopsy," Manx said, the world gradually coming back into focus.

"If we don't have a backup in the waiting room, I should have a preliminary report by sometime tomorrow."

"Any way to put a rush on that?"

Hardy peeled off his protective gloves. "Things have certainly become interesting since you came on the scene, Manx. They do say trouble has a way of following some people around."

"Don't believe much in superstition," Manx offered.

"Wise man. How's the murder investigation progressing?"

"Slowly," Manx said. "With fisherman Dick silenced for the duration, we're back to square one."

Hardacre slipped awkwardly from his over-suit, steadying himself on the ambulance. "In my experience, the dead often have a way of shining a light into the living," he said, swathing a generous helping of antiseptic gel through his fingers and palms. "See you around, Manx, but let's not make it a habit, eh? I'm too old for this kind of excitement," he said, pulling shut the ambulance doors.

Chapter 12

PC Priddle took a sip of warm tea, and looked towards the bungalow. "Fucking horrible, it was. The bloke's just hanging there, still swinging, piss and shit everywhere. Nearly lost my bloody breakfast."

"I heard you did lose it," Morris said. "All over Dick's footprints."

Priddle noticed the faintest trace of a smile on her face, but chose to ignore it. They were sheltering under the narrow canopy of the temporary incident room.

Priddle leant closer, and whispered, "That's just between you and me, like. You know what Nader and the others are like, take the piss for months, they would."

"If they hear anything, it won't be from me," Morris reassured him, but suspected it would be the talk of the station before day's end.

"Did you get a good look at him?" She asked.

"Who?"

"Dick Roberts, after, you know, they cut him down?"

"He was dead. I'm not hanging around taking fucking selfies," Priddle said, stepping back from Morris as if she were contagious.

"It's just I was reading the other day about how peoples' faces look after they've been a victim of a violent death," Morris continued.

Priddle wondered where she was heading with this line of conversation.

"Do you remember when you were a kid, and your mam used to tell you not to pull faces, because if the wind changed, it would stay like that?"

"Yeah. Didn't stop me though," Priddle said, sipping at his tea.

"Right rebel you were, I bet," Morris said. She noticed his pale, smooth skin blush at the remark. "Anyway, it says in this book when someone dies violently, their face stays in the same position it was the moment they died. It's like, they're reacting to the pain, and it's their last expression, or something. I pulled some photos from old police records in the archive. Make your blood curdle, they would, Priddle," she added, nudging him in the stomach.

Priddle swallowed hard; he was still feeling woozy from lack of food. "What were you doing looking at stuff like that anyway?" he asked.

"Further education, Priddle. It's not all bloody *CSI: Miami* out there. You know those scenes when they pull back a sheet to identify the victim, and the face looks all peaceful, like they're just taking a nap? Movie magic, Priddle, that's all that is. Apparently, undertakers have a bugger of a time fixing the faces back to normal. That's why they ask for recent photographs of the victims; make sure they get it right."

Priddle swallowed his tea too quickly and coughed. "Bloody hell, Morris, you need a boyfriend or a cat or a fucking budgie or something."

Morris laughed. "I've booked in for a cadaver workshop at the mortuary next month. You should sign up. I could stand behind you with a bucket, just in case."

Priddle looked at her, his mouth slightly ajar, which had the effect of collapsing his chin even further into itself. "Fucking sick, you are," he said, and walked off.

"Everything all right?" Manx asked.

"Fine," Priddle said stiffly. He walked over to the patrol car, and sat in the driver's seat, sipping at his tea, and looking out to nowhere in particular.

"Taking it badly?" Manx asked Morris.

"His first dead one, at least human, I think," Morris said.

"And you?"

"Growing up on a farm, you get used to it. Life, death, it's just nature's way. Anyway, it's part of the job, isn't it? You're probably used to it by now, too, sir."

Manx thought for a moment. No, he wasn't used to it, not even close. He could distance himself from the horrors he'd witnessed, but he'd never become numb to them. When he first joined the Met's serious crime unit, he believed he could be an impartial observer, that distance and detachment would make him a better copper—it didn't. What it did make him was a worse human being. He looked at Morris. *What was she, twenty-three, twenty-four?* For a split second, he saw something of himself in her eyes, something of his younger self, a steely determination and emotional distance. It unnerved him. He wanted to take her by the shoulders, and shake it out of her, like the stuffing from a rag-doll.

"You don't ever get used to it, Morris, not ever," Manx finally said, looking her directly in the eyes with an unswerving gaze. "Don't let being a good copper get in the way of being a decent human being. Learn to deal with it, but don't get used to it. Ever."

Morris mumbled something that sounded like an apology, but it was a reflex action; no meaning behind it, just a get out jail phrase she could pull out, when required.

"What's your plan, Morris? Next steps in the investigation?"

"Erm, door-to-door? See if anyone saw anything suspicious?"

"Take a couple of those community officers along. The road's probably full of curtain twitchers. Someone saw something; find out what."

Morris nodded, and scurried past Manx, like a rabbit running from the glare of oncoming headlights.

Chapter 13

Mandy settled herself into her armchair, and looked out over the Lifeboat Station towards the anxious swell of the Irish Sea. No matter how many degrees she turned up the central heating, or how many blankets she wrapped around herself, the flat always seemed cold. It wasn't Mexico, that was for sure, but she'd be back there soon, once this was over. *Mañana*, as they liked to say to her, *mañana*. She whispered it out loud; the word felt familiar and warm on her lips.

It had been a year now, since he asked her, no, *demanded* of her, that she move here and mind the shop, as he called it. He'd offered the old lady who had owned it twice what it was worth. Olive Jarman had taken the money, without a backward glance. Taking care of his business was the easy part; it was the other matter which nagged at her. The matter had always been there, knitting itself into her thoughts, clicking like needle on needle. It would be the final nail in the coffin, he had promised her. It was an apt description. Years ago, she had yearned for this, ached to feel the weight of the hammer in her palm and the steely reassurance of the nail between her fingers. Now, with the head finally poised to strike, she was rife with doubts. *What good would it do?* It was just another act of finality, which proved nothing, and fixed even less. Maybe the years she'd spent in the ease of Puerto Vallarta had softened her, or maybe she was just older, and the ripples of anger had gradually lost their echo. But, she had promised him this one last act of contrition—the final drawing down of the curtain.

It would happen soon; he had told her. She had merely nodded her silent compliance over the phone. She knew better than to ask how. "Church and state," the phrase her husband had often used, came to mind. It had served them well—she being the church, he being the state, and neither complicit in the affairs of the other. He had laughed, a sound like distant thunder rolling through the phone line, when she suggested he should forget the past, move on. He placated her, speaking a litany of proclamations as to why there was no turning back now, not for either of them.

Mandy remained in her armchair for an hour afterwards, unable to move lest the slightest realignment of her position would trigger a series of events now all but beyond her control. It was some minutes later when she finally pushed the folds of the lamb's wool blanket from her hips, and reached for a cigarette. Her hands shook as she struck down on the lighter. She tried again; the flint caught on the third attempt. She brought the tip to her lips, steadying her elbow against the wing of the chair. It was out of her hands now, but at least it would be over soon. "Mañana," she whispered to herself, *maybe mañana.*

Chapter 14

Shanni pushed back the Capri's front seat, peering over the shimmering lights of Amlwch Port, and towards the black expanse of ocean beyond. To the east, a firework shattered silently in the sky in a blossom of green and red shards weeping downwards like the branches of a willow. He prodded tentatively at the bulbous head of bandage wrapped around his finger and winced; it was still tender. The doctor had said he'd probably feel the phantom presence for a few weeks. It wasn't hard for Shanni to imagine his finger was still whole and attached to the knuckle, just waiting to be unwrapped. The doctor had also cautioned Shanni not put his hands inside an engine for at least another six weeks. In the meantime, Shanni had hired Lloyd Lug Nut, an amateur mechanic at best, but one who didn't mind getting his hands dirty. Maybe if this Scuttler bloke wasn't blowing smoke up his arse, he could make up the wages he was shelling out, but he wasn't holding his breath. The man seemed as unpredictable as he was dangerous.

Shanni had done some cursory detective work, but the name "Scuttler" had drawn a blank. It was as if he'd materialised out of thin air—a ghost. Shanni wasn't even sure if he'd hear from him again, and if it wasn't for the brutal reminder of his bandaged finger, he might have imagined the whole episode was a bad dream. But, yesterday, he had called, his measured words relaying very clear instructions to meet him here at nine o'clock at the edge of the abandoned copper mine, on time, and alone.

The rain had held off, but the wind contained an urgent howl, as it swept up from the deep basin and through the disused windmill at the quarry's edge. The unearthly eeriness of the old copper mine swept around Shanni like a cold chill. The landscape was like no place else on the island. The rust-coloured terrain looked as if it had been baked too long under an alien sun, and glowed angry and red from the ancient copper deposits still visible across the surface. As his eyes became accustomed to the darkness, he could make out the faint outline of the quarry below. *It was like one of those impact craters on the Discovery Channel,* Shanni thought, the ones made by large meteors: wide, deep and mysterious.

Shanni switched on the radio to distract his thoughts, but heard nothing, save the crackle of static. He'd been working on the car's electrics earlier today, and had almost snipped off the aerial, as he tried to handle the metal cutters. The strip of masking tape had secured the base, but left a weak connection. He rummaged around the glove compartment. The previous owner was obviously a metal-head, judging by the collection of Status Quo, Judas Priest, and Def Leppard cassette tapes. For a few minutes, Shanni lost himself in the memory of his teenage years, as he listened to Status Quo plod through the twelve-bar predictability of "Caroline and Paper Plane."

The milky glow of headlights in his rear-view mirror jolted Shanni from his thoughts. He watched as the lights drew closer. *Let him make the first move,* Shanni thought. Anyway, he'd called the meeting, and the less time he had to spend out in the cold and wind, the better.

Shanni's mobile vibrated across the passenger seat. He glanced over to the back window of the Mercedes Diesel 450. Scuttler's face was an apparition, blurred and foggy behind the layer of condensation which had settled on the back window.

"How's the finger?" Scuttler asked.

"Ask your fucking dog," Shanni said, lifting the bandaged finger.

Scuttler laughed; a controlled, sharp outburst more akin to a bark. "You came alone?"

"Yes, but what the fuck am I doing here?" Shanni asked.

The temperature had dropped several degrees since Shanni had left the house an hour ago, and the wind felt as if it was slicing through all three layers of his clothing. He walked towards the quarry and peered down over the edge into several hundred feet of deep, black nothingness.

"The kingdom of rust," Scuttler said, walking towards Shanni. "Heralded as the largest copper mine in Europe in its day…" he began.

"Jesus!" Shanni interrupted. "If it's another history lesson, can we at least do it in the fucking car, with the heater on?"

Scuttler breathed in deeply, as if he was savouring the essence of the landscape. "This whole quarry was dug out with picks and dynamite? Imagine it, Shanni. They say it saw the premature death of over a hundred men. A woefully underestimated number, I'd say." He took another meditative breath, as if he were summoning the ghosts of centuries past.

Shanni heard a crunch of footsteps—the two goons were standing guard by the open boot of the Mercedes. "Brought the brothers Grimm with you, then?" he said.

Scuttler grimaced, and headed back towards the car. He didn't ask Shanni to follow him; it was an unspoken understanding he would. The taller goon flipped open the boot. Shanni peered tentatively inside, and looked over the stack of canvas bags. Under Scuttler's direction, the goon unzipped one of them; it was filled with unlabelled pill bottles.

"Nine bags," Scuttler explained. "Twenty-five bottles in every bag, and thirty, blue money-makers in every vial. This is our test market, Shanni. I predict you should be able to sell these at five pounds a hit; any less, and you make up the difference. Understood?"

Shanni nodded. But, he wasn't listening—he was calculating.

"Let me make it easier for you," Scuttler said, taking one of the bottles in his palm. "The value of each bottle is one hundred and fifty pounds. Twenty-five bottles in each bag, equals…

"Thirty-three thousand pounds, give or take," Shanni interrupted.

Scuttler smiled. "I always knew you were smart, Shanni. And, believe me, this is just the beginning."

"What'd you dilute them with?" Shanni asked. "You got to be mixing in some other shit to get this much stuff."

"You're a business owner. Give customers quality produce, and they'll be a customer for life, isn't that right?"

Shanni nodded. "And my cut?"

"Twenty-five percent, to cover your distribution expenses. I don't care who you use; just make sure this can't be traced back to me."

Shanni did a quick calculation. Even after paying off the lads, he'd still clear well over five grand for himself. The thought made his head spin.

"Next time we meet, I expect nine empty bags, and twenty-five thousand pounds in cash. If it's not too much for you to handle."

Shanni stood to attention. "You've come to the right man. If partners, partners, right?" Shanni offered his right hand; an automatic gesture. Scuttler took it, making sure he had Shanni's bandaged finger clenched firmly in his fist. Shanni fell to his knees.

"One more thing," he said, leaning close enough for Shanni to feel the warm draw of his breath against his cheek. "Memorise that number like your life depended on it."

For a brief moment, a sliver of moonlight broke through the thicket of clouds, casting a soft glow over Scuttler's coal-black eyes. Shanni shuddered. This time, it was something more than pain, and cold chilled him to the marrow.

"After all," Scuttler said, leaning close, "this would be an incredibly lonely place to die."

Chapter 15

Manx sat to the far right of the foldout table, stifled a yawn, and looked across the crowd of around twenty people padded to the gills in scarves and quilted jackets sitting expectantly before him. The makeshift classrooms at the back of old chapels were always draughty, he remembered, as if the walls were holding onto the cold with a grim Methodist's determination. The aroma of chewing gum and pencil shavings lingered in the room, and a colourful mural of Bible parables ran like a paper tapestry across the walls. It was probably used as Sunday School, Manx guessed, and hired out in the faint hope it might convince a few lapsed chapelgoers to re-think their position and return to the fold.

Lynda Masterson, A.M.A.D. founder and chairperson, had kicked-off the meeting thirty minutes ago, with an impassioned story, long on detail but short on interest, concerning her personal struggle from Cheetam Hill, Manchester, to Anglesey. She outlined in grave detail Cheetam Hill's crime numbers (amongst the highest level of street crime in the nation), and how she had struggled to raise two boys as a single mother, studied at night school for her B.A., and was now working as a speech therapist.

Manx felt obliged to be inspired, but instead, just felt a gradual weariness cloud over him, as she went on to present a series of incidents of drug use she'd been made aware of on the Island. She showed the audience several newspaper clippings to help illustrate her point. *You can't run away from this stuff*, Manx thought. Crime didn't discriminate; it filled a vacuum, no matter what your postcode.

As Lynda outlined several "action items" for the audience to ponder, Manx slumped lower in his chair, and watched her performance. It was passionate and full of advice she'd probably cribbed from the internet. Still, the audience seemed to be responding; a series of head nods and isolated handclaps encouraged Lynda towards the finish line. Manx could imagine her practicing this speech in front of her bedroom mirror, her tightly pulled, strawberry-blonde ponytail bobbing, as she rehearsed. She concluded with a plea to the audience, followed by a more pointed request, which sounded more like a command aimed directly at Manx.

"It's our duty to keep our children safe, and we can't do that alone. We expect our local police to stand with us, help us do right by our children."

Before she sat down, Lynda steeled herself, and addressed the audience. "Dee jon, young vow," she said, for the benefit of the Welsh speakers. Even with Manx's limited Welsh, he recognised the mangled phrase: *"Diolch Yn Fawr"*— thank you very much. He noticed a few of the older members of the audience wince. *She'd need to work on that, if she was hoping to garner any real support in this community*, Manx thought.

The second panellist was introduced as Dr. Simon Vaughn, a local G.P. He was in his mid-forties, Manx surmised, and possessed a handsome but ultimately bland face, where each feature had formed in perfect symmetry, yet had failed to produce any points of significant interest. The doctor spoke eloquently about the current government policy on drug sentencing and control; both, he argued, were outdated and served to merely imprison the users and petty dealers, leaving the organised crime syndicates untouched. He asked Lynda to pass out a clutch of brochures amongst the audience. Manx suddenly wished he'd brought something with him, other than his bad mood and a fistful of pessimism.

As the doctor talked, Manx lost his concentration. His mind working its way around the case. Hardacre had confirmed Dick

Roberts's death was suicide, but how was he connected to the man found crucified to his boat?

"Detective Inspector, Manx? Inspector Manx?" Lynda repeated, throwing Manx a stiff, yet encouraging, smile. Manx willed himself back into the room.

"What is the police's strategy on the war on drugs on the island?" she asked.

Manx leant forward. "Well, we'd like to be on the winning side."

A light scuffling of shoes and coughs made Manx think he'd probably been too glib, and he expanded on his answer. "Look, the war on drugs was a headline someone conjured up to win votes. It assumes, at some point, there's a truce or a winner, and the dealers, traffickers, users hold up a white flag and surrender. I don't believe that's realistic."

Manx noticed Lynda visibly bristle, as if someone had raked the back of her neck with a rose bush. "So, we do what, Inspector? Give up?" Lynda looked to the audience for encouragement. A few of them nodded, all of them had their eyes firmly fixed on Manx.

"The best we can do with the resources we have is to manage the problem; stop it becoming an epidemic. If you, any of you, want to drop into any of our stations, we have some excellent educational literature, brochures, pamphlets, and whatnot."

"Brochures?" How about some bloody action?" someone shouted from the back of the room, inspiring others in the audience to speak up.

"I won't let my kids go to the discos anymore. I heard they're passing all kinds of drugs around in there."

"Yeah, and what about all those bloody immigrants? Coming here from God knows where. They sign on for benefits and government handouts. Send 'em back, problem solved. Not bloody rocket science, is it?"

"What you looking for, Twm? Set up a couple of Checkpoint Charlie's at the ports and bridges?"

"Yeah, not too far off the mark there, mate."

Manx had no answers—at least none which would satisfy this crowd.

Lynda turned to Manx. "Can you reassure the community the police are at least making some progress in clamping down on these dealers?"

"We're putting all available resource towards a solution," Manx offered.

"The recent murder? Was that also drug related?" Dr. Vaughn asked.

"Sorry, I can't comment on an ongoing investigation."

"I heard it was a drug boat, smuggling drugs between Holyhead and Dublin," someone else chimed in.

"Again, no comment," Manx said.

"No arrests either, mate? Bloody police! Bloody joke, more like."

"They've got plenty of resources for more speed cameras, though."

"Yeah, how about solving some real crime for a change, eh?"

"Investigations take time…" Manx began.

"Yeah, you lot drag your feet, while our kids get exposed to God knows what. Does one of our kids have to die for you lot to get off your arses?"

Manx was rapidly losing the room. Canton's words, "don't fuck up," came back to him as the audience vented. He was nothing more than a punching bag. He decided to change tact, and raised his arm.

"Inspector Manx?" Lynda said.

Manx sat up straight. "Look, I'm not saying we couldn't do a better job, but any police service is only as effective as the community it serves. I've worked in inner cities, just like Lynda described, and if there's one thing I've learnt it's that when we work together with the local community, we get results. Talk to your local community service officers; they're trained to listen and report back to us. And, when it comes to drugs, talk to your kids. Scare the crap out of them, if you have to. Better it comes from you than one of our officers at the station. By that time, it's already too late."

A low muttering rippled through the crowd. Lynda was about to respond, when a man at the back of the room addressed Manx directly.

"Inspector Manx, you're new to the island. Care to tell us what brought you here from London? The Metropolitan Police Serious Crime Division, wasn't it?"

"I don't see how that's…" Manx began. The audience shifted its gaze toward the man.

"I understand you were removed from an investigation for personal reasons? Then, suspended. Care to elaborate?" The man held up an iPhone, and thumbed the record button.

"Neither the time nor the place," Manx said.

"Surely, the people of Anglesey have the right…"

Manx scraped his chair back across the tile floor, and strode out towards the door. At the back of the room, he took a good look at the man. He was young, late twenties, with a sprout of a faint moustache. He paused, looked the man directly in the eyes, and made sure he remembered the face.

"If you really want to know how to win the war on drugs," Manx said, turning towards the crowd, "tell your kids not to buy them."

***

Manx leant on the low wall separating the chapel from the cemetery, and reached for a cigar. A spill of yellow light fell from a nearby street lamp, casting a murky haze over the headstones. He took a long, ponderous drag, and felt his heartbeat gradually steady itself. It was hardly doctor-prescribed medication, but it did the job. He watched the remainder of the crowd trickle out, followed by a communal roll of tires crunching over gravel.

"Inspector, could I have a word?" Dr. Simon Vaughn was walking towards Manx in slow, considered steps. "For the record, I agree with you."

"You'll be the first tonight."

"The more the government treats it as a war, the more it escalates. You call something a war, and it becomes one," Dr. Vaughn said.

"Give the devil a name?" Manx said.

Vaughn slipped his hands into his pockets. "You keep expecting things to change, think what you do makes a difference, but ultimately, it doesn't."

"Doesn't mean we shouldn't stop trying," Manx said. "You're still speaking out."

"Habit, maybe, but I can't *not* speak out. Feels disingenuous when I don't, so I end up throwing a few pebbles in the ocean every now and again, to see if I can make any ripples."

"Next time, try rocks, bigger splash," Manx offered.

Vaughn smiled and nodded. "Good luck, Inspector. Hope we'll come across each other again," he said, and walked back towards his car.

Manx looked over the crooked, grey teeth of gravestones protruding from the cemetery grounds to his left. *Why did he find peace in places like this? Did it put life in perspective? Was it a sobering reminder we'd all end up here one day, dust to dust, ashes to ashes?* Maybe there was reassurance in this finality. The only guarantee life offered.

As he turned to leave, he became aware of another presence to his left. It was too dark to discern any specific shape, but he guessed by the soft pad of paws on grass, and the deep growl, it was a dog, a big one. Manx stiffened. A shot of adrenaline sparked through him, as he saw a plume of warm breath manifest itself through the darkness, followed by the figure of a black dog with a head the size of a football. The creature bared its teeth and snarled at Manx, dregs of spittle falling from its jaw. The dog's eyes were dark and pitiless, as if all the compassion had been cruelly bred out them. It crouched low on its hind legs, as if it were about to pounce.

Manx stepped back slowly, and wrapped his fingers around a loose, fist-sized piece of rock. He quickly calculated how much time he would have between throwing the missile at the dog's face, and sprinting to the safety of his car. Maybe he could use his cigar, and stub the hot ember in the dog's eye. There wasn't enough time. The dog would pounce on him before he made it halfway. He tried another tack, keeping the rock firmly in his hand.

"Good boy, calm," Manx said. The animal didn't take kindly to the platitude, growled some more, and licked the drool from its lips.

Over by the chapel door, Manx noticed a motion sensor flicker to life. Reluctant to take his eyes off the dog, he briefly glanced over to the doorway. There was the outline of a man, half-lit in the darkness. He called out a one-word command, "Come." The dog ignored his master, and edged closer. The voice spoke again, this time louder and more direct. The dog reluctantly obeyed, took one last growl at Manx, ducked its head in a low, menacing bow, and retreated into the shadows.

Manx exhaled, and placed the rock, which was now clammy with his sweat, back onto the wall. He felt his mobile buzz in his pocket, and checked the screen:

Remember. Remember. Fireworks on the beach. 5th of November. Come alone. If U want answers.

There was no number or name attached to the text, just a photograph of a Guy Fawkes mask staring at the Inspector with its pale, cruel grin.

Manx glanced for a few moments at the image, before slipping the phone into his pocket. By the time he looked back up, the man had disappeared. He jogged towards the chapel entrance, but it was already deserted, save the acrid smell of recently deposited dog shit. Manx looked down, mumbled a terse "fuck it," and pulled his boots from the wet faeces.

Chapter 16

When Manx walked into the incident room the following morning, the team had their noses buried in their computer screens. He looked over the gallery of photographs—it was like piecing together a jigsaw with no picture to reference. The anonymous text and the man lurking outside the chapel had to be connected, but how? He decided to keep quiet about that, for now. He needed the team focussed, and not distracted by men in shadows.

He walked his mind through the case, slowly and methodically. This was how he liked to work—exploring the body of evidence, time and time again, searching for patterns or anomalies he might have missed. Sometimes, inspiration came quickly; other times, it could take days or weeks before something sparked a connection. It was the mundane reality of police work. The day-to-day grind, exhausting every avenue and cul-de-sac, re-tracing his steps, in case he'd missed something vital. The whole process was ingrained in him by now, second nature.

As he glanced the board, he noticed someone had scrawled the words, "Teabag Killer" in large letters across the top, accompanied by a crudely drawn pair of cartoon testicles. Manx was about to erase it, when Sergeant Mal Nader spoke up.

"Not thinking of wiping that, were you, boss? Took Minor most of the morning to draw those. Had to do it all from memory, too. Mind you, we did have to explain to her what tea bagging was. Never seen a girl turn that shade of red before."

PC Morris gave him the two-fingered salute. Before Manx could reply, Mickey Thomas made his presence known at the door.

"I've got Beaumaris on the line. Urgent, they said. Should I transfer?"

"What else would I want you to do, Mickey?"

"Rightio, then, give me a sec. What's your extension again?"

"Twenty-five."

Mickey thought for a moment. "Duck and dive, twenty-five, duck and dive, twenty-five," he mumbled to himself. Manx looked over at Nader.

"Training to be a bingo caller, for his retirement," Nader explained.

Manx shook his head. A few moments later, his phone rang. "Manx. Yes, Detective Inspector Manx." He listened for a few seconds. "Is she credible? Ok, we'll be there in half an hour. Oh, and thanks," he added, but the line was already dead.

Chapter 17

The duty officer at Beaumaris was a military-looking man with a thick moustache, which curled territorially under his top lip, as if it were looking to expand its borders. He stood to attention, as Manx and the team walked in and smiled, glad of the interruption to his otherwise mundane Wednesday.

"She came in this morning," he said. "Big grin on her face, like she's got something to tell me, but she's keeping it to herself. Didn't want to speak to a PC, she said, had to be a senior officer. That's when I called Mickey. How's he doing, by the way? Retired yet?"

"Hard to tell," Manx said. "So, do you know her?"

"Oh, yeah, everyone knows Nerys. She's a waitress over at the teahouse on Church Street, and pulls a couple of shifts on the weekends at the Bull. Takes in ironing, too, and cleans the holiday flats in the summer."

"Industrious," Manx said.

"Can't say the same for the rest of the family, mind you, spongers, the lot of 'em," the PC said, leaning forward with the palms of his hands on the desk, as if he were preparing to deliver a sermon. "If they're not getting pissed out of their heads, they're pulling some scam or other. Nasty buggers, too. Mind you, haven't seen 'em around for a couple of years now, but I remember this one time…"

"I'd love to hear more," Manx interrupted. "But, life is really too fucking short, as it is."

The PC braced himself, as if he'd just been jabbed in the eye with a sharp stick, and pressed the buzzer.

"Priddle, stay out here for now." Manx said. "Morris, you can ride shotgun, just don't ask any stupid questions."

"No, sir. I mean, yes, sir," Morris said, and traipsed behind Manx.

Nerys was lying almost horizontal in her chair. Her faded sweatshirt had drifted upwards to reveal a white expanse of stomach, and her fingers were busy poking around her navel, extracting random tufts of lint.

"Aye, aye!' Nerys said, looking up. "Bad cop and not much cop, cop!" She emitted a loud, dirty laugh.

"Very good, Nerys," Manx said. "Make that up one yourself, or did you nick it from one of your brothers?"

Nerys sniffed, and ran her fingers through her tightly permed hair.

"I'm Detective Inspector Tudor Manx, this is PC Delyth Morris.

"Bit short for a copper, aren't you?" Nerys said, casting her eyes up and down the length of Morris.

"They abolished the height requirement ten years ago," Morris said.

"Don't matter. You're still short. You want to watch out a heavy wind don't blow you away." Nerys made a long, low whistling sound. Her gaze lingered a little too long on Morris as she sat.

"The Sergeant said you had some information?"

"Depends, don't it?"

"Depends?"

"On what it's worth, like."

"Nerys, we can't pay you for information. If you're just yanking my chain, I can arrest you for wasting police time."

"Jesus, keep your knickers on. But, you better make sure you tell 'em I came in, reported it, like."

"Consider it on the record. Now, what's on your mind?"

Nerys tucked her sweatshirt into the waistband of her pants, and leant forward. "On Wednesday mornings, I do the cleaning for Ernie Stokes. He owns the antique shop up on Church Street," Nerys began. "One of them bum boy types I reckon, but that don't bother me. Always been a proper gentleman to me, no hanky panky, like. Anyway, I go over there this morning and ring the bell, like usual."

"What time was this?"

"About nine. He doesn't want me coming any earlier, likes to have his breakfast, do the crossword. Very particular about that, he is."

"And what happened next?"

"Nobody home, was there? I stood out there like a bleedin' prostitute for half an hour, freezing me arse off. Bugger this, I said to myself, so I pushed the door. I weren't trying to rob him, or anything, but it swings open, not locked or nothing. I thought the alarm was going to go off. He's got all kinds of cameras and security stuff around the place."

"Did you enter the establishment?" Morris asked.

"Never seen a mess like it," Nerys said.

"Was Mr. Stokes there?" Manx asked.

"Nah, but it looks like someone's let a prize bull loose in the place. All his stuff, really nice stuff, mind you, not this cheap junk you get in some shops, was all over the floor, smashed glass everywhere. Good job he wasn't there. Probably would have given the old bugger a heart attack."

"What did you do then?"

"Came in here, didn't I? Told PC Plod on reception what I'd seen, and he shoves me in here for an hour, with a gallon of piss-poor tea, and makes me wait for you lot to turn up."

"You didn't touch anything, Nerys?" Morris asked.

"I wasn't born yesterday," she said, sniffing indignantly.

"Smart call," Manx said. "We'll need a statement, and your fingerprints, just to eliminate them from the scene. Not planning on going away anywhere soon, are you?"

"Just to look for another job, if this one's gone tits up," Nerys said. "Not got anything going with you lot, have you? I'm very good with handcuffs," she added, folding her thick arms, and winking at Morris for good measure.

Chapter 18

PC Morris finished strapping the yellow caution tape across Stokes Antiques Emporium, and glanced down the length of Church Street. The shop was just one of several Victorian homes converted into retail space, and was sandwiched between a newsagent and a gift shop. The well-preserved medieval castle in the centre of Beaumaris ensured a constant draw of tourists during the summer. For anyone entering the town from the east, the first impression of Beaumaris would have been the single row of terrace houses bordering the town centre and painted in cool, Mediterranean blues, pinks, and greens, giving off the impression of an Italianate seaside town, which had been abducted and re-settled on a slate-grey island, far from home.

"Ugh, she gives me the creeps," Morris said, as they watched Nerys walk away, a freshly lit cigarette in one hand, yellow bucket in the other.

"One hundred per cent beer goggle proof," Priddle said.

"You believe her, boss?" Morris asked.

"No reason not to, for now," Manx said, "Any news on forensics?"

"Half hour, or so."

Manx looked down the deserted street and sighed. "Jesus, when does the tumbleweed start rolling in?"

"It's winter. Most places just shut up shop till Easter," Morris explained.

"I'm going to knock on a few doors, and see if anybody saw anything unusual, like maybe another human being," Manx said, and walked away.

Morris stamped her feet, and blew a hot clutch of breath into her cupped palms. The sun was barely warming up the day, and the low wedge of grey clouds looked as if they were there for the duration. She checked her watch—10:36am. Her stomach was already grumbling. God knows when she'd get to eat, and the enticing, aroma of freshly baked pasties from the nearby teashop was making her salivate.

As Manx turned into the newsagency, a young man brushed past him and mumbled a half-hearted apology, before turning onto the high street. Morris watched as the man crossed the road, and walked briskly towards her. She felt a prickle of unease as he passed. The man was bouncing on his toes as he walked, peering around as if he were expecting to be surprised by something, or someone. His black skullcap was pulled down tight over his forehead, and his hands were bunched into fists in anticipation. Morris stiffened. "Cold day for a walk," she said.

The man nodded but refused to make eye contact. Morris ran her fingers across the tip of her nightstick, her initial feeling of unease growing, as he came to a full stop less than a metre away. Before she had time to pull her weapon, the man had spun on his heels.

She felt the bony stab of his elbow strike her ribs and stumbled, grabbing at the caution tape as she fell. The crack of her skull against concrete echoed like a thunderclap in her head. A boot pummelled into her right kidney. She groaned, and fumbled for her nightstick, which was stuck-fast between her hip and the pavement. As the man tore at the caution tape and stepped into the shop, Morris took her chance. She reached for the hem of his jeans grasped at the denim. The man stumbled, slapped his hand on the doorframe, and kicked backwards, blindly, like a spooked horse. Morris felt the brutal force of his boot, as it sank into her stomach. Her fingers released the fabric, and grabbed at her belly. The man looked back briefly, and ran into the shop.

Morris's world faded into blur of pain. Before blacking out, she clicked on her radio, but the words wouldn't come; there was nothing but the useless crackle of static over the airways and a feeling she was sinking slowly through the concrete.

***

"Jesus! What the hell happened?" Manx said.

Morris was sitting on the pavement, her back to the wall. She attempted to explain, but it felt as if she were swallowing a sharp blade.

"Never mind," Manx said, turning to Priddle. "Medics?"

"On their way, boss," he said, as he watched the forensics team, who had just arrived, pour themselves into their over-suits. "She all right?"

"I'll live," Morris groaned.

"Tough bugger, you are," Priddle said in a tone which suggested he was convincing himself, more than he was reassuring Morris.

"Did you catch him?" Her voice was a weak, rough whisper.

Manx spun the caution tape through his fingers. "Most likely miles away by now." He peered in the shop doorway. "Whatever's in there, somebody needed it badly enough to assault a police officer. Maybe he left some partials on the tape. Was he wearing gloves?"

"Dunno," Morris said, flinching. Manx directed his gaze to the narrow street. A few shopkeepers had ventured out onto their doorways, curious as to the nature of the commotion.

"Fuck! I should have been here," Manx said.

"Can't leave me alone for five minutes, eh, boss?" Morris said. The pain in her gut was slowly subsiding, but her arm hurt like hell.

"Don't," Manx said, wiping his hands across his face. "This is my fault; I underestimated the danger. We'll get him, Morris; this island isn't that bloody big."

Chapter 19

It was late afternoon by the time the forensics team had secured the evidence. Ashton Bevan, a short, pot-bellied man, looking not unlike a dishevelled Smurf in his blue over-suit, checked the last of the bags into the evidence van.

"All yours. Just don't go nicking any of the valuables, tempting as it is on uniform pay," he said. Manx couldn't tell if he was joking, but Ashton Bevan didn't look the type prone to jocularity.

"You're new, right?" Bevan said, clambering out of his suit.

"Long story," Manx said

Bevan wiped his hand on the side of his pants, before offering it to Manx. "Ashton Bevan, lead Scene of Crime Officer." It was a weak, wet-fish of a handshake.

"DI Manx," Manx said, although it was probably irrelevant; Bevan seemed the sort of man who preferred to know the answers to questions before he asked them.

"We should have a drink, sometime," Bevan said. "Swap war stories. I'll bring you up to speed on how things get done around here. Political landmines everywhere. 'Look up, before you fuck up' has always been my motto."

There was something about Bevan which made the hairs on Manx's neck come to attention. He seemed the kind of man with a reserve of mottos he could pull out of a hat, depending on the situation.

"What are the odds of lifting prints from the caution tape? My officer says the offender's hands were all over it, probably the doorframe, too."

Bevan straightened his posture. "If there are any prints to be lifted, my team will find them," he said. His barrel chest heaved as he talked, like he was trying to liberate a particularly stubborn caulk of phlegm. Most likely smoking related, Manx guessed, as he checked out Bevan's fingers, which were tainted from the knuckles to the tips with a tell-tale, jaundiced yellow.

"What about the flat upstairs?"

Bevan clambered into the driver's seat, and rolled down the window. "We've tagged and bagged his comb and his personal effects. If you can persuade Canton to blow the mothballs from his wallet, we'll send what we have to the lab for testing. I hope you're on his good side."

"I wasn't aware he had one," Manx said.

Bevan huffed, and checked his hair in the mirror, running his fingers though the meagre strands still standing. "Big responsibility for you, Manx, this whole Island," he said.

"That's one opinion," Manx said.

Bevan turned to face him. "It's just that I hear things, Inspector. People like to talk to me, and I like to think I'm a good listener. From what I hear, the majority of the uniforms aren't too happy with all this restructuring flimflam. They wanted one of their own in charge. Better the devil you know, and all that."

"And you?" Manx asked.

Bevan smiled again, a tight, mean expression, which did little to endear him to Manx. "Just looking out for a fellow colleague. I'll give you a ring about that pint," he said, and turned over the engine.

Chapter 20

Ernie Stokes's flat was small, but immaculately appointed—one bedroom, with a striking picture window looking out over the Menai Strait.

"Christ, the wife would throw me out on my ear for a place like this," Priddle said, with a sharp intake of a whistle. Three large oil paintings, including one of the original Menai Bridge, hung along the flat's south-facing wall. A faint aroma of expensive cologne lingered in the air, like a reminder of better times.

"Notice anything unusual?" Manx asked, after a few minutes.

Priddle squinted. "Oh, yeah, no telly," he said, pleased with himself.

"Look closer," Manx said. "Every room tells you something about the person who lives there. What's this room telling you?"

Priddle thought. "Um. It's too tidy. Probably lives alone, no kids, at least not young ones. Must have a few quid, too; this stuff looks expensive."

"All good observations, but look on the mantelpiece and the tables. There's not one photograph. Not one," Manx said.

"Oh, aye," Priddle agreed.

"What kind of person, after sixty odd years on this planet, doesn't have at least one photograph of a loved one they'd want to hang on the wall—family, friends, pet Chihuahua, something?"

"Unless someone took 'em? Maybe that's what they were looking for?"

"Doubtful. Nothing looks disturbed or out of place." Manx walked towards the answering machine, displaying the number zero in large, glowing LED. "No messages either."

"Do you think he could be our John Doe?"

"Too early to tell. Check out the bedroom. Shout if you find anything that strikes you as strange, or out of place."

"Other than everything, you mean, boss?" he said, looking sideways at the explicit oil painting of a naked man hung in the hallway.

Manx walked slowly around the living room in a clockwise direction, a ritual he'd perfected over the years. He'd take note of the obvious first, then on the second and third circles, begin to look for the unusual, what was odd or inconsistent. The first thing that struck him was how neat the flat was. The man who had attacked Morris hadn't made it this far; he was either spooked before he had the chance, or didn't know Ernie lived above the shop. However, neither of those explanations got Manx any closer to the real question: what the hell was the man looking for?

"Sir!" Priddle called from the bedroom. "Would you say pornographic magazines under the bed is strange?"

"Depends on what kind, and how many, I suppose," Manx said.

Priddle walked into the living room cradling a box of magazines with a damp funk to them, and dropped them by the fireplace.

"Quite the collection," Manx said.

"Ugh. It's all gay porn, too, sir," Priddle said, taking one of the magazines by the corner and holding it at arm's length. "Sick, that is," he added, flinging the magazine back into the box.

"Well, I guess Nerys Bowen had him pegged," Manx said. "Didn't she mention he had security cameras?"

"Dunno, wasn't in the room, sir," Priddle said, wiping his hands down his trouser leg.

"If there's a security camera, there must be a recording device," Manx said, walking over to an old-fashioned bureau positioned against the wall closest to the kitchen. He pulled on the doors; they opened easily to reveal an iMac computer. Manx clicked the mouse. The screen flickered to life, revealing a patchwork of smaller, black and white security camera screens, all showing various angles from inside the shop and outside.

"Bingo," Manx said. "Let's get this stuff back to the station."

As Priddle began unhooking the hardware, Manx circled the room one last time. Over by the picture window, a small card table caught his eye. It was an ornate piece, with what he guessed was brass inlays, and a rich, red polished surface. The table seemed out of place in the overall design of the flat. Whereas everything else had a minimalist, almost mid-century aesthetic, this piece was more elaborate, and it reminded him of a card table his mother used to own. She kept it in the parlour, and, as far as Manx knew, was used only as a plinth for holding a vase of flowers. If there were ever anything as frivolous as a card game played at his mother's house, it would have stuck in his mind.

The table, if he remembered correctly, would flip and fold out. He gripped it at both ends, and carefully spun the top so it revealed the space hallow space beneath. He took a step back. The space was jammed to the corners with small pill bottles, stacked neatly on top of each other, like matches in a box. There must have been at least a hundred of them.

He took out a bottle and shook out one of the white, rectangular, pills; there was an M imprinted onto one side, and four numbers on the other. He'd seen these before; it was methadone, enough to supply an addict for weeks.

Chapter 21

"Here she is. Down, but not out, eh!" Mal Nader jumped to his feet as PC Delyth Morris walked into the incident room. She managed a weak, shrugging smile. Her left arm was cradled in a temporary sling.

"Oh, shut it," Morris said. "It's not like I did anything." She sat at her desk, her cheeks flushed at the attention.

"We should have a few pints down the Bull tonight. Who's in?"

There was a muttering of agreement from around the room.

"Champion," Nader said, satisfied it was only ten in the morning, and he'd already hatched a plan for the evening, which ensured he'd arrive back home after closing time.

Manx walked in, concentrating on a ream of papers in his hand. "Back already, Morris?" he said, glancing up from his stack of papers.

"Bored to death at home. Thought I'd do more good back here."

"See, told you she was tough," Priddle said.

"She's more man than you," Nader offered. "Here, take this." Nader reached for his wastepaper basket, and handed it to Priddle "Just in case, like. We all heard about your delicate constitution."

"My old gran's more man than Priddle, and she's eighty-three," PC Pritchard chimed in.

"Hey, I can handle myself," Priddle protested, shoving the basket back along the floor.

"Yeah, and you got blisters on your palm to prove it, right?" Nader said.

A low chuckle echoed through the room. Priddle buried his head back in his computer screen, and tended to an incoming email.

"Eh, sir," Priddle said, raising his arm. "We've got a positive on the partials from Stokes's place, just came in." The room went quiet. Priddle's lips moved slowly and deliberately, as he read the report to himself.

"Bloody hell, Priddle, don't keep us in suspenders, man," Nader said.

"The partials match a Thomas Bowen, twenty-eight years old. Lives at Cae Mawr Farm, Pentraeth, about six miles from here."

"Any previous?" Manx asked.

"Nothing but previous," Nader said, leaning back on his chair. "Probably qualified for North Wales Constabulary frequent flyer miles by now."

"What's his form?"

"Petty stuff. Likes his drink, smokes the wacky backy. We busted him a few times on possession, but nothing stuck. Did a few months in Chester, a few years back, for nicking a motor. Oh, and he insists on being called T-Bowen these days, like one of those gangster types. Thinks he's Wales's answer to Snoop Dog, or something."

"Any relation to Nerys Bowen?" Manx asked.

"Probably. The whole clan lives around Pentraeth. Slippery little fuckers, too. Don't know if they're just lucky, or too stupid to know better."

"Well, let's get him in here, see if he barks or bites," Manx said.

Chapter 22

"Sup, Holmes and Watson?" Thomas Bowen said, tapping his feet anxiously on the interview room floor. "You arresting me, or what?"

"If I had my way, I'd lock you up, and throw away the key," Nader said, settling himself in the chair next to Manx.

Thomas Bowen was the polar opposite of his sister, pencil thin and twitched constantly as if he was trying to shrug off the confines of this own skin. His face had a bony, rodent-like quality to it; an impression enhanced by the sharp upturn of his nose. Manx looked him over—black skull-cap, wound tight around his head, white wife beater vest, cut low at the chest, black faux-leather jacket that creaked as he moved, a cheap, gold-plated chain looped under his neck, and jeans pulled down low over the hips to reveal the torn waistband of his Calvin Klein boxers. Everything about Bowen screamed fake, especially the mock, ghetto-gangster slang.

"Legally, we have to inform you if you're under arrest," Manx explained. "Today, you have the pleasure of helping us out. Think of it as your civic duty. I'm Detective Inspector Manx, and this is Sergeant Nader."

Bowen sniffed loudly, and ran the sleeve of his jacket under his nose.

"Now, Thomas, as standard policy, I'm going to start recording our interview." Manx pressed the record button. "Would you like a glass of water before we start?"

"Rather have a pint," Bowen said.

"I'd rather be playing golf," Nader said, sliding a glass across the table.

Bowen downed it in one, and slammed it back on the table. "Don't have to say jack to no buzzkills, if I don't want to."

"No, you don't, Thomas, but it would be very helpful if you did, probably do yourself a favour, too, eliminate yourself from our enquiries."

Bowen leant back, puffing out his chest. His faux leather jacket crackled like an empty crisp packet. "Name's T-Bowen, now, Holmes. Changed it by deed poll. Totally legit. Call it in, if you want. I got nothing to hide."

"Right, Thomas," Manx said, making sure he stressed the word "Thomas," as he looked Bowen directly in the eyes. "Do you remember where you were Wednesday morning, at around ten thirty?"

"Probably catching some z's. Tore up a blinder the night before, didn't get back to the crib till morning," Bowen said, stretching out his arms, as if he were hoping for a more appreciative audience.

"Anybody who could corroborate that?"

"Co-what, bro?"

"Back up your story, dickhead," Nader said.

"Yea, right. The bitch was with me. Had a crackin' night. Sore as fuck after." Bowen said, pulling at his crotch to emphasise his point.

"The bitch?" Manx asked. "Your dog?"

Bowen sniggered. "Don't own a fucking dog, Holmes, my biatch; the fuckpiece. You pigs are fuckin' ignorant, man. Seriously."

"So, on a Wednesday morning, you had no reason to get up, no job to go to?"

"I'm an entrepreneur. Work for myself, keep it real."

"Doing what?"

"Music producer, emcee gigs, sell mix tapes. Starting my own record label, too. Got a ton of investors interested."

"I'm a music lover, anything I might have heard?" Nader asked.

"You serious? I'm underground, Watson, cutting edge. Don't spin shit for oldies like you."

"Underground? You mean music for the dead and buried, like?" Nader said. "Prefer the traditional stuff, myself. Hogaia'r Wyddfa, Toni and Aloma, Dafydd Iwan," he added, referring to some Welsh folk singers Manx vaguely remembered from his father's record collection.

Bowen looked at them both as if they were visiting from a distant planet, and scratched his head through his skullcap.

"So, back to yesterday," Manx said. "The incident at Stokes Antiques in Beaumaris. One of my PCs was attacked, suffered a bruised rib and a sprained arm for her trouble. Don't know anything about that, do you?"

Bowen rubbed his hands over his thighs. "Don't know zero."

"Well, that puts me in a conundrum," Manx said. "Our highly-trained forensics experts swear your grubby little prints were all over the tape and the door frame, but, here you are, bold as brass, telling me you weren't there. You're putting us in a tough spot, Thomas, isn't he, Nader?"

"Very tough," Nader confirmed.

"As you might imagine, we take the assault of a fellow police officer very seriously. What's the minimum sentence these days, Nader?"

"Five to seven, last I heard."

"Five to seven, that's a long time to be out of the record business, Bowen. Not to mention if someone lied to the police about where they were on a certain day, that's obstruction of justice, and a few more months on top of the original sentence."

Manx noticed Bowen's body language stiffen. The first sign of a dewy sweat glistened over the arc of his brow.

Manx slapped his hand down loudly on the table, startling Bowen. "Damn, and I almost forgot about the CCTV cameras," he said. "Seems Mr. Stokes was a little paranoid; installed security cameras all over the place, running all day and night. Our boys are examining the footage right now. It's just a matter of time before they identify your ugly mug, and present me with nice glossy five-by-seven your mother wouldn't be too proud to put on the mantelpiece."

Bowen shrugged, but couldn't meet Manx's gaze.

"What were you looking for, Thomas? Your sister tell you the shop had been done over, so you thought you'd do a little antiquing to fund your recording career, or were you looking for something else?"

Bowen leant forward, opening his arms as he spoke. "Like I said, I was with the bitch, in bed."

"So you said, Thomas, but here's the thing. I don't believe you, the Sergeant doesn't believe you, my Chief, who's watching this from behind that window, sure as hell is not going to believe you, and I'd bet my pension no jury's going to buy this fairy tale, either."

"We didn't tell him about the DNA yet, boss." Nader said.

"The DNA we're going to take from this glass he's been drinking from, you mean, Sergeant?" Manx said. "I'm pretty sure it's going to match the DNA we took from the scene."

"No doubt," Nader agreed.

Manx smiled and leant back in his chair. "So, Thomas, it looks like we've got a hat-trick of evidence against you—prints, CCTV, and DNA. I wish they'd all land in my lap like this, I'd be home by six every night."

Bowen kept his gaze on his trainers, and pursed his lips into a tight knot.

"For fuck's sake, Bowen," Nader said. "We've got you by the short and curlies, son. Give us a statement, and we can all fuck off out of here."

Bowen looked to the ceiling as if expecting divine providence to fall into his hands and when none came, placed his hands on the table. "You're breaking my nads, Holmes. I didn't kill no one."

"But you did assault a police officer," Manx said.

"I ain't admitting nothing, but if I talk, I need a deal, a fucking good one, yeah?"

"What? You think you're in an episode of *Law and* fucking *Order?*" Nader said.

Manx put his hand on Nader's arm in a "back off" gesture.

"Depends on what you've got to tell us," Manx said.

"I want some guarantee, impunity, like."

"I think you mean, *immunity*, Bowen," Manx said. "I can't guarantee anything, but I'll listen to what you've got to say."

Bowen leant back in his chair, and contemplated his options, before finally speaking. "There's this bloke. He's setting something up. I don't know what, but he says it's big."

"Great. Some bloke is setting up something you don't know. Give me a fucking break," Nader said. "Let's just book him, boss. The little shit's giving me a fucking ulcer just looking at him."

Bowen showed them his hands; his fingers were peppered with freshly healed scars. "The bloke was fucking psycho."

"What did he look like, this man?"

Bowen shrugged. "Dunno, it was dark."

"He paid you to break into the store? Murder Stokes?" Manx said.

"Shit, no way! I don't know nuthin' about Stokes. The bloke just gave me three hundred quid to get something for him."

"What thing?" Nader asked.

Bowen hesitated for a moment. "Pills."

"What kind of pills?"

"Don't know, do I? Aspirin?'

"Find any?"

"Didn't get the chance. Heard the fucking sirens, then ran out the back. I didn't take nothing, I swear."

"I hope you're a better record producer than you are a criminal, Thomas. You should have tried his flat; it's like a chemist shop in there."

"Fuck," Bowen said, and kicked the table leg for good measure.

***

"Nice touch with the DNA ruse, lads, completely inadmissible in court, of course," DCI Canton said, as Manx and Nader joined him outside the interview room.

"We've got enough to nail his balls to the wall with the prints. Not that the dumb fuck's sweating any of it," Nader said, and pointed towards the small video screen. Bowen was slapping his hands on the desk, nodding his head in time with the beat. "Want me to make the arrest, boss?" he asked.

Manx looked at Bowen, and thought for a moment. "No, not yet, Nader. There's something bigger going on here. We should release him," Manx said.

"You're fucking joking, right? The little shit put Minor in the hospital. Give me five minutes with him, and you'll have his confession, signed, sealed, and fucking delivered, no messin'."

"You're not seeing the big picture, Nader," Manx explained.

Nader's face turned a deep crimson. "Seems pretty fucking clear to me. If you don't do it, then I will."

Manx grabbed his arm. "Nader, if you arrest him, we'll lose the best lead we've got. Think about it. Sir?" Manx said, looking over at Canton.

"You think Bowen's connected to our John Doe?" Canton asked.

"If the John Doe is Ernie Stokes, which I'm pretty certain is the case, then Bowen's connected, somehow. We lockup Bowen, we're back at square one, but if we put a tail on him, he could lead us to the killer."

"On evidence of what?" Canton asked.

Manx took a deep breath. "It's a hunch, Chief. Bowen's a petty criminal; murder's a big career jump. We track where he goes, who he meets. If it's a dead end, Nader can have the pleasure of reading him his rights."

"You're not serious? We're letting him walk on a hunch?" Nader said.

Canton thought for a moment, as he watched Bowen on the screen, pacing around the interview room like a caged animal.

"Two stipulations, Manx," Canton said. "One, someone's tailing him twenty-four-seven. Two, if Bowen steps even a gnat's breath off the island, I'll hold you responsible for dragging him back, however long it takes."

"I wasn't planning on losing him, Chief," Manx said.

Nader lurched towards the door. "Someone should have told me it was fucking amnesty day. We've got a few more down in the cells, if you're feeling generous," he said, and slammed the door back into its frame.

"He took that well," Manx said to Canton, and went back into the interview room to deliver Bowen the good news.

Chapter 23

A thin sheet of fog had tucked itself tightly around Llangefni high street, throwing everything into a radiant blur, as if someone had cranked the world out of focus by a single stop. When Manx arrived at the Bull, just after six-thirty Thursday evening, he'd forgotten it was market day. The traders were tearing down their stalls, and re-packing cardboard boxes with off-brand blue jean several years out of fashion, and knock-off handbags.

The stench of animal faeces still lingered in the air from the livestock auction a few streets away. Manx remembered his father would bring him here when he was younger. While Tommy Manx struck up a heated debate with one of the livestock auctioneers, Manx would wander off around the pig-pens, and listen to the farmers complaining about the price of feed. His job was to report back to Tommy if the farmers let slip on any information he could use to knock down the prices; they never did.

Inside the Bull, Manx unwrapped the scarf and unbuttoned his overcoat. He shoved his way through a small group of young, turban-clad Pakistani market traders, who could speak enough Welsh to compliment a passing housewife on their appearance, or ask them what colour blouse they desired. *Glas? Piws? Coch?*

Manx peered over the mass of heads around him, and into the snug at the far end of the bar. He noticed the stocky, wide-shouldered figure of DS Mal Nader talking loudly, and pointing his finger accusingly at someone across from him. He was probably already three pints ahead of the pack. Manx imagined how the scene would play out, once he walked over—a bunch of passive-aggressive wisecracks from Nader and belly-full of restraint on his part to stop himself from saying something he'd later regret or could be used in evidence against him. He was about to turn on his heels when Morris spotted him and waved. He nodded, and pushed his way reluctantly through the crowd.

"All right there, sir?" PC Emyr Wilcox said, shuffling down the bench. "Saved you a seat. Bet Mickey a fiver you wouldn't make it."

Manx almost hadn't. There was enough work to do, and he was looking forward to a few hours of quiet in the incident room to sift through the case files, but tonight wasn't about him; it was about Morris. He was still kicking himself for leaving her, but he was more disappointed in himself for underestimating the situation—bringing a plastic spoon to a knife fight. He owed her a drink, at the very least, and he had to show support for the team; improve his people management skills, as Canton had pitched it.

"Don't suppose any of you lot want a drink?" Manx asked.

"Stupid bloody question," Mickey Thomas said, and swiftly dispensed with his pint. The rest of them followed suit, except for Nader, who stared aimlessly into his glass, as if he were looking for the answers.

"Nader? Not like you to refuse a drink," Manx said.

"Yeah? Lot of things don't seem like usual round here, boss," Nader said, still peering into the dregs of his pint glass, and uttering the word "boss" with the adequate lacing of disdain he felt tonight for the Inspector.

"Christ, you ill, or something? Take his bloody money," Mickey said.

"Got my own money," Nader said.

"Right you are, Nader," Manx said, and shoved his way to the bar.

Manx attempted to catch the barmaid's attention, but she already had four pint glasses lined-up at the pumps, and was wiping the sweat off her forehead with a beer towel as she pulled.

"Need some help, sir?" Morris asked, as she joined him at the bar.

"With your one good arm?"

Morris stepped on the lowest rung of a bar stool, and leant her weight over the bar. "Hey, Bets! Six pints for the table. There's a love."

"You're next on my list, Del," the barmaid shouted.

"Impressive. I should take you with me to every pub," Manx said.

"She lives next door to my mam," Morris explained. "Did her a favour once, with some creep who was stalking her. Don't think he'll be coming around again."

"I don't think I want to know," Manx said.

Morris shuffled awkwardly, and mumbled, "Sir, I just wanted to say," she said, hesitating before continuing, "not to let Mal wind you up, like. He doesn't mean nothing by it. He's just being Mal."

"A little Mal goes a long, long way," Manx said.

Morris nodded. "I hope I'm not speaking out of turn," she said, and then bit her top lip, about to say something, and stopped herself.

"Out with it, Morris. No place for shyness in our profession."

"Thomas Bowen. Nader's been saying you let him go. Is that true, sir?"

Manx felt his shackles rise. "I don't have to explain myself to you, do I, Morris?

"No, sir, I just heard Mal talking about it, like."

"Yeah, well, Mal Nader's got a mouth the size of the Mersey tunnel. If he charged for every word that came out of it, he'd be a millionaire by now."

Morris was about to apologise, when she felt a sweaty arm wrap itself, like a boa constrictor, around her neck. She turned. Nader was flashing a wide, drunken grin her way, his eyes a spider-web of blood vessels, with a tell-tale moistness around the edges.

"Bloody good WPC we got here, credit to the force," he said. "Takes a beating, and gets back in the saddle the next day. Probably be calling you ma'am one day, eh, Minor?" He swayed on his heels as he focussed on Manx's face, his words refusing to come.

"Whatever you're about to say, Nader," Manx said. "Don't."

Nader ignored his advice, and leant closer. Manx could smell the warm, hoppy waft of his breath on his cheekas he whispered, "What happens in London, stays in London, eh, boss?" tracing his finger across Manx's chest. Manx grabbed his wrist, and looked directly into his eyes, but Nader wasn't in. Nader wouldn't be back in until tomorrow morning, when he woke up with a hangover the size of the Irish Sea.

Manx parried his arm away. "Enjoy your evening, Mal," he said, slapping two twenty-pound notes on the bar.

As he walked through the lounge bar, he felt a tug on his left sleeve. He was about to spin himself around and give Nader the dressing down he deserved, but it wasn't Nader. This man was taller, and wearing the bespoke uniform of most farmers around the island—plaid flat cap, thick-ribbed corduroy trousers, and a tweed sports jacket, which only saw the light of day on market days and Sundays.

"Tudur Williams! Well I never!" said the man, conferring the inspector's name with the correct, Welsh pronunciation Manx had not heard in decades. The man looked expectantly at Manx, waiting for a reply. Manx looked over the man's face, but no bells of recognition peeled in assistance.

"Come on, man! Rhys! Rhys Wyn-Jones! We were in school together, form four and five, you remember!"

The man's face looked vaguely familiar, but then again, most faces around here did. "Sorry," Manx said, and began to walk away.

Rhys persisted. "It's you, no doubt. You joined the police in Liverpool, or somewhere. Your mam owns the old rectory house. What was her name again? Alice, or something?"

"Sorry. I've just got one of those faces," Manx said, and rushed towards the exit door.

The farmer, however, had saved his best shot for last. "Awful thing. Summer of eighty-one, wasn't it?"

Manx felt his stomach plummet. He braced himself for what was coming, but it didn't make it any easier to take the punch when it landed.

"The Angel of Anglesey, the papers called her, aye?"

Manx breathed deeply. The airtight vault of memories began to creak open, granting the thinnest sliver of light to edge its way in. There was a fleeting image, a few blurred seconds of a memory, which was, by now, cleaved deep within him. A girl, a beach; a bright summer day. She was nine years old, smiling directly at him, a fiery belt of sunlight behind her casting heavy shadows across her face. There was a faint burble of laughter, a childish giggle, the scrape of the ocean on the sand. Then, as quickly as the image appeared, it had gone, leaving behind it a flat expanse of mud-brown sand and the measured, steady slap of the ocean.

"They never found her, then?" Rhys asked

"No." Manx mouthed the words to himself, without giving Rhys Wyn-Jones the satisfaction of an answer.

Chapter 24

Twenty minutes later, Manx drove through the village of Talwrn. *Everywhere on the island was twenty-minute drive from somewhere else on the island,* he mused to himself, as he steered the Jensen through the hedge-trimmed lane leading to Swn Y Gywnt. "Sound of the Wind." It had always been a fitting name for the house, which had been passed down three generations to his mother, who was now the current custodian of what Manx liked to call the mausoleum.

The house was always cold. Even in the glare of the summer sun, there was a constant chill, which lingered, ghost-like, through every room. The house had been built with foot-thick grey stonework hewn from the Llanberis Mountains, and stood solitary amid thirty-five acres which held several herds of cattle and sheep. As Manx walked across the driveway towards the front door, he heard the familiar shrill of the wind lashing at the front of the house, as if it wanted in. Swn Y Gywnt stood its ground, as it always had, like its sole purpose for existing was to defy nature itself.

Manx stood at the front door, gathering his thoughts. Visiting Alice Manx-Williams always required some mental preparation. Fortunately, she wasn't one of those women who enjoyed surprise visits or impromptu gatherings. That suited Manx just fine. He took a deep breath, and promised himself to keep calm, letting whatever she said slip off his back like oil.

Alice had called him earlier in the week, and asked him to pick up some Gin; Bombay Sapphire, none of that mediocre, paint stripper rubbish, she had instructed him. He complied, more out of guilt than any sense of duty. She was eighty-two years old. *How much more damage could she do at her age?*

Alice was standing by the parlour window, pulling on a Silk Cut, when Manx walked in. She looked like a figure from an old horror movie; a tall, lean outline, with long, pencil-straight hair cascading down the length of her back, like an old, grey wedding veil.

"Put it on the table," she said, without taking her eyes from the window.

Manx complied. "They'll be the death of you," he said.

Alice drew even harder on her cigarette, so the tip glowed like a fierce, red eye in the darkness.

"You want me to turn on the lights, put the kettle on?"

"Your sister phoned," Alice said. "Said you hadn't called on her yet. She's the only sister you've got left, or are you too important to visit her these days, Detective High and Mighty?"

"Been busy. I'll drive over at the weekend," Manx said. The chances were fifty-fifty, but it made him feel better just saying the words.

"Always busy, that's our Tudor, always somewhere else to be," Alice said, turning to face Manx.

"Big case came in, you probably read about it," Manx said.

"Rubbish," Alice said, spitting out the words as she spoke. "Nothing but rubbish in the newspapers these days. Couldn't pay me to read one."

Manx felt the conversation heading into the usual cul-de-sac of diminishing returns. "You're looking well, despite the fags," he offered.

"Then, you need your eyes testing. I'm an old woman, Tudor, pickled with gin and tobacco. When they cremate me, I'll go up like a bloody atom bomb. Boom!"

Manx ignored the remark. "Need anything else while I'm here?"

"Dr. Kevorkian's phone number," Alice said, shuffling towards the fireplace, and folding herself into the leather club chair.

"He's dead, Mam," Manx explained.

"Really? God always takes all the good ones, eh?" Alice said, sighing.

"Well, you've got my mobile. Call me, if you need anything else."

Manx was making his way back towards the front door when he heard the beginning of the phlegmy strains of his mother's weeping. It was a throaty, pathetic sob he would sometimes still hear in his dreams. By now, the sound was like fingernails drawing down a chalkboard.

"She was an angel, wasn't she, Tudor? Miriam, our angel?"

"Don't," Manx said, sensing every muscle on his skeleton tighten like piano wire. He wanted to be anywhere but here, to talk about anything, other than this.

"Tell me about the day, Tudor. You still have the photograph, don't you? You haven't lost it, have you?" There was a tinge of panic in her voice.

Manx dug his fingernails into his palms. He'd talked through that day a thousand times before, churned it over in his own mind a million more. A year after Miriam disappeared, he'd left home; at the time, it seemed the only option left open to him. *Had he escaped, or run away?* There was no resolution to that particular question, but for Alice, there had been no escape, no relief. Maybe this was his penance now he was back, the benediction he was required to perform.

Manx opened his wallet, and extracted the photograph. He grasped it between his fingers, as if it were an ancient artefact recently excavated. His sister smiled at him from behind the faded yellow patina and fold marks running across the photograph. They were like creases on the palm of his hand—just as real and just as permanent. *Was she still alive?* Each time he heard of a young girl's remains being discovered, his heart would jump a beat: maybe, just maybe.

Manx dragged a chair, sat across from Alice, and re-told the story. It was a story he had narrated so often, he could no longer trust what was memory and what was myth. Not that it mattered, not any more, the only power now was in its telling.

Chapter 25

The visit to his mother's house had left Manx agitated and uneasy. Alice had that effect on him. Guilt—it was her stock in trade when it came to her son, and it passed through Manx like a dark cloud over the sun.

He'd spent the following morning examining the evidence board, and although they now had confirmation the body on the boat was Ernie Stokes, the investigation still progressed at a glacial pace, made even more frustrating by the lack of evidence and the fact there seemed to be no connection between Stokes and the lad in the hospital. There *had to* be one, but Manx needed sometime alone to tumble the ideas around in his mind. He decided to head back to Moelfre at lunchtime, and take a walk along the coast to clear his head.

He ate at the Pilot Arms, which was practically deserted, save the cadre of old codgers sitting by the window, sipping on pints of black and tan, and looking wistfully out over the Irish Sea, as if all the answers were out there, somewhere. Gwen wasn't on shift, and he didn't relish making small talk with the pimply-faced, teenager leaning sullenly against the bar, and chewing noisily on a packet of pork scratchings.

Standing in the car park, Manx reached for a King Edward. The plume of smoke warmed his face, as he drew slowly on the tightly wound tobacco. A few yards across the road, two young lads stood next to the ice-cream kiosk, which was boarded up tight for winter. A battered baby stroller was placed strategically at their feet. They gestured at Manx.

"Hey mister! Mister! Penny for the Guy!"

Christ! Things really don't change, Manx thought. That could have been him and his best friend, Rhidian Thomas, thirty years ago, standing in that exact same spot on a bitter November afternoon, begging for pennies.

"Little old to be doing this, aren't we, lads?" Manx said. The two lads must have been around seventeen. He detected the yeasty aroma of beer on their breath, as he drew closer.

"So what? No law against it, is there?" the fat kid said, pulling on the cords of his hoodie, which puckered scrappily around his fleshy cheeks.

Manx looked at the shoddily constructed effigy of Guy Fawkes. The head was a pale, cream coloured balloon with hastily drawn features scribbled in marker pen. On its head was a rangy, blond wig, cut into a bob, topped off with a bowler hat. The balloon appeared to be deflating the more Manx stared at it. The remainder of the effigy was clothed in a stained, yellow tracksuit, with scrunches of newspaper spilling out from where the feet should have been. The first image that came into Manx's mind was that of a grotesque midget Jimmy Savile.

"Put a lot of work into this, then? Must have taken you all of five minutes," Manx said.

"Come on, mate, just give us a few quid. We've been out here fucking ages!"

Manx took a long draw on his cigar. "Tell me, lads, is there anything I just said to you that gave you the impression I'm about to give you beer money for a balloon in a push chair?"

"It's not for beer, is it. We wanna buy some fireworks for the beach on bonfire night. Parents won't buy 'em, so we set up a business, like."

"Yeah, we're entrepreneurs," the fatter kid stated.

A flash of an old memory ignited in Manx's brain. "Which beach?"

The fatter kid spoke. "Dinas. We do it every year."

Of course! He'd forgotten about the annual bonfire lighting. *Remember. Remember. Fireworks on the beach. 5th of November. Come alone. If U want answers.*

November 5th was three days away. That was what the text was referring to. He let the smoke purse from his lips, and addressed the boys. "A word of advice, lads. You might want to invest in some quality control measures, before inflicting this sort of travesty on the general public in future."

The boys kicked aimlessly at the gravel. Manx squatted to inspect the Guy. "Normally, I love this kind of thing, did it myself when I was a kid. But, this? Very poorly executed, lads," Manx continued, waving his cigar to help illustrate his points. "Take your head, for instance. Apart from the fact it's deflating, there's no resemblance to any human face I've ever seen. Your stuffing's falling out, no shoes, no gloves, not even a sign. It makes me think you're just not even trying."

The two lads looked at each other, and shrugged.

"I hate to be the one burst your bubble, but...." Manx pressed his cigar gently against the balloon's wizened skin. It popped instantly. Midget Jimmy Saville buckled into a whimpering, flaccid, wrinkle. "It's just a bad Guy," Manx said. "A really bad Guy."

"*Coc owen, sais uffar!*" the fat kid hissed.

Manx remembered the insult from his schooldays: *You're an Englishman, with the manhood of a newly born lamb.*

"You kiss him with that mouth?" Manx asked the skinny kid.

The fat lad couldn't help himself, and let out a raspy, spittle-ridden guffaw, then received an elbow to his ribs from his friend for the effort.

Manx flipped open his badge. "Fun's over, lads. Must be teatime by now. Wouldn't want your mothers getting all worried, and then drive all the way to the station to pick you up, would we?"

"Fuck this," the fat kid said, and began to walk away."

Manx watched them disappear over the brink of the hill, their shoulders slumped, kicking the stroller in front of them like a football.

Chapter 26

Shanni reached for another Embassy Number Six from a pack he kept in the glove compartment, and looked over to the dilapidated terrace of council houses. After a few drags, he was ready to turn the Capri around, and forget all about why he was here, but the throbbing reminder on his right middle-finger persuaded him otherwise. He flicked the half-smoked cigarette through the window, and walked towards the corner house, the shabbiest one on the road, with a crumbling gatepost and several motorbikes in the driveway. Music was pouring out from the house, so loud it seemed as if the walls were vibrating to the deep bass line and relentless drumbeat. There would be no point in ringing the doorbell, and anyway, he knew where to find the key; Stokes had reminded him often enough.

"In case I'm ever incapacitated, Shanni, or worse, walk around the left side of the house. There's an old red racing bike chained to a drainpipe. They keep it tucked inside the saddle. Hopefully, you'll never need it, but one can't be too careful."

Shanni had always thought of Stokes as overly cautious, as if he were always expecting someone to leap out at him from the shadows—seemed like the old bugger was right. It was a fucked-up way to die. If Shanni had the balls, he would have asked Scuttler outright if he'd killed him, but that was one truth which could wait, at least for now. Stokes must have talked before he was killed, and told Scuttler Shanni was his contact. *How else would the goons have known to pick him up?* He should be angrier with Stokes, but who was he to judge? He knew what Scuttler was capable of. He slipped the key, with trembling hands, into the lock.

The first thing that struck him in the house was the smell—fresh marijuana and stale vomit. The narrow hallway was lit with red light bulbs from a series of lamps placed along the floor like runway lights. A thin figure stumbled from what Shanni guessed was the downstairs toilet, and passed by him, without giving him a second look—just another junkie joining the party. Shanni grabbed the young man's arm, which felt brittle and reedy, as if it might break if he squeezed too hard.

"JonJo?" Shanni asked

The young man looked at him, his eyes forcing the stranger into focus. He nodded towards the kitchen at the end of the hallway. Shanni let go. The man rubbed his arm, and walked toward the stairway, grasping at the bannister rails, as he hauled himself up, slowly.

Shanni pushed gently on the kitchen door, and took a cautious step forward. Inside, the air was thick with smoke. Shanni coughed as the sweet, cannabis haze caught in his throat. He counted fifteen people, if he could even call them people; they were more like feral animals, their bodies loosely draped over the floor and armchairs. No one noticed him. They were too strung out, lost in their own worlds, tripping somewhere a million miles from here. One man, though, did look up from the spoonful of heroin, or crack, Shanni couldn't be sure, he was about to liquefy.

"Here for the show?" he asked, snapping the rubber cord tight around his upper bicep, and priming his vein with his index and forefinger.

"JonJo?" Shanni asked.

"Who the fuck would you be?" the man asked, temporarily ceasing his ritual at the unwelcome interruption. Shanni threw the key on the table. The man set his tools down, and squinted at Shanni through the smoke.

"Again, who the fuck are you, and what do you want?" The man was rake thin, his face white, like a codfish, but his eyes bore through Shanni like steely blue lasers. Shanni took the only vial he'd brought with him, and placed it on the table. The man shrugged. "Got no use for your mother's old painkillers," he said. "Now, are you going to fuck off, or what?" The man sniffed loudly, and tightened the band around his bicep

"Stokes," Shanni began.

The man stopped, squinting at Shanni. "How's the old poof? Got AIDS yet?"

"He's dead," Shanni said. "Don't you read the papers?"

The man laughed, and lifted his skinny, pocked-marked arms outwards. "What do you think?" he said.

The man had a point. "New supplier," Shanni said, pushing the vial towards the man.

JonJo toppled a blue pill into his palm. "Bit light, innit?"

"Free sample," Shanni said. "Try it, then we negotiate."

JonJo raised his eyebrows. "Confident little fucker, aren't you?"

"Like I said, try it."

The man rolled the pill between his fingers, and grinned, revealing a set of rotten and chipped teeth. "Blue? What, you got pink ones for the ladies, too?"

"So you'll remember, it's called Anglesey Blue," Shanni said. It was a name he'd come up with the night Scuttler had given him the merchandise. Once your customers had a name, they knew what to ask for; it was just good business. The man popped one of the pills on his tongue and swallowed, taking a large chug of beer to help the medicine go down.

"I'll let you know. Now, you can fuck off, unless you're joining the party," JonJo said, sliding a fresh needle Shanni's way.

Shanni breathed a sigh of relief, as he left the house. Junkies made his skin crawl. They reminded him of the ferrets his "so-called-dad" used to breed. Harri Morgan kept a business of them in a cage at the back of the farmhouse. Shanni's job was to feed them and scrub out the cages. He came to hate the ferrets as much as he hated Harri Morgan; hated their smell, their long, furry backs, mottled and flea–bitten, hated how they paced around the cage, scrambling for a way out, scratching at the locks, their eyes wild and aflame, as if their gaze would be sufficient to burn through the wire. On the worst days, he'd have to pick up their bloodied teeth, rotten and worn from the constant gnawing at the metal wires, from the cage floor. The junkies were no different. The way they looked at him, with their vacant, expectant eyes, scratching at their forearms, as if they wanted to crawl out of their own skin, expecting nothing more than a fast-track to the next hit.

Despite JonJo's reluctance, Shanni knew his strategy was a winner. A free sample to get them hooked. It was a small island; word would get round. Once he had the demand, he could dictate his own price. Scuttler was expecting twenty-five thousand pounds, and that's what he'd deliver to him, no more, no less. Anything else was icing on Shanni's cake.

This was his way out, but it wasn't selfish or self-serving; he was doing this for his son and wife. They'd been married fifteen years, and what had he given her? More wrinkles than she deserved, and a mortgage to worry about every month. The garage was never going to make him rich. How long would it take his wife to realise their life would inch onwards, with the same predictable force as it always had, no matter how many nuts, bolts or distributor caps he unscrewed and reassembled. And when his wife sobered up to this conclusion, what then? She'd leave him? Take their son with her? He couldn't take that chance, not anymore. The future was like an urgent, ticking time bomb at the back of his mind, counting down to the day everything would slip through his fingers like sand.

In the warmth of the Capri, Shanni lit another cigarette. The tension he'd felt earlier in the evening was gradually subsiding. He had a plan now. Not just a plan, but a business strategy. He could sense the tick of the clock grow fainter, fading like a distant birdcall, into the shadows. He took out the pill Scuttler had given him, and turned the smooth, blue object around his fingers. JonJo could move some of the merchandise, but he was a couch-dealer; the kind that waited for customers to come to him. Shanni needed a faster, more reliable route to market. Since Stokes's murder, his lads had become anxious, ignoring his calls, and staying clear of the pubs they knew Shanni drank in. He couldn't blame them. They had day jobs, families to protect; they were just blokes, like him, struggling to make ends meet.

Now, things were different. This wasn't just pushing a few pills at the local bars and clubs for beer money; this kind of operation could set them up for life. If he had the chance to explain it to them, look them in the eyes, he could persuade them, make them see sense. After all, the lads weren't that different to the junkies crawling on JonJo's kitchen floor, and by that reasoning, he concluded, neither was he.

Chapter 27

At 6:15pm on the night of November 5th, the first firework of the evening shrieked high over the sky at Dinas Beach, shattering into a shower of sparkling embers, which fell, as if in slow motion, before fading into the blackness. A roar of appreciation rose from the crowd, their communal gaze fixed skywards. It was three degrees Celsius; the meteorologist had been uncharacteristically right. They'd also predicted the night would be rainless and windless, a rare confluence of elements for November 5th, which imbued the crowd with a buzz of anticipation Manx immediately felt as he walked onto the beach.

He looked at his phone, and read the text for what could have been the hundredth time. He surveyed the crowd. Not that he knew what, or who, he was looking for; he was here on blind faith, and more than a side helping of cynicism. It could all be a joke, or maybe he was running straight into a trap. Neither option filled him with confidence, but if he hadn't come, he'd regret it. That much he did know.

A group of teenagers had laid out a blanket by the beach entrance, and were playing music from a boom box. Manx couldn't make out the tunes, but they sounded like every other song he'd heard on the radio recently; over-produced, auto-tuned pop fodder. The girls were dancing, swinging their hips nonchalantly, and taking long, exaggerated swigs from a bottle of what he assumed was a popular brand of Alcopops. *In his day, it would have been a bottle of Strongbow*, he thought, as he watched the only boy in the group circle around the girls, his camera phone pressed to his face, and encouraging them to pout and pose into the lens.

The bonfire, still unlit, stood at around five metres from kindling to peak. Manx looked around at the families wandering along the beach, observing them with the detached eye of a policeman—a habit second nature to him by now. Fathers, mothers, and children busied themselves burying raw potatoes wrapped in tinfoil at the edge of the kindling or spearing soon-to-be overcooked hotdogs onto sticks. *Did he feel envy? Regret or relief that he'd chosen his own path? A wife, a couple of kids a detached house in a nice neighbourhood?* He could have had that, once. He'd given it a good shot. It was what had been expected—get married, get a mortgage, and get busy procreating. He'd made it on the first rung of the ladder, at least.

His marriage to Alison had lasted three years, one of them good, before he walked out. Married life had fitted him like a shoe half a size too small; every step was a pinching reminder of his mistake. He hadn't talked to Alison in decades. It was all ancient history now—a collection of memories, some good, some bad, most just forgotten or discarded. The marriage had produced no children, and the money, how little there was, had been split a long time ago. Alison had moved on, married a marketing executive, and lived on a housing estate in Birkenhead, with three kids and a toy poodle. He only gleaned that last fact when he was bored one night, Googled her name, and found himself on her Facebook page. An uneasy feeling, as if he were trespassing on someone's life, passed through him, as he scrolled down the posts and photographs. *This could have been his life*, he'd thought, before clicking off the page with a sense that was one bullet he was lucky to have dodged.

He looked up at the Guy at the peak of the bonfire, a vast improvement on the one he'd seen a few days ago. At least this one was the correct size, stiffly padded with straw and newspaper, and wearing jumble-sale clothes. From this angle, and the dim light, it was hard to tell, but Manx thought the face was a Guy Fawkes mask, the same one sent to him in the text. *Was it a sign, or merely a coincidence?*

As he looked up at the stack of wood, he wondered about the ancient ritual unfolding before him. *Why, four hundred years later, were we still burning the effigy of Guy Fawkes? Was it a basic human need to reassure ourselves evil could always be vanquished and reduced to embers? Or was it deeper than that?* Maybe, somewhere inside our psyche, we still craved the ritual humiliation of those who had done us wrong; a primal desire to sit in the front row at a public execution, and bear witness to the drawing of the final breath. Manx was deep in these thoughts, when he felt a soft hand press on his shoulder.

"Penny for them."

Manx smiled. It was Gwen. "Save your money, I'm not what you call a sound investment," he said.

"Not many people are." Gwen pulled back the peak of the baseball cap with Dubai Creek Golf and Yacht Club stitched across the front. Manx wondered if it was a gift from her ex, if he was even her ex.

"Didn't think this was your scene, or are you just a big kid at heart?"

"Came here myself when I was Owain's age. Thought I'd relive my childhood," Manx said, looking down at the boy, who was tugging on his mother's sleeve. Impatient, he slipped from his mother's grasp and ran.

"Careful, Owain," she shouted.

Owain looked back briefly, smiled, and kept running.

"What is it with boys and fire?" Gwen said. "It's all he's been talking about for days. I might have a pyromaniac in the making. Any professional advice?"

"Don't play with matches, and it gets worse before it gets better," Manx offered.

"Great comfort, you are."

"Glad to help," Manx said.

He felt Gwen chuckle. As a slight breeze blew between them, he caught the faint scent of her perfume. It smelled expensive, with a subtle aroma reminding him of vanilla and cinnamon.

"You don't talk much about yourself, do you?" Gwen said.

"Not much to tell. I was here, went away, now, I'm back," Manx offered.

"Blimey, not much of a storyteller, either."

"No, I suppose not," Manx said, turning towards Gwen. "But, I have it on good authority my case reports do make for riveting reading."

From behind them, they heard the screaming trajectory of a rocket. They turned around, as the teenage girls cheered loudly while the boy filmed the explosion of colour with his camera phone.

"Got that to look forward to in a few years, too," Gwen said, as they watched the boy light a sparkler and wave it at the girls, who ran screaming and laughing from the hissing object.

Gwen and Manx turned back to face the bonfire.

"Where's Owain?" Gwen said, with a concerned tone. "He was there just a minute ago. The little bugger's always wandering off. Got too many of his father's genes, he has."

Gwen paced anxiously around the bonfire, calling out to Owain. She approached another parent, who shrugged her shoulders, and pointed vaguely towards the ocean. Even from this distance, Manx noticed Gwen's body language shift, becoming more rigid. He walked over.

"You don't think he's gone towards the sea, do you? He can hardly bloody swim, yet," Gwen said.

Manx looked over towards the outline of the sea, beating its relentless path towards the shore. Instinctively, as if urged by something beyond their understanding, they ran.

As they neared the ocean, the crashing of the waves was like a heartbeat gathering momentum. Manx braced himself, as the first slop of seawater passed over his boots. He would have kept walking along the shore, but something caught his eye. A hundred metres or so into the ocean, there was something floating on the surface.

"Owain! Owain!" Gwen shouted into the dark emptiness. There was no reply, save the lash of waves across the sand. Gwen shouted again—this time, it was shriller, more primal.

Manx steeled himself, and ventured further, until the waves lapped at his calves. As his eyes adjusted to the darkness, they scanned urgently across the water. He stepped deeper into the sea, moving towards what he was sure was a small body floating lifelessly on the surface.

The incoming tide pushed against him, as he waded further out. He used his hands like paddles, taking long deliberate strokes, as he walked towards whatever was floating ahead of him. Strong currents scissored around him, threatening to drag him under. He felt his boots sink into the sand and the saltwater lapping at his waistline. Gwen was calling to him, but it was a faint, distant baying, lost somewhere along the shoreline. He was only a few feet away from the body now; he could almost touch the sleeve of the jacket. The water was ice-cold, but all Manx could feel was the urgent, warm beating of his own blood. Beneath him the wet sand was beginning to give way, sucking him into its briny softness.

He was chest deep in the water, when a large wave caught the underside of the body and hurled it past him. He stumbled in its wake and lunged. He grabbed a leg or an arm, he couldn't be sure. As he wiped the saltwater from his eyes, his brain took several seconds decipher what had just happened. The body had split in two, separated at the torso, leaving nothing but the debris of straw and wet newspaper.

Manx barely had time to register the scene, before the next wave spat the remainder of the debris onto the sand. He waded back to shore, his adrenaline slowly subsiding, and, immediately, felt the sting of cold numb his legs and hands. He took a large, deep breath, and looked down at the amputated effigy. The grotesque mask seemed to be laughing at him, with its cruel, wide grin.

For a few moments, Manx allowed himself the indulgence of relief; at least it wasn't Owain. He bent over, put his hands on his knees and coughed up a spit of seawater. Gwen ran towards him, gripping tightly to Owain's wrist, dragging him across the sand.

Manx looked towards the bonfire. A tall, sloped-shouldered man walked around its perimeter, dousing it with petrol from a rusty Castrol Oil can. Behind him, someone else followed with a flame, and cast it over the kindling. As the first lick of flames spiralled upwards towards the Guy, Manx suddenly felt a deep and nauseating pit carve itself in his gut. If the effigy shredded on the shore was taken from this bonfire, what was atop the bonfire now? He dismissed the thought, but then remembered the Guy, and how life-liked it looked, especially from this angle, the moonlight casting down on its broad shoulders and stiff back. He took a deep breath and ran.

"Give me your gloves!" he commanded to the man who had just laid the last flame on the kindling. He cocked his head at Manx like a confused spaniel. "Police. Now! Your gloves." he shouted. The man dragged off his gloves, and handed them over without protest.

Manx located the side of the fire with the least amount of flames and secured a solid foothold in crackling wood. The heat sear through the cheap plastic gloves, as he scrambled towards the peak. Within striking distance of the effigy, his fears were confirmed. The pale, veiny hands, the tuft of hair sticking up from the back of the mask, the leather shoes, slowly liquefying in the heat. This wasn't a Guy; this was human flesh atop a funeral pyre.

The peak of the bonfire was unstable, creaking and shifting under him, as he worked to free the body. It was bound to a metal pole, with thick wads of rope. Manx tugged at the knots, but they were pulled tight. His fingers felt thick and useless encased in the gloves. He changed tactics, and pushed at the body instead, shoving his shoulders against the pole. It relented, and broke loose from the splintering wood. With one last thrust, Manx dislodged the pole from its foundation. The body toppled, like a falling statue, and rolled over the burning shards.

Manx felt the wood give way beneath him, his right foot caught in a wedge of thick timber. If he stayed here, he'd be pulled through to the centre of the fire. He pulled, but his boot was stuck fast. He tugged again; this time his foot slipped from the boot. There was no time to react. Manx lost his balance, and felt the wood give way beneath him. He jumped as far as he could from the centre, and curled himself up into a ball—the faster he rolled down the less the fire could catch at his clothes.

The next few seconds were a blur of heat and flying embers He landed with a painful belly-flop onto the soft sand, and then, quickly rolled over to dampen the flames, before they seared to his skin.

He looked around. The body was on the ground, but the feet were still in the flames. He pulled the shoulders, but his strength was spent. As he struggled, he felt other arms gather around him, dragging the body from the fire, and laying it, face upwards, on the sand.

Manx wiped the soot from his eyes. The Guy Fawkes mask was gradually melting. He gently removed the half-dissolved guise; it peeled off like freshly roasted chicken skin. He noticed something protruding from the mouth—a piece of chewed meat, maybe? Manx carefully separated the lips, and extracted two amputated fingers, still warm. He looked at the man's hand. As he suspected, his index and middle fingers were both missing.

"Jesus Christ," said one of the men, who'd helped Manx with the body. He immediately recognised the face that, only yesterday morning, had been smiling at him from behind the length of a stethoscope.

Chapter 28

By nine forty-seven pm, the beach was cleared of the last remaining gawkers. Manx sat on the back of the ambulance, slathering lanolin on his palms, and watching the forensics team bag the remainder of the evidence. Morris and Priddle had taken the statements, and had signed off for the night.

In the car park, DCI Canton was conducting a press briefing. Manx was sure the man asking the questions was the same man who'd cornered him in the A.M.A.D. meeting. A small video crew from BBC Cymru had rigged up a bright chimera floodlight, which shone directly into Canton's face, causing him to squint. *It made him look confused*, Manx thought, as he listened to Canton reel off the standard-issue phrases police media training had drilled into officers from day one.

"Dr. Simon Vaughn. Forty-seven years old, unmarried, GP at the surgery in Benllech. Now, most definitely, deceased," lead SOCO Ashton Bevan said, snapping off his protective gloves

"Shit," Manx said. "Are you sure?"

Bevan pulled out a partially singed driving license from a plastic bag, and held it delicately at the corner. Manx looked at the bland, handsome face. "I met him a week ago. Fuck, this makes no sense." Manx rubbed his hand across his face.

"I'm not one to speculate, but this whole shebang appears to make no sense," Bevan said. "It does seem pretty medieval though—mock crucifixion, burning at the stake. Swift judgment in the name of the Lord, and all that."

"And the objects in the mouth? Any theories on that, while you're not speculating?"

Bevan smiled, which had the odd effect of distorting his whole face, as if it was being coerced into an unnatural state of being. "We found a ladder, thrown into the stream over there by the pathway," he explained. "Probably used it to transport the victim to the top of the fire. We'll trace it for partials, but don't get your hopes up."

Manx pressed the tips of his fingers together. They were still sore, and covered in an oily residue from the paraffin.

"Looks like you got off lightly. Must be your lucky day," Bevan said, as he watched Manx extend and contract his fingers in a prayer-like fashion.

"Yeah, maybe I should buy a lottery ticket while I'm on a roll," Manx said, catching a glimpse of Gwen and Owain huddled together under a police-issue grey blanket.

"Listen, this maybe something, or nothing," Bevan said. "But, my wife, Sherri, used to be the practice manager at the surgery in Benllech."

Manx stopped massaging his hands. "She worked for Vaughn?"

"She left after a few months, wanted to spend more time at home, cook dinner, dead-head the roses, you know the drill."

"Not really," Manx said.

"Anyway, she was always complaining about him, Vaughn. Still, made a nice change from moaning about me. She had a theory he was bipolar, but I'd take that with a pinch of salt. You work behind a desk at a surgery long enough, and you think you're a bloody doctor."

"Did anyone ever make a formal complaint, anything like that?"

"Not that I know of. The nurses bore the brunt of it, big mood swings, rude bastard one minute, nice as pie the next. Could just about describe any GP I've ever known. Maybe something, maybe nothing, your call."

"Would your wife be up for answering a few questions?"

"Sherri, talk?" Bevan chuckled, and reached into his pocket. "Here, enjoy the interrogation."

"Thanks," Manx said, and slipped Bevan's business card into his jacket.

"And don't forget that drink. I hear you've got a taste for the hard stuff."

Canton shook hands with the reporter, and joined Manx on the back of the ambulance. The vehicle sank a couple of inches, as Canton shrugged his generous buttocks across the lip of the ambulance floor. "Didn't you ever learn not to play with fire, Manx?"

"Must have skipped that one in basic training, Chief."

Canton ignored the remark, and watched a clutch of embers float like fireflies over the last of the bonfire. "What's that song?" he asked, flicking his finger and thumb, "Billy Don't Be a Hero"?"

"Paper Lace, 1974," Manx said, almost automatically.

"Thought you'd be over all that music trivia stuff by now. Mind you, we could always count on you on the pub quiz nights; our musical secret weapon." Canton tapped the edge of his nose with his index finger.

"Some things just get stuck in there, Chief. Can't forget them."

Canton cleared his throat. "You do realise it would have cost me a month's worth of paperwork, if you'd copped it tonight, don't you?"

"I'll bear that in mind, next time. Paperwork first, action second."

Canton sighed. "See, there's that prick-ness gene again. Can't help yourself, can you, Manx? Now, risking life and limb for a dead man. I don't know if that's fucking stupid, or really fucking stupid."

"If it's going on the record, I'd like to say it was just fucking stupid."

Canton shook his head.

"Is that my disciplinary hearing done?" Manx asked.

"For now," Canton said. "And, by the way, what the hell were you doing here? You're not exactly the family outing type. The Press is already questioning the coincidence of a senior officer conveniently at the scene of a murder, as it was being committed."

"He was already dead when I got to him," Manx said, and pulled out his phone to show Canton the text.

"Jesus, Manx. You didn't think to mention this?"

"I didn't think much of it. Thought maybe it was a prank of some kind."

"But, you turned up anyway?"

"Wouldn't you?"

Canton huffed, and brushed down the front of his jacket, where flecks of stray embers had settled like dandruff. "Friday, nine am, incident room. I want a full report. I can keep Colwyn Bay at arm's length for thirty-six hours, but don't come in tomorrow. That's an order. "

Manx was about to complain.

"Don't waste your breath, Manx. Take the day off. I need you fresh as a dew-licked, fucking daisy."

"As a daisy, boss," Manx said, looking at the phone number scrawled on the back of Bevan's business card.

Chapter 29

"It's done," the man said, easing his body into the kitchen chair.

Mandy looked anxiously through the front window, and watched the ruffle of waves fold onto the beach below her.

"You shouldn't be here, I told you," she said, folding her arms to her chest. "It's not safe."

"I expect they'll be otherwise occupied tonight," he said, smiling. It was a reedy, knife-scar of a smile that was, by now, so familiar to her, it often caught her off-guard, when, on times such as this, it could appear so cruel and pitiless. *Had it always been that way?*

Mandy leant back against the sink, and lit a cigarette. "So, that's it? Mission completed?" she said, a tone of hesitant expectation in her voice.

The man took a penknife from his pocket, and began sloughing through the build-up of black, ashy dirt under his fingernails. "Gets in everywhere," he said, sliding out the blade, and tapping it on the table.

"Use an ashtray, at least," Mandy said, handing him hers.

"Next to Godliness, eh?" the man said, shaking the fine black dust particles from his palms.

"You'll be leaving now, I suppose?" Mandy asked, wrapping her fingers around the edge of the counter, as if she didn't trust her own will to keep her upright.

The man stared directly at her—it was a stiff, unrepentant gaze. "Eventually," he said, laying down his penknife. "But, for now, I'm staying. Like he always said, never turn your back on a business opportunity when you're in the driving seat."

Mandy hesitated, choosing her words carefully. "Is that wise? Staying, after you know…"

"By the time they figure it out, it'll all be over. Finito."

Mandy felt a cold shiver run from her lower back and down into her knees. "My ticket's booked, day after tomorrow," she said, stiffly.

The man laughed. "Back to the Mexicans and margaritas? Honestly, I don't know how you can stand it, all that damned Mariachi music. Not exactly your kind of people are they, Mother. A little low rent for you, wouldn't you say?"

Mandy said nothing. Her mind was already there, on the front patio of her favourite restaurant, forking her way slowly through the catch of the day, and being serenaded by Guantanamera for the third time that afternoon.

He laid the knife on the table. "You'll have to put that on hold. I need you here, to wash my dirty laundry, so to speak. That's what good mothers do, right?"

Mandy felt her whole body stiffen. "I was never part of this pact. Never," Mandy said. "It was between you and him, some stupid promise you made. You did what you came to do. Now, just leave…"

Just leave me alone is what she had meant to say, but even now, after everything he'd done and said, that seemed unnecessarily final and cruel.

In too deep? Wasn't that the phrase? Or, was it in over her head? Both seemed to fit her situation. She was already in too deep, had been since the day he was born. There were no half measures, from that moment onwards. You loved your children unconditionally, or you didn't love them at all. There were no grey areas, it seemed to her. She did love him, unconditionally, and it scared her—*he* scared her. His voice, soft, measured and familiar, that he would brandish like a weapon to wound her, or as a blunt knife to butter her up. But, she had accepted it all, accepted him for what he was—his father's son, a chip off the old, savage block.

He flipped the penknife over in his palms. "Wheels are in motion. I'll make sure you get a healthy share, so you're not living out the rest of your retirement in abject poverty." He smiled, the implications of his words plain and direct. "And your boy, I'll need him, too. Your fuck puppet."

Mandy felt the blood rush to her cheeks.

"He's proven himself useful, and he seems suitably smitten."

"No. You can't…" Mandy began. Before she'd finished protesting, his fingers grabbed her wrist, the edge of the blade gliding across her radial artery vein, which was pulsating with life and fear in equal measure.

"It would look like suicide," he said. "A slice here, a slice there. Older woman, history of depression, decides she has nothing left to live for. All too familiar story, these days."

Mandy tried to look away, but she had chosen her side decades ago. He dropped her wrist, and reached back into his duffle bag. "Oh, I got you something," he said, taking out a plastic figurine bearing a passing resemblance to Elvis Presley, but with a Sombrero and a Mariachi costume. It reminded Mandy of a cheap Hula doll on a truck dashboard.

"Spanish Elvis," the man said.

"It's Mexican," Mandy said, flatly, "not Spanish."

"Whatever. It'll help keep your eye on the prize," he said, flipping his penknife closed.

Mandy felt a gust of cold air from the door as he left. She sat down, and poked gingerly at the figurine, which suddenly perked to life with a Spanish version of "Heartbreak Hotel," sung in a mouse-squeak falsetto. She watched as the figure swayed in a series of inevitable and predictable movements, and then repeated the pattern, this time to a different song, a version of "Don't Be Cruel." She smiled at the irony.

Chapter 30

The morning of November 6th brought with it another rainstorm. Manx had slept badly, turning over the case in his mind. Bowen was their strongest lead, so far, but after a week of tracking his movements, all they'd learned was he drank until eleven every night at the same pub, and ordered cod and chips on the way home. He was sure Bowen would slip up, at some point; it was just a matter of when.

With Canton's directive to stay home still ringing in his ears, Manx decided to drive to Benllech, and speak to Bevan's wife, Sherri. As he drove through the village centre, he was immediately taken back to his teenage years, when he worked here during the summer holidays. He'd worked in the ice cream from a stand on the beach, rented out deck chairs, and, one summer, had spent four weeks shovelling warm donkey shit from sand and into plastic buckets for a fiver a day.

Benllech, Manx had concluded, was Moelfre's slutty sister— willing to hitch up the hem of her yellow, sand skirts for any passing visitor. Moelfre, or Barren Hill as the apt translation suggested, had a stony, grey-pebble beach, which was wholly unsuitable for a lazy afternoon's sunbathing, and exuded a more puritan air, its flinty cliffs like the walls of an alfresco Methodist chapel. Benllech, on the other hand, was sand between the toes pleasure and dirty postcard innuendos, generously endowed with three chip shops, several amusement arcades, and a sand-filled beach, which fluttered its eyelashes seductively at the first spurt of sunshine.

Much of the farmland around Benllech had been converted into caravan parks and campgrounds. During the summer, they were bustling with optimistic holidaymakers, hoping for a rare break in the weather. Manx recalled summer romances with mouthy, self-assured inner city girls, brimming with sass and snide. They often came from the rougher areas of Liverpool or Manchester; daughters of factory workers and low-level managers, who had saved all year for a two-week holiday in a thirty-foot long tin can atop a hill, waiting for the sun to bless them. Manx could always spot the girls, trailing a few steps behind the rest of the family as they walked, or sitting, sullen-faced at the back of a beer garden, sipping shandy through a straw, and wishing they were anywhere but there.

He recalled a few fumbled encounters under the sea-wall when the tide was out, or, when it rained, an empty bus shelter, followed by a hurried walk back to the caravan site, and maybe another awkward, lip gloss-tinged kiss at the camp gates. There were no exchanges of addresses, phone numbers, or surnames; they were brief, easily forgotten summer romances, but without the romance and scant evidence of any summer.

***

"I wish I could help you, Inspector. It's been years since I worked there, well, since I worked at all, to be honest." Sherri Bevan paused for a moment, as if grasping at the coattails of a particularly fond memory. "Unless you count picking up my husband's dirty socks as a career." Sherri's lips curved into a curt, thin smile, which forced the fine lines at the sides of her lips to bunch up under the light dusting of makeup. "Another brew?" she asked.

Manx picked up on her use of the word "brew." Despite the flatness of her accent, he guessed she was originally from either Lancashire or Yorkshire, but the rough flanks of her vowels appeared to have been polished off for presentation purposes. He imagined, with a few drinks, she might loosen up, but at ten-thirty in the morning, Sherri Bevan was presenting herself as she wanted to be perceived—a content, dutiful housewife, who could handle unexpected guests with poise and grace.

She was dressed simply in tight fitting, dark-blue jeans and a crisp, white shirt, undone one more button than was necessary. Manx imagined she probably achieved this degree of grooming by the exact same time every day. Her blonde hair fell in thick, expensively cut layers at her shoulders. *She could have been a model, at one time*, Manx thought. She had the requisite high, chiselled cheekbones, the cool blue eyes, and she held herself stiffly, as if she were considering her every move before she executed it. She was several years younger than her husband, who was definitely punching above his weight level when he married her. *Bevan must have caught her on a bad day, or worn her down*, Manx thought, as he glanced over at the gallery of photographs on the fridge door—mostly snapshots of Mr. and Mrs. Bevan, photographed in front of a low sunset or an unfathomably blue ocean.

Sherri settled herself in her stool, and flipped her hair to the side, as if she were preparing for a camera which had long-since forgotten about her. "Ashton doesn't talk much about his work," she said, dropping her voice to a whisper. "I swear he thinks it makes him more mysterious, or something, silly old bugger. I saw the news reports, though. Sent a chill through my spine. You married, Inspector?"

"Not anymore," Manx pulled out his notebook. "You worked for Dr. Vaughn, correct?"

Sherri nodded. "I never liked him much, a very moody man. Not that he deserved to go like that, but he could be a real pain in the behind. Ask anyone who worked for him."

"Is that why you left?" Manx said.

"And Ashton. He likes a warm dinner on the table when he gets home."

"Was there ever office gossip about the mood swings?"

"It was a quiet surgery. After kids and husbands, there's not much else to gossip about. We all had our theories—drink, drugs, complicated love life. Who knows? The nurses were used to it. They just gave him a wide-berth, when he was in one of his moods. I suppose we're all at the mercy of our demons, in some way."

"But, you never saw any behaviour, yourself, you thought suspicious or disturbing?"

"Nobody caught him shooting up under the desk, if that's what you mean." Sherri leant towards Manx, and whispered, "It's not exactly a live and let live community around here. I swear, some of the old biddies would have me burned at the stake for wearing lipstick on a Sunday."

"Was Dr. Vaughn particularly close to anyone?" Manx asked.

"Like a girlfriend or lover?" Sherri savoured the word, "lover," as it slipped past her tongue.

"Anyone?" Manx repeated.

Sherri thought for a moment. "Not that I knew about. But, as I said, I left a while ago, and I was only there for a short time. He did some locum work for the doctors over at the surgery in…. Am looch? Amaloo? Christ, what is it with the Welsh and vowels? Too fancy for them, or something?" Sherri said, flitting her hands across the air, if she were fanning houseflies.

"*Amlwch*?" Manx offered.

"Well-pronounced. Didn't peg you for a native."

"Lapsed," Manx corrected her.

"Still, it never leaves you, where you come from, does it?" Sherri said. "Do you have any idea who killed him? I saw the news last night, but Ashton doesn't tell me a damned thing."

"Early days," Manx said.

"Awful way to die, though. You don't expect it in this community. It's like, you wait months for something interesting to happen, then this."

"Not too settled here yet then, Mrs. Bevan?"

"Call me Sherri; God knows no one else does. I'm always Mrs. Bevan, like I'm the lady of the bloody manor, which, I assure you, is about as far from the truth as is possible."

"I imagine being the wife of a senior Scene of Crime Officer has its perks," Manx said, flipping his notebook closed.

Sherri folded her arms, and leant forward to reveal a deep, fleshy cleavage, which Manx had yet to decide was part of the original package, or an expensive add-on.

"If I come across any, I'll be sure to let you know."

***

Manx parked at the beachfront in Benllech, and looked out over the mud-coloured expanse of sand, which had rippled like a giant, furrowed brow, as the tide retreated. Things had changed little since he was here last. The cafés along the front were weather beaten and pock-marked, their sickly pastel exteriors like a dour coating of sadness. One thing had changed, though; it was all smaller than he remembered, as if the town's significance was steadily diminishing, like the slow fade out of a song. He fired up the Jensen, and headed towards the farmlands south of the town centre.

He pulled up next to a low aluminium gate, stepped out, and looked over the overgrown acre of land, which lay past the gateposts. Fragments of memories came back to him, reflections in a cracked mirror—flashes of colour, luminous neon lights, a whirring blur sweeping through the twilight. But, it was the sounds which came to him most clearly. Loud music, laughter, screams of feigned terror, weaving together in an auditory tapestry that took him back nearly three decades.

It was the summer of nineteen eighty, and Manx was sixteen. He'd talked himself into a summer job at Hobson's Fairground Attractions; anything was better than another summer of shovelling donkey shit. Old man Hobson, a crabby, thick-knuckled man, with a constant aroma of untreated body odour and fresh engine oil, gave Manx an entry-level position, supervising the toddler rides for fifty pence an hour.

There was a dizzying energy about the fair ground, which Manx found both intoxicating and menacing in equal measure. Come sundown, these feelings would intensify, as if the night had brought with it a menace all of its own. At precisely eight-thirty, every light bulb in the fairground would be illuminated, until they buzzed and glowed against the night sky in a jamboree of colours. Manx remembered how the music would sink into him like a punch to the gut: The Big Bopper, Buddy Holly, Chuck Berry—songs of teenage longing and desire transformed into three-chord symphonies vibrating every fibre of his being.

There were smells, too. Aromas, which would linger on the thick, summer night, long after the final ride had shut its engines. If he stayed here long enough, breathed even deeper, maybe he could be intoxicated by them once again—the sickly-sweet candy floss, the warm diesel fumes spilling from the generators. By the end of the summer, he'd graduated to working on the Dodgems, but had never mastered the casual nonchalance of the die-hard carnies, who had hung, like oil-stained pole-dancers, from the back of the cars, a cigarette dangling at the corner of their mouths, their shirt sleeves rolled-up over the nub of their tattoo-speckled biceps.

The fair must have packed up and left town years ago, Manx concluded, as he looked over the wet field. A few souvenirs had remained, left to the mercy of the elements—an abandoned helter-skelter, several rusting bumper cars pushed against the far hedge, and the wooden hut, which used to house the penny arcade, lilting dangerously to one side. Manx wondered if he felt sadness or pity; it was a thin line. He had good memories here, but they were just memories. He'd interviewed enough so-called eyewitnesses to know how unreliable memories could be; memories were fluid, always shifting, adding new details as time passed. The first memory was always the purest, the most accurate. *Was that how it was with his memories of Miriam?* He'd always wondered about that. The further away he was, the harder his memory worked to re-construct what had happened the day she left. He still referred to her as having "left" rather than disappeared. It made it easier to bear, somehow, as if the mere act of leaving implied some return.

By the end of the summer of the following year, Miriam was gone, and Manx had outgrown the fairground rock-n-roll.

He'd found solace in punk and heavy rock; the music better suited his mood. Thrashing guitars, crashing drums, and angry lyrics which spat venom. If he turned up the volume loud enough, he could drown himself in the music, suffocate his thoughts, at least for a while. Thirty years on, he would still do the same. His taste in music may have shifted, but some part of him had remained here, stuck like the needle of a record jumping over and over the same groove.

Chapter 31

Manx had driven back to Benllech town centre, and pulled up outside the surgery next to the chemist, heading inside to conduct interviews with the co-workers of the deceased.

"And you can confirm no one's been in here since?" Manx began, before stopping mid-sentence. The young pale-faced receptionist, Jill, was crying again. He rephrased the question, sensing another mention of the doctor's name might trigger another round of weeping. "No one's been in here since yesterday?"

Jill sniffed loudly, and shook her head. "He gave me the only other key, so I could open up in the morning." Jill reached into her coat pocket, and brought out a small, silver key. "Who would do something so horrible?"

"That's what we're trying to find out," Manx said. "You'll have some officers coming by and asking lots of questions over the next few hours, Jill. The questions may sound personal, like they're prying, but the better picture we have of the doctor's life, the better chance we have of catching whoever did this, understand?"

Jill nodded.

"By the way, no chance of a cup of tea, is there? I'm parched."

Jill, glad of something to do, scurried back to the reception desk. Manx heard her fill the kettle, and rip a fresh Kleenex from the box.

The surgery was just as he expected. A large, wooden desk next to the window looking out over the car park, a locked medical cabinet, a small basin with a soap dispenser, and a variety of medical implements marinating in sterilising fluids. There was a green leather examination bed to the left side of the room, covered with a thin paper sheet. On the back of the door, he noticed a lab coat. He rummaged through the pockets—nothing.

He sat at the desk, and poked at the computer keyboard. The screen flickered to life, and requested a password. He contemplated calling Jill, but he'd need a court order to access anything with confidential patient files. He pulled out the narrow centre drawer—inside, several chewed pens, two packs of sugarless gum, a blank year planner with a company logo he couldn't pinpoint, probably a gift from a pharmaceutical rep. The larger drawer to his left was harder to open; he tugged a few times before it relented. Inside was a single, large brass key attached to a hastily scribbled label. Manx recognised the name. He'd seen it on a sign somewhere.

Manx pulled out his cell phone. "Priddle, meet me at Mona Storage in half an hour."

"But, Chief Canton…" PC Priddle began.

"And bring a camera, one of those professional ones the SOCOs use."

***

The owner of the Mona Storage, Owen Owens, escorted Manx and Priddle to the lockup at the end of the yard, and yanked off the padlock.

"Rented this one a few months back," he explained, lifting the corrugated metal door. "Paid six months in advance, too. Cash."

Owens stuffed his large hands into the pockets of his overalls, and gestured with a shrug of his bulky shoulders for them to follow him inside. "Wish every customer was that bloody easy."

"You know how to use that?" Manx asked, as Priddle fiddled with the buttons on the digital SLR he'd signed out of the station earlier.

"Got one just like it at home, boss," he said, slipping the lens cap into his pocket.

Owens reached for the light switch. The fluorescents flickered to life, revealing an almost empty lockup, with a musty funk.

Against the back wall, an old sofa was tipped on its side, and next to it, a dusty exercise bike, which had seen little action. On the floor, to the right, was a large, scuffed, brown suitcase, the old-fashioned type, constructed from thick leather and secured with thick, brass fastenings. Priddle rattled off a few photos, checked them in the viewing screen, and then took them again.

"Needed a flash, sir," he explained.

Manx edged his penknife under the brass clips. The case flipped opened.

"Fucking hell, sir," Priddle said, and poked the camera in front of Manx.

Manx pushed the lens away, and carefully lifted one of the fifty, or so, pill bottles stacked in the suitcase, and poured out a handful of white pills, the same type they'd found at Stokes's flat—methadone.

He looked up at Priddle. "Why does someone, who's a prominent anti-drug advocate, stash a few grand's worth of methadone in a lockup?" Manx said, not expecting a reply.

Priddle proffered one anyway. "Hiding it, sir?"

Manx sighed. "No shit, Priddle?" he said, and placed the bottle back into the case. "Call the station, and have them send someone over to Vaughn's place, pronto. Let's see what else the good doctor's hiding."

"On it, sir," Priddle said, and walked out into the yard.

"Won't want their money back now, will they?" Owens asked.

"Consider it an early Christmas present," Manx said. "But, don't touch or move anything, and you'll need to provide a statement."

Owens dragged down the lockup door. A sudden thought occurred to Manx; this had been too easy, too linear. The key, the label that led him directly here, the suitcase—it was as if he was being dragged along like an obedient dog on a long lead.

He reached inside his jacket pocket. "Is this the man who rented the unit?"

Owens extracted a pair of scratched spectacles from his side pocket. "Nah. Unless she's had one of them sex changes," he said.

"Do you remember what she looked like?" Manx asked.

"Normal, I suppose. She was wearing this hat and big sunglasses, so I couldn't really see her face." Owens paused for a moment. "I did think it was odd, mind you, wearing sunglasses when it's pissing down with rain. Still, the woman paid cash in advance, so she can bloody well wear what she wants, as far as I'm concerned."

"I take it that means she didn't leave an address, or number?"

"No. We're all above board here. We always get the contact details for

the insurance. I can get it for you, if you like," Owens said, and walked back to the front office, without waiting for a reply.

Manx looked out over the small airstrip adjacent to the storage facility. A single prop Cessna was making its approach from the east, bouncing like a cardboard cut-out model of itself in the crosswind and air currents. There was a squealing of tires and brakes, as the plane landed in a series of scrappy bounces on the tarmac, and taxied towards one of the hangers. *Someone was trying to frame Vaughn*, Manx thought. Someone with a big enough grudge to murder the doctor and ruin his reputation in the process, as if killing him wasn't sufficient punishment.

Back in the Jensen, he looked over the paperwork Owens had given him, and dialled the number for "Janice Doe." As expected, it led to a series of urgent, irritating beeps. He hung up, and made another call.

"Chief said you weren't working today. Told us to not talk to you," Morris whispered.

"He said not to come in, Morris. Not that it's any of your business."

She mumbled an apology.

"Drop whatever you're doing, and dig up everything you can on Dr. Simon Vaughn. Everything. Any lawsuits, pending or passed, any patients with a grudge, pissed off friends, enemies, girlfriends, boyfriends, Facebook profile. I want his life story on my desk by the briefing tomorrow morning."

Chapter 32

"Will you sit the fuck down, Trev, before I shove you through that bloody window." Shanni's temper was hanging by a thin, tense wire.

Trev shook his head. "We could have been followed. Can't be too careful these days, what with them satellite cameras," he explained. "Recognise your face from space, they can. Old army mate told me. It's big fucking brother out there, no two ways about it."

"Worried aliens might spot your big fucking hooter from outer space?" Shanni said.

Trev's nose twitched, as if it were trying to sniff out prey lurking on the other side of the glass. He tugged at the edge of the curtains, casually flicking a length of fag-ash onto his Wellington boots. "Don't feel right. Probably coppers fucking everywhere, tracking us like dogs."

"Fucking hell," Shanni said. "A couple of deals, and he thinks he's in an episode of *The Wire*. Jesus Christ, Trev, you're a fucking liability."

Shanni chugged down another mouthful of beer. Despite three six-packs of Boddingtons and several open packs of Marlboro Lights scattered across the kitchen table, the mood was deadly serious. The draught wheezing in from under the kitchen door only added to the chill, and Shanni could see his breath plume out from between his lips as he spoke.

"You couldn't find us a house with decent central bloody heating?" Shanni directed his question at Hywel Jenkins, seated directly across from him, and balancing on the back legs of his chair.

"You said you wanted somewhere quiet. At least we've got electricity, mate, most people shut the mains down."

Jenkins was nervous, Shanni could tell. The pitch of his voice seemed higher than usual, and he'd never called him, "mate" before. Jenkins kept his gaze fixed on the stone floor, and twisted a beer can around his palm, as if he were trying to unscrew it. Ordinarily, Hywel Jenkins was as smooth as wet plaster skimmed on drywall. He was a cocky bastard, too; the sort of man who could look someone dead in the eyes, and get them to buy whatever horseshit he happened to be selling that day. Hywel probably believed it himself; at least, for the few minutes he needed to convince someone else it was true.

"You couldn't have brought a heater? One of those portable jobs?"

Jenkins scuffed forward. "Here's the thing, Shanni," he said, resting his elbows on the table. Shanni noticed how his eyes refused to settle on any one spot for too long. It was the second thing Shanni had noticed about Jenkins—he was just like him, always looking out for the next opportunity.

"The owners moved to Jo'burg a few months back. They're asking fifty grand over market value. I'll bet you a hundred quid it'll be empty for the next twelve months. Sellers still think it's two thousand and bloody five. You try and tell them otherwise, but they don't listen. In my opinion, lads, it's all fucked up, and it's going to stay fucked up for a long time."

"Thanks for the professional insight, Jenkins. I'm sure we're all very fucking enlightened," Shanni said, taking a deep pull on his cigarette, savouring the warm cloud of nicotine as it rolled around his mouth and sank deep into his lungs. "But, looking on the bright side," he continued, "I expect we'll be done quicker, if we're all shivering our arses off. So, let's get down to business."

He blew a thin line of smoke from between his lips, and watched it drift towards the kitchen skylight. Silence, this time accompanied by a collective shrug of shoulders. *Why couldn't anyone look him in the eye?* Trevor shifted his squat, short frame from his self-appointed neighbourhood watch position, and joined the others at the table, but kept glancing over at the window every few minutes, just in case.

"Ok, I could be over-sensitive, boys, but if there's something on your minds, let's hear it, because, to be honest with you, I'm bored to fuck with the sound of my own voice."

The three men looked at each other, waiting for the other to speak up. The wind was gathering momentum outside, catching on the doors of the outhouses, and rattling them against their frames.

"Go on, Jenks. You said you'd ask him," Bug finally said.

Davey "Bug" Evans had been switched to mute for most of the evening, peering at the proceedings through his large, bulging eyes. Proptosis, an optic abnormality, had earned Davey the nickname Bug since his school days. Bug had also drunk more than anybody tonight. Seven empty beer cans were stacked up in front of him in a pyramid shape, which he'd carefully built, pushed over, then rebuilt several times over the past hour.

He looked up from behind the cans. "Well, I'm not bloody asking. I told you that. Can't go back on your word now, aye."

The more Bug drank, the more it brought out the "Bangor" in him. Inevitably, he'd begin to slur the word "aye" to the end of every sentence, whether it merited it, or not. He also had a habit of scratching at his beard when he was nervous, always at the same spot, the left side of his neck where there was the least amount of growth. Shanni had noticed the raw, pink nail marks rapidly enflaming under the collar of his crew-neck jumper.

"Jenkins? Looks like you're the spokesman," Shanni said. "Not like you to keep that gob of yours shut for long."

Jenkins shuffled uncomfortably. "All right, but it's a bit delicate, like."

"Jesus, it's not *Loose* Fucking *Women*. We're all big boys here."

Jenkins sighed. "All right. Was it you, Shanni? We need to know."

"Was it me, what?"

"Fuck! The murders, man, the fucking murders!" It was Trevor who spoke this time, and couldn't help himself from pushing back his chair, and walking back to the window. He twitched at the lace curtain, as if compelled by power greater than himself.

"Fuckin' hell, lads, that's what this is all about?"

"We're just looking at the evidence, Shanni. We all knew Stokes, and Vaughn. We didn't figure the doc for a user; he was always speaking out against the stuff. It doesn't make sense, unless he knew something, or you wanted to keep him quiet."

"Aye," Trev agreed. "They both get murdered, then you start calling us about some new product you want us to sell." He wagged his finger at Shanni. "Can't tell me that's just a fucking coincidence."

Bug peeled another ring-pull off a beer can. "Then, we see it on the telly, both of them murdered. Fucking terrible, it was, aye."

"Pretty elaborate theory for an estate agent," Shanni said.

Jenkins leant back in his chair. "If the shoe fits."

Shanni slapped his hands on the table, and laughed. "Fucking unbelievable. You all think I killed them?"

Silence. Shanni rose from his chair, leant over the sink, and lit another cigarette. He needed to wrestle back control of the room. Jenkins could fuck this all up for him. He needed to keep a clear head, be the rational one, and direct everyone back on track. If Shanni had learnt one thing in life, it was how to read between the lines of what people said, and what they really meant. It was simple information gathering, leverage he could use later for his own needs.

"Ok, Jenkins, fair dos, I can understand how you might reach that conclusion," Shanni said calmly. "But, the question you have to ask yourselves is, am I stupid and desperate enough to commit two murders a few miles from my own doorstep?"

"You tell me?" Jenkins said.

"Ok, let me put this another way, lads. Which of you seriously thinks I killed Stokes, and crucified the poor bastard on the side of a fucking fishing boat, then, a week later, topped off Vaughn, and dragged his body fifteen feet up a bonfire to show the whole world what a mad fucker I am?"

Silence. Shanni walked around the other side of the table, and rested his hands on Bug's shoulders. "Trev? Bug? You've known me since we were all shitting our nappies."

Trevor momentarily looked over from his window patrol. "It's just suspicious, like. My mam knew Stokes. Right upset, she was, when she heard. But, murder, that's a stretch, even for you, like."

"Bug?"

"I dunno. When Jenks first mentioned it, it made sense. Shanni can be a little shit, but murder, don't seem right, aye?"

"Thanks for the vote of confidence, lads," Shanni said.

Jenkins scuffled forward in his chair. "There's too many secrets, Shanni. Like what happened to your finger. You lose it chopping the veg for Sunday dinner? Too embarrassed to tell us?"

Jenkins was smart, too fucking smart, Shanni thought. There'd be time to explain everything later, but this wasn't the time or place. This meeting was about the future, not the past. He had over thirty grands' worth of merchandise stashed in the back of the car. JonJo wouldn't move his arse further than to piss in the bathroom, and Shanni needed to get the pills off his hands, fast. And that ticking, that damned ticking, in the back of his mind was starting up again.

Shanni took a deep breath, and spoke slowly. "For the record, I didn't do it. Neither of them. Now, can we move onto what the fuck we came here to discuss? Making us a boat load of money, before we're too old to spend it."

A moment of silence. Outside, the wind scraped the branches of the oak trees against the kitchen skylight.

"Good enough for me," Bug said, taking another loud swig of beer.

"Me too. Shanni's no murderer. I mean, what they did to Stokes and Vaughn, fucking sick, that was," Trev said, and spat on the floor as if to emphasise his point.

"Democracy wins out, Jenkins," Shanni said.

"But, you know who killed them, Shanni? Whoever's supplying you the drugs? Right?" Jenkins said.

Shanni felt the corners of his lips twitch. They always twitched when he was irritated. His wife had pointed it out numerous times, and he was on the cusp of becoming self-conscious about it. He clenched his fists, felt his nails dig into his palms, and smiled. "What's important, lads, is we're all up to our necks in this one way, or another. The only way to come out smelling of roses is by sticking together." Shanni looked directly at Bug and Trev. "If mates, mates. Right?"

They nodded, tentatively. Shanni continued, "What happened to Stokes and Vaughn was a bloody tragedy, no doubt, but I didn't kill them, so let's move on, and do what's right for ourselves and our families. This is just the beginning. We sell the stuff quick, and we're set for another shipment, as much as we want."

Trevor returned to the table, and threw his whole weight into the chair. "Fuck! I don't know, Shanni. It was a laugh to begin with, make a few bob on the side, but it's like serious now," he said.

"We're not flogging kitchen appliances, Trev. Of course it's bloody risky. Listen to me. There's no one up there spying on you with a fucking satellite camera. Let me worry about shit like that. Just keep doing what you've been doing, and we'll all be rolling in it. I promise you, lads, this is the real deal."

The room went silent for a moment, before Jenkins spoke up. "No amount of money's worth dying over."

"But, this amount of money is worth some risk," Shanni said. "Why the fuck else are we doing this, for shits and giggles?" He laid his hand on Trev's shoulder. "Trev, tell me, why are you doing this?"

Trev shrugged. "Money, I suppose."

"Right you are, Trev, because from what I hear, you spend more time at William Hill's than you do at home. A little too fond of the gee-gees is our Trev, in case you didn't know." Shanni leant close to Trev's ear. "Here's some odds for you to think about, Trev. Ten to one you'll have the bailiffs round the house in the next few weeks. That's not going to get you back in the missus's knickers, is it? Probably throw you out on your ear."

Trevor sniffed, said nothing, and studied the crevices in the floor.

"What about you, Bug?" Shanni walked towards the now sweating figure of Davey "Bug" Evans. "Final warning from the North Wales Water Authority for drinking on the job? Bit ironic, that, getting fired for drinking, when you work for the Water Authority. Still, you'll have more time to spend at home with the family; that'll be nice."

Bug put down his beer, and bit the inside of his cheeks, as if he were testing them for doneness.

Shanni turned his gaze towards Jenkins. "And Hywel "Wide Boy" Jenkins, estate agent of the fucking year. Takes out an expensive mortgage to develop holiday flats in Benllech, just as the economy tanks. Bad timing, Jenks. Must be like a fucking monkey on your back, mate."

Hywel said nothing, running his finger along the rim of his beer can.

"Ok, lads. Now I have your full attention, let's get down to business."

Shanni pulled a single, blue pill from his jeans pocket, and placed it carefully in the centre of the table. "Anglesey Blue" he said. "A few days ago, I gave a sample to a dealer to test the waters. Two days later, the bloke's calling me, begging me for more. Offers me seven pounds a pill. I've got hundreds of these in the back of the Capri that need shifting, and that's just for starters. I reckon we can sell at ten pound a hit to every junkie on the island. So, the question is, lads, which one of you is the stupid prick who's going to say no?"

Chapter 33

White, crushing white, falling around him, filling his mouth, his throat, his lungs. Above him, a shred of sunlight cuts through the milky surface. He reaches. He's pulled back by an invisible force, and deeper towards the black nothingness. He rolls, twisting his body in an attempt to free himself, but the force is relentless. He wants to breathe, needs to breathe. He imagines the luxury of oxygen flowing through his blood, giving life to his red blood cells again, but he senses he can feel them dying within him, flaying uselessly in his bloodstream. He opens his mouth, as if by instinct. For a second, he experiences the heady relief he longed for. Then, reality. His lungs are sodden, heavy, expanding against his ribcage. He hears nothing, save the booming pulse of his blood as it pounds, like a distorted bass-line, through his skull. Then, there is lightness. As his brain is slowly starved of oxygen, he feels euphoric; the struggle is over. His body supplicates in the water. He floats momentarily, caught in the speckled light of the sun's rays, before he's pulled downwards into the infinite darkness.

Two-sixteen am. Manx was wide-awake. The red digits of his alarm clock tripped silently to two-seventeen am. He was sweating; the clammy dampness on his skin clung to the sheets, as he groaned his way from his bed. It was the same dream he'd had ever since Miriam had disappeared. Whenever he was in the presence of death, the dream came to him, as if to remind him of his own mortality; not that he was in any danger of forgetting.

Standing barefoot on the cold, tiled floor of his kitchen, he debated between firing up the kettle, which was still full of the unused water he'd meant to boil days ago, or unscrewing another bottle of Spring bank Single Malt, his third in as many weeks.

Who was he trying to kid? He poured out a generous measure, and added a single ice cube.

He sat at the breakfast bench, fired up his MacBook Pro, and scrolled through his music collection. He paused at Lucinda Williams; it always seemed to be Lucinda Williams at this hour of the morning. "You Were Born to Be Loved" slipped easily from the speakers, filling the kitchen with its mournful Hammond organ chords, which were set back perfectly in the mix, as Lucinda's vulnerable vocals dripped, honey-like, over the melody.

Williams. Doesn't get much more Welsh than that, Manx mused, and the thought occurred to him, for the first time, that her music might possess an element of Welshness. The stripped-down arrangements and simple, pure melodies weren't dissimilar to the hymns sung at the Sunday evening services his father used to bring him along to. Tommy had the loudest voice in the chapel, a bass baritone the rest of the congregation would follow behind, like sheep to the altar. There was always a promise of divine salvation in the hymns. A deal struck with God, that, once supplicated, a sinner or saint would be granted heavenly dispensation. Manx had concluded at an early age he would be the conductor of his own salvation. Perhaps it was why he was drawn to this type of music; what the critics had classified as Americana. But, to Manx, it needed no label, just the ability to move something within him.

Amid the downbeats of minor chords, the tremor of pedal steel guitars, and bitter-sweet lyrics, there was a sense of abiding hope, running like a coal steam, through her music. Dirt tracks, gravel roads, and car wheels, they all led someplace; someplace better, someplace more hopeful, someplace you reached through your own strength and fortitude, not through supplication and prayer. As he let the music and Scotch flow freely through him, his mind began to wander. Something Thomas Bowen had mentioned in the interview niggled at the back of his brain.

He tapped his index finger on the track pad, and typed "T-Bone, music producer" into the search bar. Amidst a long list of recipes, promising the perfect grilled steak, he clicked on the one that looked most relevant: T-Bone Music Productions. The web site unfurled itself amid a garish clash of graffiti set to a heavy bass loop, which vibrated loudly around the kitchen.

The site was an amateur effort, built from a free, or at least a very cheap, template. There were numerous spelling mistakes and eccentric use of grammar, which Manx couldn't decide was the result of a poor education or street slang that had passed him by. Bowen was offering his services as an amateur musical impresario, promising state-of-the-art production facilities, song writing collaborations, and "customised mashups," but it was the Live Gigs page that drew Manx's attention. A collection of hastily taken photographs appeared on the page as he clicked. As he scrolled, one photo in particular caught his attention. Dated September 8th, it showed Bowen, with his arms around another man. They both looked worse for wear, glassy-eyed, and hanging onto each other, as if they might topple over if they let go. Manx clicked the zoom function, and focussed on one particular face, and felt the stirrings of a connection. It wasn't so much the bright illumination of a light bulb—these things rarely were—this was more akin to a thin spark in the darkness guiding him the next few steps. It was him, he was sure of it. *But, what was his connection to Bowen?* He mulled over the question, took another sip of scotch, and got to work.

Chapter 34

Friday eight fifty-three am: Major Incident Room.

The harsh, white overhead fluorescents were exaggerating Manx's already delicate physical state. He'd met the cold rise of, dawn with the fur of last night's scotch still on his tongue, and a heavy storm cloud thundering at his temples. He looked around, and pressed his thumbs into his forehead; he needed a bigger room, bigger team. Back in London, he'd have twice as many boots on the ground, and a dedicated officer to enter, collate, and cross-reference all the data into HOLMES, the Home Office Large Major Enquiry System. The five assigned officers were barely sufficient to cover one murder, let alone two, and he was relying on a rookie, PC Delyth Morris, to input all the evidence, and ensure it was all recorded by the book.

Canton had assigned another two officers to the case—PC Emyr Pritchard and PC Alyn Davies, neither of whom Manx suspected had any serious crime investigations under their belt, but seemed keen enough.

Behind him, the dim, blue light from the overhead projector flickered erratically. He tapped the head of the projector, and twisted the lens until the words "Operation Obol" clicked into focus. As he listened to Lucinda Williams in the early hours of the morning, he'd organised the evidence into thirty-one, clearly labelled, Power Point slides. It was a meditative exercise, laying out the chain of events in a logical sequence, adding the scraps of evidence to the slides as he went along.

At five o'clock that morning, he was still making tweaks, ensuring he hadn't missed something important, or included some erroneous scrap of information which would take the briefing down a series of blind alleys. This had to be an on-task operation, no distractions or tangents. Manx had figured out what he needed the team to focus on; his job now was to make them understand why.

At eight fifty-nine am, the team shuffled into the incident room, clutching their mugs of tea, and catching up on the latest station gossip. They offered a cursory "Morning, boss," before taking their seats.

"Operation Teabag gone to the dogs, then?" Nader said, as he parked himself on the desk furthest to the back, and folded his arms in a gesture suggesting he was waiting to be impressed, but wasn't holding his breath.

DCI Canton entered the room. There was a communal shuffling of chairs, and straightening of backs. "Nice of you all to turn up. And on time, must be a first," he said, and signalled to Manx to dim the overheads.

"Operation Obol," Manx began, looking over his audience. "What's the significance of Obol? Anyone?"

There was a general shaking of heads, and shrugging of shoulders.

"Charon's Obol," Manx said, clicking on an illustration he'd copied from the internet of a tall, sickly-looking man in Grecian robes, standing by a boat at the banks of an underground river. "In Greek Mythology, Charon was the ferryman of Hades. His vocation was to escort the recently departed over the river Styx to the next life. Charon's Obol was considered a necessary bribe, a coin placed in the mouth of the corpse by the dead man's family, to guarantee the soul's safe passage into the afterlife. If you couldn't pay, the soul remained in purgatory, until the debt was paid."

"Jesus, do you think the killer's that bloody well-educated?" Nader said.

"It's a starting point, Nader. Our killer is either referencing Greek mythology, or he's screwing with us. The murders have two things in common—objects left in the mouth, and a sense of the theatrical."

"Victim Number One: Ernest Stokes, owner of Stokes Antiques, Beaumaris." Manx continued to the photo of Stokes's body. "He died from asphyxiation, before being tied to the bow of a fishing boat, and violently pummelled against the harbour at Cemaes for several hours."

He clicked to the next slide. "Victim Number Two: Dr. Simon Vaughn, GP at Benllech Surgery."

"Any COD for Vaughn yet?" Canton asked.

"Not conclusive, but he was dead before the fire touched him, and there was a high concentration of methadone in his blood stream."

"The stuff they give heroin addicts? "Morris asked.

"Yes, but a lot cheaper and easier to source," Manx said.

"Be easy enough for a doctor to get hold of, then?" PC Emyr Pritchard offered.

"Which would connect Simon Vaughn to Ernie Stokes," Manx said. "The pills in Stokes's flat and those in Vaughn's lockup were identical. Vaughn was pumped full of methadone before he died, which means he's either a sloppy user, or someone did it for him. Vaughn's surgery and house were swept clean; nothing, not even pain killers."

"Vaughn could have been supplying Stokes with methadone," PC Alyn Davies began, stroking his beard in a methodical manner. "Vaughn gets cold feet, and realises he could be struck off, if he gets found out, so he shuts up shop. Stokes is pissed-off, then blackmails Vaughn. Things get out of hand, Vaughn finally snaps, and bumps off Stokes to save his reputation."

"Yeah, but who murders Vaughn? Stokes's ghost?" Nader said.

Davies shrugged his shoulders in a "search me" gesture.

Manx clicked on the photograph of the fishing boat."To date, the only person who saw Stokes's body, before we did, was Dick Roberts, who, as we know, committed suicide. But, what drove him to that desperate act? Had to be something big, something he couldn't live with. We need more history on his state of mind, any connections to the victims. Stokes didn't end up on Dick's boat by accident."

Manx gathered his thoughts, and paced in front of the projector beam. "What's the significance of leaving body parts in the mouth? Ernie Stokes had his testicles removed, and Simon Vaughn had his index finger and middle finger amputated and placed in his mouth. Coincidence, or is the killer just fucking with us? Anyone?"

"Could just be a copy of the first murder," Pritchard suggested, peering over the rim of his 2.75 lenses.

"We never released the full details of Stokes's murder to the Press, so it's unlikely he'd know what to copy," Manx said.

PC Morris cleared her throat. "He could be giving them a taste of his own medicine," she began. "We know Stokes was gay. Maybe the killer cut off his testicles because he hated homosexuals, shows how disgusted he is. Vaughn was a doctor, so he cuts off the two fingers he uses to take a pulse. He takes the things that make them who they are, and removes them. It's like he's taunting them, before he kills them. He wants to make them suffer, like death's too good for them."

There was a dead silence in the room, as the four officers all turned to look at Morris.

"Just a theory, like," she added, feeling their eyes on her.

"Good theory, very good, but you're curing the symptoms without figuring out the cause," Manx said. "We still don't know why they were killed. So, any ideas on why he displays the bodies, instead of just disposing of them?"

"Sick bastard wants to show off. Probably gets a hard-on seeing his handiwork in the papers, TV, and that," Nader offered.

"It could be a warning," Priddle said. "Like he's sending out a signal. Don't fuck with me, or something like that."

"Remember what Bowen said in his interview, Nader?" Manx said.

"Was that just before we let him walk, boss?"

Manx took a deep breath, and glanced over to Canton, whose subtle nod made it clear he shouldn't rise to the bait. "Whoever paid Bowen to break into Stokes's place knew he was hiding the drugs, even if they didn't know exactly where."

"Don't forget, Bowen was also threatened. You saw the cuts on his hands, Nader," Canton said.

"Yeah, probably did that himself, when he was high as a kite," Nader said. "The little prick could be lying his tits off. We should just arrest the little shit, get it over with."

Manx kept his trump card until last. He clicked to the photograph he'd dragged from Bowen's website. "This is Thomas Bowen with our victim, Dr. Simon Vaughn, taken three months ago. If nothing else, it proves we were right to keep tabs on Bowen. Somehow, he's connected to these two murders."

Manx sat on the edge of the table, and addressed the whole team. "We need to be on the same page, one team working together. Our number one priority is finding the connection between Stokes and Vaughn. Bowen will either lead us to the killer, or by good detective work, we'll figure it out. Either way, this is the plan. Find the connection, keep tabs on Bowen, and record everything, and I mean, *everything*," Manx said.

He turned to Morris. "What about Vaughn? Can't just be this one sheet?" he said, lifting the paper, and letting it float back down.

Morris blushed. "Um, yes, sir, that's all there was. No social media accounts, nobody's suing him, no past lawsuits, either. No girlfriend, as far as I can tell, and no real friends either. I made some calls, but everybody says the same; he kept himself to himself, a bit of a loner."

"What about before he came to the island, any history there?"

"Dead end, sir. There's nothing. It's like he just appeared out of nowhere. His driving license, passport, everything was issued when he was living here. It's like he didn't exist before. I did a web search. Lots of Simon Vaughns, but none of them were our man. Searched out all our databases, too, sir, PCN, nothing in the Fingerprint Exchange Network, no DNA matches. Sorry."

"Ok," Manx said, wiping his hand across his face. "Which brings us to the obvious question; what sort of man has no back history? No friends, no family, or any timeline we can trace back further than a decade?"

"The kind of man who doesn't want to be found, sir?" Morris offered.

"But, someone did find him," Manx said. "Which means we're now searching for two people—the killer and the real identity of Dr. Simon Vaughn."

"Maybe Stokes helped him," Priddle said. "Stokes had his fingerprints removed. Maybe he helped Vaughn get a new identity, or something."

Manx had a sudden thought. The words "new identity" flashed across his mind, as if they were in neon. "Ok, here's the plan," Manx said, eager to finish up the briefing. "Morris and Priddle, keep digging up anything you can on Vaughn. Pritchard and Davies, you're on Bowen duty. Step up the surveillance, and keep tabs on him twenty-four-seven. Nader, keep the pressure on your contacts. Question anyone who knew Stokes and Roberts; there has to be a connection, we just need to find it."

Nader ran his fingers under his collar, as if he were scouring for fleas.

"That's it, briefing over," Manx said, and pressed the escape button on his keyboard. There was a communal scraping of chairs and puffing of chests, as the team returned to their desks.

"Um, Inspector? I think you should take a look at this," Priddle said, hoisting his mobile phone above his head, and tilting the screen towards Manx. "Looks like you're a YouTube sensation."

Manx felt the blood drain from his face as the dramatic, Hammond-organ chords of "Fire" by the Crazy World of Arthur Brown spilled from the thin speaker, and filled the incident room.

Chapter 35

"Jesus Christ! Can you get that on the projector screen?"

Priddle reached across, and typed in the web address. The video buffered then played on the screen behind him. "Jim, one of the Community Support Officers over at Holyhead, emailed it," Priddle explained to the team, who had by now shuffled to the front of the room for a better look. "Thirteen thousand views, and it's only been up a couple of hours."

The video opened with the blurred figure of Manx running from the ocean and towards the bonfire. Cut to a medium close up of Manx scaling up the side of the bonfire. Jump cut. Manx is now at the peak of the bonfire, shoving his body weight against the effigy. Scratch edit: he's falling down the edge of the bonfire. Reverse motion: he's back on top again, all syncopated perfectly to Arthur Brown's funk-tinged rhythm. Wide angle, reverse: onlookers standing, shouting at Manx, and waving. Slash-pan to the bonfire: Manx tumbles down; a pyrotechnics of embers illuminates the scene. Crash zoom: the camera tries to focus on a close up of Vaughn's face, as Manx begins to peel off the Guy Fawkes mask. Fade to black: the final reveal censored by a hand slapping across the lens. Fade up from black: the demonic face of Arthur Brown, rendered in slow motion, fire spitting from his mock Viking headdress. Fade out to black.

The room fell silent, as the team tried to parse what they'd seen. Nader was the first to break the silence. "Fucking hell, boss, bit beyond the call of duty, wasn't it? Wouldn't catch me climbing a bloody lit bonfire," he said. "No matter who's on top."

"I'd pay good money to see that, Nader," PC Pritchard said. "Can't see you climbing the station steps without a fag break."

"Any idea who posted this?" Canton asked.

Priddle leant over the computer screen. "Trollseeker1282, says here, but could be anyone. Probably a fake IP address."

"Fake what?" Canton asked.

"IP address, sir. It's a unique identifier from a computer. Tells you where the information is coming from. If you don't want to be traced, you create a fake IP address. Covers your tracks, like."

"He's fucking with us," Manx said. "He was there. We need to find out who uploaded this video, and quick."

"We could call SuperNaan. I bet she'd trace him," Priddle said.

Manx sighed. "SuperNaan?"

"Not met her yet? Best we got on the island, boss," Nader said.

"Best *what* we've got on the island, Nader?" Manx asked.

"She's one of those geeks, works part time at Bangor Uni," Priddle said.

"Could she help us trace this Trollseeker joker?" Manx said.

"As I said, best on the island," Nader repeated.

Manx wiped his hands across his face. "All right, bring her in. The more the fucking merrier."

Chapter 36

"Very pleased to make your acquaintance." The voice was soft, and tinged with the elegant lilt of an Indian accent. "Dr. Eshana Shukla." The woman extended a firm, confident handshake.

"Detective…" Manx began.

"Detective Inspector Tudor Manx-Williams, but they tell me you prefer just Manx? Am I right?"

"Um, yes." Manx said.

"Good," she said, and smiled.

Manx guessed she was in her early sixties, but carried herself as if she were a couple of decades younger. She was wearing a long, colourful dress that flowered out over her ankles and feet. Her face was owl-like—rounded and inquisitive. A pair of gold-rimmed reading glasses attached to a similarly coloured chain hung at her chest. Her eyes had a grandmotherly softness to them, but still retained an expressive and curious sparkle, as if they were constantly analysing everything in her vision.

"Most people just call me Eshy, but I hear the officers have taken to calling me SuperNaan, like the Indian bread?"

"Ah, sorry about that. Police humour, gets them through the day."

Eshy leant closer into Manx. He could smell her perfume, jasmine maybe. "Really, I don't mind. After all, we should all be super at something. It bestows our lives with meaning and purpose, don't you think, Inspector?"

"And what is it exactly you're super at?" Manx asked.

Eshy laughed, a girlish-like giggle, and pulled a laptop from her bag. "Hacking the hackers," she said, settling the object on his desk. "Recent economic circumstances have opened doors for people like myself, freelance consultants ready to help our local constabulary at the drop of a hat. Zero hour contractors, I think is what they call us. Not the most flattering of titles."

"Qualifications?"

"Ah, of course. Let me see. Applied mathematical degree from Cambridge, and an advanced doctorate in computer science from Stanford. Twenty-four years in Silicon Valley, working for a global security company as a cyber threat analyst. I'm also a board member of ICANN, that's the International Corporation for Assigned Names and Numbers. Then, several years at Manchester University, as professor of advanced computer engineering, before I semi-retired, and began working with White Hats."

"White Hats?"

"Reformed hackers. When they're ready to jump the firewall, so to speak, I become their sponsor. Hackers tend to be most vulnerable in their late thirties, when they're not as young or idealistic as they once were. I train them to work with large corporations, hack their company firewalls, and find any open doors they may have overlooked. After all, who better to hack the system than a hacker?"

"Tracking down this Trollseeker should be a walk in the park, then, Doctor?"

"Call me Eshy, and yes, I'll require less than an hour to deliver what you need."

"Oh, there's also this."

Eshy glanced at the text message on Manx's mobile. "And you don't recognise the sender?"

"No idea."

"I'll need to clone your device to my laptop, and run some diagnostic software."

"I don't think…" Manx began.

Eshy sensed his hesitation. "Believe me, Inspector Manx, if I wanted to extract any critical data from the North Wales Constabulary, I would find a more efficient manner than through your cell phone. And, before you ask, DCI Canton did insist I sign a non-disclosure contract and a plethora of other official documents, so I think your Facebook account is safe in my hands."

Manx was about to protest he didn't have, and was never likely to have, a Facebook account, but Eshy had already taken the phone from his hand, and was attaching it to her laptop.

"And, if it's not too much trouble, a cup of tea would go down a treat. I believe Mickey knows just how I like it—strong, six sugars," Eshy said, and sat down at his desk, her eyes smiling at him over the rim of her glasses.

Chapter 37

Concluding his office would be otherwise occupied for the next few hours, Manx decided to pay Thomas Bowen a visit, and present him with the contents of his own website. He might be more forthcoming on his own territory, but Manx held out little hope he'd get more than a few grunts and more mock-gangster slang he might have found amusing, if it wasn't so damned irritating.

The first sound he heard as he opened the Jensen's door was the metallic click of a safety catch being disengaged. The second was Bette Bowen's gravel-toned voice, threatening him from behind the pommel of a Webley and Scott twelve-gauge shotgun.

"You might want to think twice, goo'boy, before you step away from that fancy car of yours."

Her south Wales accent was calm as she spoke. She aligned the barrels of her gun, and hoisted the pummel to her shoulder. Manx was familiar with the weapon; the Webley was considered a gateway firearm, easy to obtain, minimal kickback, and light enough to hold for long periods. The gun wasn't known for its accuracy, but it could blow a hole the size of a dinner plate in someone's chest from twenty feet away; approximately the same distance Manx guessed he was now standing from Bette Bowen. He slowly raised his arms, and took a couple of tentative steps away from the car, keeping his body protected behind the Jensen's open door.

"Mrs. Bette Bowen?" Manx asked.

"Depends who's asking, don't it?"

Manx quickly processed the situation. He didn't think Bette Bowen would shoot, but so far, the Bowen family had given him little reason to put his guard down. He looked around, and assessed the environment. A mile-long, one lane track leading from the main road at Pentraeth was the only access to and from the farmhouse. To his immediate right were two large static caravans propped up with breezeblocks, and parked close to one of them, a bright red Ford Fiesta. The car seemed out of place in the muted brown hues and hardening deposits of cow-shit scattered on the ground around him. To his left, several out buildings and a Land Rover Discovery, the number plate splattered in thick mud. Chained to the farmhouse wall was a scraggy Irish wolfhound, snoring loudly in his sleep. And, directly in front of him, Bette Bowen, the Webley hitched securely into the saddle of her armpit, surrounded by a brood of chickens, pecking at the ground.

"Are you Mrs. Bette Bowen?" Manx asked again.

"Like I said, depends who's askin'." Bette snorted, dislodged a large glob of phlegm, and spat it to the ground.

"North Wales Constabulary, Mrs. Bowen. Please put down your weapon. I'm not a threat."

Bette emitted a throaty cackle, and raised the barrels a tick higher. Manx noticed the family resemblance; it was like looking at Nerys Bowen's older, and larger, twin-sister. The tight, frizzy perm was a giveaway, and mother and daughter shared the same body-type—both as short as they were wide. Bette Bowen was optimistically sporting a pair of tight, grey jogging pants, and over her wool sweater was a food-stained apron with the words "World's Best Mum" printed across the front. There was one detail Manx couldn't draw his gaze from; Bette Bowen's baby-blue mule-slippers, each with a rabbit's face sewn into the toe area and four, large plastic eyes that bobbled and rattled as she moved.

"Just wondering if I could have a word?" Manx said.

"Police, is it?" She spat out the word, as if it were an affront to have it pass her lips. "Prove that, can you?"

Manx began to reach inside his jacket pocket. Bette re-aligned the Webley, and waved the barrels in a steady, deliberate motion, left to right.

"Steady now, goo'boy."

She shouted towards the farmhouse door. "Nerys! Need you out here, pronto luv."

Manx stared down the barrels of the gun, and kept his arms aloft.

"Come on, girl. I haven't got all bloody day."

The Wolfhound yawned, rose itself sleepily from the ground, and began barking at Manx. "And you can shut your trap, too, useless bloody mutt." The dog sulked back towards the wall, lying down with a grunt.

Nerys appeared in the doorway. "What's up, Ma? I was out back."

"Well, you're needed 'ere, now," Bette told her, and nodded in Manx's direction. "Go over and check his identification. Says he's from the North Wales Cuntstabulary." Bette chuckled loudly at her own lousy joke. "Never seen a policeman with a posh motor like that, unless he's on the take, like."

Nerys shuffled from the farmhouse door towards Manx. He noticed she had the same slippers as her mother, but in pink, the plastic eyes rattling like loose pennies, as she walked towards him. She stopped a few feet short of Manx, and turned to her mother.

"No need to, Mam, I knows him. Spoke to him at Beaumaris a couple weeks back."

"Why you talking to the likes of him behind my back, girl?"

Manx noticed Nery's shoulders slump, and her gaze fall to the ground. "Thought I'd make a few quid, tell him about Stokes's place."

"He give you any?"

"Said he'd arrest me. Waste of fucking time, Ma."

"You need money, you come ask me, girl. You got that?"

"Yes, Ma," Nerys said, stuffing her hands in the pockets of her hoodie.

"Didn't lay his hands on you, did he?"

"Not so as I remember. He had another copper with him though, a girl. Not here, is she?" Nerys asked, peering into the car window expectantly.

"No, afraid not, Nerys. She got jumped outside Mr. Stokes's shop, just after we talked to you. Someone beat her up pretty badly. Don't know anything about that, do you?"

Nerys was about to speak, when Bette interrupted. "She knows nothing," she said, disengaged the gun, and rested it in the crook of her elbow. "Now, tell me why the fuck you're here. Nerys, you can go back to whatever you were doing. I'll deal with you later, girl."

Manx felt a momentary pang of sympathy for Nerys, as he watched her skulk back towards the farmhouse, her feet shuffling awkwardly in the mule slippers that slapped loudly against the skin of her heels as she walked.

Manx stepped slowly towards Bette Bowen, and offered her his police identification. "Detective Inspector Tudor Manx…" he began, before Bette interrupted.

"Manx? You related to Alice Manx, over in Talwrn?"

Jesus, this island really was too fucking small. "Mother," Manx confirmed.

Bette cast her eyes over him, as if she were sizing him up for butchering. "Yeah, I see it. Both of you look like a long streak of piss. The old cow still alive?" she said, in a tone implying she didn't care either way.

"Last I checked," Manx said.

Bette gestured in the general direction of the farmhouse. "We rented this place from Lady Muck for a couple years, then she decides she wants to sell it off. Put all we had into this place, still fucking ripped us off. It's not like she needs the bloody money, is it? That where you got that fancy car? Mummy buy it for you?" Bette snorted, a phlegmy inhalation, causing her to splutter loudly at the back of her sinuses.

"Actually, Mrs. Bowen, it's your son, Thomas, I came to talk to."

"Everybody calls me Ma Bowen. Unless you consider yourself too hoity toity for that, you being Lady Manx's son, and all?"

Lady Manx? He hadn't heard that for a while. It still grated, like an unhealed scar. "OK, Ma Bowen. Can I please speak to your son, Thomas?"

"He's sleeping."

"Think you could wake him? It's important."

"Important to you, aye, not important for us, goo'boy. He works nights, needs his sleep, so I'd come back later. I'll tell him you called, though."

Bette turned on her heels, and headed towards the farmhouse.

"I assume all your paperwork's in order?"

She turned around with a sigh. "What bloody paperwork?"

"For the firearm," Manx said. "I assume you can produce a gun license when I ask you for it?"

"We're farmers. Need it for hunting rats and the like," Bette said. "There's all kinds of vermin that comes sniffing round here that needs putting down." A thin, crooked smile played across her face, as if she'd just said something she was particularly pleased with.

"The question wasn't why you have the gun, but do you have a license for it?" Manx sat on the bonnet of the Jensen, and continued, "Thing is, Ma Bowen, I find myself in this kind of situation at least twice a week. Farmer Jones, Williams, Roberts, whoever, forgets to renew his gun license, Maybe he's lost it, or maybe the dog ate it. Believe me, I've heard them all. If he can't produce said document, then it's my duty, as a police officer, to haul this poor bloke from his milking, or whatever he's doing, escort him down to the station, take his statement, get him fingerprinted, and then send out another couple of PCs to search the house, and make sure he's not hiding any other illegal firearms. Puts a big dent in my day, not to mention the unlucky bugger I've dragged in. The public really has no idea of the amount of paperwork involved, until they've sat in a station for five hours waiting for us to fill it out. Sign of the times, I'm afraid."

Bette thought for a moment, and bit her lower lip, as if contemplating a particularly troublesome mathematical calculation.

The problem having been solved, she hoisted the Webley to her right shoulder, snapped the barrel into position, and pointed the gun skywards. Manx braced himself. The bullet casing struck the branches of a large oak tree over one of the caravans. A couple of jackdaws bolted from their nest. Bette kept the gun pointed skywards, the handle still nestled in the nub of her shoulder.

"Thomas! Get your ass out here now. Someone wants to talk to you."

A few moments later, Thomas Bowen appeared on the steps of the caravan furthest away from the farmhouse, rubbing his eyes against the daylight. He was wearing boxer shorts, a stained t-shirt, and had a thick, gold medallion hanging low over his chest.

"What the fuck, Ma! I was sleeping."

"Language, Thomas. The copper here just wants a word. Be a good boy, eh, and have a chat."

"Didn't wake you, did I, Thomas?" Manx said.

Bowen slapped the side of the caravan with the palm of his hand. "Jesus! Can't you lot leave me the fuck alone?"

"Must be your irresistible charm," Manx said.

"Fucking…" Bowen began.

"Now, Thomas, just talk to the copper, luv. We don't want no trouble here. Keep a respectable home, don't we?"

Bowen recognised the tone in his mother's voice. He'd heard it dozens of times before, and he knew better than to argue. "Can we do this in the van, Holmes? I'll freeze me bollocks off out 'ere."

***

Manx ducked, as he walked through the low doorway into the caravan. "Jesus, it's like the Tardis in reverse in here, Thomas," Manx said, taking stock of the cramped living quarters, which consisted of a single pull-out bed, a two-burner stove swimming in grease, and a couple of narrow bench seats stacked under the back window.

"What's that supposed to mean?" Bowen said, leaning against the sink.

"Dr. Who? The Tardis? Bigger on the inside than it looks on the outside," Manx explained. "But, this? It's the reverse—smaller on the inside than it looks from the outside. Just an observation."

"Yeah?" Bowen pointed towards the thin, plywood doorway dividing the caravan."I put a divider in, for me equipment. Computers, sound mixing boards, electronic shit. I keep it back there." Bowen liberated a couple of Marlboro Lights from a crumpled pack on the stovetop, and offered one to Manx.

"Thanks, but they're not my vice."

"Vice? They're just fucking ciggies, Holmes," Bowen said, sitting at one of the seats next to the orange Formica table. Manx joined him, and wedged his thighs uncomfortably against the underside of the table. Bowen bounced his right leg on the caravan floor, as if he were keeping the beat.

"Nervous?" Manx asked.

"Waste of time, you coming here. Don't have nothing new to say," Bowen said. He kept his gaze fixed on the farmhouse as he spoke. "You got Ma all pissed off, too. I'll have to deal with that shit, till she knocks back a couple of pints and calms the fuck down," he added, his leg jittering wildly.

"Well, at least I accomplished something today,' Manx said. "Now, tell me about you and Dr. Simon Vaughn."

"Doctor Who?" Bowen said, grinning and blowing a trail of smoke through his teeth.

Manx shook his head. "Think you're a joker, right, Thomas? The class clown? Got you far in life, has it?" he said, waving a finger around the caravan. "Twenty-eight years old, still living with your mother, no real job to speak of, unless we count beating up female police officers, of course? Not quite the upward career trajectory you'd hoped for, I bet."

Bowen scrubbed the palm of his hand over his cropped scalp, as if he were scouring for lice, and leant closer. Manx could smell the fag-ash and stale booze on his breath.

"Why are you here, Holmes? I told you, I got nothing for you."

"Dr. Simon Vaughn, GP at Benllech Surgery. Someone plugs him full of methadone, then grills him over a bonfire until he's well done. Know anything about that?"

"Jack shit."

Manx placed the photo he'd printed out from Bowen's website on the table. Bowen gave it a cursory glance, and leant back with his arms crossed.

"Means nothing. He was just there, at a party. I reckoned he was one of them, you know, a gay, like. But, what do I give a shit. They can do whatever they want in their own bedrooms, yeah?"

"Very liberal of you, Bowen. Is that why you killed him? He came on a bit too strong?"

"Fuck no! Weren't me. Police harassment, this is."

"Did he take a shine to you, Thomas? Was he into bad-boys? Liked a bit of rough?"

Bowen looked at the looming grey clouds hanging over the horizon, and chewed his upper lip.

"Ok, here's the deal, Bowen," Manx began, but was interrupted by the loud techno ringtone coming from Bowen's mobile.

"Need to take this, hang on a sec," Bowen said, checking the caller ID. As Bowen lifted the phone to his ear, he felt himself being yanked forward, and the sharp pain of his ribs smacking hard into the table edge.

"What the fuck!"

Manx curled Bowen's gold chain around his fist, and pulled hard until he felt the cheap, gold-plated chain links buckle under the strain. Bowen struggled, and reached for Manx's hands. Manx yanked harder, hauling him further across the table, and made sure the chain was cutting painfully into the back of Bowen's neck.

I'm only going to tell you this once," he whispered. "Put down the fucking phone."

Bowen immediately did as he was told.

"And stop shaking your bloody leg." Manx reached under the table with his other hand, and placed a vice-like grip around the soft tissue between Bowen's knee and thigh. "Or, I swear to God, I will *fucking* break it."

Bowen's face turned scarlet. Manx relaxed his grip, but only slightly. "What you don't seem to have grasped, Thomas, is that, at the moment, I own your arse. I gave you a temporary pass on the beating you gave my officer, but that's all it is, temporary, as in not permanent, open to change. Understand?"

Bowen nodded. Manx relaxed his grip a little more. "Dick Roberts, tell me about him."

Bowen hesitated. "My da's uncle. Don't have much to do with that side of the family no more. Ain't seen him for yonks. I thought he'd been dead for years, till I saw it on the news."

"OK, so you admit you knew Roberts."

"I'm not admitting to nothing," Bowen sneered.

"We'll revisit your family tree later, Thomas. Right now, I'm more interested in your friendship with Vaughn. It shouldn't take me long to convince my Chief there's a direct link between you and the Doc. We issue a warrant, search this shit hole, turn your mam's house inside out, then for the icing on the cake, I'll make Sergeant Nader's day, and have him take another crack at you." Manx released his grip. The cheap, gold chain relented, snapped at the clasp, and clattered onto the table. "Your call."

Bowen coughed, and rubbed his neck. "Fucking police brutality, that is."

"Come down to the station later. I'll take your statement."

Bowen slumped back in the chair, and worked the chain through his fingers. "The doc and me, we had something going, like," he offered.

Manx raised his eyebrows.

"No, nothing like that. Jesus! Told me he used to work in a drug clinic, knew all kinds of shit about every drug, I hadn't heard of most of them. He reckoned those drugs they use to get people off the hard stuff aren't no different. Same chemicals, he said, they just give it a different name."

"Methadone?" Manx asked.

"It were just a few bottles here and there to start with, test the waters, like. I'd make an appointment at the surgery, pretend I was some junkie; receptionists didn't know no better. Then, we'd do the same with some mates of mine. Get enough methadone to sell on the streets. Made a few quid out of it, not much, but Vaughn wanted to increase productivity—them were his words, like. He told me he had some contact who could supply us with all the shit we wanted, if we could sell it. That's the last I heard from him. Said he had a plan all figured to make us rich."

"What kind of plan?"

"I don't know, do I? Kept it to himself. Didn't want me knowing nothing. That's the last time I saw him, at the party. He told me it was all in the works. Next time I see him, he's all over the fuckin' news."

"And what about the man who did *that* to you?" Manx said, pointing at Bowen's fingers.

"Told you, never met him before."

"You think he might have something to do with Vaughn's murder?"

"You're the police, Holmes, you tell me."

Bowen looked out through the window, and saw his mother marching towards the caravan, her chin jutting forward, full of purpose. A blast of cold air entered the caravan, as Bette Bowen snapped open the door, and the thin linoleum floor vibrated, as she stomped across it towards Manx.

"Don't you ever knock, Ma?" Bowen said. His tone lacked conviction. He was flexing his muscle for Manx's sake. Not that Bette Bowen was impressed, or cared.

"Paperwork," she said, handing over the crumpled gun license.

Manx glanced briefly at the document. "Must have turned the whole house over for this."

Bette folded her arms. "You can leave, now. Nothing to stay here for." She moved towards the sink to give Manx room to pass.

"I'd keep that somewhere safe," Manx said, handing back the license. "Just in case your friendly, local constabulary makes an unannounced visit."

Bette Bowen stayed silent, her thick arms crossed over her chest. She kept her eyes fixed on Manx, as he walked from the caravan, and into the yard. Ma Bowen followed a few feet behind, her slippers echoing like the clomping of an old donkey. She kept watching as the Jensen exited the dirt-track road, and joined the main road. Manx finally lost sight of Ma Bowen at the peak of the hill, as she faded into his rear-view mirror.

***

Thomas Bowen paced around the caravan, pulling hard on his second fag of the day. *Fucking pigs*. He'd had a bellyful of them for one week; schoolyard bullies, that's all they were. He flipped the lid off an old Cadbury's hot chocolate tin, retrieved a plastic bag, carefully sprinkled a line of fine white power onto the mirror he kept in the kitchen drawer, and cut at it with the edge of a razor. He sprinkled a line onto the back of his hand, and inhaled. The powder shot through his sinuses, contracting the thin cartilage with a momentary stab of pain both familiar and startling, before igniting his prefrontal cortex like a firework. Then, the pure moment of clarity—the perfect moment of invincibility.

No streak-of-piss copper could touch him; he was legit. *Fuck 'em all*. He was the real deal. Everyone else was faking it, living a lie, all except for her. She was a gem, a diamond, the only one that cared.

Bowen slid open the thin plywood divider leading into the bedroom. She was still there, waiting for him, lying on the bed, her arms folded behind her neck, reading one of his music magazines. His Ramones t-shirt looked good on her, made her look younger, somehow.

She smiled. "Chuck me a ciggie, would you, love? I'm gasping."

He threw a Marlboro Light her way.

"Jesus. I thought he was here for the duration," the woman said, shivering. "But, you did a great job, Tommo. You're a natural."

Bowen nodded. "Yeah, fuck da police," he said, with a swagger.

"You do know it's bloody freezing in here, right, Tommo? You should get yourself a proper heater."

A heater? Yeah, he'd do that. A heater. Good fucking idea. Keep her happy. Tommo: he liked that. No one else called him that. Only her.

She lifted her arms, and slipped his t-shirt effortlessly over her shoulders. "If you're going to be entertaining more often, that is."

She was fit, for an older woman. *A MILF? Isn't that what they called them?* She had great tits, too, even told him how much she'd paid for them. Got them done abroad somewhere, not that it mattered. She could have self-assembled them from IKEA, for all he cared. He'd never imagined he'd be doing a fifty-seven-year-old, though. Yeah, he preferred older women now. They were less bother and they were always fucking grateful. They knew what to do, knew what they wanted; they even asked for it.

The woman tousled her bleached blonde hair into a bun, and skewered a short knitting needle through the top. She turned onto her front; affording Bowen an unadorned view of her buttocks and the pale stretch of her thighs. The late morning light fell through the caravan's net curtains and onto her skin. She was like a painting, like one of those nudes he'd seen in the only art gallery he'd ever visited; a school trip when he was ten.

"Rapido, Tommo. Got to open the shop soon," she said, flipping open the sheets, and patting down the bed with her hand. "Wool's not going to sell itself."

Chapter 38

Eshy handed the phone back to Manx, and exhaled a deep, considered sigh, along with an apologetic shrug of her shoulders. "Problem," she said. "Have you ever heard of a CryptoPhone?"

Manx looked at her, blankly.

"I'll explain," Eshy said. "Most mobile communication hardware that claims to offer deep encryption technology are, at best, only telling half the story. They use proprietary algorithms and passkeys to encrypt and decrypt the data travelling to and from the device, so any infiltration should, in theory, be detected and blocked, before any information is extracted." She stopped, sensing she'd lost Manx somewhere around the word, "algorithms."

"Think of it as a code. Like the ones used to transmit secret messages during the Second World War."

Manx nodded.

"You could only decode the message, if you knew the formula. Digital information is much the same, just a series of zeros and ones. If your device has the code to unlock the encrypted information, then the message is decrypted—simple. Got it?"

"So far, I think," Manx said.

"Good. Now, the problem is the algorithms in these so-called secure devices were developed and marketed by the very same companies and government agencies people buying these devices are trying to hide from. So, to an amateur hacker with the right infiltration tools, these devices are about as secure as your iPhone, Inspector."

Manx rubbed his hands together. "So, we'll be able to trace the text back to a phone number? Problem solved."

Eshy bit her lower lip, and tutted softly. "Not solved, unfortunately. Your text originated from one of those CryptoPhones I mentioned earlier, and that is all I could find. A dead end, I'm afraid."

"You can't, what did you call it, decrypt the data? Find the source?"

"CryptoPhones come with their own encryption and decryption source code, so users can test and block any backdoors into their devices. Plus, they use two algorithms to encrypt the data, a form of multi-blind key encryption. Add a TOR browser, which adds multiple layers of even more encryption, and the device is all but impenetrable."

"Bottom line, we don't know who sent the text?" Manx said.

"Unfortunately, correct, Inspector. There's very little chance, even with my software, and considering your department's limited budget, that we'll ever trace the sender." Eshy sighed, and pulled off her glasses. "Not always so super, after all."

Manx sat on the edge of his desk, and flipped his phone in his hand. "But, these are sophisticated phones, right?" he said. "And from what you just told me, of which I probably understood about half, we're looking for someone with a pretty good grasp on technology, and a reason to keep their communications secure and anonymous?"

"And they'd need to have money. They can cost up to two thousand euros, before you even start with the data charges. You won't find these at your local Curry's, put it that way. People who buy a CryptoPhone buy them for a reason,"

"They don't want to be traced."

"Not ever, "Eshy said. "The NSA, GCHQ, and the like would love to drive them out of business. As you can imagine, they're a huge hit with global terrorist organisations."

"I doubt we're dealing with al-Qaeda in Anglesey," Manx said. "But, it's not some amateur by the sounds of it. What about that YouTube thing?"

"Better news." Eshy's face brightened. "Took me fifteen minutes. I must be slowing down in life's late hour. He was using a free Proxy service, and routed his IP address through remote offshore severs. Entry level IP masking." Eshy handed Manx a paper with a name and address.

"A word of advice, don't go too easy on him. I've seen this before, and it never ends well. Covering their digital footprint is just the start, and before you know it…"

"CryptoPhones, and God knows what else," Manx said.

Eshy smiled, gathered her bags, and handed back her empty teacup. "Please tell Mickey thank you for the tea, but a little more sugar next time. At my age, I'm less inclined to sacrifice the things that bring me joy. Anyway, I'm almost positive it helps with my concentration," she said, and walked gracefully out of the incident room in a flounce of jasmine and silk.

Chapter 39

Eshy was right; he was a kid, sixteen at most. He was sitting in the interview room, nervously flipping his cell phone from palm to palm. Manx recognised him immediately—the same kid he'd seen taking photos of the girls at the bonfire. Next to him was his mother; he recognised her, too—Lynda Masterson, head mouthpiece and ponytail-in-chief of A.M.A.D. *This is going to be interesting*, Manx thought, as he sat across from them.

"Hello again, Mrs. Masterson. Thanks for coming in. You must be Adam?" Manx said, extending his hand. Adam hesitated, then shook.

"It's Ms. Masterson," Lynda said coldly. "Will this take long? Only Adam has a lot of studying to catch up on; as I'm sure you're aware, mock O Levels are just around the corner."

Manx wasn't aware, and turned his attention back to the boy. "Bit of a computer geek, are you?"

Adam shrugged.

"Cut the modesty, Adam," Manx said. "Our specialists were very impressed with your skills. Didn't understand half of what they said myself."

Adam looked to the floor, shuffled his feet.

"Really, Inspector," Lynda protested. "He just posted a video. Don't you have some real criminals you should be questioning?"

"A man was murdered, Adam. There could have been crucial evidence on that video—a clue to the identity of the murderer, something my officers may have missed at the scene. By withholding that evidence, you're obstructing an ongoing enquiry. That all depends on the judge, of course, but they're keen to nip this sort of behaviour in the bud. Or, have you already crossed that line, Adam? What do you call yourselves, Black Hats?"

"I was just messing around with my new editing software; I didn't mean to…" Adam's voice cracked as he spoke.

"I'm guessing you don't have children of your own, Inspector, which is why you're talking to my son as if he's a career criminal," Lynda said. "He's sorry he didn't let you know about the video earlier, aren't you, Adam?"

"And sorry he masked his own internet address and IP. That's what you call it, right, Adam? In fact, he disguised it so well, we had to bring in a specialist to track him down."

Lynda's eyes widened, as she listened to Manx. "Adam, is this true?"

Adam looked to the floor. "All my mates do it. It's no big deal."

Manx looked directly at the boy. "Keep thinking it's no big deal, Adam, and someday, you'll be in here being questioned by someone far scarier and uglier than me, and your mum won't be sitting next to you and telling you everything's going to be all right. Understand?"

Adam swallowed. Manx noticed the dewy pool of tears in the corner of his eyes; his work here was done.

"Adam, I'll need your phone to download the video. You'll get it back tomorrow. In the meantime, I'm sure your mother will figure out a far more suitable punishment than I could."

Lynda nodded her understanding, and handed over the phone.

Manx placed a thick wedge of business cards on the table. "I meant to give you some of these at the meeting, but I left in sort of a hurry,"

"More like a huff," Lynda said.

"Yeah, well, here's a stack of them. Do with them what you will."

Manx excused himself, and gestured for one of the duty PCs to escort Adam and Lynda back to reception.

Chapter 40

Cadwalader Walden-Powell pushed his thick glasses back over the bridge of his nose and blinked rapidly—a nervous tick Manx remembered well. Age had bestowed little kindness towards Powell; his middle-aged paunch spilled messily over his belt, and he'd sprouted a bushy, greying moustache which hid his lips. Powell reminded Manx of a pale, flustered walrus.

"No, Manx. Absolutely not. It's…it's…"

"More than your job's worth?" Manx said, leaning against the reception desk standing between him and the secure evidence room in the basement of North Wales Constabulary Headquarters.

"It's not just that," Powell mumbled.

"Your reputation?" Manx interrupted, his eyebrows rising.

Powell cleared his throat, and ignored the remark.

"One name, Wally. Can't be that hard, surely?" Manx said.

Powell leant over the desk, and whispered, "Don't call me that, Manx, took me years to get that monkey off my back. If I hear, 'Where's fucking Wally?' one more time…"

"Got it," Manx said, smiling.

Powell composed himself. "There's a protocol—guaranteed anonymity. I doubt I can even access that sort of information with all the damned security on the network. They'd trace it back to me in seconds."

"That's why I came to you, Powell. All those rooms full of filing cabinets back there, who better to follow the paper trail than the man who laid it to begin with?"

"Cameras," Powell said, pointing to a lens in the corner of the ceiling.

"Didn't bother you back in the day."

Powell stiffened. "That didn't take you long," he said, wiping his ink-stained fingers. "Twenty-five years ago, Manx. Jesus Christ."

"There's a statute of limitations on favours?"

Powell rubbed his eyes, and blinked some more. "How did you know I'd still be here? Could have been anywhere."

"You never struck me as the kind of man with wanderlust. More slippers-under-the-table kind of copper. Never completed those twelve steps, either," Manx said, pointing at Powell's trembling hand. He slid a scrap of paper across the desk. "I believe this man entered the program around nineteen ninety-six."

Powell looked at the name. Manx caught the subtle flicker of recognition in his eyes. "And, I don't need to tell you, this is confidential."

Powell handed it back to Manx. "Impossible. These people are afforded protection; they're not meant to be found."

"Ah, right, but someone did find him."

"I'd never…"

"I know. It's beyond the scope of your imagination. But, someone did. So, I need to know who Vaughn was in a former life. And, seeing as the poor bugger's already dead, where's the harm?"

"Family?"

"As far as we know, he has none."

Powell slumped. "You're not leaving until I say yes, are you Manx?"

"Now, we're making progress."

"I do this, we're even? You won't darken my doorstep again?"

"You have my word."

"Might take a while."

"I'm not going anywhere," Manx said, taking a seat.

Cadwalader Powell: the cadet most likely to go nowhere. Manx hadn't given him a second thought, until the spark of an idea came to him during the briefing. Powell was in the same year of basic training as Manx, and even then, had the makings of a career bureaucrat. The force was always in need of coppers like Powell—steady hands on the rudder and a compulsion to instil order and process where little existed. For Powell, however, that sense of order and discipline had failed to translate into his personal life. Manx had lost count of the number of times he found Powell sobbing into his pint glass in a corner of a pub somewhere in Colwyn town centre. The favour? Truth be told, Manx only had a vague recollection. It involved one of Powell's day-long drinking marathons which almost got him thrown out of the force before he'd walked his first beat. Manx had stood as a character witness for Powell at his disciplinary hearing. What he said, or did, to convince the jury was hazy, what mattered was Powell remembered.

After thirty minutes or so, Powell returned, clutching a large flask. He glanced up at the camera as Manx leapt to the desk, anticipating good news.

"Don't think I can help you after all," Powell said, shaking his head.

Manx was about to protest, when he noticed Powell slowly turning the coffee flask around on the desk, and shifting his eyes downwards. Manx followed his gaze. He could clearly read the name, written in thick pen on a strip of masking tape on the side of the flask. The wheezy, old bureaucrat had more imagination than Manx had given him credit for. Manx committed the name to memory, and shrugged his shoulders in an overly dramatic fashion for the cameras, leaving Cadwalader Powell to his paperwork, and whatever beverage he kept in his flask.

***

Manx waited until he was clear of the car park, and called Morris. "Dr. Patrick Metcalf. That's all we've got. Looks like you've got a busy evening, Morris. Order yourself a pizza, or something. I'll pay."

Chapter 41

At six o'clock on Sunday night the village of Moelfre was already tucked in for an early night. As Manx walked towards the pub, he could hear the slow slap of the Irish Sea, as it whipped at the rocks in steady, rhythmic measures. Winter had barely begun, and he was already looking forward to the first warm breeze of summer. He wasn't one for wishing his life away on the whims of the seasons, but being back on the island had that effect on him. He always found himself longing he were someplace else; somewhere that exerted no hold on him, other than his desire to be there.

"Bit early for you, isn't it?" Gwen said, as Manx walked to the bar.

"It's not when you start, it's when you finish, Gwen," he said, sitting on one of the threadbare stools.

"Usual, then?"

Without waiting for a reply, Gwen pulled down on the pump, and drew the first pint of the evening. The barrel spat out a frothy phlegm of complaint. She twisted the tap head, and yanked the pump a few more times. "New barrel, gets temperamental," she explained.

Manx glanced around the empty pub, and rubbed his palms together. "Just an idea, but it might fill up in here, if you turned up the heating a bit."

Gwen tutted. "Don't tell me, tell his land-lordship. The cheap bugger won't let me near the bloody thermostat."

She slid Manx's pint across the bar. "Them supermodels finally had enough of you, then? Buggered off back to Monaco, or wherever they migrate for the winter?"

"Just waiting for someone," Manx explained.

Gwen raised her eyebrows, which had the effect of making her eyes appear even larger. *Someone could lose themselves in those, if they're not careful*, Manx thought.

"I'd heard a hot cup of tea was more your kind of thing,' Gwen said.

"Depends who's making it." Manx smiled, and took a long sip of his beer. It felt good; the first drink of the day. The familiar yeasty froth tingled like sherbet on the rim of his lips.

Gwen grabbed a beer towel, and wiped it across the bar. "Still able to hold a pint, I see."

"It's a struggle, but I'm coping," Manx said.

"Right! Walking bloody wounded, you are. Still, don't expect you'll be going near too many bonfires for a while. Owain was very impressed, mind you. He's telling everyone at school you're his new best mate now. Number one fan," Gwen said.

"Nice to know I've got at least one," Manx said. "He's not too traumatised, is he? You know, after…"

Gwen smiled, and leant her elbows on the bar. "Don't know much about kids, do you, Inspector?"

"About as much as I know about women."

"I swear the little bugger's tougher than me sometimes," Gwen said.

Manx noticed a slight break in her voice as she spoke, which she tried to cover up by speaking faster. "He misses his dad, that's all, but we're better off without him. Men? Who'd bloody have them, eh? More trouble than they're worth."

Manx noticed a glassy sheen had formed over Gwen's eyes as she spoke.

"Listen to me, getting all bloody sentimental." She rubbed the under-side of her nose with her finger. "Your bloody fault, that is, asking questions," she added, smiling.

"Occupational hazard," Manx said. "Listen, Gwen, I've been meaning to ask you…"

Gwen sniffed, and looked directly at Manx, as if she were expecting something more profound than what he was about to ask.

"Many tourists been around here recently?"

"Oh, helping with police enquires now, am I?" Gwen smiled. "It's been dead for weeks. Not many people want to pay to watch the rain; they can get that at home for free."

"OK, let me be more specific," Manx said. "Have you seen two men, both probably around six feet tall, wearing dark overcoats? From their appearance, I'm guessing they're not local, but I could be wrong."

Gwen bit her lower lip. "Come to think of it, a couple of blokes came in at lunchtime, a few days back. I don't usually do the afternoon shift, but his landlord-ship was desperate, and I could do with the extra. I thought they were a bit odd at the time; the type of blokes I wouldn't want to meet in a dark alley. They ordered a couple of pints and a plate of chips, and sat by the window for about an hour. Never said a word, just kept looking out the window, like they were waiting for someone."

"Did you speak to them?" Manx asked.

"Just when they were ordering."

"Locals?"

"I only spoke to the older bloke, sweaty face, sounded like he was from Manchester, really thick accent, called me "luv." Real charmer. Thought they might have been one of you lot actually— similar haircuts."

Before Manx could reply, he felt a hearty slap on his left shoulder, followed by an immediate and over-powering aroma of cheap cologne.

"Chatting up the barmaids are we, Manx? Can't leave you Welshies alone for a minute, like rats up a drainpipe." Ashton Bevan dragged a barstool, and sat next to Manx. He took a long look up and down the length of Gwen, as if he were assessing her for evidence. "Scenery's much easier on the eye than in my local, though. Maybe I should switch my allegiances," he said, as he looked around the pub. "But, I'm too loyal; that's my weakness. Loyalty first."

Bevan leant in closer to Gwen, and rubbed his palms together, as if he were attempting to light a fire. "So, what about you, sweetheart? Have a weakness for anything?"

Gwen leant forward. "Short, older men, who should know better."

Bevan said nothing, then let out a loud, unexpected laugh that rattled around the bar like a sack of old bones dragged across an iron fence. "Be a sweetheart and pour us a pint, would you? I'm parched," he said, and licked his lips, as if to emphasise the point.

"One of yours, is he?"

"He doesn't get out much."

"Explains a lot." Gwen slid the pint across the bar.

"So, what's so important it couldn't wait until tomorrow, Bevan?"

"Straight down to business? Well, I wouldn't want to bore the pants off the lovely barmaid," Bevan said, lowering his voice, and looking around the bar. "Think we could find an empty table in this place?"

"If you and prince charming want to take the seat by the window, I'll bring your drinks over," Gwen offered.

***

"What is it they say around here, yacky da?" Bevan said, raising his glass.

"*Yechid dda*," Manx corrected him, surprised he could still wrap his tongue around the cluster of consonants. "Means good health."

"Does it? I never knew," Bevan said, in a tone implying he couldn't care less. He took a slow sip on his beer, watching Manx as he drank. "This is cosy. About time we got to know each other better." Bevan smiled; it was an expression that didn't improve with age.

"You said you had information. The blood sample from the boat?"

Bevan cleared his throat. "Oh, plenty of time for that," he said, slipping back in his chair, and shoving his hands deep into his trouser pockets. He gestured towards Gwen. "That barmaid. Not bad looking, if you're into that whole dark, brooding, Celtic type. Personally, I prefer my women like my life, uncomplicated."

Manx bristled at the remark. "I'm sure Sherri mentioned I called."

"Highlight of her day," Bevan said, crossing his legs.

He was a blank sheet, Manx thought, impossible to read.

"So, tell me about the life and times of Inspector Tudor Manx. Born and bred on the island, is what I hear. What brought you back?"

"The friendly locals."

"Listen, Manx," Bevan said, dragging his chair closer. "Why don't I show the first hand, just to move things along?"

"Be my guest," Manx said.

Bevan cleared his throat. "I think that if it wasn't for your long-standing bromance with DCI Canton, you'd be making paper-clip chains and sharpening pencils in some back office in the Met, until they pension you off. Am I warm?"

"There are worse ways to make a living."

"Oh, I'm not buying that," Bevan said. "I'd imagine it's like castration for you, being tied to a desk. You probably wouldn't have come within pissing distance of the DI position, if it wasn't for Canton, which makes me think you've either got something on him, or you are as good as everybody says you are?"

"Everybody?"

"Turn of phrase. The thing is, Manx, I've been on the island for a few years now. People talk to me. I like to think I'm a good listener. Bottom line, I'm told the line of coppers more qualified for your position would circle the island, twice. And let's not forget, you've been away for thirty-five years."

"Thirty-four," Manx corrected him.

"Yet, here you are, DI over an island you left thirty-four years ago. Bit of a come down from the Met, wouldn't you say?"

"Why is this any of your business, Bevan?"

Bevan sipped at his beer in short sups, as if he were drinking from a mug of hot tea. Manx's own pint was down to the last couple of fingers.

"Did you know I used to be a constable?" Bevan began. "A trainee, actually, Bramshill Staff College. Took me eight months to figure out I'd made a mistake. I dropped out, went back to school, knuckled down, and did well enough to get a placement on a three-year Chemistry degree."

"A little over-educated for a SOCO, isn't it?" Manx said.

Bevan forced his mouth into a rictus smile. "It's all about advantage. Once I put my mind to a task, I make sure I'm top of the class, the best informed."

"Why forensics?" Manx asked.

Bevan leant back in his chair, as if he were about to deliver a long oration. Manx immediately regretted the enquiry.

"A few months at Bramshill made an impression. There's nothing quite like the rush of solving a crime, but all that PC Plod bullshit? Walking the beat, sucking up to the hierarchy, I just couldn't see myself kowtowing for thirty years, so I threw my lot in with forensics, and never looked back. As a free agent, I avoid the politics, and have no one to answer to on a daily basis. Plus, I always had an excellent eye for detail."

Bevan took a small sip of his beer, and continued, "It can be a heady form of power, public service, don't you think?"

Manx downed the last of his pint, and waved to Gwen to pour him another. "What's your point, Bevan?"

"My point?" Bevan coughed. "I understand police officers, Manx. Take the rank and file, for instance—constables, sergeants, even those community support officers. There has to be a symbiotic relationship between my team and the officers doing the grunt work, so I make sure to keep that relationship intact. I take them out for a drink every now and then, my treat, of course. It does wonders for morale, and I'm rewarded with some valuable insights. Do you know what the most valuable insight of all was?"

"Enlighten me," Manx said.

"Uncertainty. Every one of them, without exception, finds any level of uncertainty or vagueness in their leadership a potential threat. Ironic, if you think about it. For a service tasked with solving uncertainties, they are certainly wary of ambiguity in their own ranks. And you, Detective Inspector Manx, are a six-foot-three mystery, who has them all spooked."

"Where is this going, Bevan?" Manx said wearily.

"It's common knowledge you were involved in some nasty business with an East-European child trafficking operation making inroads into the U.K., am I right?"

"Nothing you couldn't find in standard police records." *Or the papers*, Manx was about to add, before Bevan interrupted.

"Incomplete, or heavily redacted. All I know is the Met's investigation was shut down pronto, with no explanation, and you disappear off the face of the Earth for a few months. Then, you turn up here, like the proverbial bad penny, or maybe the prodigal son, who knows?"

"So, you're asking me to release classified police information, over a beer, because it's good for morale?"

Bevan expelled a rough, snorting sound from deep within his lungs, bringing with it a sharp cough and a mouthful of phlegm, which he secreted into a paper napkin.

"Sherri's swearing me off the death-sticks, just my body's way of reacting to the good news," Bevan explained. He took a sip of beer, and composed himself. "Listen, you seem like a good enough copper, Manx. I guess the island will make up its own mind when, or if, you solve these murders, but rumours are like a cancer; they spread. They can kill a career; I've seen it happen."

"So, this is a warning?"

"I'm not the enemy, Manx. The rank and file trust me, because I'm an open book, easy to read. Drop me a few details, help me fill in some of the blanks, and I'll make sure people get to know. Word will spread soon enough, and that veil of mystery you've cloaked yourself in begins to lift. It would make your life a lot easier, I can guarantee you that, Inspector."

"Who says I'm looking for easy?"

"Oh, trust me. The martyr position is very over-rated."

Manx felt Gwen's arm brush against him, as she took his empty glass.

"Brought one for you, too," Gwen said.

"I'd take whatever you're offering, sweetheart," Bevan said and looked Gwen up and down, from her skirt, black tights, and high heels.

"You want to be careful where you're looking, or you'll end up wearing that," Gwen said, placing the beer on the table. Bevan didn't take his eyes off Gwen, until she'd positioned herself back behind the bar.

"I've heard those Welsh girls can be pretty feisty in the bedroom," Bevan said, winking awkwardly at Manx in a manner suggesting he rarely committed himself to such affectations.

"I wouldn't know," Manx said.

"Not much for conversation are you, Manx?" Bevan said, exasperated.

"So I've been told."

Bevan sipped his pint, and ran his tongue along his top lip. "Have it your way, but think about what I said. You've got my phone number, if you change your mind."

"You'll be the first to know, Bevan. Now, about the blood?"

Bevan pulled a thin piece of paper from his pocket. "The DNA samples from the boat were intriguing." He folded out the paper to reveal what Manx recognised as a genetic sequence printed across the centre.

"From the miniscule amount of blood my team scraped from the lobster basket, we're confident it's a young male, but here's where it gets interesting. Are you familiar with the Genghis Khan gene?"

Manx sipped at his pint, and shook his head.

"Neither was I, until today. Seems one of the lads at the lab is a gene nerd—a self-proclaimed expert on genome sequencing.

Mentioned he'd had his own DNA sequenced, and predicts he's going to live to ninety-three, if he swears off chocolate digestives, but I digress. As we all know from our schoolboy history, Genghis Khan was probably the single most sociopathic individual whoever lived." Bevan paused, and traced his finger across the table, as if he were plotting a route from one corner to the other.

"Khan raped and pillaged his way through central Asia all the way to the Polish borders, ensuring his dynasty would survive centuries after he'd popped his Mongolian clogs. Legend has it, he slaughtered any man who stood in his way, then proceeded to fuck their widows, their mothers, their daughters, hedging his bets the Khan dynasty would prevail. Looking at it dispassionately, it was a genius plan. Father several thousand offspring, and a few generations later, there's a few million more to continue the family name. But, here's where it gets interesting. It's estimated that over sixteen million men now carry this Genghis Khan Y chromosome—sixteen million offspring. Quite staggering."

"And our sample is…" Manx began.

"Exactly. So, I asked myself, why are there traces of a gene native to central Asia on a fishing boat on a small Welsh island, that's about as diverse as a Methodist picnic?"

"Random chance?" Manx offered.

Bevan shook his head. "The odds are ninety-nine-point-nine percent the person on that boat originated from somewhere in central Asia. I looked it up on the map. The furthest west they've traced the gene is Khazistan, maybe into central Georgia. I guess it's now your job to figure out who's it is, and where it came from." A self-satisfied grin spread, like a slow-moving worm, across Bevan's face.

Manx already knew. He was about to leave and thank Bevan for the information, when Bevan leant in close to Manx.

"'The greatest joy for a man is to defeat his enemies, to drive them before him, to take from them all they possess, to see those they love in tears, to ride their horses, and to hold their wives and daughters in their arms'—Genghis Khan."

"You look that up, too?" Manx asked.

"Oh no, I had that one already memorised," Bevan said, tapping his index finger lightly on his temple.

Chapter 42

Manx called the team in for an early morning briefing. He'd spent the previous night mulling over Bevan's information, trying to re-construct a believable narrative that would have concluded with a young, Eastern European man, with a bullet hole in his right shoulder, ending up in a hospital bed in North Wales. All he knew for sure was the man had been shot off the deck of Dick Roberts' boat somewhere in the Menai Strait, then the trail had run ice-cold. After a six-hour operation, the surgeons had successfully extracted the bullet; a nine-millimetre Makarov, probably fired from a Makarov PM, a Russian-made firearm specifically designed around the bullet it was intended to house. It was unusual to find the weapon this far west. Manx had come across them only a couple of times in his career, usually in the hands of some low-ranking, Eastern European gangster trying to make his mark in mainland Europe.

"Last night, the senior Scene of Crime Officer presented me with a promising lead," Manx began.

Nader, who was in the far corner of the room, emitted a throaty laugh. "Who was that, then? Bread of bloody Bevan, I bet. Take you out for a drink, did he, boss?"

"Thinks he's God's gift, that one," PC Pritchard offered.

This was followed by a short, impromptu rendition of "Bread of Heaven" changed into "Bread of Bevan" by three members of the North Wales Police Male Voice choir, which included Nader as their reserve tenor. Manx allowed the room to settle, before he continued.

"To bring you all up to speed, it's likely our patient was aboard Dick Roberts' boat when he was shot. The blood found on the lobster basket has a unique DNA traceable to someone of Eastern European descent—reading material's all here." Manx slid a thin, manila-coloured folder across the table. Morris reached for it, and began flipping through the pages.

"To date, everything points to the blood sample matching our patient. Good news, but it doesn't bring us much closer to solving our case."

"Just so we're all preaching from the same hymn book, like, and to help Priddle catch up," Nader said, "you reckon the bloke at the hospital was on Dick the Fish's boat before we found Stokes's body?"

"Correct," Manx said.

"Then, someone on the boat, maybe Dick, shoots the bloke. The bloke either falls or gets pushed over the side into the Strait, and survives twenty-four-hours in thirteen-degree water, before jumping some random windsurfer? Which makes our prime suspect Dick the Fish?"

There was a communal nodding of heads.

"I'm not buying it," Nader said, straightening his posture. "We don't even know if Dick was on the boat. He's too old, for one thing, and look at him. He's five foot three; bloke in the hospital's built like a brick-shit house. I'd put my money on Dick the Fish ending up in the brink before he would."

"I agree with the Sarge, sir. Dick Roberts doesn't seem the type," Morris said.

Manx nodded. "Only one way to find out. Pritchard, run a check on Dick's history. The bullet we pulled out of the patient's shoulder was fired from a Russian-made Makarov revolver. Dick could have picked one up on holiday. Probe into his travel itinerary over the past decade. Flag any holidays in the Balkans or former Soviet countries, specifically Georgia and Khazistan. When did he go? Who did he go with? Did he meet anyone? If he pissed in an alleyway in Prague, I want to know about it."

"Yes, boss," Pritchard said. He scribbled on the back of his hand.

"Are you still in primary school, Pritchard?" Manx asked.

"Er, no, sir?"

"Well, get yourself a bloody notebook, man."

Prichard mumbled an apology, and reached across his desk for a scrap of paper.

"Morris, you combed through Dick's accounts. Read us the headlines."

"He was up to his eyeballs in debt. Credit cards, store cards, local bookie, the usual. He was also three months behind with his mortgage. The company financing his boat haven't received a payment in six months, and started legal proceedings last month."

"Shit on a brick," Nader said. "Half the fucking island's in hock. Anyway, what's the motive? Unless shooting this bloke was going to solve all of his financial problems."

"The point being," Manx said, "is you can never predict what someone's capable of when they're about to lose everything."

The room fell silent until Morris spoke up. "It says here the DNA has a ninety-nine percent probability the owner came from central Asia. Do we know where exactly yet, sir?"

"More than likely he came into British waters from Eastern Europe," Manx said. "His wedding ring looked new, so there's probably a young wife, who's blissfully unaware of her husband's condition. Check the records for any freight ships leaving European ports in the last two weeks, on a route past the east of the island. Contact the shipping lines for missing crewmen, unscheduled dockings, that kind of thing."

Manx was about to dismiss the team, when Mickey Thomas blustered into the incident room, red-faced, having run from the reception desk. "Reese just called, boss," Mickey panted, leaning his hand against the wall to support himself. "Needs you at the hospital. Pronto."

Chapter 43

The ECG machine continued to beep, a steady, rhythmic pulse confirming what Mickey Thomas had told Manx earlier. The lad's condition had improved, and he was now breathing without the aid of a respirator.

"Might have guessed you'd turn up sooner or later," the doctor said, casting a cursory look in Manx's direction. He was the same doctor who had first attended the patient, and still looked as if he hadn't slept for days.

"PC Chatterbox outside told you the news, I suppose," the doctor said, nodding towards Reese, seated on a plastic chair to the left of the doorway.

"Just doing his job, like the rest of us," Manx said.

The doctor ignored the remark, and cleared his throat. "The patient's pupils look normal, so I'd say there's minimal chance of brain damage. Still, I'm hesitant to rush into a diagnosis, until he's completely out of danger."

"Has he spoken?"

"Just mumbled a few words, not any language I'm familiar with. He's still incoherent at this point, so I wouldn't get your hopes up."

"Don't suppose there's an outside chance you'd give me your expert opinion as to when he might be up to answering some questions?"

The doctor removed his bifocals, and swept the inner-corners of his eyes with his thumb and index finger. He was about to make himself abundantly clear to the Inspector, when he noticed something. The man's eyelids were twitching, as if a small current of electricity was travelling through them. He glanced over at the ECG. The man's pulse was racing at 120bpm. Beads of perspiration had appeared on his forehead, and his legs were moving in violent spasms. He began to speak, the words exhaling off his tongue in a soft, dry whisper. Manx rushed to his side and leant in closer. He could discern an accent, thick and slurred, and requiring a full, fluid rolling across the tongue. Manx's first instinct was Russian.

He turned towards the doctor. "Just on the off-chance, anyone here speak Russian, or any eastern European language?"

"Probably one the of porters, or a cleaner. We employ a fair amount of Poles, these days. But, I wouldn't recommend..."

"He's trying to communicate. We at least need to try to understand what the poor bugger's saying," Manx interrupted.

The man's voice grew louder, as he strained to make himself understood.

"Get one of them up here as soon as you can," Manx said.

The doctor hesitated.

"That's not a request," Manx said, looking the doctor square in the eyes.

A few minutes later, the doctor returned with a stout, dark-skinned man. The tag on his blue overalls stated his name—Teo Baranski. Teo had a dark complexion and brown eyes, which were set deep into his brow and darted around, not knowing where to settle.

"It's OK, Teo," Manx said reassuringly. "We just need your help, shouldn't take too long. You're Polish, right?"

Teo couldn't look Manx in the eye, but nodded his affirmation. "Warsaw?"

"Gdansk," Teo's voice had a matter-of-fact tone to it.

"Ok, Teo, it would really help us out if you would listen to what our patient is saying, see if you can identify the language."

Teo looked at the doctor, as if waiting for permission. The doctor nodded abruptly. Teo leant in, tilting his head so his ear was close to the lad's mouth. The same phrase was still flowing from his lips; sometimes loud, sometimes in a hoarse whisper crackling like firewood as he spoke. After a few moments, Teo turned towards the doctor.

"Not Poland," he said. "I think Slovenia." Teo looked at the door, and wiped his hand nervously on the side of his overalls.

"And you don't speak Slovenian?" Manx said.

Teo turned to face Manx, looking him directly in the eye this time. "I speak four languages—Russian, Polish, English, and Slovene. I have a first-class education," he said, pulling his back to stiff attention.

For the first time, Manx noticed an edge to his voice, a direct, unrepentant tone signifying pride, and maybe the only tangible shred of dignity Teo had left in the world.

"He is, how do you say, like a broke record?"

"A broken record?" Manx said.

"Yes, a broken record. Same thing over and over: *sledijo jutranja zvezda, sledijo jutranja zvezda*. No literal translation, but something about the morning star? Follow the morning star? I'm not sure. His voice is very hard to hear."

The room fell silent again, save the comforting beep of the ECG. The man's voice had now retreated back to the familiar rhythm of a heavy, elongated breath, as if he'd finally been understood, and could now rest.

"Are you sure that's what he said?"

"One hundred per cent," Teo said, testing out a phrase he'd heard recently on a TV show.

"Does it mean anything to you?" Manx asked.

"Only what I tell you, a translation. Maybe when he wakes up again, then I can come back."

"We'll know where to find you, Teo," the doctor said, placing his hand on his shoulder, and guiding him through the doorway.

***

Before heading back to the island, Manx took a detour, and drove down the twisting road leading to the Bangor pier. He needed to focus on the lad's words: "Follow The Morning Star?" Maybe he was hallucinating, spouting some religious gibberish. He knew from experience knocking on death's door could do that to a man.

At the entrance gate, Manx threw a pound coin into the honesty box, and walked to the end of the pier. It was quiet here, nothing but the sound of the tide sloshing hypnotically against the wooden struts. He leant against the metal railing, and lit up a King Edward, his first of the day.

At one-thirty in the afternoon, a sliver of sunlight afforded Manx a clear view across the Strait, over to Menai Bridge and Beaumaris. *The last defence of the Druids against the Roman invaders*—it was among the handful of facts which had caught his imagination as a school-kid. *The Strait was essentially a twenty-five-kilometre long moat*, Manx thought to himself, as he looked over the stretch of water, which had, in recent years, become a playground for the owners of the expensive waterfront houses now dotting its banks. The sliver sunlight reflecting across the surface of the strait imbued it with a deceptive calmness. Manx imagined he could skim a pebble across its surface, and the whole body of water would ripple out to the Irish Sea.

He drew on his cigar and let the ash scatter in breeze. Something Frank at the Lifeboat house had said came back to him. Something about the speed of the currents, the whirlpools and eddies, they were all there, but below the surface, churning centuries of silt and sediment from one end of the channel to the other. That's what Manx had to do. He had to go below the surface of the case, find out who, or what, was shifting the currents and pulling the tides. But, for now, a mile and a half across the strait, the six hundred square kilometres of Welsh rock was keeping its secrets.

Chapter 44

From inside the Jensen, Manx heard the loud, effortless shrieking of children playing. He looked over at the small, neat cottage set back a few metres from the road. Six multi-coloured balloons, tethered with a long strip of ribbon to the gatepost, danced aimlessly in the breeze, adding a burst of bright nursery colours against the dark-grey stonework. Maybe this wasn't the best time to call. Nobody likes a gate crasher, but he was here, and had no better place to be at three-o'clock on a Saturday afternoon.

As he walked towards the cottage, he noticed how uncharacteristically blue and cloudless the sky was for this time of year. The air was still cold and brittle, and felt as if it might break in two, if Manx made too rapid a movement in any direction. To the left of the cottage, a large, metallic dome-shaped building seemed out of place with the natural, stonework surrounding it. Under the apex of the dome, a simple, blue and yellow sign with the words Morgan's Motor Repair had been hung with two loose lines of chicken wire. Six cars were parked outside on the gravel lot, two of them raised on blocks, their wheels removed, and the other four had "for sale" hastily scrawled in white pen over their windscreens.

A crisp patch of stubborn dawn frost crunched easily under his boots, as he walked towards the porch. Manx tried to remember the last time he was here, before realising he'd never visited Sara at her home. The last time he saw his older sister she was dancing in a long white gown to Jennifer Warren's "Power of Love," resting her head on the shoulder of her husband of three hours. Manx had left soon after. He'd paid his respects at the church service, and then drank himself into a stupor as an endless parade of relatives offered their congratulations. He'd done his brotherly duty, and the thought of spending another four hours in the company of Nick Smart's Mobile Disco was a sobering one. He had slipped out before the first dance, looking back just once to see Alice Manx-William alone at the head table, throwing back a full glass of champagne, her eyes glazed, and her gaze fixed directly on Manx, as he turned his back and left. It felt like a lifetime ago.

He pushed gently on the cottage door, and felt the welcoming rush of warm air greet him, as he stepped into the living room. A large TV hung like an over-sized painting on the wall over the fireplace. On the floor, several boxes were still unopened: X-Box, DVD Player, a 5.1 surround speaker system, along with several unopened presents. Manx looked towards the kitchen, and saw Sara. She was fussing over a large birthday cake, her back to Manx. He stood for a moment, watching his sister as she pushed several candles into the wet icing, then wiped her hands down the front of her apron. From this angle, she looked just like Alice. Her back was long and rigid, with the same lean, stiff physique. She'd cut her hair short, so it came to rest on her shoulders blades. From this angle, he couldn't tell if it suited her, or not.

Sara sensed someone was watching her and turned. Manx noticed her catch her breath when she saw him, but quickly regain her composure, and return to decorating the cake. "Might have guessed you'd turn up empty-handed," she said, directing her words towards Manx's faint reflection in the kitchen window.

"I'm not sure what..." Manx began.

"Bloody useless as ever, Tudor," Sara said. "Dewi's birthday. Your nephew?" She gestured towards the large, patio window, and the flurry of kids scrambling over the garden. "He's the one in the cowboy hat, in case you're wondering."

Manx watched as the scatter of kids screamed their way onto a wooden play-structure. "How..." Manx said, before he was interrupted.

"Six," Sara said, placing the last of the candles on the cake.

"He looks like you. You had the same colour hair at that age."

"I'm surprised you remember," Sara said, facing Manx. He could see the raw edges of himself in his sister, as if she were the sketch that held the blueprint for his own features. She had the same light-blue eyes, though her face was rounder and more freckled. She looked tired, the dark circles under her eyes were like life's tell-tale smudges.

"Didn't know you were entering *The Great British Bake Off*," Manx said, looking at the cake; a reasonable approximation of the *Millennium Falcon*, complete with Dewi's name iced across its bow.

"You're pulling my leg, right? Asda special, ten quid. They write the name on for free."

"Who knew?" Manx said.

"So long as it's chocolate, and there's a few candles to blow out, he's happy." Sara hoisted the cake off the counter, and edged awkwardly past Manx. "Shift yourself. I don't want Dewi to see it yet. Can you?" she said, nodding towards the fridge.

Manx opened the door. The cake slid easily onto one of the empty shelves. "If I'd known it was the kid's birthday..."

"Forget it, Tudor. We gave up expecting anything from you years ago."

Manx said nothing, and shoved his hands deep into his jean pockets.

"You always used to do that when you were in trouble," Sara said. "Hide your hands, like they'd give you away, or something."

Manx shrugged, and burrowed his hands even deeper into the warren of his pockets.

Sara leant her back against the sink. "Mam put you up to this?"

"She mentioned you were asking about me," Manx said.

"Yeah, well, *asking* might be putting it a bit strong," she said, washing her hands. "What's this, then? Another one of your guest appearances? Like the wedding? Fulfilling your duty?"

"Take it day-by-day, you know."

"Always so bloody mysterious," Sara said, shaking her head. "Like a bloody ghost. Turn-up when you want, then disappear, like you were never here. Must be nice, no responsibilities, right, Tudor?"

Manx stiffened—it was a softer blow than he'd expected. Sara had a knack for wielding her tongue like a well-honed knife. Maybe she'd smoothed off the edges over the years, or maybe it was just a warm-up routine.

"Mam looks well, considering," he said, eager to shift the subject.

"Considering, what? Her age, or the bottles of Gin she puts away?" Sara said. "By the way, you didn't…?" Her eyes flashed a spark of concern, as the thought crossed her mind.

"Just the one," Manx said, shrugging.

"Jesus! We've kept her off the booze for months. Once she starts, she's a mess! Starts remembering things she'd be better off forgetting."

"Drinking to remember? That's new," Manx said, with a mild trace of a smile. Sarah caught sight of it, and immediately set to work wiping it off.

"If you'd been here to help, you'd know. Cleaning up her piss and sick at all hours of the night, it's like taking care of an eighty-year-old child. If she'd lost her marbles, I could put her in a home, but she swears she'll be carried out of the house in a wooden box. At least you'd be home to help with that, eh, Tudor? Put Mam in the ground, once and for all?" She turned to stare through the kitchen window, as if she couldn't bear to look at her brother.

There it was, blow number two, direct hit to the solar plexus. Manx rolled with it, not that he had much to spar with. Sara was right; he had no idea what it was like. He'd caught a glimpse the other night, but chalked it up to a one-off, just Alice turning up the melodrama for his benefit.

Sara turned back, and took a deep breath. She wasn't finished. Manx imagined she'd been waiting years for this moment, to spit out her long-festering bile at Manx. On this occasion, however, he was spared. His brother-in-law was tugging aggressively on the patio door, his face turning red as he pulled. It finally relented, and a gust of cold air rushed into the kitchen, adding to the already icy atmosphere.

"Bloody hell, it's brass monkeys out there," he said, waving his hands above the kitchen radiator. "Don't know how the kids can stand it."

"Look, Cledwyn," Sara said, in a pragmatic tone. "Prodigal son's returned."

"Come again?" Cledwyn asked, as he looked over at the tall figure leaning casually against the kitchen wall. It took approximately two seconds for the penny to drop into place. "Bloody hell fire!" Cledwyn finally said, rocking back slightly on his heels. Manx noticed the red-blush of his cheeks subside quickly, and the blood drain from his face.

"Didn't think we'd see you round here again," his brother-in-law said. "Real turn up for the books," he added, and blew out a breezy whistle, as he walked towards Manx.

"Been a while." Manx extended his hand. His brother-in-law grimaced.

"Eh, sorry, mate, health and safety and all that," he said, and held up a heavily bandaged finger.

"Looks nasty," Manx offered.

"Aye, Sara got a little too handy with the carving knife. Good job she wasn't near the crown jewels eh?" he said, making a snipping motion with his fingers at the fly of his jeans.

"I don't know how you can joke about it. Could have cost you your job, the garage. What use is a bloody mechanic without his fingers?"

"Ah, still got another nine, haven't I?"

"Well, it's good to see you anyway, Shanni," Manx said.

"He doesn't go by that stupid name anymore," Sara said, with a well-honed tartness. "It's Cledwyn now."

"Oh, don't listen to your sister," Shanni said, waving his hand dismissively. "She's trying to make a respectable man out of me. Bit bloody late in the game for that, if you ask me." Shanni laughed nervously.

Sara said nothing. The withering look she threw in her husband's direction said more than words ever could.

No matter what his sister insisted, he'd always be Shanni to Manx. The short, wiry, exotic-looking kid he remembered from school. Even now, looking at Shanni, he could almost smell the sawdust from the woodworking room, and sharp pungency of the grease and iron filings strewn across the metalwork benches. They were the only two classes he remembered attending with his brother-in-law. Shanni had always stood out from the other boys—dark skin, good teeth, and a knack for talking himself out of trouble as often as he talked himself into it.

"Want a beer? If you're staying a while?" Shanni said, opening the fridge door. "Got a couple of Boddingtons left," he added. Manx accepted the ice-cold can.

In the living room, they formed an awkward triangle. Shanni and Sara opposite ends of the sofa, Sara clutching a shot glass of Bailey's, one ice cube, and perched on the edge of the cushion, as if she were about to launch herself from it. Manx sat on the wide, leather recliner, which felt two sizes too big for even him. He shuffled his feet on the thick fireplace rug and struggled, unsuccessfully, for something benign to say.

Shanni shattered the uneasy silence with a bark of pleasure as he chugged at his beer. "Ah! Needed that," he said, wiping a bubble of froth from the corner of his lip with the back of his hand. Sarah remained silent, unmoving, her gaze directed towards the fire.

"Business must be good," Manx said, gesturing towards the electronic equipment sprawled across the floor.

"Aye, time to catch up with the rest of the modern world. I'll get it all fixed up when the boy's gone to bed tonight,' Shanni said.

"Waste of money, if you ask me," Sara said. "Plenty of other things need fixing here, before spending on more toys."

Shanni grunted, then turned his attention to Manx. "Saw you in the paper, like. You involved in them murders, then?"

"Senior Investigating Officer," Manx explained

"Fancy title," Shanni, said, taking a large slug of beer.

"Just means I get bigger headaches," Manx said.

"Still, nasty business, though, if what the papers are saying is true. Mind you, I don't know what to believe these days," Shanni said.

"We give them the facts; we can't control what they do with them."

"Aye, I suppose they've got to sell papers, somehow."

Sara continued sipping, directing her steely gaze into the fire.

"So, they bring you in just for this business, or you back for good?"

"There's the million-pound question, right, Tudor?" Sara said.

Manx shrugged. "Take it day-by-day," he repeated.

"That's convenient," Sara said. "Wish I could pick up sticks when the mood took me."

"Jesus, love, leave the man alone. He's having a beer with his family, give it a rest." Shanni was irritated, and his voice was tense, as if he were speaking through clenched teeth. Sara was never one for holding her tongue, and by the way she had her knees locked together, Manx could tell she was working hard to contain herself.

"Thirty fuckin' years," Shanni said, shaking his head, and balancing the beer can on his knee. "Where does it go, eh?" He leant back in his chair, and expelled a large gust of air. "Remember when we were in school? Form four, I think it was, year before I dropped out. Roland Jones taught Geography; we were all scared shitless of him. Mean bastard, he was, wound tight like a fucking distributor coil."

"I think I probably got a clip round the head from him a few times. Par for the course, those days," Manx said.

"Bloody psychopath, if you ask me," Shanni said. "Lobbed a wooden T-square at me from his desk, one afternoon. Would have stuck in my skull, if he'd been wearing his glasses," Shanni made a sweeping motion with his hand past his forehead. "Anyway, poor bugger died a couple of months ago," he added, and gazed at the large living room window, as if the past were somehow playing on the glass in glorious Technicolor. "Locked the garage door and tied a hose-pipe to the exhaust of his Mondeo. The engine didn't stop until it ran out of petrol."

"Jesus," Manx said.

"Yeah, poor bastard. I bet you come across worse than that, though, in your job?" Shanni said, gesturing with his beer can towards Manx.

"They give you special training, trauma counselling, that kind of thing," Manx explained.

"So, you have any idea who did these murders? Any leads, like?"

"Only what you've read in the papers. It's an ongoing investigation, so I can't talk too much about it."

"No, no, totally understand, mate, just wondering like. It's all too close to home. Should we be worried, me, and Sara, Dewi? Are they targeting anybody specific, like?"

"Unless you're heading up a major criminal operation on the island, I don't think you need to worry," Manx said.

Shanni paused in mid-sentence. Manx noticed the colour drain from his face for the second time that afternoon. "Ha, funny bugger," Shanni finally said. "Not locking me up for passing a few dodgy MOTs, then?" he asked, swallowing another chug of beer, and winking at Sara for good measure.

Before Manx could answer, there was a loud crash of glass. From the edge of his vision, he saw a dark object fly through the living room window. Sara screamed. Shanni instinctively threw his body over hers, cupping his hands over his wife's head.

Manx watched as a lump of rock, about the size of a bag of coffee, rolled and stopped six inches short of his Blundstone boots. Seconds later, Manx was at the window. The hole was about three-feet across, with shards of glass falling off its outer edges and onto a row of photographs. The temperature dropped quickly, as the cold air found the path of least resistance, and flowed unobstructed into the living room, causing the curtains to flap like flags in a stiff wind.

"Fucking hell," Shanni said. "You all right love?"

Sara nodded, still in shock. Satisfied she wasn't injured, Shanni ran to join Manx at the window. They could hear the loud roar of a motorcycle peel off into the distance. It sounded like a dirt bike, with a strained, high-pitched whine, and out of their hearing seconds later.

"Unhappy customer?" Manx said.

"Who the fuck knows?" Shanni said, looking across the green expanse of fields, then at the rock on the floor. Sara joined them at the window.

"Who'd do something like this, Cledwyn?" She was crying softly, and allowed Shanni to fold her into his arms.

"Probably kids. Fuck all else for them to do, so they cause trouble."

"Doubt we'll catch them," Manx said, "I can file a report, if you like."

"Fix my window, would it? Filing a bloody report?" Sara said.

At that moment, they heard the kids rush into the kitchen. Sara ran, eager to stop them, before they came into the living room.

"I'll give you a hand clearing it up," Manx offered.

"Er, don't worry, mate," Shanni said, glancing again at the rock. "Maybe

best if you clear off. Sara's not herself, you know. Stress and everything."

"Yeah, I probably should have called."

Manx stood at the doorway, and looked over the acres of sun-blessed fields stretching before him. He stayed for a few minutes, until a blotch of low, grey clouds rolled over the sun, and flattened out the scenery. As he walked back to the car, a strong gust rushed over the front garden, and unhooked the colourful bulge of balloons tied to the gate. Manx tried to catch the length of ribbon that bound them, but it was just out of his reach. As he drove off, he could still see them, spiralling skywards, buffered by the unpredictable November winds.

***

Fucking prick! "Major criminal operation?" What the fuck did he know? Nothing. He was just pissing in the wind, that was all; making conversation, trying to be funny. He shouldn't read anything into it. It was an off-hand remark, a throwaway line, nothing more.

Shanni was in his office at the back of the garage, dragging anxiously on a Marlboro Light. He took the rock from the table, and ran his fingers over the blue, crude letter S painted on one side. It wasn't subtle; Scuttler hadn't wanted it to be. It was a blunt reminder he knew where Shanni lived. Shanni had spotted the "S," and made sure his brother-in-law had left before he'd seen it. There would be too many questions to answer, too many lies to tell.

Not that lies were troublesome. It was Sara who was the problem; she wouldn't have let it go. He could have bluffed his away around his brother-in-law, but Sara knew him too well. And, anyway, it was better to hide it, say nothing. There had been too many lies in his family, too many to remember.

Shanni had suspected when he was around ten Harri Morgan wasn't his real dad. Harri had given Shanni his name and a roof over his head, but nothing more. One glance at the Morgan family album told that story. Shanni was the runt of the litter. He wasn't even the black sheep; that would have been a step-up. The gossip was his mother had slept with someone from a Gypsycamp when Harri was out at sea, and Shanni was his coming home present. Harri arrived back, saw his wife was pregnant, made a quick but accurate mental calculation, and struck her about the face until her right, upper molar flew from her mouth. Harri insisted she keep the baby, more out of a twisted sense of revenge than forgiveness. Shanni would be a constant reminder of her betrayal.

202

He was the gift that kept on giving, Shanni thought, and laughed. *What kind of fucked-up family was that? What other outcome could there be?* He was an outcast. It was his destiny, forged the day his mother spread her legs to some passing gyppo.

He looked at the map of Anglesey pinned to the wall, next to the Pirelli calendar. The lads were in, all of them. The results were already promising. He'd told them to give all the junkies they knew one free sample—all repeat prescriptions would be full price. Ten pounds a hit. There was a rush of orders. He smiled at the thought, and rolled the blue pill in his fingers. Curiosity niggled at him, but the dealer never became the junkie; it wasn't good for business. There was only one new fly in the ointment that needed to be taken care of—his brother-in-law. Scuttler didn't need to know. Not a lie this time, just a necessary silence.

Chapter 45

PC Delyth Morris leant back, stretched out her arms and yawned loudly. She glanced at the clock; five fifteen—another two hours before she could clock off. She'd spent the last four hours of her Sunday afternoon scrubbing through both the Police National Computer and DNA Databases, and cross-referencing any partials in the Fingerprint Exchange Network; there were no matches to Dr. Patrick Metcalf. If he couldn't be found in classified police databases, maybe she could track him down in a more civilian manner, via the web. She was ready to dive into the first string of results, when the incident room shot open, clattering loudly against the wall. She jumped, spilling her tea.

"Mal? What the hell?" she shouted at Nader, who looked equally as shocked to see Morris at her desk, wiping herself down with a paper towel. "Can't you just open a door like a normal person?"

"Didn't know you were in here, Minor," Nader said, "or else I would have waited for a bloody invitation."

"What are you doing here, anyway? Your day off, isn't it?"

Nader walked to his desk, and took something out of the drawer, stuffing it into his backpack. "Forgot something," he said. "The missus is out gallivanting with some Chapel thing. Better off out of it, if you ask me."

"I didn't ask you," Morris said.

"What? Oh, yeah, right," Nader mumbled.

He appeared dazed. Maybe he'd been drinking: a few too many at the pub at lunchtime "Want a coffee or something, Sarge?" Morris asked.

Nader contemplated the question for what seemed like minutes, before shaking his head. He was about to leave, when he changed his mind, and sat back down with a heavy grunt, his shoulders sloping forward, as if the burden of the world had suddenly slipped across them.

"Why did you join the force, Minor? You got a few O-Levels, right? A-Levels, even? You could have gone to college, got a proper career?"

Morris shrugged. "Lots of reasons, I suppose. Wanted to do something worthwhile, you know. All my mates, they were going to away to University or Tech College. I didn't fancy another four years with my nose in a book. Being a copper seemed the right fit."

Nader leaned forward, his palms on his knees, and looked Morris in the eyes. "You know, it's all going to shit, don't you" he said. "The whole fucking world, and we're just the shovels they use to scrape it up."

"Not sure what you mean, Mal," Morris said, cautiously.

"Loyalty, standing up for your mates, you know, stuff that used to mean something?" Nader continued. "Don't count for anything anymore. Now, it's all about bloody results. How much shit you can clean up, before the bloke behind you brings in a bigger shovel than you. That's all they care about. We're glorified shit-shovelers, Morris. We deal with the shit and rubbish no one else wants to touch."

Nader sat back and chuckled to himself. "You're ambitious, right, Minor? Career women, you call yourselves? Wouldn't find you taking up with those hippy dippy freaks, pissing off to India, trying to find who the fuck you are with marijuana and medi-fucking-tation?"

Nader paused for a second, as if to organise his thoughts, then spoke in a low, conspiratorial whisper. "Thing is, Morris, it's all bullshit. Best to let sleeping dogs lie, if you ask me, understand?" Nader tapped the tip of his nose, and slunk down further in his chair.

No, Morris didn't understand. This wasn't Nader sitting across from her; this was some other person, someone more diminished: a puppy suddenly dropped at the side of the road, and trying to figure out what the hell just happened. Nader sat, biting his top lip. Suddenly, as if he'd been called to attention, he sat up, and grabbed his backpack.

"Fuck this, eh? Working on a Sunday. Bet you'd rather be home cooking for your bloke."

"Don't have a bloke," Morris said.

"No matter. We're very liberal these days, Minor. Very accepting of the lesbian of the species in here, we are. Attended a course on it, and everything," Nader said, throwing the backpack over his shoulder and muttering to himself as he left.

By six forty-five, Morris was ready to call it a night. She rubbed her fingers into her eyes, and saw the last four hours of text, photographs and searched documents hover in her periphery like holograms: faint and untouchable. She switched search engines to "Duck Duck Go." Eshy had mentioned it a few months back as an alternative to Google; more likely to throw up more relevant results, without all the ads. She typed in Metcalf's name, for the final time today, she promised, selected her region, and clicked on the images prompt. A checkerboard of faces flashed on screen. Fifteen minutes, that's all she'd give it, then she was shutting down, and going to the pub for a pint before going home.

At six fifty-three, she zoomed into one photograph, which had caught her attention—two men standing at a ribbon cutting ceremony. She clicked on the link that connected to the archive pages of the *Manchester Evening News*, 1996. As she read slowly through the accompanying article, a shiver of triumph and relief buzzed through her veins. If Nader were still here, she would have explained to him this is why she became a copper; this moment right now, when she felt touched by lightning. She called Manx immediately. This wasn't the sort of news that could wait until morning.

Chapter 46

At nine-thirty on Sunday night, Sergeant Mal Nader sat in his Volvo 740, stabbing angrily at the buttons of the heater pumping out nothing but a breathy stream of tepid, stale air. He slid the driver's seat back a few inches to relieve the pain shooting up his sciatic nerve. If he wasn't warm, he could at least be comfortable. He reached over for the picnic blanket his wife had bought a couple of summers ago, after she decided they should spend more time outdoors. *Enjoy the countryside, Mal,* she'd enthused. If he remembered correctly, they'd used it just once; it had rained that afternoon, and for several weeks afterwards. He brushed off the remnants of the Cornish pasty he'd eaten earlier, and pulled the blanket over his thighs; it smelled of wet dog and mayonnaise.

For the next two hours, Nader waited. He was parked outside the Pentraeth Arms. From here, he could see who was coming in and out of the pub, not that it was particularly busy; few pubs were, these days. People were more cautious, stocking up with cheap, supermarket beer, and getting drunk in front of the TV. Nobody wanted to pay over the odds for anything, least of all beer and fags. The whole fucking world was going to hell. *If a workingman couldn't afford to nip down the local for a couple of pints, what the fuck was life about?* Nader thought. Still, he'd be retired in a few years, a solid police pension to look forward to; he wouldn't need to worry about paying for a few rounds down the local, every now and then.

Truth be told, and it was a truth kept to himself, the prospect of his impending retirement filled him with a gradual and cumulative dread. He was a copper, it was in his blood, all he knew, and all that had really mattered to him. He wasn't like Mickey Thomas, counting down the days to a second career as a part-time bingo caller: "Turn of the screw, sixty-two?" Another seven years, and DS Malcolm Nader would be nothing but a memory, and what did he have to look forward to? Falling asleep in front of the TV, with a can of beer in his hand? Tend to his greenhouse tomatoes? More wet picnics with the wife? The prospect made his blood run cold. It did him no good, thinking this way. It led to bad thoughts, thoughts which swept over him like a storm, thoughts making him want to loop a length of rope over the timbers of his own shed. He threw the blanket from his legs, and walked towards the Ford Focus parked a hundred metres away.

Nader rapped his knuckles in a loud, purposeful fashion on the window.

"Jesus, Nader, what the blazes are you doing here? Scared the bloody life out of me!" PC Alyn Davies said.

"Just making sure you two aren't getting too cosy," he said, with a wink, and leant his elbows on the window frame. He caught the faint, oaky aroma of whisky. "Haven't been drinking on-duty now, have we, gentlemen?" Nader asked, and gestured at the silver hipflask jammed into the cup holder.

"Who us? Never," Davies said, passing the flask. Nader sniffed it, took a large swig, then wiped his lips with the back of his hand.

"Good stuff, that," he said.

"Single malt. Not your cheap blended rubbish," Davies explained.

Nader nodded, and gestured towards the Pentraeth Arms. "Long night?"

"Too fucking right," Davis said. "Third night I've been on bloody duty. The wife's threatening to go back to live with her mother."

"That right? Better make sure we get you another week of nights, then, eh? You'll be foot loose and fancy free."

Davis laughed nervously.

"Listen, lads,' Nader said, leaning further inside the car. "It's your lucky night. I had a word with the boss, and he's letting you off early. I've not been sleeping anyway, sciatica's playing up like a bugger, so I told him I may as well do something useful."

"You serious, like?" The other officer, PC Pritchard, asked.

"As the grave, mate. Give him a call." Nader offered his mobile.

The two officers looked at each other, and shook their heads. "Good enough for me, you're the Sarge. If you want to take over, it's all yours."

Nader leant back, palms on the small of his back. "Anything to report, before you both bugger off?"

"Just the usual," Pritchard said. "He's still drinking. I expect he'll nip in the chippie after, then head back home. Creature of habit, is our Bowen."

"Then, it'll be a quiet night," Nader said, slapping the roof of the service car. "I'll see you tomorrow, and give your wife one from me, eh, Davis?"

Davis was about to say something, but Pritchard had already turned a hard left, and pulled off onto the main road.

Nader waited until the lights had disappeared into the darkness, before returning to his car. He felt a cold shiver pass through his veins. He glanced at the clock—ten-fifteen pm. They'd be calling last orders within the hour. He tuned the radio to Radio Cymru; he preferred their music selections at this time at night; they didn't play any of that modern rubbish. At this hour, they'd always spin the classics; the close harmony singing of Hogia'r Wyddfa gentle folksy stuff, with angelic female voices over lightly picked guitar, maybe some old protest songs from Dafydd Iwan. He sat back, and let the music flow over him, strumming his nerves into a place of calmness, and preparing himself for what needed to be done. No police regulations, no by-the-book procedure. Tonight, he was just a copper, looking out for one of his own.

***

June 7th 1982, the Falklands Conflict. Nader had always hated that phrase. A conflict was something you had with your neighbour or your wife; this was a fucking war. Nader was a sergeant in the Welsh Guards, had signed up at seventeen—walked into the recruitment office the day after he left school. It was a decision spurred more by a lack of direction, rather than any deep-rooted sense of duty to serve Queen and Country. At twenty-three years old, along with three hundred fellow Welsh Guards, part of the 5th Infantry Brigade, that commitment duty was about to be put to the test.

Fourteen hundred hours GMT. The *RFA Sir Galahad*, a four-thousand-ton landing vessel, was preparing to unload three hundred and fifty British troops onto the coarse beach at Port Pleasant. Then, it came, out of the blue. The screaming death-knoll of a five-hundred-pound retarding tail-bomb, dropped from three-hundred feet by an Argentinian A4-Skyhawk. Seconds later, another one fell, striking the bow of the *Sir Galahad,* and shooting a thick wall of smoke, metal fragments, and shattered bone through the line of infantrymen positioned to the fore of the landing deck.

Nader had picked himself up from the floor, and looked at the devastation. Severed limbs, shards of bone punctured through skin, the sickly, charred stench of burning flesh. As his mind had struggled to make sense of the wreckage, there was another explosion, this time to the aft. The blast blew through him. He had felt his ankles buckle, and fell onto the smouldering body of one of his fellow infantrymen, a faint trail of yellow, gassy smoke still rising through his uniform. Then, darkness, deep and thick, and a thudding pulse of silence echoing through his veins.

Twelve months later, Nader was issued with his discharge papers. Back home, it felt as if his brain had tuned into a different wavelength, like wind passing over piano wire; everything seemed to affect him. The change in the weather, a dip in air pressure, the sad ending of a TV show or film. One Saturday, in W.H. Smith's in Bangor, he'd been reading the sickly, sentimental verses, while looking for a birthday card for his mother, and noticed he was crying; large, salt-wet tears falling on the envelopes. He ran out, and found a dark corner of a pub he could hide in for a few hours.

After a couple of odd jobs, he applied to join the North Wales Constabulary. The force was desperate for new cadets at the time, and his army background helped him sail through the official training. Ten years later, after being referred to a police-therapist (a gentle, older woman with a pronounced lisp), Nader finally gained some insight into what was happening. It was his amygdala, the therapist had explained, a small part of his brain, which controlled the major emotional functions. The amygdala was often hyperactive in combat veterans, functioning in over-drive, twenty-four-seven. Nader's was not a particularly severe case, she reassured him, and was easily managed, if not cured, with the right, low-level dosage of drugs.

All Nader knew was one minute he'd be fine, the next minute something, or someone, would trigger a reaction, and he'd forget the next few minutes, as if they'd never happened. There was no thinking, no rationalisation. It was raw, primal instinct. The way the doctor explained it had made sense. He was trained to fight, not to think. In the hell of combat, you just reacted. A noise, a movement in the corner of your eye, you faced it, shot at it, without a second thought. There was no re-programming once this had been activated, no self-destruct mechanism. Nader had learnt to live with it, took meds to help control it, and attended yearly psychological evaluations to ensure he wasn't going off the rails, but sometimes, the darkness would cloud over him, just like it did right now, as he stood over the groaning body, trying to piece together exactly what he'd put Thomas Bowen through for the past few minutes.

The police-issue nightstick slid from his hand and onto the dirt-track road, making a dull thud, as it hit the ground. He quickly ran through the train of events, arranging them in sequence. Talking with Davis and Pritchard; observing the handful of punters walk out of the pub; spotting Bowen by himself crossing the road; waiting for Bowen to leave the chip-shop, following him down the narrow road leading to the farmhouse. He remembered Bowen's grey hoodie hanging like a sack over his back, felt the polished, cold metal of nightstick expand in his hand, and then what? Nothing. Nothing but a deep, black hole swallowing the last five minutes of his life, as if they had never happened.

Nader removed his balaclava, and took in the cold night air in quick, hungry breaths. He clutched at his stomach, and retched a clear, whisky-tinged pool of vomit. Thomas Bowen was moaning softly, blood seeping from the corner of his mouth. Nader wiped the sick from his chin, and looked around. Silence. Darkness. *Where had he hit Bowen?* His mind shot back to his basic training. Avoid striking the suspect's skull, spine, sternum, or groin area, or anywhere that could result in permanent damage. *Where was he meant to hit?* The peroneal nerve, that was it, just above the knee. Then, you targeted the large muscle groups, quadriceps, biceps, just enough to immobilise. He looked at Bowen; he was beyond immobilisation, way beyond. The bile in his stomach rose northward again. He bent over, his hands on his knees, swallowed hard, and kept it in check.

Immediately, he felt the first stirrings of one of his migraines—the familiar pinch of pain in the back of his neck, the urgent pressure of his blood vessels at the wall of his skull. There would be no relief from this, not for several hours. He had to leave, before someone saw him. It was the first coherent thought he'd had all evening. He picked up the nightstick, and slipped it back inside his backpack. After one final glance, he stepped over Bowen's groaning body, and walked briskly back to his car.

Nader sat behind the steering wheel, folded his balaclava, and wiped it across his brow. His breathing was fast and shallow. He heard a faint rumbling in the distance—the fat, whirring turbine engines of a large military aircraft bearing down on him. He squinted through the condensation. He could see the aircraft's landing lights to the east, ready to discharge its payload.

He had to take cover, protect himself. Responding to a command only he could hear, Nader threw himself across the front passenger seat, cupping his hands over his ears. The roar from the jet engines vibrated through every cell of his body. A bright, blinding light burst through the windscreen filling the car with a stark, colourless wash of white. But, all Nader saw were the flashing strobe lights flickering across his field of vision, as he shut his eyes tighter, and braced his body for the inevitable impact.

The sixteen-wheeler sped past him, its horn shattering the silence. The Volvo shuddered as the draft from the lorry buffered violently against the car. Then, silence, save the sound of Nader's own breathing. He stayed down, held onto the picnic blanket, and pulled it tight. He was shivering, but he wasn't cold, not even remotely. His body was burning up, sweat dripping from his forehead, stinging his eyes, which were, by now, wide-open, staring blankly into darkness.

Chapter 47

It was early Tuesday morning when Margaret Lockwood, ex-Detective Chief Superintendent of the Greater Manchester Police, returned Manx's call. An hour later, he hung up, checked his notes, and spent the remainder of the morning cross-referencing the names, dates, and facts she'd provided. He printed out the photographs the GMP had emailed over, and then set about organizing all the information in a linear narrative. Just after one thirty, he called the team in for an emergency briefing.

"Gentlemen, we should all thank Morris for a significant lead in the case." Manx gestured at the PC, who blushed, as was customary for her to do under any undue attention. There was a light ripple of applause.

"See, told you we'd all be calling you ma'am one day, eh?" Nader said.

"Be happy if you'd just stop calling me bloody Minor."

"Grow a few more inches, and I might."

"Right, straight to business," Manx said. "There's a lot of ground to cover, so stay focussed." He clicked through his first slide. "As we suspected, our murder victim, Dr. Simon Vaughn, was not who he claimed to be. I spoke at length to a senior officer from the Greater Manchester Police earlier this morning. She confirmed Vaughn was, in fact, Dr. Patrick Metcalf, a specialist in drug addiction at Manchester Royal Infirmary. After providing testimony leading to the imprisonment of a local businessman, Metcalf was admitted into the witness protection program, and relocated to Anglesey. The fact no one saw fit to inform the local constabulary about this is testament to the sorry state of the U.K. Protected Person's Service."

Manx sat on the edge of his desk, and continued, "As stipulated in the Serious and Organised Crime Act, Metcalf was given a new life, in exchange for critical information and evidence against a suspected gangster he was affiliated with, one Charles Blackwell."

Manx clicked to the next slide. "Yesterday, PC Morris found this photograph in the *Manchester Evening News* archives. Morris, give them the print out. You can read the gory details later."

Morris passed the pages to the other officers.

"Centre frame, we have Dr. Patrick Metcalf, to his right, Charles Blackwell, behind them, a brand spanking new Drug Rehabilitation Clinic, funded and built by Blackwell's construction company, BK Holdings."

The next slide: a mug shot of Blackwell.

"The GMP Serious Crime Squad had long suspected Blackwell of heading a crime ring, operating under the name Scuttler 2000. A name inspired, so I'm told, by Manchester's original street gang from the eighteen-hundreds, The Scuttlers."

Manx clicked to another mug shot. "Blackwell's laundry list of criminal activities include: Class A drug trafficking, illegal gambling establishments, racketeering, money laundering, and a whole litany of other human misery you'll find in the print out. Blackwell, probably vying for legitimacy as a local businessman of the year, enlisted the support of Dr. Patrick Metcalf, an outspoken and passionate voice against the government's drug policies, and offered to fund a series of Drug Clinics, over which Metcalf had full autonomy."

Manx clicked to a photograph of Metcalf in one of the clinics, posing with a group of patients and aides.

"A couple of years into this business arrangement, Metcalf discovers Blackwell is using the clinics as a shopping mall for the junkies in the immediate area. His crews begin selling anything they can, within a few streets of the clinics. The phrase, 'shooting fish in a barrel' comes to mind. Eventually, with pressure from our colleagues in the GMP, Metcalf agrees to turn Queen's evidence.

Until twelve months ago, Charles Blackwell was still in the dark as to who turned him in. That's when our story gets interesting."

Manx clicked a video file taken from a CCTV camera. "This footage was taken just over a year ago. A man is seen visiting Blackwell in prison."

Manx froze the frame on the image of a hooded man entering the prison gates. "Here he is again, in the waiting area, being very careful to make sure he's not recognised."

"They have any idea who it is, boss?" Nader asked.

"Not a clue. But, fast forward a couple of months, and Charles Blackwell is found dead in his cell, overdosed on crack cocaine. Officially, it's recorded as a suicide. The GMP had their doubts, especially because the month before, Blackwell had made a special request to speak to someone in the serious crime division, and offered them information, hoping to get his sentence reduced. What that information was, we'll never know."

"So, did Blackwell find out Metcalf's new identity and where he was living?" Morris asked.

"Whoever gave that information to Blackwell had to have gained access to the secure files in the Witness Protection Database—no easy task," Manx said. "And, to add another level of complexity to this mystery, the Chief Superintendent at the time relayed a vital piece of information, which was kept from the Press. Before his arrest, Blackwell was suspected of a series of murders in Manchester's Northern Quarter, mostly scummy low-life scallies, no one but their mothers would miss. They were all murdered, then showcased. A grotesque, bloody carnival, I believe is how they colourfully put it."

Manx brought up a montage of still images of the men. There was a collective groan from the team, all except Morris, who was studying each face carefully. "All five bodies were put on show, each one of them with a bodily item in their mouths, or an object personal to each of the victims. Each of these men had a connection to Blackwell. Each murder was a warning to the next victim."

Priddle's arm shot up. "We might have one of them copycat killers, sir?"

Nader chuckled. "See that on *CSI:* bloody *Miami*, did you, Priddle?"

"I don't think he's killing to emulate; he's killing for revenge," Manx explained. "We need to focus on two, clear objectives. Finding out who murdered Stokes and Vaughn, and who leaked the witness protection records to begin with. My guess? We're looking for two different people, which is why I'm having all the case files flown down from Manchester. They'll be here by tomorrow morning. Call your wives, girlfriends, dogs, cats, whoever, and tell them you're going to be missing-in-action for a few days."

Chapter 48

As he walked into the station reception later that afternoon, Manx heard a familiar voice shouting his name.

"Said his name was Manx. Lady Muck's son. Drives a posh motor. Don't tell me he's not here, or I'll go to the papers! Tell 'em everything."

Bette Bowen was standing her ground, stabbing her finger at Mickey Thomas, who had reluctantly emerged from behind his desk in an attempt to calm her down. It wasn't working. Bette's anger was bouncing off the station walls like a squash ball. She spotted Manx. "That's him! Bastard!" A shower of spittle sprayed from her mouth, and onto her quilted rain-jacket. "Nearly killed my boy, he did. You should lock him up, chuck away the fucking key." She waved her hands towards Manx, as if she was throwing a Gypsy curse.

"What's this about, Mrs. Bowen?" Manx asked.

"Don't fucking insult me, goo' boy," Bette said.

Manx saw a familiar look in her eye. It was a look he'd seen plenty of times before; the prelude to someone punching his lights out. Her fists were already clenched, as if in preparation for the deed, the crimson peaks of her knuckles breaking through her skin. She lunged with her right arm. Manx dodged the punch, feeling the gentlest of breezes, as it passed by his cheek. She was about to wind up another one, when Mickey Thomas stepped in, with a surprising balletic move, involving crossing in front of Ma Bowen, grabbing her wrist, then spinning her around so her arm was twisted upwards along her spine.

"Fuck! Police brutality, this is!" Bette struggled, but Mickey was strong, and kept one arm around her neck and wedged her elbow up her spine. It took Bette only a few moments, before realising she possessed another weapon. She stamped her heel into Mickey's left toe which was already home to a festering, weeping bunion.

"Shit!" Mick shouted. He immediately let go, and stumbled against the lip of the reception desk, hopping on his one good foot, as Bette broke free and lunged. This time, Manx was ready for her, and sidestepped the attack. She faltered and fell into the chest of DCI Canton, who made a speedy assessment of the situation, spun Bette Bowen around, pushed her to the ground, and cuffed her hands behind her back.

"Didn't think you still had it in you, Chief," Manx said.

"Mind telling me what all this fuss is about?" Canton asked, as he kept his palms pressed down on Bette's back.

"Fuss? Attempted murder, that's what it is, you fucking bastards." Bette was wheezing as she spoke, and sounded like a cheap extra in an action movie. Canton eased off her back, but kept his knees on her legs to stop her from kicking.

"Why don't you ask 'im over there, Lady fucking Manx's boy," she spat. "Came round my place to force my boy to confess. Bastard didn't get what he wanted, so he waits till dark to jump him. Nearly killed my boy. You identify him, Thomas, right now. That's the bastard right? That's him?"

In the commotion, no one had noticed the medicated presence of Thomas Bowen. He was sitting on the narrow wooden bench, his right arm in a sling, his face peppered with cuts, and his eyes swollen like over-ripe plums.

Sergeant Mal Nader walked in, curious as to the nature of the commotion. "Been in the wars, eh, Bowen? Who'd you piss off this time?"

Bette Bowen struggled, and turned on her side. "He didn't piss off nobody. We knows you've been watching him; we're not fucking stupid."

"Nobody said you were, Mrs. Bowen," Manx said in a composed, assured tone.

"You left my boy for dead. You're a disgrace, man. No better than animals, the lot of you!"

"When was this?" Manx asked.

"Sunday night. Like you don't fucking know."

"Pritchard and Davis were on shift, right, Nader?" Manx asked.

Nader shifted uncomfortably. "I gave them the night off," he explained. "I couldn't sleep, on account of my sciatica, so I thought I'd do something useful, if I'm awake."

Manx looked over at the Sergeant. "I never approved that."

"Didn't want to bother you, boss. The lads needed a break, you know."

"Not your call to make, Nader," Manx said.

"We'll deal with that later," Canton said, wiping the sweat from his brow.

Thomas Bowen remained quiet, as if he were observing the proceeding from afar.

"Well, what you going to do about it? Or is it all cops together, like bloody usual?" Bette said.

Canton eased up on her, and guided her to the seat next to her son. "Sit here. When you calm down, I'll take the cuffs off. No funny business, or I'll put you in the cell for a night. Understand?"

Bowen turned her head away.

"Mickey, keep an eye on her."

"Aye, boss," Mickey said, and looked warily over at Bette.

"Nader, Manx, my office," Canton said, turning towards the door.

***

"Not been overstepping the mark, have we, Manx?" Canton asked, as he trimmed a couple of errant leaves off a Bonsai tree.

"I interviewed Bowen a few days ago, Chief. He was in good shape when I left," Manx said.

Canton sat, and motioned for Manx and Nader to do the same. "Tricky situation here, boys," Canton began, as they sat across from the Chief. "There's a standard policy for this kind of thing, but I'm going to ignore that for now, and ask you again if you had anything to do with Bowen's injuries. Either of you?" Canton waved his finger back and forth between Manx and Nader. "I know things can sometimes get out of hand in the heat of the moment. I'm not without understanding when it comes to these things, but I need honest answers, no fuckery. Understand?"

Manx leant back on his chair. "I showed Bowen the photos I downloaded from his website. He admitted he and Vaughn were planning to sell some methadone, but the doc was murdered before they could get it off the ground. But, it doesn't add up. Vaughn had no prior, and his surgery and house were both clean, nothing more addictive than Panadol. It's all in HOLMES."

Canton turned his attention to the Sergeant. "And what about you, Nader? Why did you take over the shift that night? Wanted some quick justice, hoped no one would notice?"

Nader leant forward, and rested his elbows on the desk. "The little shit had it coming, but plenty people have got it in for Bowen. I'd have to join the back of the fucking queue and take a number." Nader laughed, an insignificant snort catching in the back of his throat.

"Glad you find it so amusing, Sergeant, maybe you'd like to take me through your movements pertaining to Bowen on the night in question?"

"You serious, like, sir?"

"Not as serious as I am, if I have to start the paperwork on this bloody mess and conduct an internal investigation," Canton said, pulling out a thick file from his desk drawer.

Nader coughed. "All right, but it's a bit private, like," he explained, and looked over at Manx.

"For God's sake, neither of us will be calling O.K. Magazine with a scoop on your personal life, Sergeant," Canton said.

Nader sniffed, straightened his posture, and talked in a volume just above a whisper. "Me and the missus, we've been having problems. Usual stuff, the job, money, wants to take a bloody three-week holiday in Mexico next year." Nader's shuffled his feet, and looked down at the floor as he spoke. "I hate fucking tacos."

Canton shook his head, and motioned for Nader to continue.

"Anyway, we had a massive blow-up that night, worse than usual. She chucks me out. So, I think to myself, if I'm going to spend the night in the car, I may as well be some bloody use, so I drive to Pentraeth, tell Pritchard and Davis I was taking over for the duration. I see Bowen leave the pub at about eleven, he goes to the chippy, orders cod and chips, eats them outside on the bench. About ten minutes later, he gets up, walks towards the farm. I reckon he's going home at that point, so I grabbed a blanket and waited to see if he came back out. I dozed off, woke up a few hours later, freezing me bollocks off. I drove back home at about two, slept on the sofa, left in the morning, before the missus woke up."

"And you saw no one else follow Bowen, or drive towards the farm?"

"I was dead asleep, Chief, sorry."

Canton hunched over his desk. "This is a kid-glove situation, lads. So far, I have one officer who was around Bowen the time he was jumped, and another that was questioning him at his home, a few days earlier. It doesn't look good. I doubt if Bowen will press charges, he's facing a few years as it is for assaulting a police officer, and breaking and entering. He's not going to take that chance."

Canton reached for the morning paper, and laid it out on the table. The headlines were bold and spoke a truth they all knew too well. "Anglesey Killer Still at Large: No Leads, Say Police."

"If Bette Bowen has it in mind to blow this up, she'll be on the phone with the *Post* before we have time to deny it. If someone makes enough noise, we know they'll print any damn thing, if it sells. Upshot, gents, we back off Bowen, it's not like he's going anywhere for a while."

Manx felt his neck hairs prick. "He's the best lead we've got, Chief. We can keep our distance, be more covert."

Canton shook his head. "We're not exactly MI5 trained around here, Manx. The family knows we're watching, we back off, starting now."

"Give me a couple more days. I think I can crack him," Manx urged.

Canton sighed, his chest expanding like a balloon. "Bowen is an invalid doped up on meds and God knows what else, whose mother is convinced one of the boys in blue, specifically you Manx, it seems, beat the living daylights out of her son. You've been trailing him for two weeks, and you haven't delivered any evidence to support your case."

"It's ongoing," Manx said, as optimistically as he could.

"Yes, ongoing, like my bloody lumbago. Bowen is out of bounds, understand?" Canton gestured for them both to leave.

Manx couldn't be sure, but he was almost convinced there was a faint trace of a smile on Nader's face, as he edged past him and into the corridor.

Manx splashed a palm full of cold water across his face, staring into the mirror. His face was red, blotchy, puffy—he should stop drinking, maybe that would help, or maybe he should drink more, and keep the illusion going. The toilet door swung open behind him. Nader walked in, and stood against a urinal.

"Ah! Second best use for your cock," he said, over the cascading torrent of urine. He had his right arm above his head, resting on the wall and his forehead set against his forearm. Manx remembered the posture from the carnies at the fairground: sound insurance, in case someone had it in mind to walk up behind you, smash your forehead against the wall, and steal whatever cash or fags you had stuffed in your back pockets. Manx wiped his hands on the paper towel, and threw it into the bin.

Nader walked over and washed his hands. Manx noticed his knuckles were scraped, raw, where the skin had been stripped from the bone.

"Looks nasty," Manx said.

Nader looked into the mirror at Manx, or was it through him? Manx couldn't be sure.

"Replaced the gearbox on the Volvo last week, fiddly fucking job," Nader said, dabbing at his knuckles with the towels. Small dots of blood spread like ink blots on the surface.

"Didn't know you were a mechanic," Manx said.

"Learnt in the Army. A trade for life," Nader explained.

Manx watched him closely for any sign of wavering—a twitch or an eye movement, but there was nothing. He tried a different tactic, leant back on the sink, and folded his arms.

"You know, I used to have this detective in my division, down south, fancied himself a real vigilante type. Thought he was Charles Bronson, but without the charm or a decent script."

Nader wiped his hand across his face, and patted his thinning hairline.

"Now, there's two ways to deal with a man like that. You can try and channel his energies to more positive outcome, keep him on the streets but keep him in check. Alternatively, you can put him behind a desk until he retires, or he decides to hand in his notice because the tedium's killing him, whichever comes first."

Nader hitched up his belt, and checked his fly.

"The problem with this particular officer was neither of those two options appealed to him. So, he decided to make up his own; not the best life choice, let's say. That officer is now serving his fifth year in Durham Prison. He's a broken man, they tell me. I can't imagine what it must be like to be a former copper doing time, must be like a walking death sentence."

Nader chuckled. Manx sensed a twinge of nervousness in the laugh. "A warning, is it?"

"Just a cautionary tale," Manx said. "If we're not upholding the law, Nader, everything we do goes to shit."

Nader leant his hands on the sink, and looked at Manx through the reflection in the mirror. "Assuming the whole fucking thing hasn't gone to shit already."

Manx leant closer into Nader. "Just in case I was a little too subtle for you, Sergeant, if I find out you had any part in Bowen's condition, I will consider it my personal pilgrimage to crucify you *and* that police pension you're holding out for."

Manx was still staring at his own reflection, as he felt the sharp gust of a draft from the door Nader had just slammed behind him.

Chapter 49

The plastic figurine on Mandy's dashboard sang, as Thomas Bowen looked across to the flickering lights on the opposite side of the bay. They reminded him of the Christmas tree lights his dad would bring home around this time of year. Fairy lights, isn't that what they called them?

Fell off the back of a lorry, Da? He'd ask.

Ask no questions, get no beating, was the standard reply.

He liked it here, Red Wharf Bay. He could found peace at the harbour, watching the steady swell of the sea, away from Ma Bowen scolding him for something he'd done, or hadn't done; it was usually the latter.

She was like a fucking terrier, all that bloody yapping. *Didn't she have an off-button? Yeah, that's what he needed, a "shut-the-fuck-up" button.* She was like a TV on full volume—the CNN of complaining, the worldwide leader in fucking nagging—that was his ma. He laughed to himself at the analogy. *Fuck her, he'd get his own place soon enough. And why did she drag him down to the cop shop like that?* If he'd had the strength, he would have told her to fuck off. That's the last place he wanted to be, in the pigpen. He thought about Manx, and what he'd said in the caravan. The long streak of piss was right. He was twenty-eight years old, and had done nothing with his life—hadn't even travelled any further than a day trip to Chester Zoo. A man needed a goal in life. Yeah, he'd make that his goal. Move out, get his own place, travel more. *A life-plan, isn't that what those self-help books called it?*

He listened to the wind buffering through the rigging of the boats. The sound reminded him of his childhood, falling asleep to the sound of boats jangling in a harbour. *Where was that again?* A family holiday, Tenby probably. They holidayed there every year since he could remember, at least until the one year when his Da had said unless he could pay for half the rent on the static caravan, he should stay the fuck at home and leave him and his Ma in peace for a week. If he remembered correctly, he was about eleven. Next to him, in the driver's seat, Mandy lit her third cigarette that night.

"Mandy fag," Bowen said, and snorted a self-satisfied laugh.

Mandy turned to look at him. "Fuck you, Tommo," she said, and blew a thin line of smoke upwards, so it clouded under the sunroof.

"Open the bloody window, at least," Bowen said.

Mandy complied. A rush of cold air gusted through the Fiesta.

"You could be nicer to me, Tommo. Is that too much to ask?"

Bowen looked at her. Yeah, he could be nicer. He could be a lot of fucking things, but tonight he didn't feel like being nice, didn't even want her here, but he had no choice; in his condition, he couldn't drive. The drugs weren't helping either. Fucking Tramadol—it was like taking Smarties. He could swallow them by the handful, and everything still hurt like hell.

"I came as soon as I heard, didn't your mother tell you?"

"Yeah, she mentioned it," Bowen said.

He glanced at Mandy. The harsh, light from inside the car was unforgiving. She looked her age; he noticed the deep wrinkles around her mouth and the spread of crow's feet around her eyes. *Laughter lines they called them, right? Nothing much to fucking laugh about*, he thought, as he looked Mandy over, as if for the first time. She hadn't even bothered to doll herself up. No makeup, no lipstick, her jacket zipped up to her neck, and pressing her tits flat against her chest. She looked like any other older woman, pushing a trolley around Tesco.

"I care about you, Tommo." She placed her hands on his cheek. Bowen flinched. "Sorry, luv. Still hurt, does it? Should I be gentler? Like this?"

Mandy took her fingers, and traced a line up and down Bowen's thigh. "I'm good to you, right, Tommo?" She was whispering in his ear, her tongue flicking around his neck, her teeth tugging tenderly at his lobes. He wanted her to stop. He didn't want her to stop. Wanted her to stop.

"No one else looks after you, like I do."

He felt her hands reach across his chest, down to his waist, tugging at his belt buckle. His cock responded, stirring and unwinding in his boxers. Her fingers coiled around his shaft. He leant back into the car seat.

"That's it, Tommo, relax," Mandy said, placing her cigarette on the dashboard, as Spanish Elvis's performance came to an end.

"Can't fucking relax, hurts like fuck," Bowen said, trying to find a more comfortable, submissive position to let Mandy finish what she'd started.

"Have you been taking the painkillers?"

"Waste of fucking spit," Bowen said.

Mandy reached for her handbag on the backseat, and pulled out a small vial and a half-bottle of Bells Whisky. "Makes everything better," Mandy said, shaking a handful of pills into her palm. "I'll take some, too. Makes it all go away, all the pain. Vicodin," she explained. "The Mexican happy pill, cheaper than booze over there. Start with three or four, see where that takes you."

Bowen nodded. A few hours of escape would be good, then that would be his last hit. After this, he'd get his shit together.

"Stick your tongue out." Mandy positioned three pills on Bowen's tongue, as if she were ministering a communion wafer. Bowen swallowed, took a swig of Scotch, and watched as Mandy did the same.

"He's a fucking psycho, or whatever they call 'em these days," Bowen said, relaxing back into the seat.

Mandy placed her hands on her knees, and talked to her reflection in the windscreen. "No, you're wrong," she said. "He only hurts those who hurt him. He likes you, he told me himself, he needs you."

Bowen examined the cuts on his hands. "Don't feel like it."

"Poor Tommo," Mandy said, stroking his forehead with the back of her hand. "We'll drive back to the flat afterwards, get some sleep. I'll make you breakfast, anything you want."

"Will he be there?"

"No, love, he's in Liverpool, on a business trip."

"Does he know about us?"

"He knows what he needs to know," Mandy said, reaching over to stroke Bowen's thigh.

"Yeah? And when he finds out, what then? He'll do worse than this."

"Oh, luv, forget about him. It's just you and me now."

"Things were all right, before he came," Bowen said. "You and me, we were doing all right, then he comes, and puts his nose in. I did everything he asked, everything. Nearly got myself arrested, then, he does this to me. What was it, a warning, like? To stay away from you?"

"He wouldn't..." Mandy began

"Aye, so you keep saying, but it don't make me feel any better. I wish he hadn't fucking come. If I'd known what he was going to do to Vaughn..." Bowen said, his thoughts trailing off.

"He had his reasons; punish those who deserve it, an eye for an eye."

"And what about me? I could end up the same."

"I wouldn't let him, Tommo, you know that. He'll be gone soon, and it'll be just you and me. We'll go away, somewhere, for good. Leave this place."

Bowen felt himself softening—maybe it was the drugs, or Mandy's words. "Yeah," he said. "Where to?"

"Anywhere you like."

"Close to the sea, has to be close to the sea," Bowen said.

The numbing effect of Mandy's painkillers was now flowing easily through his veins. He was sure Spanish Elvis was winking at him, as he closed his eyes. He felt himself sink slowly and deeply through the fabric of the car seat, melting into stone floor of the harbour, before yielding to the soft, embrace of the sand and silt below.

Chapter 50

"Does anyone have some good news to share this morning?" Manx asked, walking into the incident room the following day. "Anyone?"

Morris raised her hand. "The logs came back from the shipping companies," she said, and handed Manx a sheet of paper. "Twelve vessels passed north east of the island around the time we think the bloke fell in. Could be any of them. If we knew what day..."

"We don't," Manx interrupted, and cast a careful eye over the list. Nothing jumped out. They were just a list of ship names, most of them foreign, registered in Europe and North Africa. "One more for the gallery, then, Morris." He pinned the paper to the board. "So, what the fuck are we missing?" he asked.

The more he looked over photograph and notes, the less they seemed to make sense. It was as if they were falling further from his understanding the closer he examined them. He looked back and forth at the photos of Stokes and Vaughn. They still hadn't made the connection between them. Maybe they had a partnership that went south. *But, where did Dick fit in?* He was a distant relation to Bowen, with money trouble. Maybe he'd loaned them his boat. The lad at the hospital had to be a part of the puzzle, too; maybe a piece that had been discarded along the way. Manx removed the list of ship names from the board, and handed it to Morris.

"Morris, humour me for a moment, and read these out, aloud."

"Sir?"

"The names, just say them, slowly, out loud."

Morris shrugged her shoulders, and began. Manx concentrated on the photograph of the lad, as Morris read out the list. Nothing clicked.

"Again," Manx said.

Three quarters of the way through the fourth reading, he stopped her "Go back, read that one again."

"*Jutranja Zvezda*?" Morris stumbled over the pronunciation. "Not sure if I'm pronouncing it right."

"One more time, Morris."

She repeated the name.

"Fuck! That's what he was trying to tell us. It's the name of the bloody ship."

He grabbed the paper from Morris, and typed *Jutranja Zvezda*, then 'translation' into the Google search bar.

"That's it. That's fucking it!" he said, grabbing his jacket. "The Morning Star. Follow the Morning Star! Who's on-duty at the hospital?"

"Stan Reese, I think," Morris said.

"Radio him. Tell him we're coming over."

"On it, sir."

"Nader, you're driving, the rest of you, work the phones. Call every available number for this Global Oceans Group shipping outfit. Find out where the *Jutranja Zvezda* is headed, what kind of ship it is, who's the captain, and get every crew name from the first mate down to the cook's assistant. By the time I come back, I want the results on my desk nicely printed on A4, with a fucking pink bow wrapped around it."

Chapter 51

Outside ICU Room 304, P.C. Stanley Reese slouched in his seat, rubbed his hands over his thick, red beard, and checked his watch; the third time in twenty minutes. It was eleven-thirty am; another two hours before his shift relief came on-duty. The night before had been quiet and uneventful. A critical emergency or even a chat with a passing cleaner who could speak English would have been a welcome distraction, but instead, he had to be content with his own company, and the silent witness in the room behind him.

He slapped his fleshy cheeks with a light pat to keep awake. It wasn't working. His head drooped to one side, and a light snore fluttered from his nostrils. As the doctor and two nurses walked out of the ICU and directly past him, he stirred momentarily, but quickly dozed off again, oblivious to the man in a white lab coat walking purposefully towards him. He may have stirred slightly, as the pinprick entered his neck, but by then, it was too late. He fell the floor. The man carefully stepped around him, and was about to draw the syringe from Reese's neck when he heard a crackling sound beneath the chair, and a woman's voice breaking up over the static. He squatted, smiled at his good luck, and clicked the button off. Silence. *Good, now he could finish it. No witnesses. Was it that difficult to follow instructions?*

***

Manx rapped his fingers impatiently on the dashboard of the car. "Where the hell is Reese?"

"He's not answering, sir." Morris explained from the backseat, and tried slapping the police radio into cooperating.

"I'm well aware of that. Why isn't he answering is the fucking question."

"Um. I'll keep trying," Morris grumbled.

She continued to fumble with the radio. Nothing but the grinding, emptiness of static came back.

"Fuck! Reese better be taking a piss break," Manx said, looking anxiously out at the fast-moving waters of the strait, as they crossed the bridge to the mainland.

Chapter 52

Over the weeks, or was it months, their shapes and voices had become as familiar to him as family. The tall, curt man, who he surmised was his doctor; the attending nurse, an older, stout woman with a resolute and efficient manner about her; and the younger nurse, hesitant in her motions, as she tucked in the sheets or bathed him. She had a light, friendly voice, though it sounded distant, as if she were speaking to him from underwater.

Blurred, inconsistent figures were all he could discern of these people, as they buzzed at his bedside, and busied themselves with the machines beeping around him like living creatures. He was cold, always so cold. He was inside his body, somewhere, but there was no sensation of skin and muscle attached to his bone, or any sense of his limbs pressing into the mattress. At the beginning, he had panicked, wanted to scream, grab them by the throats, and let them know he was in here, but that had passed now. A gradual peace had gathered within him, an acceptance he would be free of this, eventually. *How else was he to survive this?*

After a few minutes, the figures left, followed by the soft swoosh of the door, and the dimming of the lights. Minutes later, an unfamiliar shape materialised in the doorway. The figure entered, paused for the door to close, then stood motionless at the foot of his bed, as if waiting to be introduced. He felt a bolt of panic. The figure walked closer, silent and sure in its movements.

***

Manx and the team charged into the hospital reception area and looked around; it was just the usual business of hospital waiting rooms, administering to the sick and those merely seeking attention.

"You two go and check with the receptionist on anyone suspicious entering the hospital," Manx said, "Keep trying Reese, and meet me at the ICU." He ran over to the lifts, pressed the call button, waited for a few seconds, before opting for the stairs.

A couple of years ago, he would have sprinted up them, without a second thought. But, now, at the second floor, it felt as if a long, serrated blade were drawing itself across his chest, and there were still three more floors still to climb—the thought made him dizzy. He stumbled and reached for the railing. His palm, sweaty and warm, slipped from the cold steel. He fell, his knees slapping hard against the sharp edge of the steps. He felt the anxious twitching of his muscles, and vomited a clear, thin liquid. He wiped the sleeve of his jacket across his mouth, and looked up. The stairwell revolved around him, as if he was looking at it through a monochrome kaleidoscope. He couldn't stay here; he had to keep moving, keep climbing.

***

He heard the ripping of the pads, but felt no sensation as the fingers peeled them from his chest, and placed them carefully to the side of the bed. The machines beeped urgently. The fingers then moved quickly and deliberately, upwards, towards his face. The figure was leaning over him, close enough he could smell its breath. He saw, from the corner of his eye, the fingers lift again, hold steady in place, then stroke his cheek, though he couldn't sense the touch; it was merely the memory of the sensation. A voice cut through the room, both distant yet terrifyingly close.

"Not long now," it whispered. "Not long.

***

Manx stumbled through the stairwell door, and onto the fifth floor. He rested for a moment and caught his breath, before scurrying towards the main corridor. The pain in his knees threw him off balance. By the time he noticed the hospital porter wheeling the empty gurney, it was too late. One of the metal side-barriers struck Manx directly in the lower abdomen, temporarily knocking whatever wind he had left out of him. He held onto the gurney, and grasped at his stomach. The porter mumbled half an apology, and scuttled past. Manx ran.

The four people inside the room turned at once to look at the Inspector. He was leaning against the doorway, breathing heavily. A wild glare clouded his eyes. It took his brain about a few moments to register the scene. The patient was wide-awake, alive, and conversing with a doctor and two nurses standing at the foot of her bed. Manx tried to speak, but it felt as if someone was taking a belt-sander to his larynx. He tried again.

"The patient…" He began and stopped to catch his breath. "Where is he? Police…" Manx didn't even know if he was making sense, but one of the nurses seemed to have understood.

"Oh him. We moved 'im yesterday. Private ward, third floor ICU."

***

His final thoughts in this lifetime were banal, everyday thoughts. His wife, his parents, his hometown; a dog he once owned; an old motorbike he once restored but never rode. A shadow passed over his face, then a familiar smell; his own essence, urging itself upon him. The hospital pillow which, seconds before, had been his support, would now become the soft machine of his death. Blackness came rapidly, followed by a flash of panic, then supplication, the definitive letting go. The concluding movements of the fingers were swift and precise. The tips brushed his eyelids gently, drawing down the shutters for one, final time.

***

Manx almost body-slammed the emergency medical team, as he stumbled into the room. They immediately got to work. A well-oiled, well-practiced machine, barking orders back and forth, and frantically reconnecting cables, pads and switches. It was too late; deep in his gut, Manx knew it. This was nothing but a resuscitation sideshow that had to go on. He slowly resigned his way out of the room to the chair outside. Reese, who had been propped up against the wall, was slowly regaining consciousness, a duty nurse attending to his vitals. Nader and Morris ran down the corridor.

"Jesus, you look like shit. No offence, boss," Nader said, looking over at the defeated figure of his inspector, his face beet-red and the thick, blue veins on his temple bulging.

"Maybe they'll be lucky," Morris offered, craning her neck. "They can work miracles these days," she added, inching her way into the room for a better view of the proceedings.

Manx said nothing; there was nothing more to say. He'd come so close. If he'd figured it out five minutes earlier, he'd have caught him. *Five, fucking, minutes.* He sighed deeply, rubbed his forehead. As he sat back in the chair, his body began to surrender, his adrenaline stores reverting back to empty. He put his hands between his knees to stop the walls folding in, and noticed something familiar underneath the chair. He reached down, and pulled out the police radio. It felt heavy and cumbersome in his hands. He looked at the useless metal brick, and then threw it down the corridor. It bounced several times over the floor, splintering into a heap of wires and circuit boards. The main casing of the radio stopped short at the end of the corridor, and caught on the sleeve of a discarded lab coat.

The next few minutes were a blur. Manx caught his second or third wind of the day, and made a run for the emergency stairwell. He pounded down the steps. At the first floor, he peered through the small rectangular window looking out to the reception area. *If he wanted a quick getaway, where would he go?* The front entrance was too risky. He looked around for a clue. Another sign caught his attention. He picked up his pace, and ran.

The force of wind from outside worked against him, as pushed hard on the heavy metal door to the Ambulance Bay. He heard the screech of tires spinning against tarmac, and thrust harder. He squeezed his body through the narrow opening. The cold air hit him like a sucker punch. He ran to the ramp leading to the parking bay, and looked around—nothing but an empty space with large "emergency vehicles only" lettering painted onto the floor. The unmistakable smell of recently burned rubber and diesel fumes still lingered. To his left, he heard a sound—a loud groan of someone in pain. He ran towards the paramedic; the man was alive, but a long syringe protruded from his jugular vein.

At that moment, Manx's world began to spin. He felt his legs buckle. He reached for the lip of a large oxygen tank to steady himself. There was a hollow grinding of metal against concrete, as the tank quivered in place before it followed Manx's exact, downward trajectory. He yelled out in pain, as one hundred and sixty pounds of air and metal fell on his chest. A wave of nausea passed through him, then a thick, liquid blackness crept over him; and above, the promise of blue, as always, just out of reach.

Chapter 53

Manx sat up and reached for the remote control. The TV piqued to life. He scanned the channels and settled his attention on the local news.

"And now, a special report on a troubling new drug that's making waves on a familiar North Wales beauty spot. BBC Cymru's Peter Evelyn has more on the story," the anchor announced, and cut to a video report from a field outside Holyhead's South Stack Lighthouse. Peter Evelyn walked into frame in a dramatic fashion, his fingers pressed together, as if in prayer.

"They call it Anglesey Blue, a small, potent pill that's selling for mere pounds a hit. Little is known about how these blue pills came onto the island, but doctors and law-enforcement have confirmed they do contain a particularly concentrated form of methadone, a dose far more potent than that available to addicts, and far more addictive, and, some would say, a lot deadlier. Although no deaths have been directly connected to Anglesey Blue, experts say the victims have so far been lucky, and it's just a matter of time. And, with two recent murders on the island, the public is asking if these incidents are connected to the drug, and why, after several weeks, has the North Wales Constabulary made so little headway in solving the cases?"

He was about to switch channels, when Evelyn segued into a sit-down interview with DCI Ellis Canton. *Shit*, Manx thought, it must have been recorded just hours ago. "Let me begin by stating no firm connection has been made between the recent murders and what the media is calling Anglesey Blue," Canton said.

"But, you have to admit, it's suspicious," Peter Evelyn prodded. "Drugs and murder often go hand-in-hand."

"Suspicion, maybe, but no evidence. We solve cases on evidence, not media speculation."

"And Anglesey Blue, as it's being called. How is it being brought to the island, distributed? Are you getting any closer to an arrest? Or should the public still be worried their children might be exposed to this?"

Canton shuffled uncomfortably; Manx felt a pang of sympathy for the Chief. Canton would never have purposely put himself in the firing line; he must have been pressured. Manx didn't hear Canton's reply. His Chief was there in person, standing at the doorway of the room, holding a well-leafed copy of *Cosmopolitan Magazine* in his hand.

"Think they got my good side?" Canton asked, as he walked over.

"You have one?" Manx said.

"Didn't knock the prick-ness out of you, more's the pity," Canton said, settling into the chair next to the bed. "What do you make of this Anglesey Blue bullshit?"

"It's all connected, has to be. Two murders, then the Island's suddenly flooded with it."

"You think the murderer and the supplier are one and the same?"

"I do now."

"HQ is of the same mind. They're very results oriented, these days, like cases shut down quickly, good PR," Canton said.

"And this is good PR?" Manx said, gesturing towards Peter Evelyn, as he sat on the edge of his interview chair, and pointed at an increasingly uncomfortable and sweating Canton. "Any junkie, or impressionable kid with a mind for experimentation, is going straight out after this prick's finished his report, looking for a hit. We could have contained it, but that train's already left the fucking station."

"Maybe, but it's beyond our control. Public Relations are driving the media strategy; it's all about how we're perceived by the public, Manx. In the meantime, let's concentrate on solving the case."

Manx was groggy, and short-tempered from a heavy night's sleep and a cocktail of painkillers and sleeping pills. "I assume he wasn't apprehended, then?" he asked, shuffling under his bedclothes.

"The ambulance was dumped in a ditch, just outside Caernarvon."

Manx groaned, as he attempted to elevate his body to a sitting position. Every bone and muscle felt like it had been beaten with a large rock.

"I'll give you a hand." Canton leant over, and pressed the bed-raiser.

"Could have done that myself," Manx said, shifting to a position which hurt the least.

"We've put security outside your room, just a formality," Canton said.

"Not Reese, is it?"

"He's recovered. But, he'll be taking over Mickey's reception duties for the foreseeable future. Not much he can fuck up there."

Manx doubted the accuracy of Canton's remark, but let it go anyway. "The paramedic?"

"Drugged, nasty cut to the head, but he'll live."

"Morris and Nader?"

"They located that ship, the *Morning Star*, off the west coast of Spain, Carballo, I think. Should be docking in Lisbon in about three days, depending on the weather."

Manx saw a glimmer of hope in what had been a few hours of bleak, unrelenting darkness. "We should fly out there. Land someone on the ship, question the crew, someone must know something."

"Tell you what, I'll call the Royal Air Force while I'm at it, shall I? The department's rolling in cash these days, shouldn't be a problem to scramble the jets on your behest."

Manx was about to protest.

"Save it. We've already alerted the local authorities to put the screws on the captain after he docks. No jollies to the Algarve for you, just yet."

Manx shifted his position. "I should get back to work," he said, and attempted to swing his legs from the bed. They felt like lead weights.

"Think again, boyo," Canton said. "Minimum of two days' bed rest according to Nurse Ratched, and she doesn't look like the negotiating type." Canton nodded towards the solid figure of the senior nurse at the window. She glowered, and tapped her wristwatch. "A few days' rest will put things into perspective, actually help you see the forest, not just the trees."

Manx relaxed. Maybe Canton was right. His body didn't seem to be co-operating, anyway. He'd give it a few hours, discharge himself, and head back to the station later.

Canton slapped his thighs, and made a gesture to leave. "Right! As you haven't quite shifted off this mortal coil just yet, I need to get back. Paperwork up the yin-yang," he said, and slid the magazine across the sheets. "Fascinating article on how to make your man happy in bed," he said. "Frankly, I expected a bit less on the mechanics and more on the practicalities; who gets which side, maybe some breakfast recipes, that kind of thing. Goes to show you what this old fart knows, eh?"

"I'll be sure to read it," Manx said.

The nurse opened the door, just as Canton left the room. She said something to him, and wagged her finger. Canton scooted out of her way sheepishly. Manx felt a sudden and overwhelming sense of weariness; maybe it was the drugs, or maybe he really was that tired. He held the magazine; it felt heavy, like an old family bible. He briefly scanned over the front cover, but the print was blurring in and out of focus, as he read. He closed his eyes, just for a second.

His sleep was deep and satisfying, and he dreamt of nothing. It was as if his brain needed to re-boot itself, switch into a state of hibernation to prepare for whatever was coming next.

PART TWO
The Gathering Storm

Chapter 1

As Ryan Adams poured out the debris of his broken heart, Manx finished off another glass of Springbank, and hoisted the two boxes of evidence Morris had dropped off earlier onto his kitchen table. Twenty-four hours in a hospital bed had been all he could take; he had discharged himself the following day. Canton was adamant he should stay at home, but had offered no resistance when Manx insisted on sifting through the GMP files in the relative comfort of his kitchen. Manx read carefully through the witness statements and court records, focussing on Dr. Patrick Metcalf's sworn testimony, his name heavily redacted throughout the records. The GMP was nothing if not thorough.

Several hours later, after Ryan Adams had concluded "Love is Hell," then come full circle to affirm his alternative country roots with "Dirty Rain," Manx's own needle had barely shifted. There was nothing in Metcalf's testimony that helped him. The papers were mostly from 1996, and included long transcripts of recorded conversations, confidential witness statements, and notes taken at secret meetings in shadowy car parks in the Greater Manchester area, all diligently recorded and catalogued, though of little value to Manx.

"Three Lions" was the soundtrack to the summer of '96, if Manx remembered correctly—a jingoistic slice of pop to bolster national pride ahead of the European Football Championships. He was living in London, scrapping his way through the ranks of the Met. That summer, the city was humming with anticipation and an unfamiliar chord of optimism, which could have been attributed to England's first round victory in the European

Championships, or the early signs the Conservative party was finally losing its grip on power. He'd be hard pressed to remember who lifted the cup that year—however, he was sure it wasn't England. Optimism, when it came to the English football team, was like the air inside a balloon; sooner or later, it would start to leak, slowly, until it was thoroughly deflated. Manx tried to recall the trial, and subsequent sentencing, of Charles Blackwell. He had some vague recollection, but this had happened in Manchester, before the ubiquity of the internet and twenty-four-hour news. There was little attention paid to matters beyond the Met's jurisdiction, in those days, unless it directly affected a case they were investigating.

He dumped the stacks of paper back into the box, and took out a thick manila envelope. He scattered the contents across the breakfast bar—two dozen black and white surveillance photographs of Blackwell, taken with a long lens, spilled out. The photographs were unremarkable, and taken at face value, they chronicled the banality of daily life. Blackwell entering and exiting his car, eating lunch, meeting other businessmen, buying coffee, opening his front door. One photograph, though, caught his attention. It probably wouldn't have struck the investigating team, at the time, but nearly twenty years later, it triggered a thought. There were several photographs of Blackwell taken on the weekends, according to the date stamp. He was accompanied by a young boy, no more than twelve, Manx imagined. The boy's face had been blacked out, as if with a marker pen; this wasn't unusual; the boy was a minor, and the jury wouldn't have been permitted to see his face. *But, what about today?* The boy would be at least thirty by now.

What if, before he was killed, Blackwell had informed someone else, someone close, that Metcalf was the snitch? It would have to be someone who was both willing and capable of carrying out Blackwell's instructions from beyond the prison gates, or, as it had turned out, from beyond the grave.

An old saying came to him, as he slipped the photographs back into the envelope, the apple doesn't fall far from the tree. *Maybe that was especially true of the rotten ones*, Manx thought, before logging onto the Virgin Trains website, and booking himself a day return to Manchester Piccadilly Station.

Chapter 2

Retired Chief Superintendent Margaret Lockwood's dining room had been converted into a temporary campaign headquarters. A baize throw, resembling a cast-off from a snooker hall, had been pitched over the mahogany table and three easels, each cradling a glossy poster of now Councillor Lockwood, were positioned randomly throughout the room.

A new hope for Manchester- one headline proclaimed.

The Lord Mayor Manchester Deserves- read another.

A career civil servant, not a career politician- stated the third.

The Councillor's face was stern, yet compassionate, her head slightly tilted towards the lens to give the impression of casual authority, and her arms folder under her chest in what Manx understood to be a 'power pose.'

"Which one?" Margaret Lockwood asked, striding into the room. She gestured with wide, expansive arms towards the poster mock-ups. To her immediate right, a young, pixie-haired girl babbled into her mobile, while simultaneously harvesting random tufts of lint from Margaret's jacket, much like a young monkey preening its elder.

Manx shrugged, not having spotted any discernible difference between any of them, other than the taglines.

"Typical man," Margaret said. "No useful opinion on anything that matters." She gestured towards the poster in the far-right corner. "I like this one, but it looks like I'm shoving my tits up to my chin." She folded her arms, and pushed them up until her bosom rested, plump and comfortable, on her forearms, to emulate the pose.

The pixie-haired girl, impounding her mobile for the moment in the crook of her armpit, walked over to the poster. "We could go closer," she said. "Make it a head and shoulder shot, just above the bust. That should work." She illustrated her point by tracing a square across Margaret's face with her hand.

Margaret scraped her bottom lip with her teeth. "Maybe," she said. "Too bloody busty, that's my problem. My mother was the same. Blousy, they used to call them back in the day. Try it, Jilly. More close up, less tit."

Jilly nodded, thumbed a note in her phone.

"I have ten minutes," Margaret said, turning her attention back to the inspector. "Photo op at the Town Hall in a half hour." She sat across from Manx, picked up one of the brochures left for her approval, and flipped through it, waiting for Manx to speak.

"Charles Blackwell," Manx said. "You were head of the Serious Crime Division at the time of his arrest."

"Career highlight," Margaret said, and then, as if she'd just remembered something important, gestured at the pixie-haired girl. "Jilly, make sure we're on point on this story. I'm not letting the Press own the conversation. Stress the outstanding work the team did on the case. Give them some sound bites to chew on— the streets of Manchester are now safer, we stopped the escalation of serious crime, the usual bollocks they like to print. But, don't milk it. I don't want it to look like I'm relying on past victories."

Jilly nodded, and thumbed furiously at her phone.

"I told you everything I remembered about the case, Inspector. I haven't dug up any fresh evidence in the past week, if that's why you're here."

"I wanted to talk to you about Blackwell's son. He was around twelve years old at the time of his father's arrest."

"Protected minor. We couldn't put him on the stand, even if we wanted to. Same with the wife, of course. Though we suspected she was up to her neck in her husband's business, we could never prove it."

"Understand," Manx nodded. "I'd just like you to confirm this was his son. Callum Charles Blackwell, born September 13th, 1984?"

Margaret glanced over the copy of the birth certificate, then handed it back. "Cal, I think they called him. Sweet boy, if I remember. You'd like to think the kids won't be affected when tragedies like that happen, but, if wishes were horses, beggars would ride, isn't that what they say?" Margaret pushed one of the brochures across the table. "It's why I'm doing all this, providing an alternative to our disaffected youth."

"Sounds like a campaign pitch," Manx said.

Margaret sat back, placed her hands flat on the green baize. "It all begins with responsible parenting. After that, it's my personal opinion society has a moral obligation to provide support structure for young people. All this "enterprise culture" bollocks they keep banging on about these days. It's got every scally and toe rag thinking they're the next Steve bloody Jobs. Where's the sense in that? I blame the internet, myself, but bugger all we can do about that now, is there? Kids need rules and structure, not a free market economy."

"Seems a worthy cause," Manx offered, eager to shift the conversation back on track.

Margaret huffed. "You sound like one of my opponents. He's portraying me as one of those Victorian, busybody do-gooders."

"Tough on crime, tough on the causes of crime?" Manx said, gesturing to one of the posters.

Margaret smiled. "You didn't come all this way to confirm Callum Blackwell's identity, did you?"

"Your key witness in the case against Blackwell, Patrick Metcalf."

"Bloody tragedy, after all the good work he did for us," Margaret interrupted.

"We believe it's directly related to the Blackwell case—not a random act."

Manx had the Councillor's rapt attention for the first time that morning. "Your evidence?" Margaret asked, her eyes widening.

"The personal objects in the mouth of the victims. Similar calling card to Charles Blackwell."

"Jesus Christ. You didn't see fit to tell me this when you called?"

"I wanted more evidence, which I now believe we have."

Margaret's hands crept across the table, as if she were grasping for something. "Fuck it," she said. "Bad time to give up the ciggies." She placed one hand over the other and pulled them back. "Nobody on the team knew his new identity. It was a by-the-book WPA program."

Manx lowered his voice. "I came to ask you in person, because…" he began, but Margaret had already beaten him to the punch line.

"You suspect someone on my team? That's why you're here?" Margaret turned to the girl. "Jilly, go make us a cup of tea or something, will you, luv?" Jilly complied, and shuffled off.

Margaret rose slowly from her chair, collecting her thoughts as she did so. She leant against the dresser on the far wall. "It used to be a damn sight easier, running for public office," she said, looking out towards the perfectly mowed patch of lawn to the rear of the house. "You put yourself out there to the public, explained your positions, your beliefs. If people liked you, they voted for you. These days? It's a bloody media circus. Dirt gets dug, shit gets flung; nobody comes out clean. That's why the blandest, least offensive candidates get into positions of power; sour milquetoasts without an original thought or a grain of character between them."

"Let he who is without sin," Manx said.

"Hell's bells, don't get biblical on me, Inspector. It's way too early in the morning for that kind of discourse." Margaret paused. "I ran a tight ship; too tight, some might say. Maggie's farm, they called it," she laughed. "Old hatreds take a long time to die up north."

"Thatcher?"

"The gift that never stops giving," Margaret said. "Listen, if I suspected anybody on my team was leaking confidential information, believe me, I would have taken a truncheon to their balls, and escorted them out of the building myself. You couldn't be subtle back then; not like today, all P fucking C and trauma counselling. These were professional Yorkshiremen, or born and bred Mancunians; they didn't do subtle."

"Did you have your suspicions about anyone?"

"Operation Hightail took over two years to bring in Blackwell, but without Metcalf, we didn't have a case. Seventy-five assigned officers worked around the clock. Some came, some went. You hear things, but that's not the same as evidence, as we both know."

"Any name come up a few too many times?

Margaret shook her head. "It was a long time ago. Names, faces, they fade, mostly for good reason."

"You retired soon after Blackwell's sentencing."

Margaret's body language stiffened. "I see where you're going with this." She waved her finger accusingly at Manx. "No, I was not pushed out, neither was I forced to resign. Our case was airtight. No scandal, no bent coppers, no bruised balls."

"As far as you know," Manx said.

Margaret relaxed, resigning herself to imparting the next fragment of information to Manx. She walked back to the table. "I took early retirement, because I found my husband was shagging my neighbour six doors down. I thought, more fool me, that if I was at home more we could repair some of the damage this job does to a marriage. Six months later, the cheating bastard runs off with his fancy woman. I got the car, the house, and a Christmas card every other year, if I'm lucky. I needed something to take my mind off murdering the little shit, so I moved into politics, and now I'm running for Mayor. Does that answer your question?"

Manx nodded. It wasn't exactly news. He'd heard variants on this narrative from just about every copper he'd worked with, male and female.

"The job takes the best years of your life, then you wonder what the hell was it all for," Margaret said, a distant look in her eyes.

"I just wanted you to know," Manx said. "If we do find the leak at the WPA, and its traced back to your team, it's only a matter of time."

Margaret smiled; it had a resigned, weary quality. "So, this is an early warning? Painting the devil on the wall?" she said, reaching for a pen, and writing on the back of one of the brochures, sliding it towards Manx. "The Chief who took over from me, Darren Sutton, you should speak to him. If there's any information on Callum Blackwell, he'll know, or at least know who to talk to."

Jilly walked back into the room, tapping her wristwatch, and folding Margaret's rain jacket over her forearm. The Councillor nodded.

"You'll keep me informed, won't you, Inspector?" Margaret said, extending her hand, and guiding Manx towards the front door.

Chapter 3

Darren Sutton stood at the large, third-floor window of his office, and looked out over Manchester's King Street. "Used to be the centre of the north-west banking industry at one time," he said, gesturing at the now pedestrianised thoroughfare. "All fancy boutiques and wine bars these days."

"And expensive office space," Inspector Manx said, casting his eyes over Sutton's loft-like office conversion, complete with exposed brickwork, and a view, which held in its frame the majority of Manchester City Centre down towards the River Irwell.

Sutton turned to face the Inspector. "We lost track of Callum Blackwell soon after he left Manchester University after his first year," he explained. "The GMP had no budget, nor any tangible evidence to keep tabs on him, and anyway, we had bigger fish to fry. Gang violence, drugs, cheap firearms on the streets. Callum became a low priority, and eventually, fell off the radar completely. These things happen."

Sutton sipped on a freshly-pressed cappuccino drawn from a chrome espresso machine in the corner of his office. "Sure I can't offer you one, Inspector?" Sutton said, flashing Manx a wide, frothy smile. *This man is the sort of man who finds smiling as natural as breathing*, Manx thought. His demeanour and dress sense gave the same impression of a man as comfortable in his own skin as he was in the perfectly tailored suit he was wearing.

"Thanks, but I'm more the tea and biscuits type," Manx said.

Sutton nodded and smiled; this time it seemed more pitying than frothy. "But, here's what's interesting," he said, taking another sharp sip. "Not long after I left the force and became a consultant, I received a request from an unidentified person asking about Callum Blackwell. They wanted to know his whereabouts, address, occupation… that kind of thing. I wasn't intending to set myself up as a private detective, stalking missing persons, snooping cheating spouses, but I was just starting out, and she paid well."

"She?" Manx asked.

"I never knew her name, at least her real name. Janice Doe, she called herself. Dark sense of humour, I remember thinking at the time."

A cold shiver ran through Manx's spine. "What else did she tell you?"

Sutton thought for a moment. "She lived abroad, South America, I imagined, and wired her payment through an international bank direct to my account. Everything paid in full, up front."

"Did you find anything?" Manx asked, sensing his body edging forward on the Herman Miller chair.

Sutton hesitated. "Quite a lot, actually. More than she, or I, had bargained for," he said. "He's a bad seed, Inspector Manx, that much I can tell you. We traced him to Eastern Europe, Transnistria, a rogue state between Moldavia and the Ukraine. From what I could gather, he was extending what his father had started. Expanding the BK Holdings enterprises into new territories."

"How did you find all this?"

Sutton laughed. "You make a lot of friends in my position. When the National Crime Agency was founded, many of them made the leap. I'd always been more of the entrepreneurial type, so I chose a different direction. Now, I consult with the GMP, NCA, Homicide Working Groups, and Firearms Units. Everyone needs a second opinion; I'm their CYA Policy. Cover Your Arse, before someone kicks you out on it."

"And Callum?"

"He was on the NCA watch list—had been for some years. Interpol had their eye on him, too. I don't think there was a criminal activity he wasn't involved in. I, of course, gave what information I could legally disclose to this Janice Doe, and never heard from her again."

"Do you have any photographs of Callum? Recent, not so recent."

"Afraid not. I handed it all over to the NCA. I'm sure they'll have everything logged and filed; they're very thorough over there. I could make a call," Sutton offered.

Darren Sutton probably spent the majority of his day offering to make calls on people's behalf, Manx thought. And would, at some point in the future, expect the favour to be returned.

"A number, and a name, would be great," Manx said, offering a smile of his own.

Sutton wrote a name down on a Post-it note. "If you ever think of giving it all up, Inspector, I'm always in need of seasoned officers. I don't think we have anybody covering the North Wales area." He handed Manx his card.

Manx ran his finger over the glossily, embossed card, and slipped it into his pocket.

"Think about it," Sutton said, guiding Manx past the window and towards the door. "You don't get a view like this working your arse off for the North Wales Police."

There it was, that smile again—wide, frothy and completely unreadable.

***

Manx boarded the Bangor bound train at Piccadilly Station, settled himself with his iPhone playlist and notebook, and took a window seat in coach class. The journey had been worth it. The evidence pointed directly to Callum Blackwell, now confirmed by two people who both knew him. He had the motive, revenge, but Manx was missing the opportunity. *Did Callum come back into the country undetected? Was he on the island right now? And was he the connection to Anglesey Blue? Had he brought it onto the island? If so, who was distributing for him?* He'd call the contact at the

National Crime Agency, as soon as he got back to the island, and have them send over any information. This was now a manhunt, and he could sense he was slowly closing in on Callum, one small piece of evidence at a time.

The train shunted noisily out of the station, leaving behind the charcoal-sketch sprawl of Manchester, and into the damp, mottle-green fields of the Chester and the Wirral. Two hours later, the train was skirting the North Wales coast. To his right, the Irish Sea was an expanse of cold, grey soup, and to his left, the stalwart regiment of mountains rose, flinty and midnight-black, into the thick, expectant clouds stirring restlessly at their peaks.

Chapter 4

At times, it seemed as if every room in the farmhouse carried in its thick walls the echo of his ma's screams and the crack of hard fists against soft bone. This had been the soundtrack to Thomas Bowen's childhood since he could remember, and had only ceased when his da finally took off for good. Bowen had just turned thirteen. There was no ceremony or long goodbyes; it was as if Terry Bowen had walked out to buy a pack of cigarettes, and then decided not to return. That was fifteen years ago. He could barely remember what he even looked like anymore. Ma Bowen had burnt all the photos of his da in a bonfire the day after he left. *Where the fuck did the time go*, he thought, pulling back the cheap fabric curtains, and peering through the caravan window. Fifteen years, and he'd barely moved a few feet from the house. But, that was changing. He had a plan now; a plan which made his bones ache with the realisation of it.

Ma Bowen was out in the yard, throwing chicken feed, and calling at her brood. *HERE, CLUCK CLUCKS, BREKKIE, BREKKIE*. His sister, Nerys, appeared at the front door with a large dog-bowl, and laid it out next to the wall. The wolfhound scoffed it down in seconds. His ma motioned for her to go back inside, probably assigning another chore.

This had been the same, well-worn scene since he could remember; it depressed him just looking at it. But, today was different. Amongst the dour grey brick of the farmhouse and sodden fields beyond, there was now a bright, red counterpoint to the scene; the Ford Fiesta which had been parked outside since yesterday evening. Bowen smiled, and flicked back the curtain.

He lit a joint he'd rolled last night, but never got around to smoking, and sat at the narrow, pull-out table. The smoke flowed easily through his body like an anaesthetic. Since the beating a couple of weeks ago, he'd been unable to sleep for more than a couple of hours at a stretch; at least the grass mellowed out the pain. He flipped through a European Road Atlas he and Mandy had glanced over last night.

They'd earmarked a page; Spain and Portugal, closed their eyes, stuck in a pin; it had landed in somewhere called San Sebastian. Mandy said she knew it. Bowen asked if it had a harbour, Mandy insisted it did, along with a beach. And it was in Basque Country, she had explained, almost its own separate country. Bowen liked that. *They're like the Welsh of Spain*, he had thought to himself, as he read more about it on the internet later that night. There was nothing to miss back here. Nothing. He could work on his music anywhere; all he needed was his laptop and a pair of headphones, and weren't Europeans always following the UK trends anyway? Fuck it, he could be a celebrity DJ over there, make a mint, like that Calvin Harris bloke.

He heard Mandy stir from behind the partition. She slid back the thin plywood screen, and stretched her arms upwards, as if performing a sun salutation. The Day-Glo Happy Mondays t-shirt rode up her thighs to reveal a thin tuft of pubic hair. "Breakfast of champions?" she said, pointing at the joint.

Bowen smiled, and handed it to her. She took a short, snappy pull, and squeezed into the other side of the table. He loved the way she looked in the morning. She seemed younger, as if her face hadn't quite fallen completely into place yet.

"Not too keen on me, is she?" she said, looking at Ma Bowen.

"Not too keen on anybody," Bowen offered.

"Never mind, eh, Tommo? We've got a new life to look forward to now." She cupped her hand over his. He smiled, and took another drag on the joint. No one had taken the time to understand him before, not like Mandy. *So what if she was older? Age was just a fucking number, right? Isn't that what they said?*

He'd be old one day, too. Bowen reached over the table, and stroked her left breast with the back of his hand.

"Let's fuck," he said. He felt her nipple respond favourably, as he traced his index finger around its edges.

"Randy little bugger this morning, aren't we?" Mandy said. She stretched her leg under the table, and stroked his crotch through the thin cotton fabric of his boxers. "No satisfying you, is there?" She felt him harden.

"I meant what I said, you know, Tommo." Her expression was serious, but her eyes told him something else. It was as if she was asking for reassurance before she went any further.

"About what?" Bowen asked.

"Getting away from here, Tommo. I can get a renter for the shop, and I've got some money put by. You need to get away. We both do."

Bowen felt something akin to a sudden lightness fill his body, as if he'd been underwater for years, and was now just beginning to re-surface. Maybe this was what love felt like; he didn't know enough about it to make an educated guess, so he kept his thoughts to himself, at least for now.

Chapter 5

Manx called the team in for a late afternoon briefing. He directed his audience towards the photograph on the projector screen—a Manchester Metropolitan University ID card. He allowed the team to take in the boy's handsome smile and his dark, onyx-black eyes staring defiantly at the camera.

"Thanks to our colleagues at the National Crime Agency," Manx explained, "we now have a far clearer picture of our prime suspect, Callum David Blackwell, only son of Charles Blackwell; deceased. Callum was educated at the most prestigious public schools in the Greater Manchester Area. It's astounding the quality of education a life of crime can buy. Callum, known as Cal to his friends, studied, or more likely dabbled in History and Business. By 2003, Callum's father had already served eight years of a life sentence at the high security prison in Wakefield; an easy Sunday drive from Manchester for some father and son bonding time."

Manx clicked to the next slide, a blurred, long shot of a woman at a bus stop, kneeling and fussing around the buttons of a young boy's jacket.

"Callum Blackwell was brought up by his mother, Amanda. Once Callum flew the nest, Amanda also picked up sticks, and moved away. Current whereabouts, unknown."

Manx clicked back to Callum's student ID. "Callum dropped out before his second year, citing mental issues, though he never supplied any records to his counsellors. The GMP suspected, around this time, he was running errands for his father, but without proof, or a warrant, they hit a brick wall, and ceased surveillance. For the best part of a decade we lose track of Callum Blackwell, until, in 2013, when he's noticed entering the country under a false passport."

Manx brought up a CCTV shot of the arrivals gate at Gatwick Airport. "Callum Blackwell was making noises in Eastern Europe, loud enough for both Interpol and the National Crime Agency to take note. They suspected Callum was cultivating a network of contacts, and cashing in on the newly opened borders. As we know, the trade agreements between European counties are not limited to what the EU sees fit to regulate—sex trafficking, child slave labour, drug cartels, and, of course, the manufacturing of narcotics, and smuggling said contraband into UK Ports, and beyond."

Manx clicked onto another photograph; a Google map of several buildings on a dank, grey industrial estate. "The Camenca district of Transnistria, a small, breakaway state located on the border between Ukraine and Moldavia, a state within a state. It's corrupt, lawless, the UN won't touch it, and it makes Afghanistan look like a fortnight in Benidorm. Chief exports include military-grade weapons trafficking, human cargo—mostly young, white girls. In the Camenca district, to the east, their preferred activity is drug manufacturing. Hot-house marijuana, Oxycodone, Vicodin, heroin, coke, and recently, methadone."

Manx brought up the CCTV footage of the man visiting Charles Blackwell in prison. "Remember this character?" he said, freezing the video on the hooded man in the prison waiting room. "I had the techies enlarge the image; it's not conclusive, but I'd say this bears a pretty close resemblance to Callum Blackwell."

"If that's right, then Blackwell could have told him who turned evidence against him," Nader said. "Then, gave him the orders to kill Metcalf."

"OK. Let's assume he does tell Callum Metcalf turned Queen's on him, then guilts his son into doing his dirty work. How does Callum find Metcalf? He's been in the witness protection program for over fifteen years, the records are sealed, and no one should be aware of his new identity. Where does Callum start?"

"Maybe Callum bribed or threatened someone at the Witness Protection Agency," Morris offered.

"We can't prove that," Manx said. "A warrant could take weeks. The WPA has a very long, clear-cut procedure when it comes to revealing protected identities, which we don't have the time to follow, or the wherewithal to circumvent."

"What do we do next then, sir?" Morris asked.

"Solve the case with the evidence we have, not the evidence we'd like to have," Manx explained. "I'm convinced Callum Blackwell killed both Stokes and Vaughn, and had a hand in Dick Roberts's suicide. There's a lag of a year between Callum's return to the U.K. and the murder of Vaughn. Enough time for Callum to track down Vaughn, and confirm he is, in fact, Patrick Metcalf. After all, they'd waited over a decade, what's another few months? As a final tribute, Callum signs off the murders with his father's trademark signature."

"But, what about Stokes and the lad in the hospital? Connected, or just coincidence?" Nader asked.

"Coincidence is just a connection we haven't made yet," Manx said. "Stokes may have been in the wrong place at the wrong time. He was selling drugs, albeit in small quantities, so maybe Callum was sending out a "don't fuck with me" warning to the competition. It's all conjecture, at this point."

"Jesus," Priddle said. "Could he be behind all this Anglesey Blue stuff?"

"Supplying, maybe. He doesn't have local knowledge. Someone must be helping him distribute. We need to find that person, quickly."

"Bowen," Nader said, his tone gaining an edge of excitement. "We should arrest the bastard, proper this time, lock him up."

"No evidence, Nader. We can't go arresting him on a hunch. His mother's already out for blood. Give her another taste, and she's on the phone with the *North Wales Daily Post*, with a story they won't take the time to corroborate."

Nader shook his head, the blood rushing to his neck.

Manx pulled out a stack of blow-up photographs of Callum, and placed them on the table. "This is the man we are now putting all our efforts behind finding and apprehending, Callum Blackwell. I don't want to see this photograph anywhere but on your person," Manx said, pinning a copy to the incident board. "This face is for your reference only. I don't want to see it left in the pub, in the back of a patrol car, or God help us, in the hands of the Press. If Callum Blackwell finds out we're onto him, he'll run. If he thinks he's safe, he stays put. Everybody clear?"

There was a communal nodding of heads.

Manx stood still in the middle of the room. "Remember, Callum Blackwell has likely murdered three people, put a police officer and a paramedic in the hospital. If you run into this man, call for backup. Do not try to apprehend him, unless you want to be front-page news of the unfortunate variety," Manx concluded.

For the first time that day, the incident room fell silent.

Chapter 6

"Lynda Masterson, from A.M.A.D. I need to speak to Detective Inspector Manx, please. It's urgent."

PC Reese glanced up from his copy of the *Daily Post,* and squinted through his thick glasses at the intense looking woman standing before him. *Good looking,* he thought, *but stern, especially with her hair pulled back into a tight ponytail.* She reminded him of a whippet he once owned.

"Anglesey Mothers Against Drugs?"

Reese shook his large, square head, and shrugged his shoulders.

Lynda sighed, speaking slowly and deliberately. "Inspector Manx said I could call on him anytime. He gave me his card."

Reese held the card, examining it over the rim of his glasses. "And who are you?" he asked, addressing the sullen boy standing next to her.

"Adam. My son," Lynda said sharply.

"All right, there?" Reese said, warily. Having never fathered children of his own, Reese was always unsure as to how to act around them, and frequently defaulted to a detached, authoritarian stance. Adam nodded, then offered a belated, resigned smile. Reese handed back the business card.

"Inspector's busy, doesn't like being disturbed in the middle of an investigation."

Lynda was about to impart a well-honed retort, when Reese addressed Adam again. "Your mam brought you in to read you the riot act, did she? We got a couple of PCs not doing much, they'd be happy to oblige," he said, and winked at Lynda for good measure.

The gesture however, was miscalculated. Lynda composed herself, flattened her hands on the reception desk, and spoke to the officer, as if she were addressing a troublesome schoolboy.

"Constable Reese, I'm sure you have a very important job here, interfacing with the public, but I've driven all the way from Dinas in the pouring rain. I just need two minutes of the Inspector's time. Trust me, he'll want to hear what I have to say. And if you don't, I can guarantee your supervisor, and anyone else who's ranked above you, will get to hear about it." Lynda finished with a wide, open smile.

Reese rubbed the palm of his hand across his thick, ginger beard, and debated the best course of action. Manx was still bearing a grudge since the incident at the hospital last week, but if it were as important as she claimed, and he didn't call him, he'd be in a worse pile of shit. Lynda Masterson didn't seem the sort of woman who took no for an answer. He'd experienced enough of those in his lifetime to know.

"Hang on," Reese said, picking up a phone on one of the desks behind him. He nodded a few times, and replaced the receiver.

"He'll be out in a mo. Take a seat," he said, sheepishly, and turned his gaze back to his computer screen, as Lynda yanked the elastic tighter around the nub of her ponytail.

***

"Adam, what was your impression of events?" Manx asked, and rubbed the back of his neck. It was still sore from where he'd landed crookedly on the ambulance bay. He imagined old age would feel something akin to this, though worse and unrelenting. "Adam?" he repeated.

The boy shuffled his trainers over the interview room floor, and kept his gaze facing southwards. Manx looked at Lynda.

"We talked about this, Adam. Tell the Inspector what happened."

Adam pursed his lips. "Like I said, this bloke walks up to me on the way back from school, and asks if I want to buy some blues."

"Blues?"

"Anglesey Blues. The stuff they've been talking about on the news."

"Was this man familiar to you?" Manx asked.

Adam shook his head. "The older lads knew him, I think."

"So, why did he approach you?"

Manx saw Lynda's body language stiffen. Adam shrugged his shoulders; the universal teenage sign for "dunno."

"Were you curious, Adam? Looking to purchase some for yourself? Or maybe sell it on the internet. Wouldn't be too difficult for you."

Lynda quickly interjected, "My son is not under suspicion here, Inspector. We came in to report a crime, not to be interrogated."

Manx relented. "OK. What happened next, Adam?"

He looked at his mother before talking; she nodded her encouragement.

"One of the six formers told me to sod off, so I went around the corner. I saw the bloke hand over an envelope, and the kids gave him some money. Then, he got in the van, and drove off."

"What kind of van?"

"A work van. It had a blue and green logo on the side. Here, I took a picture." Adam handed over his cell phone. Manx studied the picture. It was blurry shot, but he recognised the logo painted onto the back door: Dwr Cymru, Welsh Water Authority.

"Is this the only photo you have?"

Adam nodded. Manx tore a page from his notebook, and picked up his pen. "This is my email. Send me the photo."

As Adam entered the address into his phone, Lynda straightened the elastic at the foundation of her ponytail. "This is not one of those incidents that's going to be swept under the carpet, is it, Inspector?"

Manx's phone beeped, as Adam's photo arrived in his inbox. "Not on my watch," Manx confirmed.

As Lynda rose, she offered Manx her hand. It was a firm, confident handshake. "That business at the meeting the other week," Lynda said, "I had no idea. We've never had the Press show an ounce of interest before."

Manx shrugged. "Celebrity culture. It'll blow over in fifteen minutes," he said, and escorted them both to the station reception. He thanked Adam for his good citizenship; it raised a brief, if weak, smile from the boy.

"We'd like you to come back, for a line up, if we find him, okay, Adam?"

The boy looked at his mom, a slightly nervous look to his face.

"One step at a time. Adam and I will discuss it." Lynda guided Adam through the door, her hand pressing gently on the small of his back.

Manx glanced at the photo on his screen, and walked back into the incident room. "Priddle, you seem to know what you're doing on this computer malarkey. Fire up that new equipment in the surveillance centre, and see if you can blow up the number plate on that photo I just emailed you."

Chapter 7

The air in the interview room was stale and warm. Manx and Nader sat across from David Griffiths, a nervous man with bags under his eyes, and thin lips he kept swiping his tongue over, like a dog licking at a hot-spot.

"What?" David said, flickering his eyes left and right between the two policemen who had been questioning him for the past hour.

"Just wondering, like," Nader said. "How stupid you have to be to sell drugs outside a fucking school? Takes some balls does that."

The man laughed nervously, and placed his hands, palms up, on the table. "I told you. I don't know anything about any drugs, honest."

Manx leant forward. "OK, let's go on the merry-go-round one more time," he said, gesturing at the print out on the table. "Your van was seen in Amlwch yesterday afternoon, just outside the boundaries of a school zone. My witness says you approached him, offered to sell him drugs, Anglesey Blue. Got anything you might like to add to that?"

The man leant back in his chair, and shook his head. "Wrong bloke, mate. Told you, I wasn't even on shift that afternoon."

Manx smiled. "And while we're checking that out with your boss, can you enlighten us as to where you were, if you weren't selling methadone out of the back of your van, like Mr. fucking Whippy?"

David cast his eyes around the room, and shuffled his feet.

"Come on, David. The longer you drag this out the worse it gets, you know the drill," Nader said.

David licked his lips again, and leant in, so his elbows were resting on the table. He spoke in a whisper. "Can we keep it between us, like?"

"Something you don't want the wife to find out about? Dirty bugger," Nader said.

"No. Nothing like that," David said, with a tone of regret, implying chance would be a fine thing, if it were "something like that."

"I got this part time job, like," he began.

"Yeah, we figured that," Nader said, smirking.

"Water Authority don't allow us to moonlight, but I needed the cash."

"What kind of work?" Manx asked.

David looked at both of them again, licked his lips some more. "Fuck it!" he said, exhaling loudly, as if he were unburdening himself. "I was fixing some water metres for some mates."

Nader laughed. "Fuck me! Talk about pissing on your own doorstep."

"Boss don't need to know, does he?" David said. "The wife would murder me, if I got the sack again." A single line of sweat trickled steadily down David's forehead and onto his cheek. He brushed the dampness away with the back of his sleeve. "Why's it so fucking hot in here?"

"Faulty thermostat," Nader said. "New building, too. You'd think they'd get that fixed, eh?"

There was a knock on the door. PC Morris walked in, and handed Manx a scrap of paper. He read it, and placed face down on the table.

"OK, your boss confirms you were not on shift that afternoon."

David visibly relaxed in his chair. "Does that mean I can go?"

"Hold your horses, King Canute," Nader said. "Just because you weren't on shift, doesn't mean you weren't there."

"I don't get it?" David said. "If I was selling drugs, why would I do it out of the company van?"

"Because you're a stupid fucker?" Nader offered.

"The yard where they keep the vans, where is it?" Manx asked.

"Near the reservoir at Llyn Alaw."

"How many employees are authorised to drive the vehicles?"

"Not sure. Six or seven, maybe?"

"Is there any way of knowing who took which vehicle, and when?"

"Boss makes us hang keys at the end of the shift, then hands them over in the morning when we start."

"So, someone else could have taken the van?"

"Yeah, maybe. But, I don't know…"

Nader interrupted. "Seven blokes, boss. Wouldn't be too hard to track 'em down, bring them in."

Manx nodded, and looked at David. "Anything else that you might want to share, David, while you're here?"

David bit his lip, licked it, and contemplated for a moment, before answering, "There's security cameras in the yard," he said. "Company runs 'em all fucking day and night. Suspicious buggers, don't trust no one these days."

He smiled at Manx, the irony of his own remark having completely passed him by.

Chapter 8

"Don't understand how people can live in places like this. Drive me bonkers, it would, everybody on top of each other," PC Morris said, as she and Manx took a sharp right turn from Llangefni high street onto the Cefn Glas Estate.

"People have got to live somewhere," Manx offered, but even he had his reservations about Cefn Glas. The development was meant to be completed in early two thousand and eight, just before the housing collapse, and was squeezed into a discarded patch of land in between the nearby Leisure Centre and the industrial estate housing the Ready Chick, chicken-processing plant.

As they drove through the estate, Manx felt a familiar sense of weariness. Every other home had a For-Sale sign spiked into the front lawn. A number of houses had already been vacated, their windows boarded up, and the gardens left for the remaining neighbours, who cared enough to keep up the appearance of the estate to tend. At the end of the road, where the land backed onto open fields, several houses had still to be completed. *It was like a project someone had started, but lost interest half way through*, Manx thought as they drove past the rows of identical bungalows, differentiated only by the brand of car parked in the driveway, or the species of flowers planted around the perimeters of the garden.

"Everything used to be farmland when I was a kid," Manx said, and pulled over the Jensen directly opposite number seventy-three.

"Should have left it like that," Morris said, and wiped a sop of condensation off the passenger side window with the side of her sleeve. "Give me an old farmhouse and a couple of acres of land any day."

Manx could barely imagine what he'd do with a beer-towel-sized patch of land to tend to, let alone a couple of acres.

"Is there a strategy, sir?" Morris asked, as she slipped her fingers into a pair of black, woollen gloves.

The wipers chafed noisily across the glass, as Manx looked out. It was seven-thirty in the evening, and a heavy darkness had been poured, like a thick stew, over the island. A couple of lampposts along the road were still working, although one of them flickered on and off, as if it were about to give up the ghost. A thin film of evening fog had begun to roll in, and the temperature had dropped several degrees since sundown.

"A strategy?"

"For apprehending the suspect. I've never done an arrest before, except in basic training, like," Morris explained.

Manx looked over at the bungalow. Like all the dwellings on the road, its main selling feature was a large, square window occupying most of the front wall. The curtains were open, which afforded Manx a clear view into the living room. The TV was switched on, and a woman and young child were playing some kind of board game on the floor.

"We'll do it outside, discreetly," Manx said.

Morris nodded, and breathed deeply.

"Nervous?" Manx asked.

"No. Calm, sir, very calm," she offered, and took several more breaths to convince herself she was as relaxed as she claimed.

"Might be our man," Manx said, pointing at a pair of headlights turning into the estate. They watched as the van pulled into the driveway of number seventy-three. "Bingo," Manx said. "Just follow my lead, and don't fuck up," he added, and stepped out into the brittle night air.

"Thanks for the pep talk," Morris mumbled, following close behind.

The headlights reflected off the white garage door, and filled the driveway with an overly bright pool of light. The driver was about to exit the van, when he noticed Manx's face smiling at him through the window. The man mouthed what Manx guessed was, "what the fuck?" Manx took out his badge, and tapped the glass. He felt a rush of stale air across his face, as the man rolled down the window.

"North Wales Constabulary. I'm Detective Inspector Manx and over in the blue corner, PC Delyth Morris."

Morris nodded at the man from the passenger side window.

"Let's make this quick, Davey. You know why we're here, don't you?"

The man unbuckled his seat belt. "Dunno. Overdue parking ticket?"

"Thanks for bringing that to our attention. We'll add it to the list. Now, do me a favour and switch on that interior light, would you?"

Davey snorted heavily, as if he were suffering from a bad cold, and complied. He was dressed in blue work overalls, with a Dwr Cymru logo stitched into the chest pocket. There was a faint stench of sewage coming from inside the car, but it was the man's eyes which caught Manx's attention. They were unnaturally large and bulbous, like a couple of Christmas baubles pushed into sockets several sizes too small to house them. But, there was something else in his eyes, too, something Manx knew well. Fear. He caught it the instant Davey rolled down the window; his eyes were darting wildly, searching for an escape.

"Now, Davey, let me explain to you how this is going down," Manx said, resting his elbows on the window frame. "We're going to do everything in slow motion, like in the films, right?"

Davey kept his gaze fixed on the garage door, and nodded his agreement.

"Good, because I've had a shit few days, and you're about the only good piece of news I've had. And, just so you know, I'm short on sleep, which makes me very bad tempered, just ask Morris here."

"Running on a short fuse, he is, no talking sense to him when he gets like this," Morris confirmed.

Davey's fingers coiled tightly around the sheepskin steering-wheel cover.

"Glad we all agree, "Manx said. "Now, I'm going to back away from the door, Davey, and you're going to slowly, I repeat slowly, exit your vehicle, keeping your hands where I can see them at all times. Got it?"

Davey nodded again, his fingers wrapped tighter around the wheel.

"Morris, get ready to cuff him. He's a big boy, so come around to my left, while I turn him to face the car."

Morris unclipped her handcuffs, and walked to the right side of the car. Davey groaned, as he squeezed his girth through the narrow gap.

"Easy now. Remember, short fuse," Manx said.

Davey said nothing. He was resigned to complying with the Inspector's instructions, at least until he caught a glimpse of his wife and child through the window, oblivious to the commotion outside. He turned to Morris. "Can I just tell the wife, so she's not worrying, aye?"

In the second it took for Morris to glance Manx's way, Davey grabbed the slim window of opportunity.

Manx felt the shock of the impact, a hundred kilos of steel door pummelled into his upper abdomen, hurling against the wall, and ricocheting the back of his head off the brickwork. Davey hunched his shoulders forward, and charged at Morris like a bull. He ploughed into her shoulder, spinning her one hundred and eighty degrees, before she dropped to the floor like a bowling pin. He made a break towards the narrow pathway, looking behind him as he ran.

Morris scrambled to her feet, and saw Davey huff his way down the narrow alley between the garage and the adjoining house.

"Keep your radio on," Manx said, but his voice was a hoarse murmur lost somewhere in his throat. He leant back against the wall to catch his breath, and hoped Morris was as fast as he imagined she was.

Manx was right, Morris thought, as she scrambled through the narrow opening leading into the back garden, Davey was a big lad. She could hear his heavy, laboured breathing, as he ran a few metres ahead. If she kept a steady pace, she was sure she could tire him out.

As she emerged from the side alley, she felt the terrain change underfoot; she was on the back lawn. A motion sensor over the patio illuminated the square of green. Davey was gone. She scanned the scene—a swing set, a half-built shed, and to the left, a section of fence, splintered and still swaying.

She clambered over the wood into the adjoining garden. There was no motion sensor; the house had been abandoned some time ago. She waded through the thick weave of wet grass toward Davey. He was still breathing hard. She could hear the squelch of his footsteps, as he tore at the wooden slats of the opposite fence. She needed to pace herself, let him do all the hard work. Directly ahead of her the pale, yellow light of the Leisure Centre spilled over the canopy of oak trees at the entrance to the estate. One more garden, and he'd be out in the open.

By the time Manx had caught his breath, he'd lost sight of both Davey and Morris. He unfolded himself to standing, and looked around him, debating which direction to follow. To the right, he decided, back towards the main road. If he were Davey, that's where he'd run—back to the town where he could easily lose himself in one of the pubs, or hide out in a back garden. He took a deep breath, and jogged towards the Leisure Centre.

Morris stopped, permitting herself the luxury of a brief rest. It was quiet; too quiet. She couldn't hear Davey's breathing. Maybe he'd taken a different route. She clicked her radio.

"Do you have visual on the suspect, sir?" Morris said.

"Not a fucking chance. You?" Manx said.

She was about to reply, when she heard the familiar rasp of heavy breathing. But, this time, it was directly behind her. There was no time to turn. Davey already had the wooden post of a discarded For-Sale sign in his hand, and brought it down on the back of her head. Morris fell forwards, twisting on her wrist, as she stumbled on the wet grass.

She saw a flash of feet, grabbed at the outside of Davey's ankle, then pulled. His boots slipped across the wet grass. He faltered for a second then dropped to the ground with a heavy grunt. It was a fleeting victory. He kicked Morris's hand away, and scrambled back to standing. Morris watched him flounder, like a drunk, his legs buckling under him. *He'll run himself ragged*, Morris thought. She brushed herself down, and followed. There was no need to run; she'd catch up with him soon enough.

Davey staggered into the car park in a zigzag manner, which implied he would drop at any second. The loud fritz of the car park lights startled him, but not as much as the narrow beam of light snaking towards him. As his eyes became accustomed to the brightness, the tall figure of Manx came into focus. Davey fell to his knees, and gulped large mouthfuls of air. When he looked up, Manx was looming over him, his torch searing his eyes.

"Guess that's what you get for letting your gym membership lapse, eh, Davey?"

Davey heard a sound to his left. Morris was walking towards him from the opposite direction.

"OK, here's what's going to happen," Manx said. "I'm going to place my knee in your lower back, pull your arms back, and Morris here is going to cuff you. You got that?"

Davey nodded. Morris drew the cuffs from her belt for the second time that night, snapped them onto Davey's wrist, jerking his arms upward so they pinched hard into his shoulder blade.

"Fucking hell!" Davey screamed

"Was that really necessary?" Manx asked.

Morris shrugged her shoulders, and put her hand at the back of her head to wipe away the trickle of blood flowing down the nape of her neck.

"Pay back's a bitch, isn't it, Davey?" Manx said, as he grabbed him, and hauled him up to standing.

Chapter 9

Shanni was singing along, in full-throttle voice, to the old Judas Priest hit, 'Breaking the Law.' He felt good, like he did after a few pints, but just before the point where he became too drunk to enjoy being drunk. Even his finger seemed to be in on the good mood, and had stopped its constant throbbing. The bandage was due to come off next week. Shanni dreaded what lay under the swaddling: an ugly, useless, stub of bone and flesh he'd have to learn to live with. He banished the thought from his mind—nothing was going to bring him down tonight. He pushed harder on the accelerator, pumped up the volume until the speakers rattled, and Rob Halford's voice distorted through the tweeters like static interference.

Last night he'd met with Bug, Hywel, and Trev. At least the mood was better than the last time; it was hard for him to imagine it being any worse. Even Trev had taken the night off from sulking around the window like an anxious puppy. Shanni wasn't sure how the meeting would go down, especially after the last fiasco. He'd done his homework, that was all. He half expected the lads to back off, bottle out, but they'd all stayed, not that they had much choice. He smiled at the memory. How they all listened, mouths wide open like broken gates, as he rattled their skeletons, one-by-one, in front of them. After that, the motivation was easy—just show them the money. How they moved the merchandise was of no consequence to him, so long as he had the twenty-five grand in his hands before he met with Scuttler again, which would be in about an hour from now; that was all that mattered. He had the cash, all of it, stashed in an old gym bag in the boot of the Capri. His icing on the cake? That was a different matter. He'd hidden that. Eight grand of pure profit. Scuttler would never need to know.

Shanni had underestimated the demand for the pills, and his marketing strategy had worked. People were asking for it by name: Anglesey Blue; *Got any Blue? How much for more Blue? I need the Blue, mate, really fucking need it!"* He felt a flutter of pride, as he thought of how well the whole scheme had panned out. They'd offloaded everything, every single blue pill sold in four weeks. The lad's eyes had lit up like Christmas, as he divided out the cash. They'd all crossed the point of no return now, each one of them carrying equal risk and responsibility; it was just the beginning.

"Fuck yeah!" Shanni shouted, and tweaked up the volume. In four weeks, he was up eight grand, but down by half a finger. If that was the price of entry for a better life, to provide for his family, so be it. It was a small sacrifice.

He slapped the palm of his good hand on the steering wheel. It was time to kick all that runt-ish behaviour he'd been exhibiting recently into touch; from now on, he was adopting the Alpha dog posture. No one was going to fuck with him, no one.

Chapter 10

There was a persistent drizzle, like a sheet of constant wetness, obscuring the Capri's windscreen. Shanni flicked on the wipers. The scene wiped to the exact same view as it did thirty seconds ago—an empty airstrip with several storage containers marking its perimeter. A sharp, cold wind had begun to push across the runway, agitating the bright orange windsock on the control tower, until it buffeted in place like washing on a clothesline.

Ten minutes later, Shanni watched the yellow glow of headlights, as they turned slowly into the airstrip. He stiffened. The Mercedes pulled up in front of the Capri, and kept its engine running. His cell phone buzzed. *Scuttler knew he was here for fuck's sake; why did he need to call?* He ignored the ringing, and stepped out into the sharp, cold air. *Alpha dog stance*, he reminded himself, and leant as casually as he could on the wing of the Capri.

The light from the headlamps shone like the cone of a projector beam, illuminating the thin belt of mist and drizzle falling between the two cars. Scuttler appeared a few moments later, easing himself from the back door like a snake emerging from behind a rock. The interior light flickered. Shanni could make out a figure in the backseat, probably one of his goons. He hoped he hadn't brought the Mastiff along for second helpings.

Scuttler stood in front of the Mercedes, the beams smouldering behind him, and casting deep, heavy shadows across his face.

"Shanni, here we are again, enjoying the Welsh weather together."

Shanni's body stiffened, as he listened to Scuttler's slow, sonorous tone that he imagined, depending on the circumstance, could either calm a restless child or lull his victims, as he drove knife a through their guts.

"Should come down here in summer, like Hawaii, it is," Shanni offered.

Scuttler laughed. The same, short, bark-like laugh which prickled Shanni's neck hairs. "Maybe I'll do that." Scuttler nodded to the goon to his left, the fatter one with the shaved head. He walked towards Shanni, patted him down, and handed Shanni's mobile over to his boss.

"Good," Scuttler said. "Let's get this over with quickly. I'm sure we've all got families to get home to, right, Shanni?" He pawed his way through Shanni's phone, opened the back, and removed the battery. Shanni felt his Alpha Dog stance begin to weaken. Maybe he wouldn't get away with this, after all. Doubts crept over him, just like the goon's hands had done seconds before—unwelcome and predatory.

"Money's in the boot," Shanni said.

Scuttler gestured for the goon to go fetch it. He brushed by Shanni, nudging his shoulder as he passed. Shanni stumbled, and felt his Alpha Dog balls shrink some more in his briefs.

"You know what I love about you Welsh?"

Not another fucking history lesson, Shanni thought. He was cold and wet. He wanted to get to the nearest pub, sink a few pints, go home, fuck his wife. *Was that too much to ask?*

"Our sunny disposition?" Shanni offered.

"Quite the opposite, actually," Scuttler said. "That dark, brooding pessimism, your distrust of outsiders. I guess that's what comes from centuries of oppression and conquering, am I right?"

"Dunno, before my time. Failed my History GCSE, anyway."

"Maybe you just had an uninspiring teacher. The thing is with history, Shanni, it teaches us about the present. Some lessons are hidden in plain sight; you just need to know where to look."

The goon dumped the bag of money on the bonnet. "It's all there, twenty-five grand, like you said. Took my cut already," Shanni explained. He felt a quiver of nervousness in his voice. "Like we agreed, aye," he added, this time in a more confident tone.

Scuttler smiled. "Well, I suppose we should call this the start of a beautiful partnership."

Shanni felt as if a weight had suddenly been lifted from his shoulders. He allowed himself the luxury of releasing a long, deep breath "Aye, well you got my number," Shanni said, gesturing at the mobile.

Scuttler flipped the phone over in his palm. "Indeed, I do, Shanni."

For a few moments, there was silence, save the flapping of the windsock and the faint sound of muffled music coming from inside Shanni's car—Def Leppard, "Pour Some Sugar on Me." He named the tune in one.

"Right, I'll be off then," Shanni said, turning towards the driver's door. "Any chance?" he asked, pointing towards his mobile.

"History lesson number one, Shanni, learn from past mistakes," Scuttler said, handing the phone back to the goon. "Do you recall that fun game we played a few weeks ago, Redneck Roulette?"

"Fun for you, maybe."

"Every game needs a winner, Shanni, otherwise, what's the point of playing. The purpose was to illustrate a point, a little heavy-handed maybe, but I often find subtlety in these kinds of negotiations leads to vagueness and time wasting."

"Sorry, I thought we were done here," Shanni said. He could feel his voice faltering. "I got all your money, twenty-five grand, like you said."

"And the rest?"

Shanni tried to swallow, but his mouth was packed to the gums with sand. "There is no rest. Twenty-five, straight up, no bullshit," Shanni said, but the words were like dry pebbles in his throat.

Scuttler turned towards the Mercedes, and waved his right hand in an impatient, fanning motion. There was a moment of dead air, before the back door swung open with a slow ponderous creak. First a boot, then a leg, then the full length of body and a face Shanni had sat across the table from, less than twenty-four hours ago.

Chapter 11

It took Shanni less than a second to register the tall, well-groomed man being pushed from the back of the car, the butt of a revolver pressed against his left temple—Hywel Jenkins. Shanni wiped a clammy palm across his face, and watched as the other goon shoved Jenkins hard in the back. Jenkins was in his shirtsleeves, shivering like a wet dog, his hands tied behind his back. He kept his gaze to his feet, not once raising his head to look up. He looked petrified. *Welcome to the fucking club*, Shanni thought.

"Jenkins? What the fuck?" he shouted.

Jenkins kept his head bowed. Shanni promptly decided he was in need of an escape plan. Things were about as bad as they got, but if he hung around any longer, he imagined they'd get a whole lot worse, and quickly.

Scuttler walked behind Jenkins, and grabbed the nape of his neck. Jenkins winced, and hunched his shoulders further forward, a lock of his damp hair falling across his face.

"Jenkins, here, loves to talk," Scuttler said.

Shanni swallowed hard, and tried to keep his bladder in check. He could feel the pressure building; fear, it did that to him, made him piss his pants, had done ever since he was a kid. A tiny light bulb, the size of a Christmas tree light, sparked in Shanni's brain. He tensed his pelvic muscles, and felt for the base of the car aerial just to his right.

"I don't know what angers me the most, Shanni," Scuttler said. "That you think I'm stupid enough not to care how much you're selling my product for, or that you thought I wouldn't find out."

"Don't know what you mean," Shanni said, twisting the nub of the car aerial in his fingers.

"I only ever asked for loyalty, Shanni," Scuttler said, and nodded towards the goon who had pushed Jenkins from the car. The goon reached inside his jacket pocket, and pulled out a revolver, feeling its weight in his palm, before aiming it at Shanni.

Shanni's legs shook. He steadied himself on the car bonnet, and felt a gradual warmness drip down his thighs. He looked down. A tell-tale patch of dark blue spread across the crotch of his jeans. By the time he looked back up, the revolver was pressed against his forehead, the cold steel rubbing against his skin, as if it wanted in.

Chapter 12

If there was one sliver of education that had stuck with Shanni it was this: never back down from a fight. Even tonight, with a cold gun grinding into his forehead, his instinct was to fight. He'd already made up his mind. He wasn't going to die tonight, not here, not with his crotch full of piss, and Sara and Dewi waiting back at home for him. It couldn't end like this.

He assessed the situation. Jenkins, Scuttler, and the goon with the shaved head were at the front of the Mercedes. The other goon was directly to his left, scraping the barrel of the revolver against his skull. He had a big, stupid grin on his face. *He didn't look like the sharpest chisel in the box*, Shanni thought, as he twisted the car aerial between his fingers, and applied a few grams of pressure.

"Who's first?" Scuttler said. "Jenkins, who sold you out, or you, Shanni?"

Scuttler released his grip on Jenkins, and continued, "You, Shanni, most definitely you."

He pointed to a patch of green to Shanni's left. "In a couple of days, they'll find your body, next to that scrub of grass over there. Your story will make the newspapers, maybe even the nationals. You'll be famous for a while—famous but dead. Then, after your funeral, life goes on. Your family will miss you, but they'll learn to live with it. Your wife re-marries, someone younger, better prospects. Your son gets used to calling someone else 'Dad,' and you gradually fade from his memory. That's the tragedy of life; it always moves on, despite our departure. And you, Shanni, will be a footnote in all this. The mechanic who got overambitious, too greedy; a desperate weakling, with desires above his station, which is a shame, because if you'd heeded my initial warnings, things could have been so different."

Scuttler nodded. The goon pulled back the cocking mechanism. Shanni tensed. He needed to do this now, right now. He reached for the aerial, and snapped it clean from its temporary housing of masking tape. By the time the goon's brain had registered the action, Shanni had whipped the jagged end of the aerial, like a fast uppercut to the goon's neck, rammed home the thin metal rod into his throat, and only stopped pushing when he felt the resistance of bone. The goon attempted a scream, but all that came out was a muted, thick gargle, as the blood quickly pooled in his larynx. He immediately dropped the gun, and reached both his hands towards his neck. By the time he'd extracted the metal, Shanni was gone. Not that the goon cared. Blood gushed from his jugular in a jet of crimson. Having been on the other side of this equation on numerous times, the goon quickly calculated he had only a few minutes left to live. And, judging from the look on his boss's face, he didn't expect the welcome wail of sirens of medical assistance anytime soon.

Chapter 13

Shanni was fast—the best cross-country runner in the county, if he applied himself, according to his secondary-school gym teacher. Of course, Shanni hadn't applied himself, that would have entailed too much graft and kowtowing to authority, neither of which he was fond of. Tonight, though, as his boot soles struck the shallow, rough grass at the edge of the runway, he applied himself as if his life depended on it.

A few hundred metres to his east, the A5 rumbled by, like passing thunder. If he made it to the road, he'd follow the perimeter, and head down to the low marshes leading into Pentre Berw, and then onto Gaerwen. He'd hide out at the phone near the bus stop, call Sara, warn her, not that he knew what to say; he'd figure that out later.

He was three hundred metres from the control tower, when he stopped dead in his tracks. The echo from a single gunshot broke through the cold night air, and echoed through his head. He stood still, waiting for another shot, which never came. The silence returned just as quickly as it had been shattered. The bullet wasn't meant for him; that one had Jenkin's name carved into its casing. He'd heard of people's blood running cold, but this was the first time he'd experienced the phenomenon. It was as if his blood was gradually being replaced with ice water, from his head to his legs. He tried to wrestle the image of Jenkins slumped over the bonnet of the Mercedes, his eyes, cold and lifeless. Shanni took a deep breath, applied himself, and ran.

***

He hadn't run this hard for years, and it showed. Sweat gushed into his eyes, and his lungs ached with every hurried, hard-earned inhalation. He clambered over a low wall leading into the nearby marsh. The wet ground gave way easily under his boots, which were already sodden with rainwater, as he moved deeper into the marsh. The infrequent strobe of car headlights provided the only light, scanning across the darkness like searchlights. A thin tissue of fog had begun to roll like a transparent carpet across the morass, and floated eerily a few feet above the ground.

A few minutes ago, escape was his only goal, but now, as the adrenaline slowly subsided, his mind ticked back to the last hour. Jenkins was dead, and Shanni was a killer, running for his life like some feral animal. Not that his life was worth much, anyway; maybe his family would be better off if the goon had put a bullet in him. Sara could claim the life insurance; she'd be well taken care of, her and Dewi. He was worth more dead than he was alive. It was a sobering thought. He stopped momentarily to catch his wind. As the breath poured from his mouth like steam, another thought hit him, as fast and startling as the rock that had shattered his front window. For the second time in the span of ten minutes, his blood ran cold. Scuttler knew where they lived. Shanni ignored the stitch digging into his right side, and kept on running. This time it wasn't for his own life; it was for something far more important.

Chapter 14

After twenty minutes of hard running, which took every spare breath he possessed, Shanni reached the end of the marsh, and clambered over a wall onto the main road. Five minutes later, he was at the public phone box. He threw his back against the squares of glass and steel, and slumped to the ground. His feet were soaking, and his stomach churned with excess bile. He coughed—the effort scratched his throat like a cat's claw

When was the last time he'd used a public phone box? Must have been years ago, the familiar aroma of plastic and warm piss was strangely comforting. He fumbled for a few spare coins in his pockets, poked them impatiently into the slots, and began to dial. *Shit! What was his home number again?* He always had it on speed dial. It took him three attempts, before he got the right combination of numbers. Sara picked up almost immediately. Shanni took a deep breath, and began to speak.

"What's wrong, Cledwyn? Where are you?"

Where to begin? His mind raced through an inventory of half-truths, excuses, and lies, before settling on a combination of all three.

He began by explaining, as calmly as he could, what had just happened; or at least a version of events which would imply the severity of the situation, without sending his wife into an irreversible panic. He'd been a witness to a murder, he explained. Some blokes had seen him, chased after him, but he'd lost them. In a panic, he'd left his cell phone and the car behind. The blokes would find his home address, either in his phone or in the glove box. She needed to leave right now, with Dewi, just to be safe.

He was sure nothing would come of it, but it might be a good idea if she and Dewi stayed with her mother tonight, just in case. He'd contact her tomorrow. He was sure it was all a misunderstanding, but she had to leave right now.

Before the rapid, urgent beeps cut them off, he was sure she agreed, but he could never be certain with Sara; she had her mother's stubborn streak, but this wasn't the time to showcase the Manx-Williams family traits. All he could do was hope, for once, Sara would do as she was asked.

Shanni slumped down in the phone box. He smacked the back of his head against the glass, a slow, rhythmic movement. A car passed by, slowly, as if it were looking for someone, then sped up again. Shanni let out the breath he'd been holding in, and focussed on his next move. Staying here wasn't an option; it was too public. He needed somewhere hidden. A mile or so back, he remembered passing a narrow dirt track. The road had a few cottages along its verge, maybe he could hide in one of the gardens, before he remembered the old railway line which cut through the back fields. It was unused and probably overgrown by now, but there was an old tunnel there; it would be closer and safer.

He stepped from the telephone box, and felt the immediate sting of cold slap across his face. He waited for a clutch of cars to pass by, then ran across the road. The stitch dug into his side like a voodoo pin, reminding him of what a fucking idiot he'd been. Shanni may have cried at this point, or maybe, it was just the cold pricking at his eyeballs; it was difficult to tell.

Chapter 15

"No. Fucking. Comment." Davey Evans folded his tree trunk-like forearms across his chest, and looked directly through Manx, as if he were glass. The Inspector ran his finger across his eyebrow, and glanced at the court-appointed solicitor, Fraser Davenport, sitting across from him, and chewing absent-mindedly on a cheap biro.

"My client has supplied you with all the statements he's willing, or required, to make at this time." Davenport extracted a moist splinter of pen from his teeth, and set it down on the table. "If you insist on asking him the same questions, hoping for different answers, I will have to terminate the interview."

"We have a witness who saw you selling narcotics close to a school, Davey. Not the smartest of locations to dump your stash," Manx said.

Davey stayed mute, his wide, bulging eyes staring at the back wall.

"So you mentioned, Inspector, many times," Davenport said. "But, without him, or her, present to identify my client, you have no case, and obviously little evidence, or you would have charged him already."

Davenport was getting under Manx's skin. The solicitor was older than he had expected, with rosebud-pink cheeks, and a fleshy expanse of neck, which draped like raw pie crust over his shirt collar.

Manx leant forward. "Your client ran when we attempted to question him, and he assaulted one of my officers. So, my question is, Davey, why?"

"Naturally, he panicked. Being accosted by two police officers in the vicinity of his own home, anyone would feel intimidated. He is extremely sorry for that, aren't you, Mr. Evans?"

Davey nodded. "Yeah, sorry, aye," he muttered.

Manx sighed. He wouldn't get any further with Davey tonight. "Interview with the suspect, Davey Evans, and Detective Inspector Manx terminated at twenty-one hundred hours."

The solicitor gathered his papers. "Forty-eight hours, Inspector, then you'll either have to formally charge my client, or release him."

The solicitor looked pleased with himself, too bloody pleased. Manx had tried to coax something out of Davey for the past two hours, and all he'd managed to extract was either, "no comment," or "no fucking comment." Davey was the first tangible connection they'd had, and one which had to be handled with kid gloves. He suspected Davenport to be the anally retentive type, and unlikely to turn a blind eye to any minor infractions by the North Wales Police.

"We'll continue this in the morning, bright and early," Manx said, as one of the duty PCs escorted Davey back to his cell. Unless he was a hardened criminal, which Manx doubted, a night alone with his own thoughts and the prospect of a few years of the same might just scare Davey enough to cough up more information come the morning.

"Oh, before you go, Davey," Manx said, raising his six feet three frame from the chair. "Just so you know, the typical jail time for possession, with intent to supply, is around ten to fifteen years, and you can add another five to that number for selling to school kids—juries tend to come down hard on that, for some reason. You'll be what, sixty-five when you get out? Kids left home, got kids of their own, wife probably divorced you, moved on. Then, you'll need a job, not easy for someone with a criminal record. Just something for you to mull over, while you enjoy our hospitality."

Manx thought he detected a ripple of panic flutter in Davey's eyes, but he couldn't be sure. Davenport exchanged a few hushed words with Davey, before his client was led off towards his studio suite—complementary mints and turndown service not included.

***

Back in the incident room, Manx looked over the litter of evidence pinned to the board. He placed Davey's mug shot onto the expanding pile of photos, documents, and scraps of ideas. *How did Davey Evans fit into all this?* The permanently sloped shoulders, the way he shuffled rather than walked, all pointed to Davey Evans as a bit player in this drama, and he'd been stupid enough to sell drugs close to a school zone in his work van. *If Davey was a cog in a bigger machine, could he build on what he knew, slot the small pieces into place, then pull back far enough so the big picture would reveal itself? Who was running the distribution?* It certainly wasn't Davey, or Bowen, and with Bowen off limits, for the time being, Manx's best hope lay with the bug-eyed mute. It wasn't a reassuring thought.

Manx stepped further back from the board. As he did so, an idea stuck him. He removed the portraits of the men and pinned them to a secondary board. This made sense—separate the players from the action, and observe them as single entities, rather than part of the big picture. *What did he know, or rather, what* didn't *he know about them?*

Stokes had a criminal past, and had served five years in Northumberland Category C Training Prison for fencing stolen antiquities and artworks. For the last few years, he appeared to have kept his head down, running the antique store in Beaumaris, and selling methadone on the side. Maybe someone from his past had come back. Men, like Stokes, often made life-long enemies. The lad in the hospital (Manx's heart still sank when he thought of him) had probably witnessed something he shouldn't have, and paid the ultimate price for being in the wrong place at the wrong time. Dick Roberts's death was a suicide, but maybe someone had pushed an already vulnerable man over the edge. He was still looking over the board when Morris came back, touching the back of her head, as she crossed the incident room.

"All fixed up, then?" Manx said.

"Aye. An hour and a half at the emergency room for a couple of stiches and a prescription; God bless the National Health," Morris said.

"We should call Lynda Masterson, bring in her boy for a line-up."

"I can call her before I leave," Morris offered.

"No, it'll be better coming from me," Manx said. "Good work, tonight," he added. "I had you figured for a sprinter."

"Helps when the bloke's overweight and asthmatic," Morris said, and grabbed her jacket from the back of the chair. "Even Nader would have caught up with him, eventually."

Manx was about to reply, when his mobile vibrated. "Got to be on our top-game, tomorrow, Morris. Can't fuck this up at this stage. We've got one shot with Davey."

Morris nodded, and headed towards the door. Manx looked down at the number, and sighed. He didn't need this tonight. He answered anyway; there was no point in delaying whatever his sister was complaining about now.

"Manx," he said, which sounded more like a weary exhalation, rather than his own name. He listened for a few seconds.

"Just hang tight. I'll drive over," he said, scooping his jacket from the back of his chair.

Chapter 16

Shanni scrambled over the steep embankment towards the railway tracks. He flipped up his jacket hood, and walked towards the tunnel. Close to the entrance, he smelled fire. A cacophony of laughter and loud voices carried towards him. It sounded discordant and distant, as it echoed off the tunnel walls. He knelt beside a thick bramble bush, and looked to his east.

The voices were coming from a group of gypsies, five of them, sitting on milk bottle crates around the fire. Several tattered and dirty caravans marked the perimeter of the camp. These were not the romantic, brightly coloured horse-pulled Romany caravans, but the kind of beige, ordinary caravans, which bottled-necked the roads on the island during the summer. These caravans weren't travelling anywhere soon; their wheels had been removed and replaced with several stacks of house-bricks.

The fire had long, healthy flames flicking skywards, though Shanni was too far away to reap any of its heat. A young girl entered the circle. One of the men picked up a guitar. The girl began to sing; some old Gypsy melody, Shanni imagined. She had a pretty voice, which seemed to impart a haunting stillness to the scene, as if he were looking at an old photograph captured in time. *Why didn't he know about the camp?* Or maybe he did and hadn't really taken any notice before. It was at that point he remembered; a long-buried memory suddenly resurrected.

The camp had always been here. He recalled visiting with his mother when he was a kid, probably around age six or seven. Every few weeks, she'd get her cards read by Mrs. Locke, or Madam Locke, as the garishly painted poster in her caravan window preferred to address her. She was an old woman, back in those days, a small, fragile figure, with what Shanni always imagined was a flowered napkin wrapped around her head and large, looped earrings. *She must be long dead by now*, he thought, as he sat on the wet ground.

He felt the sickening weariness of hunger and tiredness ripple through him. Eventually, he fell asleep. When he woke, an hour or so later, all he could hear was the gentle crackle of the fire, and the snorting of a couple of old ponies shackled to the caravans. The camp was empty, but the fire was still burning, albeit low and steady.

He walked tentatively towards the slowly dying fire, and crouched beside the embers, rubbing his hands against its warmth. The camp smelled of bad sanitation and burnt wood. He hated it when his mother dragged him out here, usually when his "so-called-dad" was away on the ships. Shanni would hang outside on the caravan steps, while the Gypsy kids taunted him, or gawked at him, as if he were a specimen in a zoo. They never gave him too much trouble, though, maybe because he looked a little like them. It was probably around that time the pieces had begun to fall into place for Shanni. He looked more like the gypsy kids than he did his own family. But, he kept those suspicions to himself. Thirty-five years later, it remained an unspoken truth. Still, the revelation had provided clarity for Shanni. Why his "so-called-dad" always treated him like a lump of dog shit on the heel of his boots, and how his mother would be overprotective of her youngest son, the way she never acted with her other children.

From the back of one of the caravans, he heard the sound of scratching. He stiffened, waited for it to stop, but it became louder, more insistent. He walked tentatively around to the back of the camp.

Two wooden cages, about four feet off the ground, covered with a thick, green tarpaulin were stretched along the length of the caravan. He immediately knew their purpose. He lifted the right hand corner of the tarp. The scratching intensified. The familiar stench of rodent faeces rose from the flooring, and

Shanni quickly pulled the remainder of the tarp from the cages. The ferrets scuttled towards him, clambering over each other to be the first to be granted their freedom.

There must have been ten of them, clawing at the cheap metal cage fencing and biting at the frame, splintering the wood with their teeth. He stood, transfixed for a few moments, as the ferrets scratched. They were focussed on one goal—escape, which, for a moment, Shanni contemplated granting them. But, there were more pressing matters to deal with, like the heavy footsteps he'd failed to notice until it was too late. When he turned around, two men were standing a meter or so away from him. Father and son, Shanni guessed. They looked to be cut from the same cloth, that cloth being dark, thick and roughly hewn

"What the fuck you doing here?" the older one said. He was slapping a long, thick pool cue against the palm of his hand. Shanni said nothing; he was out of conversation, out of fight, and shit out of luck, too, he guessed, by the way the two men were staring him down.

"Fuckin' robbin' us, that's what," the younger one said, who also had some form of weapon in his hand, maybe a baseball bat.

As he swung it, Shanni realised it wasn't a baseball bat, but a cricket bat. The absurd image of a bunch of gypsies in cricket whites suddenly crossed Shanni's mind. The thin edge of the bat struck him directly on the temple. The pain rattled through his skull, shaking it like a snow globe; white flakes swirled around his eyes. He fell to his knees with a groan.

"Fuckin' thief," the older man shouted, jabbing Shanni's abdomen with the bat. Shanni doubled over, and felt the wind exit his body.

The ferrets screamed louder, as if they were enjoying the spectacle. As the men turned around to give them the futile instruction to "shut the fuck up," Shanni took his chance, and ran. After a few hundred metres, he figured they weren't following him, probably happy enough to give him a scare before getting back to whatever they did in those flea-ridden caravans.

He returned to the railway bridge, his whole body shivering with cold, apart from one warm spot on his neck, where the blood from his temple ran in a slow-flowing trickle. He scuffed along the damp grass, folded himself into a foetal position, and considered his options—stay here, or head back to the house and face the consequences? There was little to debate. He knew what needed to be done. He scrubbed the back of his sleeve across his eyes, which had begun to sting, and blew a glob of mucus onto the damp earth. He ran a finger across his cheeks. This time, there was no doubt. These were tears, and he let them flow, comforting and warm, over his face.

Chapter 17

Shanni arrived back at the cottage the following morning. It had just turned six. He'd spent the night under the bridge, but it was a restless and troubled sleep, punctured by the frequent appearance of Hywel Jenkin's bloodied face. His forehead hurt like hell, and there was the beginning of a head-cold gathering in his sinuses. As he walked the narrow pathway, he noticed the front door was slightly ajar. A gentle south-westerly cuffed at the door, like the hits of a light hammer. Shanni felt his stomach churn. It could have been his hunger, or, more likely, it was the object which had just caught his eye to the left of the driveway. Sara's car was still there.

He carefully pushed open the cottage door, and took a couple of tentative steps. He held his breath. The house had been turned over. *No,* Shanni thought, revising his initial impression, *the house had been trashed.* The sofa and chairs were on their sides, cushions scattered to the floor. The phone was ripped from its wires and stamped on, so its components were now spilling from it like electrical guts. The bookshelves, although they contained mostly knick-knacks and the pottery figurines Sara was fond of collecting rather than actual books, had been ripped from the wall, and their contents trampled into the carpet. The TV had a yawning, black hole where the screen should have been, and the X-Box and DVD player lay in pieces.

Shanni felt something scrunch underfoot; a photograph of him Sara and Dewi at Alton Towers was still in its frame, but the glass was now shattered into a fine line of a cobweb. He trod cautiously over the debris, his heart pounding and a dry sickness in his stomach, as he edged towards the kitchen.

What Shanni surmised to be the sum total of all the crockery they owned, was now scattered on the floor, shattered into millions of tiny fragments. He detected the faint aroma of souring milk and rotting food; the contents of the fridge and freezer were rapidly defrosting on the floor. Shanni didn't even bother to walk over the mess; there was no point. He did a one-eighty, and headed towards the stairs.

The twenty steps to Dewi's room felt like the longest climb of his life. He steadied himself on the railing and took each step slowly, quietly. Eighteen. Nineteen. Twenty. He stood on the landing outside Dewi's bedroom. A messy, hand-drawn, "*Privit Keep Out, No Girls Arlowd*" sign was hung, lopsided, on the door. Shanni traced his finger along the thick, waxy letters, before gently pushing down on the handle. The door clicked open.

He exhaled a long sigh of relief. The bedroom was just as he left it two nights ago. *Or was that a lifetime ago?* It was beginning to feel that way. The life he had once known was slipping slowly from his grasp. He could feel it, could almost touch it, as it faded off into the distance.

Before going back downstairs, he checked the master bedroom. Sara had abandoned a pile of her clothes on the floor. Maybe she had packed in a rush; it was a comforting thought. Yes, he was sure she and Dewi had escaped, before Scuttler got here, but her car was still in the driveway. *Maybe she'd called a taxi?* Yeah, Sara was practical that way, and she hated driving at night.

Before he turned to leave, something on the bed caught his eye; a thin rod, about a meter in length, silvery, and with what looked like dried blood at the tip. He steadied himself against Sara's dressing table. Scuttler was a sick fuck. As Shanni took a moment to compose himself, he heard a noise from downstairs, as if someone was walking across broken glass. He reached for the aerial, and closed the door quietly behind him.

Whoever was in the house was making little attempt to cover their presence. He held his breath as he walked down the stairs, being careful to avoid the step that creaked. Sara had been nagging him to fix it for months; another thing he wished he'd done right.

Whoever was in the house had now moved to the kitchen. He could hear the sharp crunch of china underfoot. A long, thin shadow traced itself across the length of the wall. *Should he call out? Or maybe surprise was the best defence?* Shanni waited, heard the striking of a match, then a plume of smoke drift out of the kitchen. He barely had time to register it as cigar smoke, when his brother-in-law stepped out, casually, into the living room.

"Fuck! Tudor. Fuck!" Shanni was so relieved, he could have hugged the Inspector, but resisted the temptation.

Manx looked him over. "If you're challenging me to a duel, you're going to need to find me a weapon," he said. Shanni dropped the aerial to the floor, kicking it to the side of the skirting board.

"Long story, Shanni?" Manx asked.

"You wouldn't fucking believe it, mate," Shanni said.

"Try me," Manx replied and gestured for Shanni to sit down. "Probably best we do this here, rather than down at the station."

Shanni had only had one question. "Sara and Dewi?"

Manx settled into the wide, leather chair. "Sara called me, probably just after she hung up on you. I picked her and Dewi up as soon as I could, and took them to Alice's place."

Shanni would have smiled, but he was too anxious. His mind was whirring through a multitude of scenarios. *What should he tell Manx? The whole story?* He'd probably arrest him on the spot. Family or not, he was still a fucking copper, and he'd never had much luck with them in the past.

"Are they...?" Shanni began, before Manx interrupted.

"Sara's upset, not surprisingly, but not half as upset as I'll be, if you don't tell me what the fuck is going on," he said, taking a considered pull on his cigar, as if he was settling in for a long fireside chat.

Shanni executed a split-second decision. He wouldn't tell the whole story; not now he knew Sara and Dewi were safe. He still had a chance to salvage something from the shit-storm he'd created.

He launched into his recollection of events, the same story he'd related to Sara, but with added embellishments and details he'd concocted the prior night, as he lay under the railway bridge. Manx listened intently as Shanni spoke, only interrupting every now and then with some clarifying questions.

"What were you doing at the airstrip at that time of night?"

He had a lock-up there, Shanni explained, which was true, although it held nothing more than a few engine parts. He needed a part for a car he was working on, an old Fiesta MK 2.

"And it couldn't wait until tomorrow?"

He was passing anyway; it would save him a journey in the morning.

"How many men?"

Three. He was sure there were three of them. And a car, too, an old Mercedes, Shanni told him.

"Talk me through what happened, slowly and in detail," Manx said taking another puff on his cigar.

Shanni cleared his throat, which felt dry as A-grade sandpaper. He was making his way out of the lock-up, waking towards his car, when he heard the Mercedes. It stopped about a hundred metres away, and kept its engine running. He was about to walk back when he heard voices, then two blokes walked out of the car and dragged someone out of the backseat. The bloke was shouting, but he couldn't make out what he was saying.

Suddenly, he made a break for it and ran. One of the men pulled out a gun from his belt and shouted at him to stop, but the bloke just kept on running. That's when they shot him straight through the head. At least, that's what he thought, but he couldn't be sure, because it was dark and the bloke dropped like a sack of potatoes. Shanni had panicked, dropped the engine part, a head-gasket, he was carrying. It bounced on the tarmac, made a hell of a racket. The men turned, saw Shanni. They fired a warning shot. Shanni didn't think, he just ran. He was always a fast runner; remember, in school, he reminded Manx.

Manx nodded. "Then, what happened?"

Shanni explained how he made it to Gaerwen, called Sara, then spent the night under the old railway bridge.

"I was terrified, fucking terrified," Shanni was shaking. "I didn't know what else to do."

"Call the police?" Manx offered

Shanni hesitated. "Not thinking straight, was I? I'd just seen some bloke murdered. You might be used to it, but it scared the crap out of me." Shanni leant in, as if here were revealing a confidence. "Sara and Dewi, you know, I was just thinking about them. If family, family. Right, Tudor?"

Manx didn't care for what Shanni was implying, but let it go for the moment. After a few moments silence, Manx spoke. "OK, this is what's going to happen. I want to do right by my sister, but that doesn't mean I'm going to put my job on the line for you. I'll get a team over to the airfield. If what you're telling me is true, I'll make sure you, Sara, and Dewi get full police protection, until we figure this out."

"Thanks, mate that's a load…" Shanni began.

"But, if I find out you've been shovelling me with bullshit, I swear, I will cuff you myself, and march you down to the station. Understand?"

Shanni nodded, swallowed a thimbleful of saliva, and wondered if he'd done the right thing. There was an opening. Manx was offering him an out; he just needed to take it.

"I swear, God's own truth," Shanni finally said.

Manx nodded. "All right."

"Where am I going to go?" Shanni said. "I can't stay here."

"You can bunk at my place for tonight. Don't phone anyone, or leave the house, until I give you the all clear. Got it?"

Shanni nodded.

"Good," Manx said, but his mind was thinking otherwise. This wasn't good at all. In fact, it was so beyond not good he was beginning to wonder how much he could trust his brother-in-law. Keeping Shanni on a tight leash seemed the best plan.

"I've got a few calls to make," Manx said, walking towards the door. "I'd clean up, if I were you. Don't want Sara coming home to this," Manx said. Shanni nodded, and wiped his palm across his face.

***

Manx made two calls. The first was to Sara, to let her know her husband was safe. Not that she offered much of a reaction. She sounded distant, as if she were already disconnecting, hoping for the best, but preparing herself for the worst. The second call was to Nader. He instructed the Sergeant to meet him at the cottage in twenty minutes, and be ready to call forensics, and maybe Hardacre, if the situation demanded it.

He watched Shanni through the window of the cottage, busying himself cleaning up, as Max had suggested. *What did he really know about his brother-in-law?* They knew each other at school, but that was about it. Shanni was an odd kid, an outsider, but if every odd kid Manx had known in school had grown up to be a criminal, the island would be over-run with them. He thought back to a few weeks ago, a day or so after the first murder. The way Shanni's blood seemed to drain from his face when he saw Manx, and asking that question about him and Sara being safe. He wanted to give his brother-in-law the benefit of the doubt, even if it was just for his sister's sake, but he knew Shanni had always been the runt of the family, and the problem with runts was they were always out to prove themselves.

Chapter 18

"Why are we out here again, boss?" Nader asked, zipping up his rain jacket.

"Searching for a body," Manx said, without much conviction, and kept walked the perimeter of the airstrip until they reached the Capri. The light south-westerly had picked up momentum, and was now gusting across the runway. Manx felt the beginnings of a light rain peck at his face.

Nader kicked at the remains of a seagull, which had sounded its final caw some weeks back. "Human, is it, boss?" he asked.

Manx ignored the remark, and walked slowly around the car.

"1984, 2.8 injection, bloody good nick, too," Nader observed, nodding in appreciation. "Used to have one of these myself, back in the day. Went like the clappers. Wife made me get rid of it, when we got married. I agreed, like a bloody fool." Nader ran his hands gently over the back-wing, lost in some youthful recollection.

"What do you make of this?" Manx asked, pointing at the broken aerial connection on the passenger-side wing.

Nader huffed. "Electrics were always a bastard on these. Maybe he got some new digital what-you-may-call-it in there, junked the aerial."

"Maybe. But, why make such a botch of it? Looks like he's just snapped the bloody thing off, then stuck it back on with masking tape. The rest of the car's immaculate, why leave this eyesore?"

"Dunno, boss. He's your brother-in-law," Nader offered.

Manx knelt down, and traced his finger across a series of dark splatter marks, in a cone-shape, spreading out from the wing of the car and onto the tarmac. "Take a look at this."

Nader groaned. His arthritic knee joints cracked like dry twigs, as he squatted. "Oil from one of the planes, or a dodgy radiator?"

"It's too random. Oil or fuel spills are more uniform. I'll get forensics down here, get their take on it," Manx said.

"Champion," Nader said, groaning himself to standing. "An early morning callout, and Bread of Bloody Bevan." He walked around the Capri, and stood a few feet away, as if admiring an artwork.

"Looks heavy on the back end, mind you," Nader said.

"What was that?" Manx was speaking with one of the SOCOs, the wind gusting over the open airstrip was making it hard to hear.

"Heavy," Nader shouted. "Like there's something in the boot." He walked to the rear of the car, and clicked his thumb on the circular, chrome lock. The boot was stiff, and it took him a few pulls before the mechanism released. It sprung up quickly, narrowly missing his chin.

"Jesus Christ!" Nader said. He stepped back slowly from the bloodied, contorted body which had been squeezed into too tight a space, with too little air.

"Boss, you'd better get Hardacre down 'ere, too," he said, wafting away the foul stench rising from the boot. "Looks like your brother-in-law's carrying some extra baggage."

Chapter 19

"Morning, Inspector," Mickey Thomas said, in an overly cheerful fashion, when Manx returned to the station later that morning.

"Got a solicitor who's none too pleased with you, threatened to leave a couple of times already," he added, taking a large slurp of his steaming hot tea.

"Seems everybody's in a hurry to leave this place," Manx said.

"Aye, don't understand it, myself. Brand new digs, warm bed, hot breakfast, and a cuppa in the morning, what's not too like? You get the invitation by the way, in your inbox thing?"

Manx had a vague memory of something cartoonish landing in his mailbox a few days ago, but had immediately deleted it, suspecting it was one of those inter-departmental missives, which attempted to promote a head-office initiative in a humorous manner, and regularly failed in its objective.

"Retirement party. Week on Saturday, back room at the Bull."

"Oh, right, almost forgot." Not that Manx had any recollection of looking at the invitation.

"You'll be there?"

"Got nowhere else to be," Manx said.

"Aye, that's what we all reckoned," Mickey said, grinning over the edge of his over-sized mug.

As Manx walked into the interview room, Frasier Davenport and Davey were sitting by the table, neither of them looking thrilled to be there, especially Davey, who in his unshaven, crumbled state looked as if he'd been incarcerated for weeks. *Good.* It was the effect Manx hoped for.

Davenport, however, looked spritely and freshly scrubbed; he could have done without that. Manx himself had woken up dog-tired, with a bank of miasma creeping around his head, the sort of dense fogginess coming from too little sleep and too much worry. It had taken him the best part of three hours to talk Sara off the ledge last night, and then, there was Shanni to deal with earlier this morning.

"I've been waiting for over an hour, Inspector," Davenport said. "I do have other clients who need my representation."

Manx sat. "Many of them on a triple murder charge?"

Davenport began to protest, but Manx interrupted, "Morning, Davey. Well-rested?" Manx noticed the corner of Davey's lip twitch, as if he was about to say something but thought better of it.

"Triple murder, really?" Davenport said, shaking his head in an over-dramatic fashion.

Manx flipped opened a folder, and dealt out five photographs across the table. Davey grimaced at the images—a man's body stuffed into a car boot, his throat punctured, and beads of dried blood baked onto his neck and upper chest.

"What's with the Penny Dreadfuls?" Davenport said, pushing back the photographs.

"This man was found this morning, murdered, probably sometime yesterday evening, sharp implement rammed into his throat."

"Well, that rules my client out. He was in here, enjoying your... accommodations."

"Correct," Manx said, sitting back in his chair. "However, according to our pathologist, this man's been in the boot of that Capri all night."

Manx noticed Davey's body language stiffen. "Know someone with a Capri, do you, Davey?" Manx asked.

Davey looked to the floor.

"Last night's temperature was around three degrees Celsius. Temperatures that low tend to slow down the rate of decomposition.

We won't know for sure until we get the full pathology report, but we'd expect the time of death to be early evening, just before we picked you up, Davey."

Davey exhaled a nervous, twitchy laugh.

"Three murders. Must have taken a hell of a lot of planning."

"You apprehended my client in order to question him on a specific drugs charge, not murder," Davenport interjected.

"Open season on what I ask, until he's charged."

"Weren't me," Davey said.

Manx smiled. "Innocent men don't usually run, and you probably already know what we found when we impounded your van."

Davey stiffened, as did Davenport. "Two thousand pounds in used bills. You been fixing water meters, like your mate, Edwards?"

Davey focussed his eyes on the opposite wall.

"Or is that what you were paid to bump off this bloke?" Manx said, stabbing one of the photos. "Two grand? You operating a bargain basement assassin service on the side?"

"I never killed nobody," Davey said.

"Then, who did?"

Davey was about to reply, when Davenport interrupted, "Inspector, my client knows nothing about this supposed murder."

"Murders," Manx corrected him. "Maybe, but Davey knows something, and if he's not spilling the beans, then I'm inclined to propose my own theories. Want to hear one?"

Davey kept his gaze on his shoes, like a small child being reprimanded.

"I'll tell you, just to pass the time," Manx said. "You don't have the brains or stomach for murder, Davey. I'm amazed you made it so far without being caught, a bad reflection on this department, if nothing else. Still, you have to agree, bloody stupid move, peddling drugs so close to a school zone."

"Allegedly," Davenport interrupted.

"My theory is you're a minor player, whatever the fuck this operation is." Manx shuffled closer to Davey. "I don't know how far down the food chain you are, plankton level I suspect, but you're obviously protecting someone. A pact, is that it? Honour amongst idiots?"

Davey twiddled his thumbs, as if knitting them into a scarf of nail and skin.

"Listen, Davey," Manx said, easing back in his tone, finding the calm, reasonable Manx he often accessed for situations like this. "I don't think you killed these men; you don't fit the profile. My Chief, however, has a different take. Now, I hate disappointing my boss, and telling him I think he's wrong. My theory? You're covering for someone; someone who probably wouldn't give a shit if you rotted behind bars for the duration."

Manx leant in across the table. "I've seen this before, Davey, this misguided loyalty bullshit, and I always ask the same question. Would the person you're protecting do the same for you, if the situation was reversed?"

Davey's brow glistened with sweat.

"Admit to the dealing, supply me with a name of who you're working for, and my DCI puts in a good word for you at the Crown Prosecution."

"Again, Inspector, evidence?" Davenport piped up.

"We can dig up a lot in twenty-four hours," Manx said.

"Twenty-two, to be precise."

"Best not waste any more time, then," Manx said, and stood up. "You need to go to the bathroom, or anything, before we get set up?" he asked.

"Set up for what?" Davenport said.

"Davey's big close up," Manx explained. "You've seen how this works on TV, Davey. I put you in a room full of blokes as ugly as you are, and someone identifies you as the person pushing Anglesey Blue outside Amlwch School. Old fashioned, but effective."

Davey looked over at Davenport, who responded with an "it's out of my hands" shrug of the shoulders.

"After you," Manx said, and followed close behind, as Davey and Davenport shuffled out of the interview room.

Chapter 20

Priddle had delivered Shanni, as directed, to Manx's house just after ten-thirty that morning. By eleven o'clock, Shanni had showered, shaved, and made a well-needed deposit in Manx's bathroom. He changed into the only clothes he'd grabbed from the house—a pair of faded jeans and hooded sweatshirt. By eleven-twenty, he was pacing down the narrow corridor that passed for Manx's sparsely furnished kitchen, like a caged animal.

He spent a few minutes poking around the house, searching for something to read; there was nothing, not even a newspaper or the back of a cereal packet. Manx's computer was giving him a come-hither look from the kitchen table, but as he pressed the keyboard, the animated screen saver whooshed to the background, and the password prompt teased him to venture further. He resisted the temptation; Manx was a stranger to him, as impenetrable as the MacBook Pro beckoning for him to at least give it a try.

His brother-in-law had told him nothing about what they found at the airstrip, other than confirming they'd located Shanni's car, which had been impounded, and was now being combed over by forensics. The way Manx relayed this information, in an official, detached tone of voice, had made Shanni anxious. Maybe he was being over-sensitive. Last night's events had rattled his nerves. *Was Manx deliberately keeping information from him, or was it standard police procedure to keep people in the dark? Sweating them out, isn't that what they called it?*

Shanni hadn't even noticed his hand was trembling, until he held a mug under the tap. He drank the water quickly, hoping the shaking would subside, and held out both his hands over the sink, watching as they trembled like the loose exhaust pipe on a truck. They were working man's hands, soiled with the oil and grime his job demanded, but now, he reminded himself, they were now also the hands of a murderer.

His mind shot back to last night. *What had happened after he ran?* He'd heard the gunshot, Jenkins had to be dead, the goon, too. *Had Scuttler and the other goon then taken both bodies, and dumped them somewhere?* Or had they discarded them, like used condoms on the side of the airstrip, along with Shanni's car, implicating him in the murder of both men. As the theory began to take shape in Shanni's head, which was now humming like a well-tuned racing engine, a deep, hollow pit opened in his stomach.

He sat on the two-seater sofa, the only item of furniture in Manx's living room, stretched out his legs, and let out a long exhalation. Last night, in the phone box, he'd extended himself too much credit. He hadn't just been stupid; he'd been the Taj fucking Mahal of stupidity. A thought, like the snagged end of a thread, began to unravel in his mind.

Manx was going to finger him for the murder of both Jenkins and the goon, he was sure of it. Manx hadn't believed a word of what he'd told him this morning, he was sure of that, too. The way that lanky, steely-eyed bastard looked at him, as if he were dog shit on his shoe; the same look his "so-called-dad" used to give him; still did. And the way Manx squinted his eyes and visibly tensed when Shanni mentioned the word "family," as if he'd poked his brother-in-law in the eye with a sharp stick. Sara had mentioned Manx was a cold fish, especially where his family was concerned. *What kind of man turns his back on his family, anyway?* Manx would never understand why Shanni did what he did. He was taking care of his own. *How could he understand something like that?* Nobody was depending on him; no six-year-old boy who believed the world began and ended with his dad. Shanni was just another suspect to him, family or no family.

Shanni could almost feel his brother-in-law's breath, warm and accusing on his neck, as he sat in his house, surrounded by his belongings, frugal and minimal as they were. Manx was probably poking around for evidence right now, turning over the house, asking questions. Maybe he'd even drag Sara down for questioning, Dewi, too.

He switched on the small, portable TV on the coffee table. The set took a while to warm up, and when it finally reached its optimal operating temperature, it offered only a grainy image of Loraine Kelly twittering on in her soft, Scottish brogue. After a few minutes, thick, grey bars began scrolling up the screen; it was as if the TV itself was rolling its eyes at him.

"Fuck this," Shanni muttered to himself, and jerked the cord from the socket. He checked his watch—opening time. He'd sink a couple of pints, calm his head, get some food inside him; he hadn't eaten since yesterday afternoon. Yeah, to hell with Tudor fucking Manx. He wasn't going to hang around waiting for him to come back, with a car full of pigs and a hard-on for an arrest. No. Fucking. Way.

***

As he walked towards the Pilot Arms, the Irish Sea lolled, like an old drunk, to and fro against the rocks. A sharp line of sunlight flared from behind the clouds like a searchlight, and fell onto the window of the wool shop across the bay.

As he looked over, he noticed two men leaning against the window frame, their thickset figures like solid shadows over the white pebbledash. *It couldn't be*, he thought, as he squinted his eyes against the momentary brightness. He pulled back his hood. The two goons were standing in front of the shop, not five hundred metres from him, smoking, hanging around like bored teenagers looking to cause trouble. *Had they followed him here? Had someone tipped them off? But, the more disturbing question was, what was one of them still doing alive?* Alive and smoking, as if last night had never happened. For one glorious moment, Shanni thought it might all have been a terrible nightmare, but the sickening emptiness in his belly and the bruise on his temple, courtesy of the gypsy with the baseball bat reminded him otherwise. *So, why wasn't the big goon dead, or at least lying in the hospital with a tube rammed down his throat?* Shanni didn't wait to answer his own question. Instead, he quickly gathered the thick hood back around his face, turned his back to the sea, and jogged the final few metres to the pub.

Chapter 21

Lynda and Adam Masterson stood close to each other, as the curtains covering the large picture widow were drawn open. Both mother and son took a small, tentative step backwards, as the six men shuffled awkwardly into the room, and looked to the floor. Lynda took a short inhalation, and made the sign of the holy trinity across her chest.

Manx pressed the intercom button. "Hold your numbers up, please, and look directly in front of you."

The men did as they were instructed, one even smiled, an unnecessary action, given the circumstances, but it made Adam chuckle. His mother immediately ordered him to shush.

"Do you recognise any of these men, Adam?" Manx said.

Adam scrunched his eyes, and looked over the men from left to right, then back again. "Number four," Adam said, pointing at the shabby, bug- eyed figure of Davey Evans.

"Is this the same man you saw selling Anglesey Blue, three days ago, in the vicinity of Amlwch School?"

"Yeah, that's the dude," Adam said.

Lynda rolled her eyes at her son's use of the word, "dude."

"All right, you can take them all out now, Constable." Manx turned to the boy. "You've been very helpful, Adam. You're probably a little too old for a lollipop and a plastic police hat, but if there's anything we can do to help you or your mother, let us know."

"Tiwzz... he'd like a hat," Adam said, raising his head slightly as he spoke.

"Tiwzz, I mean, Danny, Adam's younger brother," Lynda explained. "He's five, likes to be called Tiwzz. We're all hoping it's just a phase."

"Mickey will sort you out at reception," Manx said, and offered his hand. Adam took it willingly, although he blushed deeply as he did so. Lynda rubbed her son's back, a gesture of warm motherly pride, which the teenager attempted to shrug off, though Manx saw little effort behind Adam's action, as he permitted Lynda to keep her hand on his back, while Manx escorted them back to reception.

Chapter 22

Why wasn't he answering? Trev always picked up on the third ring; it was their code. Shanni tried again—nothing. On the sixth ring, he picked up, his tone of voice falling somewhere between mildly anxious and terrified. He asked a laundry list of questions, one of which included asking Shanni if he needed the van for anything illegal, and if so, he'd have to say no. Shanni laughed, and almost told Trev to shove the favour up his arse, but persevered until Trev finally agreed to loan him an old Ford Escort van. It was a good runner, Trev informed him, but the interior was knackered.

"Good enough." Shanni hung up, and called the taxi number on one of the business cards stuck on the notice board.

Trev had left to pick up his wife from a W.I. meeting, but he'd left the van parked outside his garage, with the keys stashed on top of the front driver's wheel. It started first time, but Trev had been wrong about the condition of the interior; knackered was a woefully inadequate description. There was only one seat still remaining, thankfully, the driver's, and the majority of the critical instruments were either missing, or useless. It also had a pungent aroma of cow-shit. Trev probably used it to transport manure to his allotment at the back of the cottage; a pastime he'd told Shanni, on more than one occasion, he felt more wed to than his own wife. Shanni wondered how Trev's wife would have reacted to that remark, but his guess was she already knew.

Chapter 23

"You want me to authorise what?" DCI Canton asked, thrusting his body-weight into his office chair, which squeaked with complaint.

"Release a sketch of Davey Williams to the Press. Tell them he's our prime suspect." Manx explained.

Canton pulled out a pair of butterfly shears from his desk, and began to snip delicately at the branches of the Indoor Chinese Elm. "That's what I thought you said, but then, I thought to myself, that couldn't be right. Why the hell would I authorise releasing a sketch of an innocent man?"

Canton quickly corrected himself, and grunted, as he nicked at one of the leathery leaves, and let it fall onto the damp soil. "A man, who, as you just explained to me, is unlikely to have committed these murders, and then inform the world and his dog we're searching for him, when he's already in custody. That's not what you're asking, right, Manx?"

Manx leant forward, making sure to explain himself in as clear and logical way as he could. "If Callum Blackwell gets wind we're onto him, he'll bolt. If we release Davey's ugly mug, Blackwell stays put. Davey, on the other hand, sweats it out on a triple murder charge, and eventually tells us who, and what, he knows, which leads us to Blackwell."

"You hope," Canton said, rising slowly from his chair, and snipping at the mini-copse of six Bonsai trees lined up in perfect symmetry on his wall cabinet. "What if Davey clams up?"

"He'll talk, but if he doesn't, we nail him on the drugs charge, and Blackwell stays on the island, until we find another way to bring him out in the open."

"Still a gamble, though, Tudor," Canton said, lopping an errant branch from a Juniper Bonsai.

"I always took you for a gambling man," Manx said. "That prostitute killer in Tiger Bay, back in the nineties? You staged a copycat murder, leaked it to the Press, and got the killer so riled up, his ego got the best of him. Just about walked into the station to complain, is what I heard."

"Is that where you got this crackpot idea, Manx?"

"You're an inspiration, Chief, what can I say?"

Manx noticed Canton's back straighten. "Hardly the same thing," Canton said. "We commissioned a full psychological profile of our suspect. What do we have with Blackwell? A couple of photographs and a classic need to please his father. Flimsy, at best."

"We'll contain it, make sure only the immediate team is in the know, but the authorization needs to come from you, for credibility."

"Not exactly by the book, is it?" Canton said.

"Just an alternative interpretation," Manx offered.

Canton sighed, and sat back down. "Listen, Manx, I've kept you out of this, because, quite frankly, I want you focussed on solving this case." Canton placed his elbows on his desk, and spoke softly. "I'm getting pressure from the higher ups at Glan Y Don. They're making noises about drafting in some new blood from South Wales C.I.D. to oversee the investigation. Probably just rattling my cage, but this gorilla's too long in the tooth to care. Told them so, too. Don't think it went down too well." Canton chuckled.

"It's a good plan. Either way, we win."

Canton attended to a stray clump of lint on his sleeve. "Maybe, but it's about perception. If this scheme of yours falls on its arse, I'll be tarred as the officer who authorised the leak of a sketch of a man who's already in custody. It's not going to look good. Perception, Manx."

"Since when did looking good appeal to you, Chief?"

Canton leant back in his chair, and shifted the photograph of his wife a few centimetres to the left. "In six years, I'll be out, pensioned off. Got big plans in the works. World travel, villa on the Costa Del Sol. If the wife ever got wind I jeopardised my full pension, she'd never forgive me. I don't expect you to understand, but Marjorie's been a policeman's wife for forty-five years, and I owe her not to step on any landmines on the home stretch. So, my answer is no, Manx. Find another way, something that's not going to get me marched out of here under a thundercloud and half a pension. I'd make a shitty security guard. I hate the bloody telly, as it is. Nothing but attention seeking idiots and those damned Nordic police dramas. I get enough of that at work."

Manx was about to complain, when Canton raised his hand in a stop gesture. "Save it, Manx. Remember what I told you at basic training? A threat can often be as effective as the action, sometimes more so?"

Manx nodded. He remembered exactly.

Chapter 24

Shanni arrived at his parents' small-holding, just after one thirty that afternoon. He unlatched the iron-gate, and walked to the main house. His "so-called-dad" would be working the day shift at Holyhead Port for the next few hours, punching tickets on the Stena Line ferries. His mam would be at work, too, probably clearing up the dishes after lunch at the old people's home. He called out, anyway, with a few loud "hellos," just to be sure. He received nothing in return, save the cackle of cormorants, as they passed under the ceiling of grey clouds.

He took a diagonal path across the cobblestone yard towards the east side of the barn, and squatted down at the narrow drinking trough. He reached underneath, and ran his fingers along the lichen-covered curves, feeling the cold outline of a key in his fingers.

Inside, the barn was dark and empty, with an overwhelming aroma of rotting wood and stale hay. He looked towards the ceiling. Shafts of thin, pale light fell through the cracks in the stone and roof. As his eyes became accustomed to the darkness, he saw the object he was looking for—a tall, grey, metal cabinet propped up against the far-right corner.

He reached, almost automatically, for the torch which had always hung on the left of the door. To his left, something caught his eye—a long, wooden box missing the mesh of wire, which would normally have surrounded it.

A shudder ran through him, as his mind raced back three decades ago to a day not unlike today, the air still and heavy, as if it were waiting for something big to happen. Shanni was seventeen, and had just endured what he swore would be the last beating he'd ever suffer at the hands of his "so-called-dad."

That night, he'd made up his mind to leave. He packed up some clothes, and quietly closed the front door behind him. But, there was one last chore still to complete—one final act of release.

Even today, when he couldn't sleep, their sounds would sometimes haunt him. The high-pitched screeches of sixteen black, sable-mitt ferrets falling over themselves, as they leapt from their cage, and ran in circles around the farmyard, clueless as what to make of their freedom. Then, as if they'd finally gathered their collective wits about them, they ran westward, towards the open fields. Shanni had watched them, made sure they'd cleared the yard, and then set off in the opposite direction, down the dirt track, and over the gate to anywhere. Anywhere had to be better than here.

Shanni reached under a plant pot on the shelf for the key. The metal door swung open with a slow, ponderous creak, as if it were asking Shanni if he really wanted to do this. He did. He'd never been more sure of anything.

He unzipped the gym bag, and counted the eight grand just to make sure it was all there; it was. He was about to close the cabinet door, when another object caught his attention. A 9mm Glock 19 revolver. Harri Morgan had bought it on one of his extended sea voyages, or had won it in a card game, Shanni couldn't recall. He slipped the weapon from its holster, and felt its perfectly balanced form in his palm. He attempted to curl a finger around the trigger, but the thick bandage caught in the housing. He tried his left hand; the gun felt loose and unbalanced. There was only one option. They were meant to come off next week, anyway. *What difference would it make?*

He reached for a rusted pair of rusted pruning shears, and snipped the knot. Layer by layer, the white bandages fell, and sloughed from his finger, like a conjurer's endless handkerchief trick. They fell in a thick spill of snow at his feet. His finger, or what was left of it, protruded like a small nub of red bone from his knuckle. It felt as if his finger was still attached, the joints perfectly aligned, the nail still chewed to the nub and dirt-filled; a phantom of a life he once had, and could still feel, but could no longer touch.

Chapter 25

Manx tossed Callum Blackwell's photograph across the table. It spun a hundred and eighty degrees and settled, face up, directly in front of Davey.

"Ring a bell?" Manx asked.

Davey glanced briefly at the photograph, and shrugged his heavy-set shoulders. "Never seen him before."

Manx slapped the table hard. "Look closely," he said, leaning the full stretch of his body across the table, until it loomed like a thin shadow over Davey Evans.

Davey snorted, and picked up the photo for a closer look. "Still don't know him," he said, and laid it back on the table.

Manx smiled. "Call it police intuition, but I had a feeling you'd say that. "Manx reached inside the other envelope, and laid out a piece of paper, face down, on the table. "Know what this is, Davey?"

"Not Darrin fuckin' Brown, am I."

"Turn it over," Manx said.

Davey shrugged, and did as he was told. If it was at all possible, Davey's eyes grew even more bulbous, as he recognised the sketch.

"Can't draw for toffee, myself, failed O Level art," Manx said. "But, even I can appreciate a good likeness when I see one."

Manx watched carefully, as Davey looked over the portrait drawn by the police sketch artist, less than an hour ago. "It's a little rushed. The chin's off and the nose could be better defined, but he's got the eyes down pat, don't you think?"

Davenport leant over Davey's shoulder to look at the sketch. "Where's this going, Inspector?" he asked, stifling a yawn.

Manx sat back, and dug his hands deep into his jean pockets. "In approximately three hours, the North Wales Police will be holding a Press conference. I'm not usually the media circus type, but for you, Davey, I'll make an exception. During this circus, I'll be announcing to the good people of Anglesey due to their assistance, we now have a detailed description of the man we believe is our prime suspect. I will go on to explain while, as yet, we don't have a name, we believe our suspect bears a striking resemblance to this gentleman right here. At this point, I'll bring up this sketch, nice and big on the monitors."

Davey flinched.

"I'll also confirm our suspect is extremely dangerous, should not be approached under any circumstances, and if anyone knows or sees this person, to call the police hot-line as soon as possible."

Davenport shook his head, and snorted. "This makes no sense. Not to mention, it violates my client's civil rights."

"Possibly, but even we make mistakes. But, by the time we admit ours, and apologise profusely, somebody will have recognised you; a relative, work colleague or friend, maybe even your mother? You have a close relationship with her, Davey?"

Davey put down the sketch, and looked directly at the wall.

"No matter. We're sure someone will call in; it's just a matter of time. Then, let me tell you what happens, Davey. Press start calling you all hours of the day and night, Welsh Water lays you off, with no pay, your mam finds her boy's been dealing drugs all over the island, probably selling to her friend's kids. Tough for her to live that down, in a small place like this."

Davey kicked at the table leg. "I keep telling you, I never killed no one,"

"But, you know someone who knows the killer, don't you, Davey?"

Davenport shook his head. "Empty threats, Mr. Evans, and in my opinion, skirting the outer edges of the law."

"Do you trust me not to go ahead with this plan, Davey?"

Manx noticed Davey's eyes were glistening now.

"Let me make this easy for you," Manx said, stabbing Blackwell's photograph. "You're probably not aware of this, but you were selling drugs on behalf of this man, Callum Blackwell. I suspect you were too low on the food chain to ever meet him, because, if you did, you'd remember. But, whoever is heading up your tin-pot, methadone cartel does know him. I need that name, Davey, or your ugly mug is all over the six o'clock news. How's your wife and kid going to feel about that? Your mother?"

Davey wiped his sleeve across his sweat-soaked brow.

"One name," Manx repeated.

Davey's eyes were like glassy barbules protruding from their sockets, the beginnings of a tears forming at the corners. He drove his thumbs into his eyes, and wiped away the moisture.

"I'd recommend you say nothing, Mr. Evans," Davenport said.

But, Davey wasn't listening. He swallowed hard, and whispered a name.

"Can you repeat that?" Manx said.

Davey spoke the name again, and then again, each time louder, rocking like a toddler attempting to soothe himself. By the sixth time, Davey repeated the name, it was like the dead smack of a hammer on steel. The revelation didn't provide Manx with the relief he hoped for. Instead, on the seventh repeat of the name, he felt a deep, nauseating pit form in his stomach, and a sharp flood of blood rush to his head.

Chapter 26

"Shanni Morgan!" The name Davey had offered up was still reverberating in his brain with a furious intensity.

His own bloody brother-in-law! Fuck! How could he have been so stupid? But, looking back, the pieces fell into place. How Shanni turned almost white when he first saw him in the kitchen that Saturday afternoon; the way he became flustered when Manx made the joke about running a major criminal organisation on the island. Then, the brick through the window, there was no way that was a coincidence. It must have been a warning. Also, there was Shanni's missing finger; his explanation was too vague, too flippant. And last night's events. He was already suspicious of what Shanni had told him, which is why he'd wanted to keep him close for a few hours. And then, the body in the boot, stabbed with a sharp object. *Was Shanni holding the murder weapon, when Manx confronted him this morning?* He suspected Shanni might be dipping his toes in some petty crime, but he'd failed to grasp the extent of his involvement.

He brought the Jensen to a juddering halt, wheels half on the curb, and ran into his house. He tore through the first floor of the semi-detached in a matter of seconds, calling out Shanni's name, and receiving nothing but the silence. He took the steps leading to the upstairs two at a time. *Where the fuck was he?* Both bedrooms were empty, and the only evidence Shanni was ever there was a damp, discarded towel on the bathroom floor. Manx threw the bathroom door closed. The bang echoed like a gunshot through the thin walls of the house.

In the kitchen, Manx dragged up a stool, took a few deep, meditative breaths, and laid his hands, palms down, on the breakfast bar. *If he were Shanni, where would he go? How would he feel right now?* Tired; he'd be exhausted, a night sleeping rough, and the stress of deception would be pressing down on him. He'd be on edge, probably had been for weeks, maybe even close to breaking down. *What had gone down last night? A deal gone bad?* Shanni always was a mouthy little fucker; maybe he'd pissed off Blackwell enough to make him want to kill him. *But, who was the dead body in the back of the car? Had Shanni killed him? Or was that Blackwell?*

Shanni's first instinct would be to protect his family. Maybe Blackwell had threatened them. He'd be tired, hungry; angry, even. *Angry at who?* Blackwell and probably angry at Manx, too, but Blackwell seemed the more likely. *But, why would Shanni leave the house?* He was safe there, no one else knew, other than the immediate investigation team, and there were no visible signs of a struggle, which meant Shanni had left of his own accord. But, he had no car, no landline, no cell phone. Then, Manx remembered. Of course, if he were Shanni, that's exactly where he'd go. Someplace with warm food, shelter, and a working pay phone.

Chapter 27

Manx ran the few hundred metres downhill to the Pilot Arms. He barrelled into two young lads attempting to extract a pack of Embassy Number Six from the vending machine, mumbled a half-hearted apology, and threw open the lounge doors. Three old codgers sitting close to the window looked up momentarily from their pints, then carried on looking out to sea. He ran through the lounge into the snug. Shanni was gone, if he was ever here. He looked towards the bar. Gwen was clipping several packages of fresh pork-rinds onto the pegs next to the mirror.

"Gwen!" he called, as he walked towards her.

She smiled. "Oh, hiya! Not seen you for a couple of days. Usual, is it?"

Manx placed his hands on the bar. "Was there someone in here earlier today? A shortish bloke, olive-skinned, dark hair, probably wearing some kind of hooded…"

"Shanni, you mean?" Gwen said.

Manx was at a momentary loss for words.

"He told me his name was Shanni, anyway," Gwen said, as she unfolded a tea towel. "Talkative bloke, bit flirty, but seemed harmless enough. He ordered a plate of chips, sat over there by the window."

"Anybody with him?"

"Don't think so. He stayed for about an hour, then asked for change for the phone. Didn't see him after that. One of your most wanted, is he?"

"Do you know the number for the pay phone? The one by the door?"

"No idea. But, it'll be on the phone, won't it?" Gwen said.

Manx pounded the bar. "Yes. Yes, it would. Thanks."

A young man was on the phone, speaking in a low voice into the receiver. He was talking to someone called Amy, and by the way he seemed to be repeating her name, with the same, pleading tone, Manx guessed he was attempting to atone for something. Manx tapped him on the shoulder. The lad turned his back, and kept talking. Manx flipped open his badge, and held it a few inches from the lad's face, miming the word "now." The lad complied, and handed Manx the receiver. The number had almost faded into the white paper, but there was enough ink remaining to make out the important digits. Manx reached into his pocket, and took out his mobile.

"Morris, it's Manx. Urgent request, top priority. Get me a list of all the calls in and out of this number today." He read out the number twice, slowly and deliberately. "And call me back the second you have it. No time to explain, just get me the trace."

Manx hung up, and handed the receiver back to the young man, who was still processing what had happened, with a confused, slack-jawed expression.

***

As Manx walked back towards the car, he contemplated his next move. His priority was to find Shanni. There was one other place he might be—Alice's house. Maybe Shanni had called a taxi, or asked a friend to drive him there. If he were at Alice's, Manx would have no choice but to take him down to the station. If he wasn't, he'd have to tell Sara the whole story, but better she heard it from her brother, rather than shop gossip, or God forbid, the six o'clock news.

Driving the eight miles to Swn Y Gwynt, he rehearsed what he would tell his sister. Even as Manx ran the phrasing through his mind, it seemed ridiculous and over-dramatic, but as he knew from experience, there was no way to sugar coat that kind of news.

A sickening feeling fluttered through him, as he drove through the narrow-hedged lanes towards Talwrn. It was a familiar sensation; the same one he'd experienced decades ago, as he shivered with cold at Aberfraw Beach, the twilight descending rapidly over what had been a perfect summer's day.

He remembered clearly the line of policemen, as they marched the length of the beach, their torches scribbling beams across the sand, and the barking of search dogs snapping at the silence. His dad, Tommy, was climbing through the dunes, falling up to his knees in the soft sand, and calling out until he was hoarse. Alice had stood close to the ambulance, calm and collected, her eyes fixed on some point on the horizon. She resembled a woman who had just woken up to find her worse nightmare had come to life. Manx had watched red, raw welts appear on her bare forearms as she pinched at the skin in the vain hope she would wake at any moment, warm in the comfort of her own bed, her children safe and still sleeping. It had seemed like hours before she spoke, and when she did, she had directed the question at her son, but kept her gaze fixed firmly on the darkening horizon.

Where's Miriam, Tudor? You were meant to be watching her. Where is she, Tudor? Where is she?

Chapter 28

Shanni reached for the key, which was always kept on the ledge above the doorframe, and unlocked the door.

As he entered the narrow hallway, he noticed how little his parents had done to the place since he was here last, which must have been a decade ago. He resisted the desire to poke around. He didn't have the time, and, anyway, he only needed one thing—a working landline.

He walked through the living room, and glanced briefly at the framed photographs gathering dust on the top of the upright piano. They were mostly grandchildren and wedding photographs. He picked up the one of him and Sara. God, they were so young then, grinning aimlessly at the camera, their whole lives ahead of them. Dewi, too, in the photo next to them, a wide, open smile illuminating his face, as he sat on the old tractor parked outside the farmhouse. He felt a lump gathering like a ball of wax in his throat, as he crossed the hallway into the kitchen.

The afternoon light cast a grey pallor over the kitchen. Shanni sat at the table, reached for the phone, and dialled his own mobile number. Blackwell let it ring five times, before answering. Shanni took a deep breath, and laid his demands out clearly and slowly. He'd hand over the extra money, all of it, more, if he wanted, on one condition; he had to swear to leave his family alone. Blackwell muttered something about Shanni being in no position to negotiate, but would consider his offer, if he met him tonight, seven o'clock, at the easterly point of Parys Mountain. Shanni was about to protest, but thought better of it. *Come alone,* was the final instruction Blackwell offered, before hanging up.

Shanni slumped back in the chair, and felt the cold handle of the Glock urge itself into his lower back. He pulled it out, and rested it on the table. He swept his finger across the barrel in a swift motion, so the gun spun in place. Shanni had forgotten how quiet it was here—nothing but the odd baying of a cow or sheep, and now, Shanni's own pulse, which was thundering at his temples with a deafening thud. He squeezed his palms either side of his head to lessen the effect, but it only served to amplify the sound, which now seemed to travel from his head, and echo through every atom of his body. The gun stopped spinning, the tip of its barrel pointed directly at Shanni's ribcage. He spun again, and again. Each time, it yielded the same result. The dull-grey, metallic eye of the barrel always returned to the same position, as if it were daring Shanni to defy its intentions.

Chapter 29

"Got the numbers for you, from the phone at the Pilot," Morris said, as Manx walked into the incident room. He threw his jacket across the back of his chair, and snatched the scrap of paper from Morris's hand, giving it a cursory glance, before dropping it on the table.

"Just three," Morris explained. "One to an Amelia Barnes, in the Chester area. The other two were local. The first was a cell phone number, we traced it to Trevor Gibbard, lives in Gwalchmai, Priddle's getting the full address." Morris pointed towards Priddle, who had his ear to the phone, and taking down notes.

"And the other?" Manx asked.

"Mona Taxi. They confirmed a driver picked up a passenger from the Pilot round about twenty past twelve, and dropped off in Gwalchmai."

"Good. Very fucking good," Manx said, and walked over to the incident board. "Okay, our number one priority is locating Shanni Morgan. Everyone clear on that?" he said and stabbed his finger on Shanni's photograph.

"What about Blackwell? Thought he was our prime suspect of the day," Nader said.

Manx pinched the bridge of this nose. He felt a familiar weariness fall over him. "We find Shanni, and he leads us to Blackwell. We stop another murder. Simple enough, even for you, Nader."

Nader was about to offer some retort, but his attention was drawn to the large figure of DCI Canton standing at the doorway.

"Word, Manx?" Canton said, and turned back to his office, without waiting for a reply.

Chapter 30

"Your brother-in-law?" Canton was pacing around his office, picking up random objects off this desk and shelves. "And you didn't think to mention this pertinent piece of information?"

"I only found out this morning, Chief, when Davey spilled the beans."

"That would be, what? Three, four hours ago?"

"Maybe less," Manx confessed.

Canton rolled over his two index fingers in a rewinding motion. "Cast your memory back for a moment. Remember when I gave you very specific orders on this case? Care to remind me what they were?"

"Keep you informed, and no fuckery. Probably in that order," Manx said.

"So, what in God's name were you thinking?"

"It's not how it seems," Manx offered.

"Well, tell me how you think it seems, and I'll tell you if it tallies with my perception, and everyone else's perception, of how it bloody well seems."

"Chief, there's no time…" Manx began, but was interrupted by Canton's bark-like command

"Sit," he said, gesturing towards the chair. "Now, talk."

Manx took him through the series of events in rapid fire succession.

"And you didn't think of bringing this Shanni Morgan character in for questioning, even after you discovered a dead body in the boot of his car?"

"We didn't find the body, until after I sent Shanni to the house. I wasn't completely convinced by his story, but, if it was true, my sister and nephew both needed protecting. I wanted to keep him close for a few hours, see if I could get to the truth, before bringing him in. I thought he'd open up to me. I didn't think he'd be stupid enough to do a runner."

"If what you're telling me is correct, then your brother-in-law is the main distributor of Anglesey bloody Blue on the island, and possibly our murder suspect. That's quite a fucking revelation."

"We need to find him, Chief, before Blackwell does."

Canton walked around his desk, and eased himself, with a couple of customary grunts, into his chair. "Let me tell you how this looks from an outsider's perspective, Manx, and, by outsiders, I mean those over-degreed pen pushers over at Colwyn Bay. The Senior Investigating Officer's brother-in-law is found to be intimately involved in the triple murder case said SIO is investigating. The SIO finds a body in the brother-in-law's car, but instead of bringing him in for questioning, he has a police escort drive him to the officer's house. While at the house, the brother-in-law decides he's not happy with the accommodations and runs. What type of people run, Manx?"

"Yes Chief, but Shanni's not guilty of murder. He's guilty of being a stupid prick, who got in over his head."

"I applaud your family loyalty, Manx, but it's not going to play well over at HQ. They'll say you're too compromised, send in some ambitious, twenty-five-year-old, with two degrees shoved up his arse. I'm too fucking old to deal with that, Manx. Too fucking cranky and old."

"You don't need to deal with it, Chief," Manx said. "Twenty-four hours. If I don't bring in Shanni, you can call anyone you want."

"They'll need more. You know how it is. Gossip spreads like clap in a brothel around here."

Manx thought for a moment. "Formally charge Davey Williams with possession with intent to sell. Let Nader do it. He's had a hard-on to arrest someone for weeks. The Superintendent gets his face on the news. It's a successful arrest, the first in what we expect to be a series of them, and he gets to bask in the glory for a few days, while we find Blackwell and Shanni."

Canton sighed. "Twenty-four hours?"

"Twenty-three, if I'm lucky," Manx said.

"Better be very fucking lucky, then," Canton said, gesturing for Manx to leave, before he changed his mind.

Chapter 31

Trevor Gibbard answered the door on the third knock. He was outside in his back garden, tending to his potato patch. The sight of two uniformed officers and a tall, lanky detective dressed in funeral black, with an intense, shit-kicking look about him, immediately unsettled Trevor to the point of near muteness. His mouth uttered some nonsensical sounds, as they asked him about Shanni. *Had he seen him today? Did he call him? How well did he know him?*

After a few minutes of throaty grunts and mumble-core dialogue, Manx lurched forward, and asked if he'd prefer to answer questions down at the station. The threat shook Trevor from his silence. Yes, Shanni had been here, a few hours ago. He'd given him his old van. He gave them the number plate; it didn't have a license, he told them. Manx smiled, and assured Trevor that was probably the least of Shanni's problems.

"Phone in an APB on the van," Manx instructed Morris, as they walked back to the car. "I want every officer out looking for that vehicle. Did we get a trace on Shanni's mobile yet?"

"No, sir. Nothing. Either switched off, or he's dumped it," Priddle said.

"Great!" Manx said, as he slammed the door closed, and switched on the engine. Twenty hours, two hundred and seventy-six square miles of island to search, and a suspect who didn't want to be found. The odds weren't good, but then again, they never were.

Chapter 32

Manx sat at the kitchen table, watching his sister pour a can of baked beans into a pan. It was just after three o'clock, and the afternoon sun was already fading into the encroaching twilight. It reminded him he was running out of time, and the conversation he was about to have with Sara was not going to be easy, or quick.

"I saw Mam out front. Should she be carrying wood in her condition?"

"You want to go and tell her to stop, be my guest," Sara said, turning to face her brother. "You're wrong about Cledwyn, you know. People always misunderstand him. He's a good man; he wouldn't lie to me. You must have got your wires crossed, or something. Cledwyn would never…" Sara stopped when she saw her son run from the hallway and into the kitchen. "Beans on toast. OK, love?" she asked, slotting two slices of bread into the toaster.

"Broken, Mam," Dewi mumbled, and attempted to reattach the wheel that had fallen off his favourite, sixteen-wheeler lorry.

"Will Dad be here for beans, too?" he asked, raising his gaze towards Manx. "My dad fixes cars, and lorries. He's a mechanic," Dewi explained, as he forced the bent wheel back onto the axle.

Manx dragged his chair closer to his nephew. "Let's have a look," he said, and gently took the lorry from Dewi. He quickly realised his lack of mechanical skills also extended to the scaled-down version of the real thing. Dewi watched him intently for a few moments, as Manx knotted his eyebrows in frustration, fumbling with the miniature plastic object, which was far too small for his over-sized hands.

"You're my mam's brother, so you're my uncle?" Dewi asked.

"Yep, that's usually the run of things. Damn it!" Manx said, the wheel slipping from his fingers, and bouncing on the stone floor.

"Uncle Tudor?" Dewi said, as Manx leant over to pick up the wheel.

"Yes?"

"You're not a very good mechanic, are you?"

"No. No, I'm not," Manx admitted, handing back the lorry with a smile that spoke of defeat. "Listen, Dewi. Maybe your grandma has some glue or something to help fix it back on. Why don't you go and ask?"

Dewi shrugged his shoulders; a gesture which suggested he'd do as he was told, but it was ultimately a worthless task. "Dad will fix it when he gets home," he said confidently, and gathered the lorry under his arm.

"Jesus Christ," Sara said, and turned off the heat on the beans. She gripped at the edge of the counter, her knuckles turning white.

"Why don't you sit?" Manx said.

Sara's body quivered, as if someone had poured cold water down the length of her spine. "Cledwyn would never put us in danger. God knows he's not perfect, but he wouldn't do anything to hurt us. Not his family."

Manx heard the first crack in her voice, as she held back the damn of tears he was sure would break soon.

"We don't know everything yet, Sara, but the evidence..."

"Evidence?" Sara snapped. "Jesus, Tudor! Talk to me like a bloody human being, not some bloody police briefing, or something."

Manx took a deep breath; he'd have to choose his words carefully. "You're right, sorry. We're confident Shanni is heavily involved in a major drug distribution ring on the island. We have someone in custody, who has named him as..."

"Who? Who told you that?" Sara asked, and pointed her finger at Manx.

"I can't reveal that."

Sara sniffed loudly. "What kind of drugs?" she asked, folding her arms solidly across her chest.

"You've probably seen the news reports, Anglesey Blue."

Sara moved her hand to the base of her neck. "Not Cledwyn, Tudor. I'd know. Where would he get that kind of thing from, anyway?" She turned away from her brother, looked out over to the fields beyond the yard. "No, this is all wrong. It's some big police cock up, or something, or a setup. Isn't that what they call it? No, I can't accept it, Tudor, not Cledwyn."

Manx softened. "I know this is a shock, but I need your help. We think we know who's supplying him, but we need to talk to Shanni, quickly."

"He's a bloody car mechanic," Sara said, spinning back around to face her brother. "Not some bloody drug lord! It's ridiculous. Honestly, I don't know what to think, Tudor, these bloody stories of yours. "Sara's voice had shifted up in pitch, with an added tone of mockery, as if she'd found a glimmer of hope to cling to, and the mere absurdity of the situation was warrant enough to discredit Manx's accusations.

"Sara, you've got to trust what I'm telling you is the truth."

Sara held herself stiffly against the counter, and lifted her head defiantly. The gesture reminded Manx of his mother's unfortunate habit of looking down on people, with the same, dismissive manner.

"Why? Why should I trust you, Tudor, over my own husband? You're my brother, and I hardly know you. No one does."

"Shanni's in danger, Sara…"

"In danger? What does that even mean? More bloody police talk?" Sara reached for a pack of cigarettes, and struggled to liberate a single stick.

"Shanni's finger? The rock through your window? His story about being a witness to a murder? You didn't think any of it was strange?"

Sara pulled hard on the cigarette. Of course, she'd thought it was strange, but she had enough to worry about. It was just another one of those stages Cledwyn would go through. He'd latch onto a plan, dive into it with both feet, then forget about it two weeks later. She'd learnt it was better to let these things run their course.

"I need Shanni's mobile number—friends, work colleagues, customers. Is there anywhere he might feel safe enough to hide for a few days?"

Sara finally extracted her grip on the counter, and sat. "This is like a nightmare," she said, weaving her fingers through themselves, as if she were carefully massaging each knuckle and joint. "Things like this don't happen to people like us."

Manx winced. He'd heard variations on that statement for most of his career. His sister was wrong. Things like this happened to people like her all the time. It was the randomness of life. There was no discrimination when it came to grief or despair, or disappointment. It was a burden disseminated without prejudice or favour.

Sara reached for Manx's pen, and wrote down Shanni's mobile number. "I can't think clearly right now," she said, wiping a tear from her eyes.

Manx nodded, folded the scrap of paper into his pocket.

"Why? Why would Cledwyn do something like this?" Sara asked. Her eyes had begun to pool with tears. Manx saw how much they looked like his own—a steely, blue-grey hue, with flecks of brittle black around the iris. As she wept, Sara's eyes became darker, less penetrable. It reminded Manx of rain on a slate roof, and how quickly it would shift the slate's appearance from a light grey to dark ebony within minutes. He leant forward, placing his hands on his sister's; they were both familiar and strange, her knuckles like tiny, broken spines under his palms.

"Money, probably, Sara. It's the usual motive in these kinds of crimes."

Sara nodded. It was the only thing Manx has said, so far, which made any sense. She leant forward on her chair, and spoke in low, deliberate tone.

"He didn't kill anyone. Not that poor man on the boat, or that doctor. We've been married fifteen years, Tudor, I know my own husband," she said, with the same, unshakable confidence her son had expressed about his father minutes before.

Manx waited a few moments, before speaking again. "We found another body, in the boot of Shanni's car," Manx said.

Sara bit hard on her bottom lip, and wiped a sleeve over her eyes.

"Forensics are still trying to sort out what happened, but the important thing, right now, is we find Shanni."

"Cledwyn," Sara corrected him; a tense edge cleaved back into her voice.

"Yes, Cledwyn," Manx said patiently. "I'll try to keep a lid on this until we find him. You'll need to prepare Dewi, too. It could get ugly, once the Press gets wind of the story."

Manx stood up to leave; he felt heavier and wearier than he did thirty minutes ago. He pushed his hands deep into his jeans pockets, and looked at the broken figure of his sister, as she wrung her hands back and forth over each other, as if she were washing them clean.

"Sara, I'm really sorry I had to be the one to tell you this, but my hands are tied. I can't be seen to show any special favours, just because he's family. You understand that, right?"

Sara lifted her head, and spoke through a taut, reserved smile. "I'd never expect you to make any special allowances, Tudor," she said, stubbing out the cigarette butt on the side of her saucer.

There was no answer to that, and Manx accepted his sister's well-aimed blow with the pointedness with which it was intended. As Manx opened the backdoor, a gust of cold wind blew through the kitchen, ruffling the net curtains.

"Why did you come back?" Sara asked, without looking up at her brother. "Everything was fine, until you turned up again." She sniffed, and wiped her nose with her sleeve. "A couple of weeks ago, when you came round the house, I said you were like a ghost. I was wrong."

"We all say things…" Manx began, but Sara interrupted.

"I was wrong, because you're not a ghost. You're like the grim reaper. Wherever you go, death isn't far behind, is it?" Sara spoke through a dam of tears, which had chosen this moment to break. She sounded like Alice when she cried. Manx felt his skin crawl. It was a reaction he despised in himself, but one he was unable to resist.

"You're around too much death and grief. Ever since… since…"

Sara didn't need to finish her sentence. They both knew how it concluded. "Did you really hate us that much? Was it that painful for you to be with us, afterwards? It was an accident, that's all, a stupid, tragic accident," his sister sobbed.

Manx could only see Sara's back now; it was heaving and shaking with the force of her tears. He wished he had some words of comfort, but that particular well had run dry a lifetime ago, it seemed. The best solace he could offer his sister right now was to do his job. Find her husband, before Blackwell did.

Chapter 33

The darkness pressed down like a thick, gloved hand, as Shanni navigated the narrow roads leading towards Parys Mountain. There was little light coming from the van's weak, fogged up headlights, which seemed to cast their own shadows and monsters around each corner.

In the passenger foot-well, the cold, blank eye of the Glock was staring at him in the same fashion as it had a few hours ago, across the kitchen table. *One bullet, one bullet.* It seemed to be taunting him, as it clattered against the rough, steel floor; *one bullet, one bullet, one bullet.*

He rolled down the window, and savoured the welcome blast of icy air over his face and hands, although it did little to ease the galloping pain still pounding in his skull.

Maybe Scuttler was right. Shanni had stepped out of place, disrupted the natural order of things with his ambitions and high fucking hopes. *One day, one day?* That nagging voice had never truly left him, he knew that now, but that day had finally come. In some strange way, he knew it would; it was inevitable. He was going to lose everything—Sara, Dewi, the business, all of it. If he could just turn back the clocks, if only God would grant him the last month back, he never would have got involved. *Fuck!* He'd been so stupid, a fucking idiot. It was clear as daylight now. He'd fulfilled his own, worthless destiny. He was the gypsy runt his "so-called-dad" had always insisted he was.

He didn't deserve what he had with Sara, none of it. It was all make-believe. He'd merely been playing at happy families all this time. He'd lied to himself. Good things never lasted for him; they were transient, passing bequests. It was God's big joke, offering

Shanni a glimpse of happiness, and then, snatching it from his grasp at the last minute.

As much as it hurt him to admit the fact, Sara and Dewi would be better off without him, Blackwell was right about that. And maybe Alice Williams was right, too. She'd always insisted Sara had married beneath herself, always referring to him as if he were some archaic household servant or an easily discarded possession. Sara, though, had always believed in him. But, recently, Shanni had noticed a subtle shift in her behaviour. Her pointed snapping had become more frequent, and he would often see her alone, sitting at the kitchen table, looking out to the distance, as if she were imagining a life a million miles away from here. *For richer or poorer, wasn't that their vow?* He couldn't hold her to that, not for a lifetime. There was only a singular act of redemption left now. Just like the ferrets he'd liberated decades ago, he was destined to repeat his actions, but, this time, for his family. Tonight, he would end it, one way or another.

Chapter 34

The three-quarter moon hung low in the sky, casting a milky hue across the mountain. There were other lights ahead of Shanni now, faint, yellow streetlights which signalled he was in the centre of Llanerchymedd, the final town before the mountain pass.

He eased off the throttle, and kept his hands steady on the steering wheel, which was now moist with a clammy film of sweat. It was six forty-five, and the streets were deserted, save a small dog sniffing at a ball of discarded chip wrappers. A thin gauze of mist hung a few feet above street level, floating ghost-like over the road. As he circled around the clock tower, he was distracted by a woman locking up her bakery for the night, and didn't notice the police car parked outside the pub opposite.

Inside the patrol car, PC Tony Collins had just finished his last round of Angry Birds when he looked up to see Shanni's van moving far too slowly—in his professional opinion—through the town. Something clicked, as he watched the white Ford Escort van take a long right turn from the town centre. He logged onto his computer and double-checked. He placed his iPhone back into his jacket pocket, and pulled slowly out of the parking space, following.

Chapter 35

The van seemed to take flight, as it ploughed through the yawning potholes marking the narrow mountain track. His headache was pounding again, the same spot the gypsy fuck had struck him last night. *Was it only last night?* It seemed like a lifetime ago, or maybe another lifetime.

The metallic rattle from the gun scooting along the bare-metal floor seemed to be mocking him, staring him down with the same vacant expression. He tried to ignore it, ignore the pressure building urgently at the edge of his skull, but the pain came at him with little respite. Ahead, he could see his final destination—the old windmill. It extended thirty feet from the ground like an exclamation mark, the white brickwork illuminated by a faint trickle of moonlight.

He came to an abrupt stop, and killed the engine. It was eerily quiet, as if sound itself were reluctant to make the journey to the peak. He switched on his full beams. The outline of the quarry dissolved through the lights, like an alien planet whose inhabitants had long since left it to die—cold, sunless, and thick with the remembrance of death.

Chapter 36

Twenty minutes after PC Collins had called in the sighting of the van, Manx pulled up the Jensen at the entrance to Parys Mountain.

"Anyone see you here?" Manx asked, running towards the officer

"Don't think so," Collins said. "I followed the van, then parked across the road. The instructions were not to approach the driver, so I stayed put."

"Good. Any other vehicles come through?"

Collins flipped through his notebook. "Six thirty-five, sir. A brown-coloured Mercedes. Took the same road as the van. Didn't get the number plate though, too dark."

Manx looked up at the serrated outline of the mountain, the moonlight falling on the edge of the abandoned windmill.

"How far to the peak, do you think?"

"Dunno, exactly. About a mile, or two?"

Manx reached into the boot, and took out his thick, down jacket.

"You're walking?"

"They'll hear the car. Stay here until you hear otherwise, got it?"

"Um…" Collins hesitated.

"Problem?"

"Um, it's just my shift, sir. I'm not authorised…"

"I'm authorizing it. Whatever overtime you need," Manx said.

Manx zipped up his jacket, and climbed the slope, towards the windmill.

Chapter 37

Shanni sat and waited. It was ten past seven, and the cold and damp air was seeping into his bones. A strong south-westerly blew in agitated gusts over the mouth of the quarry, and pushed against the sides of the van, as if it was attempting to tip it over the edge. Beyond the northwest curve of the basin, the lights of Amlwch Port glimmered in the abundant darkness. To the east, the long, slender blades of the Trysglwyn Wind Farm chopped at the blackness, like the arms of a madman raging at the world. Across the horizon line, the lights from what Shanni assumed was a small aircraft dipped low, and circled the port, before rising back up and veering eastwards. He blew a shot of hot breath into his cupped hands, and glanced in his rear-view mirror. A pinprick of light in the far distance caught his eye, slowly edging closer, and bouncing erratically over the uneven mountain road. He took a deep breath, and reached down for the Glock.

The diesel engine clunked to a stop, and the back door of the Mercedes fell open with a slow ponderous creak. Shanni watched as Callum Blackwell walked slowly towards him, and rapped impatiently on the window.

"Going down in the world, Shanni?" Blackwell asked, kicking lazily at the front tire.

"Must be, if I'm working with the likes of you."

Blackwell laughed; his trademark, terse, snarl. "Gallows humour. Very fitting," he said, leaning on the window frame. "Why don't you step out?"

Shanni complied, walking out into the glacial night air.

"Alone?" Blackwell asked, and looked down the mountain road.

Shanni nodded. But, he wasn't alone; the cold, steel barrel of the Glock was pressing reassuringly at the base of his spine.

"And the money?"

"In the back," Shanni said, with as much bravado as he could muster, but his voice sounded distant, an echo of its usual self.

Blackwell walked back to the Mercedes, and tapped on the window. Shanni held his breath, and felt the veins in his skull throb sharply, as the one surviving goon emerged from the car, and flipped up his jacket collar. He furrowed his wide, thick forehead, and stared at Shanni with the same dead-eyed expression the Glock had been giving him all day.

"He's still upset that you killed his baby brother," Blackwell explained.

Shanni's mouth became as dry as the dust and rock surrounding him. Blackwell nodded at the goon. He walked around the back of the van, extracted the gym bag, unzipped it, and nodded.

"Makes us even, yeah? All paid up? A deal's a deal, right?" Shanni shouted through the wind, which had now begun to gust around the quarry's edge, pushing at his back.

"I have no interest in your family, Shanni, if that's what you're thinking."

Shanni felt the briefest moment of relief.

"We have bigger ambitions than that, don't we, Jenkins?" He gestured inside the car. Hesitantly, the lithe figure of Hywel Jenkins slid over the backseat, and into the dusty beams of the headlights. He shivered, as he stumbled over the uneven rocks. It took Shanni a few seconds to process what was unfolding before him.

"No!" Shanni shouted, and pointed a trembling arm towards Jenkins "You're dead. He… he fucking killed you, Jenkins."

"And yet, here he is, very much alive," Blackwell said.

Shanni felt the slow drip of a tear run down his right cheek. *Shit!* The pain was like a drill to his eye now, digging back under his eyelid, and into his forehead. He jabbed the palm of his hand into his eye-socket, and pressed hard. There was a moment of blessed relief, but as soon as he took his palm away, the pain returned, harsher and fiercer than before.

"Shanni…" Jenkins began, before Blackwell interrupted.

"We needed Shanni to think you were dead, didn't we? Just to keep him on his toes. Seems to have worked, too."

Shanni tried to understand what Blackwell was saying, but his words were being ripped to shreds by the wind and the pain in his skull.

"How the fuck do you people live in this damned cold?" Blackwell said turning towards the goon "Let's get this over with, Valdis, quickly."

The goon puffed his chest and smiled; his talents were finally being put to good use. Blackwell leant back against the Mercedes, as if he were getting ready to enjoy the show. "They're very Old Testament, these Latvians, eye for an eye, my enemy's enemy, that kind of thing. It's like a form of folk-art for them."

Valdis straightened himself to his full, six-feet four-inches, and scowled at Shanni, as if he were an ant he was about to crush. From the inside of his jacket, the goon extracted a thick bar—a tire iron for a 1983 Mercedes 450, Shanni was sure. The goon moved towards him; the crunch of his boots on the gravel chaffed at Shanni's skull as he walked.

Slap. Slap. Slap. The goon struck the bar against his palm like he was beating out Shanni's own funeral march. The goon moved closer. *Slap. Slap. Slap.* The rhythm was in sync with Shanni's own veins, as they pounded at the sides of his skull. Still, the goon kept coming, smacking the metal against his palm, his heavy boots crunching over the rocks. Now, it had to be now.

Shanni reached behind his back, pulled out the Glock, and stared the goon directly in the eyes. But, the gesture seemed futile, and was undermined by Shanni's arms, which had betrayed him, and were shaking, as if the weight of the weapon was too much to bear. The goon stopped, and assessed the situation. Blackwell slapped the roof of the Mercedes, and let out a loud, yelp-like sound.

"A gun! He brought a gun," he said. "Now, things get interesting." He folded his arms across his chest, settling in to enjoy the second act.

Shanni was desperate to say something, something threatening, but his throat was held tight in a cobra's grip. He waved the gun towards Blackwell, who performed a faux "hands up" gesture, and laughed. *Who to pull the trigger on first? Shit!* If only that pain in his head would go away he could think clearly, make a decision. The goon, it had to be the goon. He was moving again, his breath like a backdraft of fog sweeping towards him.

Slap. Slap. Fucking Slap.

Shanni curled his finger under the trigger, but the pain shot through him like lightening. He tried again, and then stopped, as a loud voice from his left distracted him.

"Shanni, put down the gun. Now!"

The voice was familiar, but not instantly recognizable. It came from the side of the old windmill. A figure slowly walked out from behind the brickwork, arms raised. Shanni blinked, as the man walked towards him. *His brother-in-law! What the fuck was he doing here?* Shanni was sweating heavily, the salty moisture seeping into his eyes. He brought up his arm to wipe away the perspiration.

"Put down the gun, Shanni, and I'll guarantee you'll see Sara and Dewi again," Manx shouted, edging carefully from the shadows.

"Who the goddam fuck is this?" Blackwell shouted.

"He's…I don't know what…" Shanni flustered. His head felt as if it might explode.

Manx reached for his badge, and held it high "Detective Inspector Tudor Manx, North Wales Police," he said calmly. "Let's put down our weapons and not make this any messier than it should be. Shanni? Blackwell?"

Blackwell stiffened at the sound of his name. Shanni's whole body was shaking, but just when he needed it most. His mind became clear and precise, his body following suit.

"No, Manx. Not going to happen," Shanni shouted. He raised the Glock, this time his arms were solid iron bars, but the sound of slow-moving thunder still rolled through his skull. He drew back the trigger.

The shot echoed through the quarry walls. The recoil yanked Shanni's arms backwards violently. His aim was off. The bullet only scraped the goon's calf, momentarily slowing his progress.

Fuck! What was that sound? It seemed to be swallowing the air around him, and there was a spotlight searing through his eyeballs, and deep into his head. He aimed again, but his focus was failing, the scene a red blur of shapes and sounds. He saw Blackwell pull out a gun.

Shanni pulled again. The Hail Mary shot punctured the rear wing of the Mercedes. Blackwell smiled, and pinched his own trigger. Shanni fell to the ground. But, it wasn't the impact he was expecting. He heard his brother-in-law scream, as Blackwell's bullet grazed Manx's right arm. Shanni felt his brother-in-law's breath on his cheek as he lay on top of him.

"Don't fucking move," Manx whispered.

Shanni's fingers scratched over the dirt towards the Glock, but it was just out of reach. He watched, helpless, as the goon's heavy boots crunched across the dust towards them. The noise was deafening, shredding the night air with its roar and boom. There was light, too; dazzling white beams lighting up the mountain, as if it were daylight. He felt the goon's boot kick into his ribs, then his large, fat hands grasped at Shanni's hood and dragged him away. Manx grabbed onto Shanni's sleeve, but the goon's boot got there first, and ground his hand deep into the earth until he released his grip.

The goon hauled Shanni along the ground, then threw him into the car. The last thing Shanni saw, before he was pistol-whipped into unconsciousness, was the helicopter, hovering and kicking up a blood-red dust storm, with its powerful down draft. Manx heard the spin of tires on gravel, and watched as the taillights of the Mercedes faded into the night.

"Everybody stay on the ground, or we will open fire," the loud hailer bellowed into the thick dust.

To his left, Manx heard a soft groan. Jenkins was in a foetal position but unharmed. Manx stumbled to standing, gripping his arm, which was seeping blood. Two figures leapt from the helicopter, and walked towards them.

"Follow them! Why the fuck don't you follow them?" Manx screamed. Then, a moment of recognition that was like a slap to the face. The men ignored him, just as they'd done that day outside the wool shop. As they moved closer he recognised the lettering on their Kevlar vests—NCA

"You! Down on the fucking ground, now."

There was a gun pointed a few feet from Manx's head, a glowering, red face behind it. "I said, get the fuck down! Throw your weapons to the ground. If either one of you move, I will fuckin' shoot to kill."

Manx moved carefully, kneeling down then spreading himself out on the ground, making sure his badge was still clearly visible. The other man walked slowly towards him and crouched down.

"We've got a local, sir," the man shouted.

The second man walked over, looked down and spat. "Jesus on a stick," he shouted. "Could this be any more fucked up? Cuff him anyway."

Manx felt the snap of the plastic cuffs around his wrists, and a deep, sinking feeling, as if he were free falling down the quarry face into darkness.

PART THREE
The Ties That Bind

Chapter 1

Manx's right shoulder was throbbing mercilessly, as if someone were twisting a fork through it. The duty nurse had sterilised the wound, sutured it, then sent Manx on his way. At nine-thirty that night, he was back at the station, sitting alone in the conference room, waiting. A few minutes later, Senior NCA Officer Derrick Garrett burst through the door, like a rodeo bull, and threw his sports jacket across the table.

"Is Jenkins talking?" Manx asked.

Garrett sat down, and slapped his boot heels on the table. He was widely built, with what Manx assumed was a permanently red face. The veins in his neck were pumping furiously; he seemed like a man continually at odds with the world.

"Your brother-in-law? That's what you told me earlier, or did I dream that?" Garrett spoke, with a thick gravy of a Yorkshire accent. Before Manx could reply, Canton and the second NCA Officer, Josh Markham, entered the room.

"Yes, Shanni Morgan," Manx confirmed.

Garrett took a deep breath, and spread his arms wide. "What the hell did we walk into, Markham? Any idea?"

"Beats me, sir," Markham said. The officer was young, with a pinched face still bearing the scars of his adolescent acne.

"Are we on the goggle box?" Garrett said, looking around in an overly dramatic fashion for the hidden cameras. "The Great British Fuck Up? Made in fucking Anglesey? Is that what's going on?"

Manx and Canton both looked at each other, confused.

"How long have you known about your brother-in-law's involvement with Blackwell?" Markham asked.

"Less than twenty-four hours."

Garrett huffed. "And the rest. Maybe you're in this together, running a family business."

Manx shook his head. "Outstanding theory, Garrett. Why aren't you out there looking for him? Blackwell will kill him, if he hasn't already."

Garrett straightened himself, stuffed his shirttail into his trousers and looked out of the window onto the station car park. "Inspector Manx, do you have any idea what we do at National Crime Agency?"

"Enlighten me," Manx said.

"Mandate number one: The NCA does not pursue petty criminals. That means we will not be extending our highly specialised resources to chase sheep-shaggers and the like across hill and fucking dale. Secondly, we investigate and prosecute large-scale, international criminal organisations—child slavery, sick fuckers with a bent for kiddie porn, arms dealers, and the such, none of which I believe pertains to your brother-in-law. Or do I have that wrong?"

Manx spoke as clearly as he could the theory that had been rattling around in his head, but had yet to articulate. "Blackwell was manufacturing cheap, highly addictive and potent methadone pills in Eastern Europe, then trafficking them into the country, probably by boat. Anglesey was his testing ground. Pile it high, sell it cheap, give it a distinctive colour and a name everyone can remember, and Blackwell doesn't have merchandise any more. He has a recreational product he can sell to anyone with a spare few quid behind the sofa. That petty enough for you, Garrett?"

Garrett huffed. "We are completely fucking aware of Blackwell's activities, Manx, the more pressing matter is you've taken a big wet shite over twelve months of detective work. If you'd stuck to arresting sheep sodomizers, or whatever else you do for kicks about these parts, we'd have Blackwell in custody, and your brother in law might wake up still breathing come the morning."

"You should have notified us of the operation. We could have provided support," Canton said.

"The NCA is under no obligation to inform local police of our actions when it falls under an international investigation," Markham said. "If you suspected your brother-in-law was involved with a known drug trafficker, then you should have backed off, and called us. We're trained in this kind of specialist operation."

"My Inspector was doing his job, following up on a lead..." Canton began.

"Oh, brav-fucking-o, Inspector. Job well done," Garrett spat, leaning closer. Manx could smell the acrid tinge of stale nicotine on his breath. "We were this close." Garrett stomped around the room, placing index finger and thumb within a few millimetres of each other. "This fucking close to nailing Blackwell's balls, before *Reservoir Dogs* here went and lifted his leg and pissed all over the case," he added, waving his arm in Manx's direction.

"So, did I take a shit on your case, or did I piss on it?" Manx asked. "Because I'm confused."

"I think we're done here," Garrett said, grabbing his coat.

"So, you'll let a man die, because it's not part of your mandate to act?" Manx said. Garrett was beginning to work his way under his skin, like the pain from the fork still twisting through his shoulder, though more visceral and immediate.

"See, you're not that slow on the uptake when you need to be," Garrett said, walking past Manx towards the door.

Manx felt his blood rise. He lunged at Garrett, grabbed his tie, and shoved him up against the thin, plaster wall until it shook. They stood eye-to-eye, daring each other to make the next move.

"Think you've got the balls?" Garrett said. "Go ahead."

Canton stepped in between them, before Manx could prove otherwise.

"You should put this fucker on a tighter lead, Canton," Garrett said, re-arranging his tie, and stuffing the back of his shirt into his trousers.

"Sit down, Garrett. This is an unusual situation, but I won't have my station turned into a cage fight," Canton said. "As the senior ranking official, the island is still under my jurisdiction. I have a responsibility for the safety of its inhabitants, even if they are stupid pricks like Morgan. Inspector Manx will receive the necessary support to locate him, with or without help from the NCA. We received intelligence on our suspect earlier this evening, Manx acted on that information, but did neglect to call for backup, an oversight for which I will be having words with him later. My perspective on this situation is this—the NCA stumbled into our investigation, and we stumbled into yours, which in my book makes us even. So, I propose a more cooperative air will benefit us all."

"How did you know Blackwell would be there?" Manx asked.

"Garrett has a CI. Provided him with Blackwell's whereabouts, then we triangulated his cell phone co-ordinates." Markham said.

"I thought he had one of those CryptoPhones, untraceable," Manx said.

"Crypto, what? I have no idea what you're talking about," Garrett said.

"Who's your CI?" Manx asked.

"That's why they're called Confidential Informants, Inspector. I didn't even tell the boy wonder, here," Garrett said, waving in Markham's direction. "So, why would I tell you?"

"Because we're on the same side?"

Garrett unwrapped a stick of Nicorette, and threw it into his mouth. "I hate this fucking gum," he said, slumping into his chair.

"What now?" Manx asked.

There was an awkward silence in the room, save the smacking of Garrett's loud, reluctant chewing.

"We could turn the screws on his mother again," Markham said.

"His mother?" Manx said.

"Amanda Blackwell. She goes by her maiden name Mandy Travis now. She owns a wool shop in Mo... Molv... Molevre?" Markham said, tripping over the village name.

"Moelfre?" Manx asked, sitting forward in his chair. "Something like that," Markham said.

If Manx's mouth had opened a millimetre more, it would have hit the floor with a loud, "what the fuck?" clunk.

Chapter 2

At ten thirty-five that night, Manx, Garrett, Markham and Sergeant Nader were gathered like a band of unlikely Christmas Carollers outside Woolly Backs. Garrett flipped the letterbox open.

"Open the sodding door, Mandy, or we'll open it for you!" He peered through the darkened glass of front window, and saw nothing but the reflection of his own tired, blood-shot eyes staring back.

"Mandy, we know you're in there!" Silence, save the soft backwash of waves breaking on the shore below.

"Fuck it," Garrett said, gesturing towards Nader. "Sergeant whatever the hell your name is, bring the big red key over, and fuck up this door."

Nader felt the weight of the red battering ram in his arms, and hoisted it from one arm to another searching for the most stable grip.

"Tonight would be nice, Sergeant," Garrett shouted.

"Clear the area, boys, coming through!"

Nader launched the battering ram at the door. The centre panels splintered, revealing a hole the size of a football. Nader wiped the sweat from his brow, aimed directly at the lock, and swung again. The steel tip did its job, pounded through the brass lock, and shattered the dead bolt. Nader gave the door a swift kick. It swung open, hanging lazily on its hinges.

"About fucking time," Garrett said. "Markham, search the immediate premises. I'll take the flat upstairs. Manx, you're with me. Stick tight, you might learn a thing or two."

The stairs leading up to the flat were steep and narrow, and Garrett was breathing heavily as he climbed. There was a pungent aroma of stale body odour trailing behind him as he worked up a sweat.

"I'll take the bedroom; you take the living room." Manx said. "Unless you need a lie down."

Garrett mumbled something incomprehensible.

Manx entered the bedroom. It was small, with a couple of distressed white wood cabinets and matching wardrobe. Manx peered inside, and saw nothing but empty, expectant coat hangers, and the faint aroma of mothballs. Mandy was gone, not just for the night; she was gone for good.

He walked back to the landing. Garrett was tearing at the cushions of the settee, with an enthusiasm which made Manx wonder if he wasn't attempting to expel some of his own demons. He left Garrett to this exorcism, and entered the kitchen.

Manx opened the cupboards—all empty. He tugged at one of drawers in an absent-minded manner, and almost missed the upturned corner of a photograph poking out from under the drawer liner. Manx held it to the light. Mandy must have overlooked it in her rush to leave. He would have dismissed it as just another photograph, if it wasn't for the gleaming, red object Mandy was leaning against when it was taken. As he looked closer at the bright red Ford Fiesta, something pricked in his memory. *He'd seen the car before, but where?* He closed his eyes, and conjured up the surrounding objects and scenery. A caravan, a dog, a dirt road, the sound of gunfire.

Manx stuffed the photograph into his pocket, and shouted, "Garrett, Mandy is not hiding down the back of that fucking sofa."

The NCA Officer looked up from his hunched position, beads of sweat peeling from his forehead. "What the fuck are you talking about?" he asked, and hitched up the waistband of his pants.

"I know where she is. Let's go."

Garrett looked at Manx, his brow knotted, and an expression in his eyes which spoke both of weariness and reluctant compliance

Chapter 3

Thomas Bowen stuffed the last of his acid-house-themed t-shirts into his duffel bag, and pulled hard on the zipper. He slid the bag under the pull-out bed, and peered through the caravan window—same shit, different time of day. Several hundred metres away, at the peak of the dirt road, a flash of car headlights broke the darkness. Maybe Mandy had forgotten something. He glanced around the caravan, but there was nothing except the suitcase she'd given him earlier—an expensive looking one, Gucci, it said on the label, with a gold-coloured lock. Mandy didn't have enough space in her car, she'd explained to him, as she slipped out of her knickers and into his bed earlier this evening. She had to drop off some old clothes and furniture at the charity shop, but she'd meet him nine-fifteen tomorrow night at Holyhead docks, in time for the ten o'clock ferry to Dun Laoghaire.

The plan was simple: catch the ferry to Ireland, one night in Dublin, then drive down to Rosslare by Sunday. On Monday morning, they'd take the boat to Spain, Gidjon, then it was a four-hour drive to San Sebastian. It felt good to have a plan. He'd only ever had schemes before, and most of those had bit the dust by the time he got around to executing on them. This time, he wasn't going to fuck it up. He was deep in these thoughts and other vague promises to himself, when a strobe of a yellow light passed over the caravan. It was quickly followed by an urgent, loud pounding on the door.

"Bowen, open up! Detective Inspector Manx, North Wales Police."

A wave of panic rattled through him, as he palmed the remainder of last night's joints into the bin, and debated his options.

Outside the caravan, Garrett scraped a glob of mud from the underside of his shoe on the steps leading up to the door. "And I thought this place couldn't be any more of a bloody shit hole," he said, spitting.

"Should come here in summer, like Spain, it is," Nader offered

"Great. I'll cancel the Costa Brava, then," Garrett said, "I'm sure the missus will be chuffed as peas."

Manx pounded on the door again. "Thomas! We're not averse to breaking down doors, wouldn't be the first time tonight."

Manx stood back and waited. Nader struck a wide-legged pose, and readied himself with the battering ram. Manx was about to give the order to charge, when they heard a loud slapping noise and a muffled groan from the other side of the caravan. "Round the back!" Manx shouted.

Behind the caravan, the large picture window was flapping in the wind, and slamming against Bowen's back, as he attempted to slip through the narrow opening. His legs were hanging outside, the remainder of his body stuck inside the caravan. In his flight to freedom, Bowen had snagged the waistband of his boxer shorts on the window latch, and they were now bunched around his knees exposing his pale, hairless buttocks.

Bowen shouted—a muffled, strained voice, as if it were coming through a pillow. "Can't you bastards leave me the fuck alone?"

"Your call," Manx said. "We can do this inside or outside, but it's my guess you'd prefer we questioned you inside, where you'll have the dignity of keeping your trousers on."

Garrett stepped around the corner. "Jesus. It's Carry-on-fucking-policing," he said, shaking his head

"Nader, give him a hand," Manx said

Nader stepped back. "What? Me, boss?"

"Yes, you. Just grab his feet, and push up. That should do the trick. We'll go back around the front, wait for him to open the door."

***

Bowen slid open the doors leading to the bedroom, and gawked at the three policemen. Nader entered a few moments later, wiping his palms on the side of his pants.

"Brought your mates around to finish what you started?" Bowen said, buckling up his belt, and hauling down his jeans to the pre-requisite distance from his waist.

"Who the fuck is this joker?" Garrett asked.

"Thomas Bowen. He's been helping us with our enquiries, haven't you, Thomas?"

Bowen sniffed loudly, and shrugged his shoulders.

"Does he know of her whereabouts?" Garrett asked.

"Told you before, don't know nothing about no one," Bowen said.

"What about Mandy Blackwell?"

Bowen hesitated. It was enough of a clue to alert Manx whatever came out of Bowen's mouth next had a ninety-nine percent probability of being bullshit.

"Never heard of no Mandy fuckin' Blackwell."

"She's also known as Amanda Travis, owns a wool shop around here," Markham said, resisting the attempt at another pronunciation of Moelfre.

Bowen shrugged his shoulders, and sat back down on the edge of the bed. "Not a big knitter myself, don't have the patience."

Manx moved closer to Bowen. "Thing is, Thomas, I'd swear that the last time I drove over here, Mandy's car was parked right outside your love shack. A red Ford Fiesta?"

Bowen shook his head, pushed out his lower lip.

"If she wasn't dropping off samples of yarn for your Christmas jumper, what was she doing here?"

"A fucking wool shop, are you lot yanking my chain?" Bowen said, sniffing loudly.

"Mandy was in here, wasn't she, when I was questioning you?"

Bowen shifted his gaze to the floor.

"Were you protecting her? You sleeping with her, Thomas?"

Bowen laughed. "Give me a fuckin' break, Holmes. Do I look desperate, or something?"

"This is a waste of time, Manx," Garrett said. "Let's call it a night."

"Yeah, listen to him, Holmes. You're wasting your time."

Manx stepped forward. "Stand up, Thomas."

"What?"

"Stand the fuck up."

Bowen did as he was told, slowly: too slowly for Manx's liking. He grabbed Bowen's belt, and slammed him against the wall. The caravan shook, toppling an empty teacup to the floor. Manx leant close to Bowen's face, and caught the stale stench of weed and alcohol. He yanked harder, until Bowen's jeans pinched at the base of his groin, and kept pulling steadily.

"Here's my delicate state of mind tonight, Bowen, just so you know the hurt I'm about to inflict on your body is not all about you"

Bowen's neck veins pulsated hard and fast.

"Today, I've been lied to, I've been shot at, I've been cuffed, and I've had to deal with these two wankers fucking up my investigation."

Manx sensed Garrett was about to offer a counter-argument, and gestured for him to shut up before he began. "A man's life is in danger, a man I know personally, and you, Bowen, are the only link I have to possibly saving him." Manx pulled up harder on the belt. Bowen gasped, and placed his hand against the wall to support himself. "So, just before I finish shoving your balls back to where they were before they dropped, you might want to reconsider your previous statement." He looked Bowen directly in the eye, an unwavering, challenging stare, which left Bowen in no doubt as to Manx's intentions.

"Jesus. All right, just put me fucking down, Holmes," Bowen gasped.

Manx relaxed his grip slightly, and backed away.

"I know her, but I've not seen her for days, like."

"Is that right?" Manx pulled up on the belt again. Bowen was sweating now, beads forming on his forehead.

"Totally legit, Holmes."

"See, Bowen, every time I hear you say the word legit, I just think the complete opposite."

Bowen ran his forearm under his nose.

"Why don't we take you down the station, and have you sweat it out for forty-eight hours? Might put a dent in your travel plans, eh?" Manx said, gesturing towards the open atlas on the table.

"Me mam wants to take one of these Euro-breaks. I was helping her."

"Yeah, she looks the type," Nader said, laughing. "Proper globe-trotter, your mam."

Bowen swallowed, a dry, painful action sticking deep in his throat.

"So, tell me about it, Bowen. Is this a 'boy toy meets cougar' kind of thing? Because, that's an image I'd rather not dwell on," Manx said, as he gestured for Bowen to sit back down.

Bowen complied, tugging at the fabric around his groin. "It's not like that," Bowen said, and slowly pushed Mandy's suitcase further under the bed with the back of his foot.

"Oh, true-fucking-love, is it?" Nader said.

Bowen said nothing.

"I'll ask you again, nicely, or I'll ask them to take over the questioning," Manx said. "And, take my advice, you don't want to fuck with these blokes. They carry very big guns."

"Very fucking big," Garrett confirmed.

"Mandy's son, Callum Blackwell, do you know where he is?"

Bowen shrugged, and shook his head, his foot bouncing erratically on the caravan floor.

"But, he knows where you live, doesn't he? Mandy probably told him over family dinner." Manx leant closer into Bowen's face.

"Thing is, Thomas, these two officers have been tracking Blackwell's movement for years, and they tell me he's left a long line of bodies in his wake. You were probably useful to him, for a while, did his dirty work, but you're expendable. The world's full of scumbags, like you, to do the grunt work. What did he pay you? A few hundred quid to spin me a fairy tale about Vaughn setting up a drug operation on the island? Did Blackwell get you to plant the key to the lock up in the surgery, too?"

Bowen wiped the palms of his hands down the front of his jeans.

"In case you're weighing up your choices, in that shoe box you call a brain, I would recommend unrestrained conversation as your preferred course of action."

Manx relaxed his grip, and took a chance on a lie he hoped would turn Bowen. "Know what else these blokes told me?" he said. "Blackwell had his own father murdered in prison. Pretty fucked up, right?"

"Dunno, maybe he deserved it. Deadbeat dad, like."

"And Mandy? Do you think she deserves to be killed, too? That's the thing with people like Blackwell—everyone's expendable, everyone's a commodity. Even family."

Bowen's neck muscles tensed. Manx noticed the flickers of fear spark in his eyes. "Honest, I don't know where Mandy is. I've not seen her for a couple of days."

"Is that right?" Manx said, relenting his grip slightly.

"Yeah." Bowen hesitated. "I saw Blackwell, though. Took me to a farmhouse, up by Penmon, few days back."

"Where, exactly?"

"Off the Beaumaris Road. Take the first left, then right, down the hill, Bryn Talw."

"That's very specific. You fucking with us?"

"No, no way. Me da used to take me there when I was a kid, when the pigs were ready for slaughter."

"Bonding experience, was it?" Manx asked.

Bowen didn't reply. The memory was still carved into him like initials in tree bark. The stench of death, the panicked shitting of the pigs, the metallic stench of blood, the anxious swine grunts. And the sound that had stayed with him most—the breathless screeches of terror when the drove finally understood why it was there. Every once in a while, one of the pigs would break ranks, and run for its life. Bowen would silently urge the animal to keep running, pray it would escape into the thick copse of trees at the far end of the field. His prayers were always left unanswered. The pig would be rounded up, beaten, and then shocked with the electric stock-prod, until it complied, and brought back into line.

Chapter 4

Derrick Garrett peered through the window of the service car at the hedges illuminated by the jittery bounce of the headlights.

"You were fucking joking about this place, right?" he said.

"Joking about what?" Nader said, glancing in the rear mirror.

"All fucking sunshine and sangria? Like the Costa De Sol? Hard to imagine."

"In the summer, aye," Nader said brightly. "The local in Beaumaris does some cracking tapas. Bit stingy on the portion sizes, though."

"It's why they call it tapas. Small plates," Markham offered.

"Yeah? Learn something new every day, eh?" Nader said.

Garrett sighed, and shook his head.

"So, what's it like, the NCA? I bet they're always in need of good officers, right?"

Garrett laughed. "You know what we say the NCA stands for, Sergeant Who the Fuck? No Cunts Allowed. But, with your door wrecking skills, they'd probably snap you up right quick."

"Yeah, but you get respect, right? Government mandated, and that," Nader said. "They treat you like you matter, like you make a difference."

"What's your problem? Inspector Skinny Jeans stopped giving you hugs and cuddles? Forget it, Sergeant. If you want unconditional love, buy a fucking dog. They're known for it, so I'm told."

"Already got a dog," Nader offered.

"Then, what the fuck are you complaining about?" Garrett said. "Won't you be retiring in a few years, anyway? You're fucking older than me."

Nader ignored him, and concentrated on navigating through the dark, narrow roads.

"What are the odds Blackwell's still there?" Markham asked.

"He's not hanging around, when he knows someone's on his arse," Garrett said. "He's gone by now, like piss down a urinal. All this? It's a wild fucking goose chase. He's like his father, a slippery little bastard."

"You knew Charles Blackwell?" Nader asked.

"Part of the original arresting team when Blackwell Senior was put away, weren't you, sir?" Markham offered.

"Bloody lifetime ago," Garrett said, sharply.

"He was undercover, for months. Infiltrated one of Blackwell's crews."

"Put a cap on it, Markham, ancient history." Garrett was becoming edgy.

"I was just…"

"Enough, Markham, got it?"

Markham shrugged. "Whatever you say, boss."

The remainder of the drive was spent in silence, but Nader's brain was a pinball machine of flashing alarms. Garrett wasn't the kind of man to hide his light under a bushel; in fact, he'd probably trample down the bushel to make sure he got the lion's share of the light. He was a boaster, a bragger, one of those coppers who made sure you knew how good he was, before anyone else could tell you otherwise. *They usually had something to hide, coppers like that*, Nader, thought, before realising maybe he had more in common with Garrett than he cared to admit.

Chapter 5

W*as it that time of year already*, Manx asked himself, as he drove the Jensen at twice the posted speed limit through the small market town of Menai Bridge. The first trimmings of Christmas had appeared almost overnight, it seemed. Loose strands of fairy lights were woven haphazardly through the trees along the high street, and several shops already had a powdery film of fake snow sprayed inside their windows to accompany the plastic, dwarf Christmas trees and the tufts of boa-feather tinsel.

It was the end of November, Manx reminded himself, the 29th to be exact. He hadn't spent Christmas on the island since he was a teenager, not that the season concerned him much. Christmas was mostly for kids, and, as he wasn't in possession of any, he found little reason to celebrate. He always volunteered to work during the holidays, and allow the coppers with families to take the time off. Come the New Year, most of them were desperate to return to the station, having had a belly-full of family and festive cheer.

When he turned off the main road, two miles later, it had just passed midnight. The narrow, hedge-rimmed road leading to Cwm Talw was steep and muddy, and the Jensen's tires scrambled for traction. Behind him, the service vehicle with Nader and the two NCA officers followed, the headlights twitching nervously in the darkness.

Cwm Talw: Peaceful Valley. It was an apt name, considering the farm was located in a shallow dip between two hills and well-hidden from the main road. Both cars cut their engines at the wide iron gate blocking the access to the farmhouse. Manx stepped out, and looked towards the horizon. The roofline of the house was visible in the darkness, and illuminated by a single light positioned directly under the eaves. Manx guessed it was about half a mile away. If what Bowen had said, about Cwm Talw being a slaughterhouse, was true, there was little sign of that now. Maybe they'd shuttered the facility years ago, and converted into holiday flats. He reached down for the padlock; it felt cold and heavy in his hands, then let it fall back against the bars.

"You going to look at that, or vault over it?" Garrett called out from inside the service car.

As Manx contemplated the question, he caught a faint whiff of burning wood coming from the direction of the house.

Nader walked up to the gate. "Think he's hiding out down there, boss?"

"It's only been a few hours," Manx said. "If he thinks he's safe, then he'll hang around."

"No way. He's fucked off, by now." Garrett said, joining them.

"I can smell smoke, probably a fire," Manx said. "He's still down there."

"Should we call for backup?" Nader asked. "He's armed, maybe got a few more blokes with him, too?"

Garrett was about to complain, and offer another objection, when he suddenly stopped himself. "Backup?" he said. "Why the merry fuck do we need backup?" He pulled his weapon from his jacket pocket, signalling for Markham to do the same. "You've got two experienced officers with ACO training, why call in the tin-pot cavalry? He's probably tuned into the police radio; we may as well send out bloody smoke signals."

"Really?" Markham said, surprised at Garrett's sudden change of opinion. "How many do you reckon are in there?"

"Two, for sure. Blackwell and the big bloke," Manx said.

"Three," Garrett corrected Manx. "Your brother-in-law. Probably in one of the windows with a shotgun, waiting to pop us off, one-by-one."

Manx breathed in deeply. Garrett was right. From his perspective, Shanni was just another criminal. But, what Garrett didn't know was how scared Shanni was. Manx had seen that himself. The way he shook when he spoke, the long horizon-bound stare, how he stood up against Blackwell, and how, if his aim had been on target, Blackwell would either be in custody right now, or laid out in the mortuary—either option would have suited Manx fine. Garrett knew none of this, but there was no time to argue his point.

"OK, three," Manx agreed. "But, nobody opens fire on Shanni Morgan, unless he's armed, and threatening one of us."

"Fair enough. Not that I'd know him from Adam," Garrett said. "You two stay here. Markham, you recon the perimeter with me. We only enter the house, if the situation warrants it."

"Fuck that," Manx said, sliding his arms through his Kevlar jacket and zipping it closed.

Garrett spat onto the ground. He was too tired to argue. "Your funeral," he said. "But, I'm not filling out the paperwork, if you decide to be a fucking hero. You heard that, for the record, Markham?"

"Loud and clear," Markham said.

There was a clunk of steel on steel, as the NCA officers took out their Walther P99s, directed them at the ground, pulled back the sliding case, and checked the vertical barrel tilt.

"Clear," they both said, and slid the revolvers back into their holsters.

"Sure this is a good idea, boss?" Nader asked.

"Good?" Manx said. "No. Best we've got? Probably."

Chapter 6

Nader watched as the three officers dissolved into the darkness. He turned back towards the car, and suddenly felt something. *A flutter of nervousness, or was it excitement?* It had been sometime since he'd felt anything that visceral. He quickly corrected himself. Thomas Bowen, buckling under his nightstick, that was about as visceral as feelings got. But, that particular incident had been deleted now, or at least stored in a small box marked, "to be forgotten," at the back of his mind, where he'd trained himself to stash those sorts of memories.

Garrett was a prick, and Markham was the wart on the side of the prick, Nader concluded, as he settled into the service car. Under the edge of the seat, something caught his eye; a flyer for Mickey Thomas's retirement party. Mickey's wide, cartoon face grinned at him from the garish artwork. It made Nader smile, but retirement? It was the last thing he needed reminding of. He scrunched up the paper, and checked his watch. His shift should have finished hours ago. Still, he'd get good overtime, and the missus would be asleep by the time he got home; not a bad result for the night.

He thought about Garrett. Something didn't fit. He made a call.

"Hey, Minor, want to stop playing Candy Crush, and do me a favour?"

"Dunno. Want to ask me nicely?"

"No time for that, luv. Dig up anything you can on this Derrick Garrett bloke. Turns out he was one of the original arresting officers on the Blackwell case."

"What am I looking for, Sarge?"

"Fuck knows, just a hunch. Call me back, soon as."

Chapter 7

The petrol leaking from the punctured fuel tank of the Mercedes fell onto the wet cobblestones with a steady drip, drip, drip, like the seconds of a clock counting down. Manx, Garrett, and Markham passed silently by the car, placing their hands on the bonnet to check if the engine was still warm—it wasn't. Manx pulled on the rear door. The interior light buzzed to life. There could have been blood splatter over the beige upholstery, Manx couldn't be sure. The tire iron was still in there, but at least Shanni wasn't laid across the backseat, with a bullet through his skull.

Garrett urged Manx to keep close as they crossed the yard and stood either side of the farmhouse door. Manx caught the same trace of burning wood that he smelled at the gate, only more pungent. He glanced up at the chimney; there was no smoke, just the rustling of the tree branches scraping across the tile roof like brushes over a snare drum.

The door was moving gently in the stiff breeze. "Open invitation," Garrett whispered, before tapping the door with his boot—it fell wide open. There was a communal holding of breaths, as they waited for a response. None came; just the slap of door against wall and the whip of wind through the hallway.

"I'm going in," Garrett said. "Markham, check upstairs."

Garrett pressed his back against the wall and held out his arms, his finger poised on the trigger. Manx followed close behind. There were two doors, both open on either side of the narrow corridor, and at the end an open area leading into the kitchen. Garrett made sure the two rooms were clear, then signalled for Manx to follow.

The kitchen was warm, the embers of a fire still glowing red in the fireplace. As Manx's eyes became accustomed to the darkness, he took stock of the room. They'd left in a hurry. There were several dishes still on the table, and a teapot still warm to the touch.

"Not long gone," Manx said.

Garrett ran his torch along the walls, over the table, to the sink, then back again. Markham's footsteps echoed through the house and creaking floorboards. He returned a few minutes later.

"All clear upstairs," he said, entering the kitchen.

"Fuck it," Garrett said. "They had another vehicle."

Manx directed his torch towards the space above the fireplace. His attention was caught by an old sketch of the farmhouse. He looked closely. To the right of the house were two barns and several outhouses, and to the left, a series of indeterminable buildings. The larger of the structures looked industrial, probably constructed of wood and steel. It was taller, with a narrow, metal chute protruding out of the main entrance. To the side of that building were three smaller, cabin-like structures, with curved roofs, like a child's interpretation of an igloo. He ran the torch along the bottom of the sketch—Cwm Talw Farm and Slaughterhouse circa 1963.

"He's still here," Manx said, and tapped the edge of his torch against the outline of the slaughterhouse. "Garrett, you're armed. Lead the way."

Chapter 8

Nader sat to attention, and dipped his rear-view mirror, as a flash of headlights appeared behind him. He watched as the lights jostled and bounced over the rough terrain, then slow as they neared the gate.

Reluctantly, he opened the door, and stepped into the stiff, cold air. The car came to an abrupt stop. There was a crunch of gears, the whine of an engine, then, the futile spin of the front wheels, as the tires dug into the wet earth and spat mud along the side of the Ford Fiesta.

Nader walked carefully towards the car, which was digging itself further into the mire with a grim, but fruitless determination. It wasn't until Nader tapped on the roof, and gestured for her to wind down the window, that Mandy eased off the throttle.

"All right, Mandy. Emergency wool delivery, is it?"

Mandy slapped her hands hard several times on the steering wheel, and screamed through her teeth. Mexican Elvis bobbed in place, took a final bow, and fell from the dashboard onto the floor, gyrating and cooing, as he left the building.

Chapter 9

The ground behind the farmhouse was soft and sodden with rainwater. Manx felt his boots sink into the mud, as they walked the soft incline towards the slaughterhouse.

There would be no holiday flats here anytime soon, Manx thought, as the slaughterhouse came into view. Pale shafts of moonlight poured onto the old building. The perimeter was marked by a low, wire fence connected by a series of rotting wood posts, and several hastily scribbled placards stuck in the ground declaring, "Danger. No Trespassing."

The smell of burning wood grew more intense, as they reached the slaughterhouse. Above them, the roof flapped and wheezed, like wet sheets on a clothesline. They edged around the north wall, and found what they were looking for. The corrugated iron door was slightly ajar, enough to squeeze one police-sized body through at a time.

It's colder inside than outside, Manx thought, but there was something more than cold here, something more ominous and chilling. The slaughterhouse hadn't been used in years, but the ghost of its past still lingered, ingrained into every crack and steel bolt. The eeriness of the place crept over him like a shadow. If Garrett and Markham felt the same, they showed no sign, as they continued to edge along the east side of the building, their backs firmly pressed against the wall.

"Markham, go left, check out the other side. We'll keep heading north," Garrett whispered. Markham nodded, and sprinted across the floor to the opposite side. From the left, Manx heard the loud crack of a gunshot, followed by a scream from Markham, as he fell to the floor, gripping his thigh, which was spurting blood like an oil-drill which had just hit pay dirt.

Chapter 10

The slaughterhouse roof groaned with complaint, as the wind cuffed at the loose wooden beams and the makeshift tarpaulin sheets. Manx and Garrett contemplated their next move. The moon offered little light, but Manx's eyes had now become accustomed to the dark, and he could discern the angular shapes of the brutal machinery scattered around the structure.

The east of the slaughterhouse was a chute, narrow enough to allow one pig in single file to pass quickly into the holding pen, where they'd suffer a single bullet to the head, before being ushered on. Above the pen was an iron track, with a row of rusted hooks dripping from its chains. Six large, black objects had been sunk into the floor. They were like over-sized cauldrons, with their lips raised a meter or so off the floor, and filled with filthy, black water, which rippled like waves, as the wind blew across the surface. Directly at the end of the building, towards where Garrett was now walking in slow, considered steps, was a narrow conveyor belt, where Manx imagined the final cuts would be butchered and sorted, before being packaged. Above this, in the only structure on the second floor, Manx noticed a small office looking down over the kill-floor. *Was there something or someone in there, a flicker in the shadows?* Manx watched for a few moments, but saw nothing more. It was most likely a trick of the light; the building was probably pregnant with them.

"Upper level," Garrett whispered to Manx, and gestured for him to follow him to the stairs. Manx heard the grinding of metal on metal to his left, and turned just in time to see the blurred, rusted shape of a hook sweeping over the track towards him. He ducked, felt the wind from the hook pass his cheek, and saw another one come at him, fast. There was no time to warn Garrett. Manx heard the crack of steel against bone, as the hook split Garrett's forehead wide open. He buckled to the floor, blood trickling from his head and onto the concrete. Manx dropped to the ground, and checked his pulse. It was still strong; Garrett was just out for the count.

He dragged Garrett towards the shadow of the wall, and reached to retrieve the Waltham, which had fallen just feet away. As he curled his fingers around the handle, he saw a vapour of breath above him, followed by the hard steel tip of a work boot jab deep into his ribs. He doubled over, struggling to keep the gun in his palm. He felt hands dig under his armpits, and begin to haul him across the floor.

Manx twisted, tried to get a clean shot, but the man was grinding him like a millstone. He could feel the harsh bristles of the man's beard against his cheeks, and his breath on the nape of his neck. The man lifted Manx, as if he were a toy, and flung him to the floor. His knees smacked into the concrete with a force which sent his brain into a momentary blackout, the gun falling from his hands. As his senses slowly fuzzed back to clarity, he realised where he was. The man had dragged him to one of the cauldrons, and was now urging Manx's face downwards into the black, rancid water.

Manx held his breath to avoid inhaling the overwhelming stench, and scrambled for the gun by his feet. He felt the tantalizing brush of his fingers across the cold barrel, before the man came down hard, stamped his boot into the back of Manx's calves, and pushed harder against his neck. Manx pushed back, but the goon's strength was like a bulldozer. Seconds later, Manx's face hit the surface. He felt the filth of water seep through his nostrils and back into his throat, where it pooled for a few moments, before seeping down into his stomach wall. He could hear nothing now, nothing but the heavy silence of water damning his ears.

The man yanked Manx's head back from the water. He struggled to inhale another lungful of air, before he was shoved under for a second time. He had to stay calm, figure a way out, but he could already feel the perilous drift into unconsciousness. If the man allowed him to come up for air one more time, he could distract him long enough to twist the gun around, but he couldn't wait that long. He needed a better plan.

Manx blindly reached again for the Waltham, which he knew to be somewhere close to his knees. He found it. This was his last and only chance. He curled his palm under the handle, and flipped the gun into his fingers. He'd never hit the man from this angle, but maybe if he distracted him, he'd get a few extra, precious seconds of life. Manx pushed back again, trying to get a clear line of sight, but the man pressed his head further into the liquid darkness. Another slime of water slid down to his lungs and stomach, bleeding through his body like poison. It had to be now.

He felt the pressure on the trigger give way, then the sound of the bullet as it struck the side of the east wall, pinging a loud metallic echo throughout the building. The man momentarily relaxed his grip, as he tried to pinpoint the origin of the shot. Manx took the opportunity, and thrust his head free from the water. The man's hand, wet and greasy, slid easily off his neck.

Manx quickly spun on his knees, looked up at the shovel-like face staring down at him, and fired his second shot of the night. The bullet found its mark, a direct hit to the underside of chin, spraying a mass of flesh and bone into the air. The man stumbled and fell backwards, with a dense thud and a crack of shattering skull against concrete.

Manx leant against the side of the cauldron, and spat out the thick wad of water, the bitter rheum filtering upwards to his throat. He felt his heart rate steadily drop, and his breath become more measured. *Where was Blackwell?* He had to be somewhere in the shadows, lurking, watching. He breathed in, slowly and quietly, listening for footsteps or breaths. There was nothing, save the bluster of the wind as it clawed at the timber roof. Manx waited a few more moments, before turning face down on the concrete, and crawling across the floor towards the safety of the back wall. He touched something warm and fleshy to his right—Garrett. The NCA Officer stirred as Manx checked his pulse.

"Gun," Garrett said, in a dry, rough whisper.

Manx showed him the Waltham in his palm.

"Kill the fucker. Needs to be finished, all of it, finished, for good," Garrett said, slipping gradually back into unconsciousness.

Manx crawled outside. The air was now thick with smoke fanning through the main slaughterhouse door. *But, where was it coming from?* The fire at the farmhouse was all but dead, and the slaughterhouse was deathly cold. *Had Blackwell started a fire in one of the fields, torching any evidence?* As Manx attempted to lock the pieces of the puzzle together, he remembered the drawing of the farmhouse above the mantelpiece. There were other buildings etched into the scene. They looked like tiny igloos drawn by a child's hand, with snake-like lines curving upwards from a hole in the roofs. They weren't for storage; they served another purpose. They were smokehouses, and there were at least three of them on the property. *But, why would Blackwell be smoking meats?*

It made no sense to Manx. Until, suddenly, it did.

Chapter 11

Nader cuffed Mandy's wrists, and guided her into the back of the service car. She complained, spat something at Nader, but he wasn't listening; he was trying to catch what Morris was saying over the bad reception on his mobile. He prodded the speakerphone icon.

"You were right," Morris said, through the thin speaker, "Garrett was one of the arresting officers on Operation Hightail."

"I knew that already, Morris."

"Bastard," Mandy shouted from the backseat.

"Shut it!" Nader said. "No, not you, Minor."

"Fucking bastard," Mandy repeated.

"Anything else, Minor? I've got me hands full here."

"Yeah, you'll want to hear this," she said. "Before he was assigned to the NCA, Garrett worked for thirteen months at the Witness Protection Agency."

Nader gave Morris's words a few seconds to sink in. "You sure?"

"Double-checked it, got all his records right here."

"Fuck!" Nader said, and hung up.

"He's a bastard," Mandy said, again.

Nader turned around. "Who? Who's a bastard? Callum?"

"No, Garrett. He's bent, like your girl said. Didn't want my husband to grass him up from prison, so he had him killed. That's why he's a bastard."

Nader laughed. "You're losing your marbles, Mandy. Manchester Police told us the whole story. Blackwell died in prison, suicide."

"They got you fooled, too," Mandy said. "The Greater fucking Manchester Police. Looking out for their own, just like the rest of you lot. You're all the fucking same." Mandy rested her head back, and looked out to the blackness. "Not that it matters now. It's done. *Que se*-fucking-."

Nader's head was spinning. He turned towards Mandy, noticing her eyes were moist and bloodshot. "You're telling me Garrett was on the take from your husband, then Garrett had him killed, so he wouldn't talk?"

Mandy quickly regained her composure and well-honed survival instincts. "Not without a solicitor and a deal from CPS, I'm not."

Nader felt another visceral flutter pinch at his stomach. This time, it wasn't excitement or nervousness; it was dread. It felt as if his stomach was pooling with a heavy, dark liquid, slowly creeping its way towards his throat.

He radioed Morris. "Call for backup, Firearms Unit, first responders, the lot. I've got a bad feeling about this, Morris. A bad fucking feeling…" his thoughts trailed off, as he clicked off the radio.

He looked through the windscreen and over to the dark outlines of the mountains beyond, contemplating his next move. Stay here, or go and warn Manx. Or, maybe, it was already too late.

"They say confession's good for the soul, right?" Mandy said, lifting her cuffed hands, and tracing the sign of the cross through the curtain of condensation. She rested her head against the window, and began to mumble to herself. "Forgive me, Father, for I have sinned…"

Nader opened the car door, letting in a gust of cold air. "Stay here," he said, stepping from the car.

Mandy lifted up her cuffed hands, and gave him a "where the fuck else would I go?" look, letting her head fall back onto the window. She might have been crying, as he slammed the door shut, Nader wasn't sure; he had other priorities now.

Chapter 12

Manx ran towards the first of the three, brick smokehouses. Plumes of grey smoke billowed skywards, and drifted like pepper spray to his face. He set his forearm against his eyes, reached for the door handle, and felt the dead weight of a padlock in his palm. It was secured by a thick, iron chain, triple-wrapped at the centre. He gripped the Waltham in both hands, aimed the barrel at lock-level, and backed up. He pulled back on the trigger, and then stopped. There was something behind him; he could hear it snorting and panting, as it padded towards him.

There was a parcel of hot breath, then a low, throaty growl. A small gust of wind scattered the smoke sufficiently to reveal the features of a large, black dog. The creature edged back, bowed its head low, and retracted its lips to expose drips of thick saliva slacking from its teeth. It growled again, back to finish what it had started. Manx lifted his gun. The dog crouched and jumped. Manx dropped to the ground: a manoeuvre the primitive brain function of the dog had failed to predict. Manx caught a fleeting glimpse of the Mastiff's muscular underbelly, as it passed over him, secured his gun in both hands, and fired. He felt the faintest trickle of warm blood drop onto his cheek, as the bullet ripped open the Mastiff's underbelly. It uttered a swansong of a yelp, followed by a dull thud, as it hit the ground. There was one last, feeble whimper, then silence.

Manx stayed down, watching his own breath dissipate into the night air, and waited for Blackwell to appear from the shadows. After a few minutes, he stood up, fixed the gun in his palm, and fired at the padlock. It shattered instantly. He slowly pushed open the door, and stepped back as a thick vapour of smoke feathered out, rolling through the cold night air.

Chapter 13

Hickory—it was the first smell which struck Manx, as he stumbled in. The second aroma had a fleshier, fattier scent, like freshly smoked ham hocks or bacon.

As the smoke cleared, he saw Shanni, tied to the wooden post cutting through the centre of the structure. His feet were bound at the ankles, and a strip of silver duct tape secured across his mouth. As Manx squatted down, he saw Shanni's face clearly through the smoke. But, this wasn't Shanni. The handsome, gypsy-like features were sloughing and curling from his face, like paper over a flame. His face was smoked to a rough, pink doneness, and his eyes were wide and terrified, pleading for release.

Manx began to work at the ropes, pulling at the knots. The smoke burnt his eyes, blurring his vision, until he could only feel the hardened lumps of knots under his fingers. His lungs were thick with ash and fumes, and his chest was pulling tight, as he inhaled the swath of burning smoke. He knelt down, and contemplated his options. He could probably last a few more minutes, maybe less, before he had to run back out and save himself, and leave his brother-in-law to suffer. Or, he could let Shanni go in peace. Perform one swift, final act of mercy.

Manx wiped his forearm across his eyes, and gripped the Waltham. A wash of broken images played out in his mind, like a reel of Super 8 film fracturing from its sprockets. He'd been here before, played this role; he knew how it ended. He placed the palm of his hand on Shanni's brow. It felt as if he were touching the final embers of a fire. He closed his eyes, and pulled hard on the trigger.

Chapter 14

Another gunshot—the third in as many minutes. DS Nader felt every nerve in his body stand to attention, as the echo vibrated through his skull, like the plucking of a too-sharp guitar string. He shook himself, as if he were trying to rid himself of a bad dream. The pain was back; the same relentless pinching at the nape of his neck which would travel his forehead and then to his face, numbing his jaw, and setting his gums on edge.

He looked out across the black horizon towards the farmhouse. Smoke spiralled from the fields beyond, though his brain failed to parse the scene. The curves and dips of the hills and mountains, where they touched the skyline, were warped, as if they were subject to their own laws of gravity and physics. The half-hidden moon seemed to adhere to the same principals, bending and twisting through the soft filter of clouds, as if he was looking at the milky satellite through water.

He leant against a damp, lichen-covered rock, and began to breathe in deep, considered breaths, just as the psychiatrist had instructed him. His mind slowly came back into focus. He had to keep going, warn Manx, save the rest of his men. That's what a soldier did—he did his duty, stayed loyal to his platoon, left no man behind.

Chapter 15

The Waltham's kickback wrenched at Manx's wrist with a sharp jolt. The first bullet entered the thick, mass of knots binding Shanni's ankles, fraying the rope into a shred of fibres. The second bullet shattered the other knot around his wrist. Manx shoved the gun into his belt, and reached under Shanni's arms. He was unsteady, scraping his boots along the floor, as Manx dragged him out into the welcome relief of frigid cold air.

He leant Shanni against the smokehouse wall, and ripped off the duct tape from his mouth. Shanni immediately vomited onto the floor, then inhaled in hurried, greedy breaths.

"Can you walk?" Manx asked.

Shanni nodded. As Manx's eyes cleared of smoke and dirt, he could see the severity of Shanni's injuries. The skin on his face was flaking off, like the peel of raw sunburn. Manx could see flecks of white cheekbone urging through the red mass of blood and muscle. He reached under Shanni's arms, and guided him back in slow, deliberate steps, towards the farmhouse.

"So much for the great fucking escape, lads."

The voice caught Manx by surprise. He spun around quickly, the revolver primed in his palm. "Fuck!" he said, letting his arm drop. "You almost got yourself a bullet."

Garrett swayed in place like a Friday night drunk, as he focussed his gaze on Manx. "You finish him, Manx? Kill the bastard?" he said, spit flying like a spray of buckshot from his mouth and onto his Kevlar jacket.

Manx noticed he had a gun—another Waltham P99, hanging loosely from his hand—probably taken from Markham.

"You okay, Garrett?" he asked, gesturing for Shanni to sit.

Garrett wiped a trickle of blood from his head with his sleeve and blinked. "Show me the body, Manx. Prove to me he's finished, that you've put this fucking thing down for good."

Manx watched Garrett's movements carefully. His eyes scanned across the horizon, without settling on anything, and he was waving his gun in the air in over-exaggerated gestures. "Put down the gun, Garrett, and we can talk about it, all right?"

Garrett shook his head. "No. Not until I see the body, not until you show me he's dead."

"We haven't located him," Manx said.

Garrett's face contorted into something between confusion and blind rage. "Not fucking acceptable, Manx. If you're too chicken shit to do it, then I will," he said, turning in place, looking, aimlessly for Blackwell to appear from out of the smoke, or maybe from the fields behind him.

"Why, Garrett? Why is it so important Blackwell dies?"

Garrett was momentarily quiet, as if the question had slammed the brakes on his train of thought. Manx turned quickly, his gun stiff in his hands as he heard footsteps and laboured breathing coming from his left.

"Boss, it's him!" Nader shouted. He was panting heavily, as he came to a stop next to the Inspector. "Garrett." Nader took another deep, painful breath, and sputtered, "He's the snitch. Worked in witness protection. Been on Blackwell's payroll for years."

Manx turned to face Garrett, the Waltham aimed at his chest. "Garrett?"

"Fuckin' bollocks," the NCA Officer said, dismissively.

"Mandy. Back of the service car," Nader panted. "Told me everything."

"Been on the sangria again, eh? Sergeant What the Fuck."

"It's Nader," Nader said, slowly regaining his composure. "Detective Sergeant Malcolm Nader."

Garrett threw him a "what the fuck do I care" shrug, and laughed. "Mandy, that old trout? Who do you think my CI was?

She'll tell you anything so Callum Blackwell doesn't find out he's been shopped by his own mother."

Manx took a couple of tentative steps towards Garrett. "Okay, then, hand over the gun, and we can get all this cleared up. We'll bring in Mandy and Blackwell, both of us."

Garrett laughed. "No fucking way. If he's still alive, my bullet's ending it," Garrett said, waving his gun towards Manx. "Scumbags like Blackwell, they don't deserve justice. See what he did to your brother-in-law? Think a few years in the slammer's going to reform him? Think he's not going to be running his business from inside, like his fucking father?"

"It's not our call to make, Garrett. You know that," Manx said, calmly.

Garrett shook his head. "Come on, we'd be doing the world a favour. One less monster under the bed, who knows how many lives saved? He fired first, we returned fire. Suspect was shot, fatally, end of story. Sergeant What the Fuck will back up the story, right? I'll put in a good word for you at the NCA. Quid pro quo."

Manx hesitated. "Dead men don't tell secrets, right?" he said. "If Blackwell lives, he'll get a few years knocked off his sentence for testifying against you. Is that what you're afraid of?"

"Why are you still talking, Manx? Let's go find this fucker."

"Then, there's Mandy," Manx said. "You'll have to get rid of her, too. That's the thing with killing, Garrett; it never stops. There's always another drop of the domino."

Garrett wiped the blood from his forehead, and edged his gun towards Manx and Nader. "Thirty-seven years. I'm not going out like this, no fucking way."

Garrett's gun was shaking, his finger poised on the trigger, waving between Manx and Nader. Manx tightened his own finger around his trigger. But, there was no need. He could see Josh Markham rushing towards Garrett, limping awkwardly across the field, one hand fixed firmly against the bullet hole in his thigh.

"It doesn't need to end like this, Garrett," Manx said, eager to keep him talking, as Markham drew closer. But, Garrett had already spun around, sensing the danger behind him. Manx was about to fire, when he felt Nader's stocky frame brush past him. Nader tackled Garrett at the ankles. He lurched forward with a deep groan, and fell face-first into the dirt. Nader stumbled, straddled his legs across Garrett's back, and pulled hard on his arms.

"Cuffs," Nader said to Manx, who quickly unclipped his own, and passed them over. Garrett struggled and shouted something unintelligible into the grass. Nader repositioned himself, and wedged his ample thighs either side of Garrett's lower back.

"Jesus, Nader, you learn that in the army, too?" Manx said.

"Prop forward, Llangefni over thirty-fives. I'll keep him occupied till the firearms unit get here," Nader said.

Manx was about to throw a well-deserved, but rare compliment in the Sergeant's direction, when he heard the clunk of a diesel engine starting, and noticed the milky spill of car headlights over the farmhouse roof.

"Stay here. I'll come back for you," he said to Shanni, who nodded his compliance. But, Shanni's eyes told another story; one, which in the pitch-dark, Manx didn't have the time, or the presence of mind, to read.

Chapter 16

Manx reached the farmhouse, breathless and sweating, just as the car's rear lights made it to the brink of the hill. He pressed his palm across the needle-sharp stitch poking into his right side. His entire body pulsed with pain; his chest, like unrelenting fist compressing around his heart; his knees, precarious and shot, with urgent, stabbing aches. As he looked up, he expected the car to have dissolved into the blackness, but it had come to an abrupt stop, its engine spluttering and impotent, as it drew the last fumes of diesel from the empty tank. Manx secured the P99 in his hand, and willed his body forward.

The car headlights illuminated the scene, like floodlights over a football field. Manx saw Blackwell clambering over the gate, and towards the service car. He called out, but his words were thick wads of cotton in his mouth. He steadied his breath, made sure Blackwell could see his gun, and tried again. "Stop, Blackwell, or I will shoot!"

Blackwell cocked his head towards Manx, but ignored the command, flipping his body easily over the gate. As his boots landed on the dirt, he turned to face Manx, and reached inside his raincoat. Manx stiffened his grip on the Waltham. Blackwell lifted the twin-barrels of his sawn-off shotgun from inside his jacket and fired. Manx hit the ground, just as the slug shattered the stone post to the right of the gate, sending a cascade of rock-chippings and limestone through the air.

Manx heard the clicking of another slug slotting into its chamber. "Put the gun down, Blackwell, and we'll both get out of here alive," he said. "I know all about Garrett. Testify against him, and you'll get a deal."

Blackwell fired again, both barrels this time. The shells pounded into the ground close to Manx, kicking up a thick divot of soil and grass.

"We've radioed for backup. They'll track you down. Nothing but open-fields around here, time to stop running, Blackwell."

"No more fucking deals!" Blackwell's voice sounded dense as he spoke, his words punctuated by the snap of another two shells falling into place.

Manx scrambled behind the gatepost, and kept his eye on Blackwell as he walked backwards, his shotgun set against his hip. He saw a flicker of light, small but perceptible, just behind Blackwell's shoulder. Mandy staggered from the car, and stepped uneasily towards her son, her hands cuffed, and held tightly at her breast.

"Do as he says, Cal," Mandy said, her voice brittle and close to breaking. "It wasn't meant to end like this. Please."

Blackwell spun around quickly, keeping the shotgun pointed at Manx.

"This is your doing?" he said, a tone of disbelief thick in mouth.

"Metcalf's dead, Cal," Mandy said. "They know about Garrett. I couldn't stand it, if I lost you. Not after…"

Blackwell stiffened. "What did you do?" His breathing was rapid and hard, as he spoke through clenched teeth. "What did you do?" he repeated.

Mandy wept, dropping to the ground, as if she'd been cut at the knees. She reached out, supplicating at her son's feet. Blackwell flipped the shotgun, now directing the barrels at his mother. The penitent words were about to leave Mandy's lips, when Manx shouted from behind the wall.

"We traced your phone, Blackwell. Bowen told us where you were. Mandy's in the wrong place, wrong time. She was coming to warn you."

Blackwell spun back around to Manx, then back to Mandy again. "Bullshit. You've changed. Being away… it's made you soft, made you forget." His voice dripped with disdain.

"No Cal, it's made me realise what's important." Mandy said, her tears cutting channels through her makeup and onto her jacket. "I'd have come back for you, so we could be together again, but not for this, not for more death." Her chest was heaving, and her breath drifted aimlessly through the cold air, like incense, as she pleaded with her son.

"Put your hands up, Blackwell. Like Mandy says, it's over. You'll get out of here alive, that's all she wants," Manx said.

Blackwell blew a snort of contempt. "Incarceration and rehabilitation, is that what you were hoping for? Come and visit me once a month, like we did with Dad? Repeat the experiment, see if there's a different outcome?"

Mandy wiped her sleeve over her eyes. "Anything so you're alive, Cal, anything. Please. For me."

"I stay alive to make you feel better about yourself?" Blackwell spat.

Mandy clasped her hands tighter, and shook her head. "No, for both of us, Cal. Some future is better than none, isn't it?"

Blackwell issued a terse, contemptuous laugh. "You were always a terrible liar, Mother. But, no matter, I've made contingencies." Blackwell aimed the gun barrels downwards, towards Mandy.

Behind him, Manx heard the click of a door opening. *Someone was in the back of the Mercedes! Shit!* He should have checked it. But, he couldn't take his eyes off Blackwell, not yet.

"No, Cal, you can't do this. Please," Mandy pleaded, her fists wedged hard under the bone of her chin.

Manx watched Blackwell, as he loomed like a dark angel over his mother. Manx heard another noise to his left; someone was scrambling in the shadows. Nader? That you?" he whispered. There was no reply. He quickly turned his gaze back to Blackwell and Mandy.

"There's no one else now, Cal, just you and me. It's always been you and me," Mandy said. "Everything I've ever done is out of love for you, don't you see that? When Chas left, all we had was each other. You were my world, and then, you left, too. I couldn't stand it, Cal. I had to leave, start over. You can't blame me; I was owed that much, at least."

Blackwell's posture seemed to relax, as he listened to Mandy, letting her words resonate through him.

"Put down the gun, Cal," Mandy said, her voice soft and consoling through the sobs. "You've done what you came to do, kept your promise. Dad would be proud of you, Cal, really proud."

Blackwell faltered, his shotgun hung loose in his hands. Manx kept his own gun steady and primed; there was no predicting how he would react. He was sure Blackwell was about to drop his weapon, when he noticed a figure scramble at the corner of his vision. He blinked, trying to discern the shape, as it hauled itself over the wall, and towards Blackwell.

Blackwell spun on his heels. Shanni Morgan was charging towards him, hatred and fury burning in his eyes. Manx shouted, but Shanni was beyond listening, beyond rational thought—beyond reach. He hoisted the tire iron above his shoulder, and brought it down.

Blackwell's head jerked violently. White flecks of splintered bone flew through the light beams, blood spraying from his head in faltering spurts. He stumbled, as if confused, and yanked back his shotgun. He discharged his final round.

Shanni's body vaulted several feet from the ground, as if pulled by an invisible rope into the shadows. Manx fired. The bullet ripped through Blackwell's chest. He stumbled in place for a moment, as if he were deciding his next move, though that decision was, by now, out of his control. The shotgun slid from his hands. He swayed in place, then fell.

A thick silence fell over the scene. It felt to Manx like the moment at the conclusion of a play, just before the final drop of the curtain. He could hear nothing now but his own, shallow breath and his blood, thumping loudly like a drumbeat through his veins. Then, darkness—the final fall of the curtain, as the battery died and the car lights slowly petered out to black.

But, there was one final act, before the players were to be dragged from the stage. Mandy stumbled and moved towards her son, wiping her eyes with her coat sleeves. She threw herself over Cal's body, her cuffed hands beating on his chest. She screamed, a long desperate wail of despair. It was a scream Manx thought would never end, as it carried over the hills, through the fields, embedding itself in everything around it, before dissipating into the insistent chop of helicopter blades and the urgent wail of sirens, as they moved closer.

Manx scrambled over the wall, and ran towards Shanni. He cupped his hands behind his brother-in-law's head, and listened. He was still breathing, though barely. Manx checked his injuries. His stomach was ripped open, and glistening with fresh blood and the pink overspill of intestines.

"Hold on," Manx said, as he took off his jacket, jammed it deep into the crimson cavity and pressed down hard. Within moments, his hands were sodden, and warm with Shanni's blood.

"Don't you fucking die!" Manx shouted, pushing down with all the strength he had left within him. "Don't you fucking dare die."

Chapter 17

The night was clear, but cold. A salt-seasoned wind blew through the Port of Holyhead, buffering against the long arms of the container cranes along the dockside. Ferries and pilot boats busied themselves with their night's work, scuttling back and forth across the narrow channel in a froth of backwash and diesel. Every few seconds, the sound of a pile driver from one of the nearby factories drummed at the earth, with a purposeful, insistent rhythm, like the pulse of a steady, strong heartbeat. In contrast, Thomas Bowen's own heart felt as if it were trying to win a race he was unaware he was participating in. He focussed on the dull thud of the pile driver, and tried, in vain, to match its composed, mechanical thumping. It was futile. He'd already taken a hit of cocaine a couple of hours ago; it would be another two before the rush would subside.

He was standing outside the Stena Line ticket office; had been for the past three hours. He rubbed his palms together, wishing he'd packed something warmer than the thin leather jacket he always wore. No matter. He'd buy a warm coat when he got to Dublin. There was no way in hell he was going back to the caravan and Ma Bowen—that life was over now. Beside him, on the harbour floor, was Mandy's suitcase and two of his own shabbier-looking backpacks. One contained most of the clothing he owned, the other housed his laptop, three pairs of jeans wrapped around it.

He checked his watch for what felt like the millionth time that night. Nine-thirty pm. Mandy should have been here over an hour ago. He craned his neck over the line of people filtering onto the ramp leading to the ferry. There was no sign. She wasn't answering her mobile, either; it switched instantly to voicemail, but he tried again anyway. He listened to Mandy's soft, motherly tone, instructing him to leave his name and phone number, and insisting she'd return the call as soon as she could. He hung up before Mandy's trademark "adios." He'd already left ten messages tonight. He doubted one more would make any difference.

The ten o'clock ferry to Dun Laoghaire would stop boarding in eight minutes, and in another fifteen, would be reversing out into the open sea. He felt his first pang of anxiety. The thought Mandy might not turn up had never crossed his mind. He'd seen her just yesterday, a few hours before that Inspector and the other three pigs had busted his balls.

He heard the boarding gates begin to swing close, and ran over to the dockside. "You can't close up yet, mate. I'm waiting for someone. She'll be here any minute," Bowen said, addressing the stocky, uniformed official manning the gate. Harri Morgan, it stated on his name badge.

"Unless she's here in about twelve seconds, she's not going anywhere. You boarding, or what?"

Bowen looked at the man, spat on the floor, and slowly backed off as the gate locked in place.

Two hours later, Bowen was still outside the ticket office. Another ferry, the last one of the evening, had departed an hour ago, and the lights in the boarding area were already dimmed for the night. The stocky man from the gate passed him, as he made his way home after his shift.

"Nothing more till morning now, lad, best get home, if I were you. Rain's in the forecast," he said jovially; too jovially for Bowen's mood. He ignored him, and lit a cigarette.

"Suit yourself," Harri Morgan said, walking towards the car park.

Bowen stood up, and took one final look over to the port entrance. It was deserted. He kicked at his bags on the floor. Mandy wasn't coming; that fact had finally sunk in. He sat himself down again, and rubbed his hands over his face. But, she'd left her suitcase with him. *Why would she do that, if she were dumping him?*

No, something must have happened. Maybe her son, Callum, or the pigs, someone must have stopped her.

A sliver of moonlight caught the gold buckle of the Gucci suitcase. He'd resisted the temptation for the past few hours, but now, it seemed there was no reason not to. He snagged a penknife from inside his jacket, and slipped the blade under the lock. It broke easily; the suitcase was probably a fake, he thought as he tentatively lifted the lid, and peered inside. Wool. There must have been over fifty bundles, an abstract of colours and textures, packed tightly to the edges.

A dark heaviness surged through his body. He took the suitcase in both hands, swung it across his body, and released it with as much strength as he could muster. It soared over the harbour's edge before landing in the black, diesel-greased water. The yarns quickly unravelled and drifted along the surface, like a thin rainbow of seaweed. Bowen stayed for a few minutes, watching the strands float around the dockside. Some caught against the rough face of the stone harbour wall, while others drifted a few feet, and became tangled in the debris littering the channel. After a few minutes, the suitcase sank out of sight.

That's all this ever was, Bowen thought as he walked back towards the port entrance, a yarn, a story—a fantasy. He hated himself for believing it, hated Mandy for giving him hope, and hated the world for conspiring to fuck him over time and time again. He was about to leave and find someplace, or something, to drown his considerable sorrows, when he noticed the rim of car lights in the distance. The car came to a stop at the harbour gates, but kept its engines running. *Probably a taxi*, Bowen thought, as he walked slowly towards the car, hesitant to even hope Mandy would be in there.

Long, thin fingers wiped away the condensation from the back, passenger side window. He saw her, Mandy, through the smeared glass. He should have trusted her. He wouldn't doubt her again, not ever. *But, why wasn't she coming out to meet him? Was she waiting for him to open the door? Did she need change for the driver?*

Bowen was about to walk the few metres to the car, when the driver's door swung open. He didn't recognise him at first, but as the figure walked towards him, a wide, satisfied grin on his face, Bowen felt rooted to the spot.

"She's a talker, your MILF," Detective Sergeant Mal Nader, striding confidently towards Bowen.

Bowen looked over at Mandy. She lifted her hand to wave. She was cuffed at the wrists, a pale, resigned look to her, as she wiped her nose with her palm. *She'd never looked older*, Bowen thought, *old and tired*.

"Spain? What a fucking loser," Nader said, turning Bowen around, and binding the cuffs tightly around his wrists. "Still, plenty of time to get over her, where you're going." He pushed Bowen against the car door, and ran the tip off his nightstick over his still swollen eye.

"In case you were wondering," he said, "you deserved everything you got. Now, let's make it official." Nader gripped his hand around Bowen's neck, and shoved his face into the window. "Thomas Bowen, I'm arresting you for assaulting a police officer. You do not have to say anything, but…"

Chapter 18

D r. Richard Hardacre rolled the gurney in a grim, funereal fashion towards the couple. He paused for a moment, before shuffling a respectful distance to allow them to prepare themselves. Manx watched from behind the glass partition, as Hardacre spoke to them in what he guessed would be a reverential, hushed tone, before gently resting his hand on the young woman's shoulder. When he felt they were ready, he slowly drew down the sheet, until it came to rest at the dead man's shoulders.

The woman brought her hand to her mouth, and began to sob. She had her back turned to Manx, but he could see her shoulders tremble, as she looked down at her husband's body. The clear, plastic bag, containing a wedding ring and a fake Rolex watch she'd picked up from the hospital earlier today, slipped from her hand and onto the floor. Hardacre bent down to retrieve it, and turned it over in his palm, feeling the flimsy weight in his hands. The man standing next to the young woman was much older and shorter than she was, and appeared to buckle at the knees as he looked at the face that, twenty-three years ago, he'd gazed down on with wonder and pride, as his son had taken his first breath in the world. The man stiffened, regained his composure, and rested his hand on the rail of the gurney. The woman ran her finger over the ghostly, pale face, and made the sign of the holy trinity. The older man followed suit, bowing his head low as he did so.

Manx felt his heart tighten. His thoughts went back to something his sister had said: *things like this don't happen to people like us.* They must be thinking the same, questioning themselves, asking how this could have happened, blaming themselves, and wondering if there was one, singular event or small utterance which would have changed the course of events. Of course there was. There were millions of chance happenings which could have changed the outcome, but that's not how the fates had aligned for Gasper Kosir. Like most things in life, it was a random series of events which led to his murder, and, in turn, led to Gasper's wife and father being here today, hundreds of miles from home, weeping over his body.

Manx was wrapped in his thoughts, and didn't hear the Detective Chief Inspector enter the hallway, until Canton was standing next to him.

"I could have handled it," Manx said, watching Hardacre handing the bag back to the woman, who held it tight to her breast.

"Part of the job," Canton replied. "He died while under our protection. The least I can do as the senior officer is to offer my condolences."

Manx sniffed, and watched the old man comfort the young woman.

"Taking the body back with them?" Canton asked.

"As soon as the paperwork's signed, then, it's like he was never here," Manx said, stuffing his hands deep into his jeans pockets.

Canton sighed, and turned. "We can only do so much, Tudor."

"Five minutes. If I'd figured it out five minutes earlier, he'd still be alive."

Canton looked at Manx with a grave expression. "Maybe, maybe not," he said. "There's no telling. Listen, Manx, we all carry the dead around with us. As coppers, we carry more than our share. The trick is to acknowledge their presence, show them respect, and move on. It's all any of us can do."

"Another Bonsai proverb?" Manx said.

"You can beat yourself up all you want, Manx, but if you want my professional recommendation, as your superior officer and an old friend, let it go. Guilt's a demanding mistress. She'll steal your heart and your soul, if you're not careful."

"Bit poetic, Chief."

"Doesn't make it any less true."

Manx knew he was right, but no matter how poetic Canton's words, they weren't providing the solace he was looking for. That was the problem with words of comfort; they fell flat, unless you were in the right frame of mind to accept them.

"Any news on the Captain they picked up in Lisbon?" Canton asked.

"We faxed over the front page of today's *Daily Post* to the Portuguese officials. He wanted proof Blackwell was dead, before he talked."

"Good. That should be the final nail in the coffin. Case closed, thank God. The higher-ups in Colwyn Bay are already singing your praises, by the way. That young NCA officer, Markham, they'll be wheeling him out too, wheelchair and all. Big Press conference, personal commendation from the Super, usual song and dance."

"Can't wait," Manx said.

Canton folded his arms across his chest. "Your brother-in-law had quite the distribution network," he said. "Been operating for quite some time, too. Don't know how we missed it."

"Sometimes you miss the shit that's right under your foot when you're looking out for the shit pile down the end of the road," Manx said.

"Pleasant analogy," Canton smiled. "Make sure your team gets the recognition they deserve. Take them out for a few pints, or something, a morale building exercise," Canton said, and patted Manx on the shoulder, before pushing open the heavy door into the mortuary.

Manx stayed for a few minutes, watching as Canton removed his hat, and shook hands with both the wife and father, expressing his deepest of sympathies. They both nodded calmly as Canton spoke. Manx had seen enough; he turned away, and walked back down the corridor.

Chapter 19

"Have you ever lost anyone close, Inspector?" Mandy asked, flicking a stray wisp of bleach-blond hair from her cheek. She looked tired, her eyes bloodshot and rheumy, her face drawn and pale. Manx, momentarily taken aback by the question, leant back in his chair, and glanced at the court appointed solicitor, an older woman called in at short notice, who already seemed bored with the proceedings.

"Back to you, Mandy," he said. "You were part of Callum's operation. Laundering his drug money and any other illegal sources of income through the shop. Am I right?"

"I'm a pensioner living frugally, Inspector. I wouldn't know how to begin to launder money. Really, it's absurd."

Manx chuckled. "Come on. Make this easy on yourself, Mandy. We've already got most of this figured out."

"Then, why am I here?"

Manx leant in closer, and placed a thick padded enveloped on the table and pulled out a photograph. "This was all about revenge wasn't it, Mandy? Your husband, Charles Blackwell, was jailed on evidence provided by Dr. Patrick Metcalf." Manx stabbed at the photo of Metcalf and Blackwell outside the clinic. "He spent years stewing on this fact. But, with Metcalf in witness protection, there was no way for Blackwell to act on whatever schemes he was plotting."

Manx pulled out another photograph. "That is, until he gets the bright idea to bribe Derrick Garrett, a police officer who's been on your husband's payroll for decades, to find the information for him, or he spills the beans on their cosy relationship. Am I close?"

'Too fucking close," Mandy said, scraping her chair back several feet from the table, and flipping over the photograph of Garrett.

Manx continued, "Garrett can't take that chance. He has connections, people who owe him. So, he calls in a few favours, and bingo. He's got Metcalf's new identity—Dr. Simon Vaughn, GP in a small village surgery here on Anglesey."

"I wouldn't know. I'm more of the self-medicating type."

"Now, Blackwell is finally in possession of the information he needs, but he's locked up for the next twenty years, how does he act on it? He turns to family—your son, Callum. Getting Callum to do his dirty work is easy. He worships his dad, will do anything for him, so he visits his father at Wakefield, and Blackwell supplies him with the name and address. Is this sounding familiar?"

"Same old, same old, if that's what you mean," Mandy said.

"But, I think Callum does more in that meeting than say yes to his father. He gives Blackwell an idea. Tell the Greater Manchester Police Derrick Garrett is as bent as they get, provide them with names, dates, in exchange for a reduced sentence. Blackwell requests his solicitor set up the meeting, but he's underestimated Garrett's web of corruption. When Garrett gets wind of this, he panics, suspects the worse, and pays off one of the guards at Wakefield to pump Blackwell full of crack cocaine, making it look like a suicide. The coroner declares accidental death, but you're not buying it, neither is Callum. That's when this mother and child reunion takes place. Am I right?"

"As I said, I just run a wool shop in a quiet village, keep myself to myself."

"Callum persuades, or threatens you, to come back from Mexico for one final act of revenge. Kill Vaughn, then kill Garrett, too, or at least, expose him. Is that what happened, Mandy?"

"A lot of shit happens in life. I can't keep track myself, these days,"

"A year ago, you take over the lease on the wool shop, as a front for Callum. He needs a false passport to get back into the country, that takes time. This gives you a few months to establish yourself as part of the community, find out where Vaughn's living, and make sure he's the man you're looking for. Is that when you started your relationship with Bowen? Used him as your lackey, and whatever else."

"I didn't hear him complaining," Mandy said.

"You used Bowen to help find Vaughn. It was too risky for you to walk into the surgery. He might have recognised you, you couldn't take that chance."

"It's a lovely story. You should write it down, someday."

"When Callum does return, I'm guessing no more than a few months ago, he hides at the farmhouse, but has minimal contact with you while he plans Vaughn's murder. But, Callum's like his dad, a chip off the old block. Killing Vaughn wasn't enough. He wanted to ruin his reputation, and showcase his handiwork, as a tribute to his dad."

"Maybe he was just a shitty doctor? Maybe a pissed off patient did him in?"

"Callum then has a stroke of luck, one Ernie Stokes. He's retired, but still dealing small amounts of methadone. But, Stokes isn't playing the game. It's too big for him. He only wants to dabble, has no interest in being part of a large-scale operation. Callum, on the other hand, has an assembly line in Transnistria, producing, amongst other drugs, methadone. Did you try it yourself, Mandy? A couple of samples?"

"I'm strictly a fags and booze girl," Mandy said. "You can take the girl out of Manchester," she added, with a tight smile.

"Callum has the goods, but no distribution, so he threatens Stokes, gets him to give up the name of his distributor, Shanni Morgan. He then murders Stokes. After all, dead men don't tell tales. Is this making sense to you, Mandy?"

"Well, you're obviously pleasuring yourself with it."

"About two months ago, Callum starts importing drugs via a container ship. Dick Roberts, a distant relation of Bowen's, who's up to his eyeballs in debt, helps transports the drugs from the ship and onto the island. Dick Roberts, racked with guilt after what Callum did to Stokes, commits suicide. Approximately six weeks ago, on the night of November fifth, Callum grants his father's final wishes, and murders Vaughn. You thought that would be the end of it, didn't you, Mandy? You'd go back to Mexico, deal done. But, Callum's got other plans. He's a businessman, sees an opportunity, and forces you to stay on, launder his money. Is that what you did?"

"A mother would like to think she'd do anything for her children."

"You didn't answer the question."

"You're right, I didn't. I knew nothing of my son's criminal activities. As I said, I'm just a retiree running a wool shop."

Manx leant forward, and spoke softly. "I reckon you were tired of it, Mandy, tired of the killings, the shattered lives. You'd seen this drama before; you knew the ending. That's why you called Garrett, told him where Callum was, but you couldn't quite bring yourself to stop him completely. You gave Garrett just enough information to pull him in, then let the NCA and us do the rest."

"If I was that smart, do you think I'd be sitting here?"

"Did he threaten to kill you, too, Mandy? Callum was unpredictable. You were scared of him, scared of your own son."

Mandy shuffled uncomfortably, the first veneer of stoicism falling from her face. "It's all facts and evidence to you, isn't it?" she said, moving her chair forward. "You want everything wrapped up nice and tidy. Case closed." She slapped her palms on her desk to emphasise the point.

"It's how it works, Mandy."

Mandy sniffed, ran her hand under her nose. "Thing is, this is just a story, not even a story; it's a laundry list of facts. Callum did this, I did that, then, he did the other. Cause and effect."

"We have proof. I just thought you might like to share your version of events. Help us help you, Mandy."

"My confession? Is that what you want? Bless me, heavenly Father, for I have sinned?" Mandy mocked, her hands pressed in prayer, her gaze directed to the ceiling. "I've lost my whole family at the hands of the police, and you think I'm going to sit here and bare my soul to you?"

"I'm a good listener," Manx said.

Mandy placed her hands flat on the table, and fixed Manx with a steely, unrepentant stare. "Fuck. You!" she mouthed, and sat back, satisfied she'd delivered the one line she'd been preparing for all morning.

Manx cleared his throat, and took something else out of the envelope. "That red Fiesta of yours, Mandy?" he said. "Forensics took the whole car apart yesterday; they found nothing."

Mandy smiled. "See. Just a retired woman running a wool shop, nothing to hide."

Manx placed the figure of Spanish Elvis on the table. "Except this,"

"Jesus, you must be desperate," Mandy said, her confidence shaken but, as yet, still not completely shot.

"We would have just thrown it in the evidence room, if it wasn't for the sound it made when one of our men lifted it from the car," Manx said, shaking the plastic figure. It rattled, as if it were full of beans.

Another twitch of nervousness flitted across Mandy's face. Manx slowly unscrewed the circular stage the King was mounted onto, and poured a stack of blue pills onto the table. Mandy's left hand began to shake.

"What was it Callum said? A contingency plan?"

Mandy's chest was heaving, her eyes wet with the first prick of tears.

"There's exactly enough methadone here to charge you with possession with intent to sell. No more, no less." Manx said, and sat back in his chair. "Kids, they break your heart, don't they?"

Manx watched the woman in front of him crumble. First, the dab of a tear, the stiff clench of the jaw, then, the quivering of the bottom lip. Her face, once stoic, softened, and became almost transparent, as if she were wiping off the day's makeup to reveal the unvarnished, crestfallen woman beneath.

"Now. Are you ready to make a statement?" Manx said, sliding the paper across the table.

Chapter 20

"*To everything, there is a season and a time to every purpose under the heaven. A time to be born, and a time to die; a time to plant, and a time to pluck up that which is planted. A time to kill, and a time to heal; a time to break down, and a time to build up. A time to weep, and a time to laugh. time to mourn, and a time to dance.*"

As rain fell, like small pebbles, onto the Chapel's slate roof, the minister continued with the reading of Ecclesiastics Chapter three, verse one; the King James Bible translation, Manx guessed, though he was no expert. The reading inevitably brought him back to the song, "Turn Turn" by the Byrd's—1965, if he remembered correctly. If there was ever a better pop song crafted from Bible verses, Manx was yet to hear it.

The chapel was packed tight. *Standing room only*, he thought. He stood at the door, his back against the wall; just another grim face in the solemn cast of portraitures. Even if there was a place to sit, Manx would have still chosen his present position, where he could observe from a distance. It also afforded him the opportunity to slip away unnoticed after the service. He came to pay his last respects, no more.

The sound of crisp bible pages being turned echoed off the walls, as the minister encouraged the congregation to join him in prayer. Heads bowed in unison. Following the minister's cue, the organist flat-fingered a run of dud notes before stumbling into the opening bars of "Calon Lan: Pure Heart." Manx remembered it was one of Tommy Williams's favourites: "*A Pure Heart is full of goodness, more lovely than the pretty lily. Only a pure heart can sing, sing day and night.*"

The congregation sang along, haltingly, at first, then in full, roof-raising voice. *Was there a more sorrowful instrument than a wheezing pipe organ bellowing its ancient, breathy notes through a funeral service?* Manx thought, as the sting of his own tears pricked at the back of his eyes.

After the final verse, the six pallbearers proceeded to carry the casket down the aisle, and towards the cemetery located at the east of the chapel on a hill overlooking Llangefni. A cutting wind had begun to whip through the graveyard, and the drizzle fell like a soft mist.

The congregation shuffled towards the grave. The women held tight to their black "Sundays and funerals only" hats, and the men, their hands buried deep into the pockets of their winter coats, looked stoically towards the horizon, as if they couldn't bring themselves to stare at the dark hole beneath them. It was too grim of a reminder they would end up here, one day, shovelled over with dirt, and left on this windswept hill.

The pallbearers settled the casket on the wet ground, and shuffled back a respectful distance. Manx stood a few metres away, under the shade of one of the oak trees hemming the cemetery. He couldn't hear the minister's eulogy, but by the way his sister kept wiping her nose with her handkerchief, he guessed the words must have touched a nerve. Alice Manx-Williams stood as rigid as the gravestones surrounding her, and took Sara's hand. There was something more between them now; a shared loss that he, Tudor Manx, had been partially responsible for. The realisation seared through him, as he watched Sara let her head fall sideways on her mother's shoulder.

As the casket was eased into its final resting place, the minister scattered a handful of wet soil into the grave. Sara did the same. Dewi, following his mother's lead, scrambled his hands over the earth, and let the soil filter through his fingers. He paused for a moment, deciding the gesture was too impersonal, then reached into his pocket, and held out the toy lorry he'd been cradling for the length of the service, the same one he'd shown to Manx, just over a week ago. Dewi opened his palm, allowing it to roll from his hands, and onto the casket lid with a dull, punctuating thud. Manx felt a thick lump form in his throat: he'd seen enough.

As Manx turned his back, the minister's words were carried by the wind into silence; they were expressions of condolence meant only for the regiment of mourners, not for him. Manx would need to find comfort elsewhere—dig further to forgive himself for what had happened to Miriam, and now, Shanni.

Maybe Canton was right, after all—we all carry the dead with us, and returning to the island had only succeeded in adding to his load. There would be no closure for him; he understood that now. Coming back had been a mistake. Whatever he was looking for, he wouldn't find it here.

Chapter 21

"Rough day?" Gwen said, as she pulled on the pump, and drew a fresh pint.

"Doesn't begin to describe it," Manx said, loosening his tie.

"You were there? At the…" Gwen began.

Manx nodded.

"Oh, that's awful. The poor bloke was standing right where you are now, not more than a week ago. Tragic." She looked down, and gently patted Manx's hand. Her touch, felt warm; like home, if he could remember what home felt like anymore.

"How's business?" Manx said, eager to shift the subject.

"Thinking of expanding my horizons, and taking over the lease on Mandy's place. Might even move into the flat. Owain needs his own bedroom."

"Good for you," Manx said, raising his pint glass.

"Bit of a gamble, but go big, or go home, isn't that what they say?"

Manx had to admire Gwen's ambition and optimism. He used to see the world like that.

"Eating tonight?" Gwen asked, pushing the Pub Grub menu his way.

"Liquid supper," he said, savouring his first sip of the evening.

"I'll keep back a ham and cheese sandwich after the kitchen shuts, just in case you change your mind."

Manx smiled. Gwen was a good woman, probably the sort he should be attached to. *But, that was one more complication than necessary, for both of them*, Manx thought.

"Owain still goes on about you, you know? Cut out that picture of you in the paper, and stuck it to the wall by his bed."

"Shouldn't he be putting up posters of Iron Man, or whatever kids are into, these days?"

"He's like his mam, more practical," Gwen said. "Prefers his heroes closer to home."

Manx looked at her, smiled, and took another sip of his bitter.

"Homework?" Gwen asked, a few moments later, gesturing towards the thick, A4 manila envelope Manx had placed on the bar.

"Last piece of the jigsaw," Manx said, "I should probably get stuck in. The boss wants a full report in the morning."

"Don't let me keep you. Just give me the signal, if you need anything," Gwen said, waving a pint glass towards Manx.

Manx moved to a window table. He slipped the pages from the envelope, and glanced over the fax cover that read, Policia de Seguranca Publica, Lisbon, with the emblem of what looked like an eagle atop a blue coat of arms with six-pointed white stars. Below the emblem, a neatly hand-written note stated: Confidential, Prepared for Detective Inspector Tudor Manx-Williams, North Wales Constabulary. Transcript of P.S.P. Special Operations Group, interrogation of Captain Robert Bayard-Hayden, of the cargo ship, *Jutranja Zvezda*.

Chapter 22

No witnesses. It was the final communication the Captain had received, before he set off from the Port of Rotterdam early in the morning of October 28th. He'd come to understand the process by now; they liked things clean and tidy, no loose ends. How long it would be, before he considered him a loose end, was a thought he'd rather not linger on for too long.

The Slovenian-registered *Jutranja Zvezda*, a twenty-thousand ton dry-cargo carrier, gradually reduced speed, as it navigated the shipping lane hemming the North Wales coastline. Three miles northeast of Beaumaris, the Captain killed the engines, and gave the order to drop anchor.

To the east, the dawn was just breaking, sketching an orange-red ribbon across the Snowdonia mountains. He wrapped his fingers around a strip of Rizalrolling paper, stacked with a line of Kentucky Select, and massaged it into a perfect white cylinder. The cigarette hissed, as he pulled on the tightly wound tobacco. There was nothing to do now, but wait. He set about rolling another cigarette to kill the time.

Below deck, twenty-three crewmen were betting their paycheques on a game of blackjack; the sort of game which didn't require too long of a commitment. They were mostly Eastern European, from the old communist bloc countries—Slovaks, Poles, Latvians. The Captain no longer cared about their countries of birth. They were all the same to him, just more muscle and brawn to add to the great Eastern European stew spilling ever westward.

They didn't ask questions, and he extended the same courtesy. If they could produce a valid passport, it was information enough to get them one crossing, and a chance to prove themselves. In return, the Captain knew none of them would question why they'd dropped anchor on a calm morning, sixty miles from port. None of them would be concerned that, amongst the thirteen tons of cargo they were carrying below, six unmarked crates had been left on deck. It was none of their business. Just like it wasn't their business to even stir when they heard a small fishing boat pull up the starboard side. And when the youngest crewmember folded his losing hand face down on the table, and made his way above deck, without a word, no one raised an eyebrow.

The Captain stepped onto the deck. He heard the faint bay of a fog-horn break through the morning, and directed the young crewman towards the six unmarked boxes placed directly where the fishing boat was now buffering against the ship's hull, some twenty feet below them.

It took less than fifteen minutes for the crewman to carry the boxes, and load them on deck. When he was done, the Captain climbed down the rope ladder, and joined him. He tapped on the window of the open cabin to inform the skipper he was done. The skipper, a short, wiry man in a yellow sou'wester, nodded, and started the engines.

The Captain pushed away the lobster basket hanging from a mechanical arm, and sat on the narrow bench stretching the length of the gunwale. He offered the crewman a roll-up. The crewman smiled, and placed the cigarette in the corner of his mouth. As the Captain attempted to strike the match for the third time, the crewman leant over and stopped him

"Bad luck, Captain," he said, and slotted the roll up inside his jacket.

As the boat made its way towards the central channel of the Menai Strait, he heard the whirr of a small dinghy. The skipper immediately thrust the engines into reverse, and held her steady. A length of rope was thrown onto the deck. The Captain moved quickly, tied it to one of the metal cleats, and signalled the crewman to start loading. The boat's engine groaned and whined, as the skipper fought against the force of the current. As the final box was loaded off the deck, the Captain walked to the bow of the boat, and exchanged a few words with the man on the dingy. The man passed the Captain a large brown envelope. He checked it by the dim light of the cabin, before untying the rope.

The skipper turned the boat back towards the open sea. As the vessel picked up speed, the crewman sat down, and pulled out his single cigarette from his pocket, placing it in the corner of his mouth.

"You have a light, Captain?" he said in a thick, Eastern European accent.

God, he was young, the Captain thought; handsome, almost Asian-like features, but with a pale, wide face and the faintest wisp of sideburns. Probably had a girlfriend or a young bride back home. They married young, these kids. He'd seen enough tearful, dockyard goodbyes in his career. It was a waste. Still, orders were orders, and the message was clear: *no witnesses*.

The Captain reached inside his jacket pocket. His fingers brushed over the cold metal of the '73 Makarov semi-automatic pistol. The crewman stiffened. The Captain gave him a reassuring smile, the one he'd used before to put them at ease. He drew the gun from his jacket pocket.

"No witnesses," he said.

The Captain pinched the trigger. A rogue wave lifted the boat several feet; his aim was off by an inch and a half. The bullet lodged itself into the crewman's shoulder. The Captain only had seconds to react. The crewman was already lurching towards him, reaching for the gun. The Captain grabbed at the metal lobster basket, and swung it. It was a clean hit, twenty kilos of rusted metal drew an immediate trickle of blood. The crewman offered little resistance, his momentum already veering towards the water. The splash was dull and anti-climactic, as he broke the black, ocean surface.

For a few moments, there was no sound other than the whine of the engine and the slap of seawater against the hull. The Captain looked away, slipped his pistol back inside his jacket, and waited for the lights of the *Jutranja Zvezda* to come into view.

Chapter 23

Manx splashed a palm full of cold water over his face, and examined himself in the mirror. He looked tired; the dark circles under his eyes were puffy, like freshly acquired bruises, and his eyes seemed to have a faraway look about them, as if they belonged to someone else. He'd come close to death; the second time in just over a year. Maybe the universe was trying to tell him something. The experience didn't improve with age. He had witnessed no angels, no gathering of loved ones around him, ushering him to towards some beatific light. *Maybe he'd feel better after a few good nights of sleep*, he thought as he wiped a paper towel across his face, but it was a rare bout of optimism he knew better than to trust.

The music emanating from the back room of the Bull suddenly increased in volume. "Come on, Eileen" echoed through the walls. *Predictable*, Manx thought, and stepped into the hallway.

He pushed open the reception room doors, and felt the overwhelming blast of heat and vibration of over-modulated sub woofers. As his eyes adjusted to the flickering strobe lights, the scene unfolded before him like some distant relative's wedding reception he'd been forced to attend. Manx took the road most travelled, walked directly towards the bar, and ordered a pint of whatever they had on draft.

By now, the dance floor was swarming with a clutch of middle-aged women in floral dresses, exerting more energy in one evening than they had no doubt done in the past year. Directly under the homemade banner announcing his retirement, Mickey Thomas was holding court, and attempting to perfect the signature moves of the Macarena, instructed by two women, neither of which Manx suspected was his wife. Manx had left it fashionably late to arrive. It was a habit of his with parties. He'd arrive when people were sober enough to remember he came, but leave when they were too drunk to remember when he left. He looked at his watch—nine-thirty. With any luck, he'd be out of here in an hour.

"Manx! You deigned to grace us with your presence," Canton said, ambling over to the bar. He was sporting a suit he'd outgrown some years ago. The sleeves were too short, and the fabric bunched around his shoulders in rough folds. Under his jacket, he wore a garish pink shirt, the top three buttons undone to reveal a patch of grey, glistening chest-hair.

"Scarlett Johansson was otherwise engaged," Manx said.

Canton laughed, his face a deeper shade of red than usual, with beads of sweat percolating from his forehead. "There was a sweepstakes, you know? Bets were laid as to whether you'd turn up, or, if you did, what time," he said, gesturing to the barmaid to pour him another pint.

"What was your play?" Manx asked.

"Somewhere between no chance, and a snowball's chance in hell. Still, goes to show, what I know?" He looked over Manx, as if he'd just noticed him. "Don't you ever change your image, Tudor? Wear something a little more, I don't know, colourful?"

"You've been reading too many *Cosmo*s, Chief."

"But, black and white? You may as well be back in bloody uniform."

"One less thing to think about in the morning."

Canton shook his head. "By the way, you're meeting with the Royal Security Detail next Wednesday. They're expecting you at ten-thirty, sharp. I'll give you the full address the morning of. Make sure to hitch up that tie," Canton said, waving his index finger accusingly at Manx's unfettered knot.

"About that, Chief…" Manx began, but was interrupted by a claw-like hand gripping at his right shoulder.

"Never took you for the party-going type, Manx," Ashton Bevan said, contorting his face into his usual, awkward smile.

"The quiet ones are always the most trouble, isn't that right, Inspector?" Sherri Bevan said, appearing as if by magic from behind her husband, and offering Manx her hand.

"Of course, you've already met my wife, Sherri," Ashton said, placing his hand on the small of his wife's back.

Manx nodded. "Nice to see you, Mrs. Bevan," he said, noticing how good she looked. *Dolled up for some better occasion than this*, he thought, before realising that occasions better than this were probably in short supply around these parts, for women like Sherri Bevan.

"Sherri, call me Sherri, for God's sake. It's not like we're complete strangers, is it now?" she said, as she took his hand. "Are you the dancing type?" she asked.

"I wouldn't like to ruin people's evening," Manx said, sipping his beer.

"Oh, Ashton and I love to dance. In fact, we're signed up for ballroom this winter. Paso Doble, Rumba, maybe even some Argentinian Tango, if Ashton's up to it. He won't miss an episode of *Strictly*, will you, Ash?"

"Unless I'm on call," Bevan said smugly. "By the way, damn good work on that case, Manx, but my condolences on your brother-in-law." Ashton thought for a moment, and shrugged. "Close to home, too, but how were you to know?" he said, with a thin, wintry smile.

"No police talk tonight, Ashton, you promised," Sherri said, snaking her hand through her husband's elbow, and leading him towards the dance floor. Ashton offered Manx a "what can I do?" shrug, and followed his wife to the dance floor. Sherri rippled her hands in the air, and swivelled her hips suggestively towards her shorter, far less rhythm-centric husband, who was biting hard on his bottom lip, concentrating on each shuffle of his feet, as if they might run away from him at any moment.

"Better go attend to my own wife," Canton said. "Not that she'll want to dance, but Marjorie gets bored with all the shop talk."

"Chief, I need to talk…" Manx began.

"If it's work related, save it till Monday. I'm officially off the clock."

"It can't wait, Chief," Manx said. "Coming back here…it was a mistake. Don't get me wrong, I appreciate what you've done for me, but…"

"Too many ghosts?" Canton asked.

"Too many living reminders," Manx explained, though both statements were probably true.

Canton rested his shovel-like palm on Manx's shoulder. "Take the weekend to think about it. Anyway, where the hell else would you go?"

"Maybe leave the service for good. Fresh start. Consulting," Manx said, realising his words sounded empty and hollow, as he spoke them.

"What? Buy a bed and breakfast on the coast? Run a bookshop in a quiet village?" Canton laughed. "If I had a fiver for each time I heard that pipe dream, I'd have my own Caribbean island by now. I told you a few weeks ago, there's opportunity, if you're willing to look for it. You've got the respect of your fellow officers and full support of the ranking officials; you did that in a few weeks; that's nothing to sniff at. Don't forget, my chair will need filling in a few years. We'll need a competent replacement."

"I know bugger all about Bonsai plants, Chief," Manx said.

"Trees, Manx, Bonsai trees. Well, you'll have plenty of time to learn, then," Canton said. "My advice? Never make a life-changing decision at the tail end of a case. Give it some time. Now, I'd better get back to Marjorie, before Mickey drags her into his harem. We'll talk Monday."

Manx watched as Canton returned to his wife, reaching down to place a small kiss on her forehead as he sat.

On the dance floor, inspired by the opening chords of "The Time Warp," Mickey Thomas slipped the tie from his neck, and swirled it above his head. In the far corner of the room, hidden from the searching glare of the strobe lights, Mal Nader was sulking into his pint glass, accompanied by a woman Manx guessed was his wife, who was sipping demurely on a coke and lemon, and looking out to the dance floor with a wistful expression. At another table, PC Delyth Morris was attempting to drag Kevin Priddle to the dance floor. He offered little resistance, and followed Morris's lead, jumping to the left, then to the right, followed by an awkward, ill-timed pelvic thrust.

This was life, Manx thought, as he looked over the gathering. The beat of the music vibrating through the floorboards, the slice of lemon in the gin and tonic, the few hours of release before you pick yourself up, place one foot in front of the other, and start all over again. *Is that why he always felt so removed from these moments? Was he too busy observing life to ever lose himself completely in it? Had he made that decision years ago, without even realising it? Was he walking towards something, or walking away, and was there even a difference anymore?*

As the smoke machine pumped a layer of fresh dry ice across the dance floor, the deejay fumbled a cack-handed segue into "Dancing Queen." It was Manx's cue. He placed his glass on the bar, and turned his back, the rousing keyboard refrains of the chorus fading slowly into the background, until he could no longer hear it.

Chapter 24

Outside the Bull's Head car park, the night was miserable and damp. Manx pulled his scarf tightly around his neck, and unwrapped a King Edward—his last of the day, he promised. A patter of light drizzle had begun to fall. He stood for a few minutes by the clock tower, looking over the now deserted town, and the narrow band of main road which ran through its centre, and disappeared into darkness at the peak of the hill.

The smoke from the cigar drifted over his face, and dissolved in the cold air. He was about to walk back towards his car, when his mobile phone pinged urgently in his jacket pocket. He took it out, and glanced quickly at the screen. There was no message, just an attachment, a photograph, the same blurry and pale Guy Fawkes mask he recognised from several weeks ago. The phone pinged again. Manx felt the King Edward slip from his fingers, and fall with a soft fizz into a pool of rainwater, as he read the short, nine-word message.

He steadied himself against the clock tower, his body shaking, as if it were doused in nicotine, and sat on the stone steps. He read the text again, focussing on the type, until his eyes hurt. Several more digital pings broke the night air like a strange birdsong, all with the same, one-line message:

MIRIAM WASN'T THE ONLY ONE.
FIND HER, FIND THEM.

THE END

A Note from Bloodhound Books

Thanks for reading *Anglesey Blue* We hope you enjoyed it as much as we did. Please consider leaving a review on Amazon or Goodreads to help others find and enjoy this book too.

Bloodhound Books specialise in crime and thriller fiction. We regularly have special offers including free and discounted eBooks. To be the first to hear about these special offers, why not join our mailing list <u>here</u>? We won't send you more then two emails per month and we'll never pass your details on to anybody else.

Readers who enjoyed *Anglesey Blue* will also enjoy

Only The Dead – The first instalment of Malcolm Hollingdrake's explosive new Harrogate Crime Series

<u>Amazon UK</u> – <u>Amazon US</u>

Unquiet Souls – Liz Mistry's best-selling and critically acclaimed crime thriller.

<u>Amazon UK</u> – <u>Amazon US</u>

Dylan H. Jones, is a native, Anglesey-born Welshman who now lives in Oakland, California with his wife Laura and daughter, Isabella. He has worked as a media executive and copywriter at various TV networks and advertising agencies both in London and San Francisco. Currently, he is owner and Creative Director of Jones Digital Media, a video content agency.

Dylan was born on Anglesey and moved away when he was seven years old to the Northeast of England. His family then moved to the Wirral for several years before settling back on Anglesey when he was fourteen. Dylan studied Communication Arts and Media at the University of Leeds, then moved to Cardiff, working for S4C. In 1993 he re-located to London as a Creative Director with Channel 4 TV. Today, he lives in Oakland, California. His parents, sister and most of his immediate family still live on the island.

Anglesey Blue is the first in a series of crime novels featuring the sardonic, sharp-witted but troubled detective, Detective Inspector Tudor Manx. Dylan's life, both on and off the island, inspired him to develop the series.

Dylan is represented by literary agent, Ger Nichol of the Book Bureau, Ireland. thebookbureau123@gmail.com

You can read more information at www.dylanjonesauthor.com

Printed in Great Britain
by Amazon